He's rich, he's s[...]
gorgeous. There[...]
works with him! And it's just [...]
to keep things...

Strictly Business

A brand new collection of
three extra-special short stories
from talented Mills & Boon® authors:

Penny Jordan,

Liz Fielding and Hannah Bernard!

C000063438

Praise for three bestselling authors –
Penny Jordan, Liz Fielding
and Hannah Bernard

About Penny Jordan:
'Penny Jordan creates a sensual tale
overflowing with emotional intensity.'
— *Romantic Times*

About Liz Fielding:
'The characters, the story and the conflict
leap off of the page'
— *Romantic Times*

About Hannah Bernard:
'[Her writing] is fast-paced and fun!'
— *Romantic Times*

Strictly Business

Penny Jordan

Liz Fielding

Hannah Bernard

MILLS & BOON®

*MILLS & BOON and MILLS & BOON with the Rose Device
are registered trademarks of the publisher.
Harlequin Mills & Boon Limited,
Eton House, 18-24 Paradise Road, Richmond, Surrey, TW9 1SR*

STRICTLY BUSINESS © by Harlequin Enterprises II B.V., 2004

The publisher acknowledges the copyright holders of the
individual works as follows:

The Boss's Marriage Arrangement © Penny Jordan 2004
The Temp and the Tycoon © Liz Fielding 2004
The Fiancé Deal © Hannah Bernard 2004

ISBN 0 263 84500 1

024-0904

*Printed and bound in Spain
by Litografia Rosés S.A., Barcelona*

CONTENTS

Penny Jordan has been writing for more than twenty years and has an outstanding record: over 150 novels published, including the phenomenally successful A PERFECT FAMILY, TO LOVE, HONOUR & BETRAY, THE PERFECT SINNER and POWER PLAY, which hit *The Sunday Times* and *New York Times* bestseller lists. Penny Jordan was born in Preston, Lancashire, and now lives in rural Cheshire.

THE BOSS'S MARRIAGE ARRANGEMENT

by

Penny Jordan

CHAPTER ONE

As ALWAYS when she had to walk past her boss's open office door, Harriet felt her body tense and she forced herself to look straight ahead and not into the room.

She should never have agreed to work for Matthew Cole, she admitted, reflecting darkly as she did so that if it hadn't been for her best friend then she wouldn't have done. That was the trouble with best friends; sometimes—too many times, in her experience—they tended to believe that they knew what was best! Her particular best friend certainly did, which was why he had coaxed, cajoled and generally used every trick in the book to get her to submit her CV for Matthew Cole's personal appraisal.

Yes, that was right, her best friend was male! She and Ben had been friends since their junior school days, and that friendship had strengthened when they had both chosen to go to the same university.

Now, four years after they'd left university, their friendship was as strong as ever—which was why she had taken Ben's advice and applied for the job at the firm of architects and design consultants, which he had insisted would be perfect for her.

And, to be fair to him, in all probability it would have been. If the job hadn't come with strings. Strings that were firmly held in the uncompromising grip of the company's owner, Matthew Cole. And strings which Matthew Cole had absolutely no compunction about pulling extremely hard when he felt like it. Take the way he had dictatorially announced that her desk was to be on the opposite side of the room from Ben's, even though they were collaborating on the same office design project.

She should have listened to her own inner feelings right from the start, Harriet admitted, her green eyes shadowing as sunlight spilled through the window, burnishing her conker-coloured shoulder length hair. The thickness of her long black eyelashes gave her eyes a certain smouldering sensuality, which was echoed by the warm fullness of her mouth.

As she passed Mathew Cole's office she let out a sigh of relief. She knew without looking in that he wasn't there. For some reason she had developed a very sensitive early-warning system that told her very explicitly whenever Matt was about.

If she had had any sense she would have paid far more attention to that stab of shocked awareness and its ricocheting fall out when he had first interviewed her. She should have done, but when Ben had asked her jovially if she had been, as he put it, 'knocked out by Matt's sexiness, like every other woman who sets eyes on him,' she had of course denied being so much as remotely aware of any such thing, never mind affected by it!

Ben had been hugely amused by her reaction, shaking his head and laughing as he told her how women normally reacted to his boss. And that had been her downfall. Because of course when she had been offered the job her own pride had not allowed her to refuse to accept it.

Despite the shock that Matthew Coles's potent air

of sexuality and masculine power had given her, she was totally immune to it—and to him, Harriet assured herself, with blatant disregard for the truth, as she walked into the open plan office she shared with Ben and other members of their team.

'Nice weekend?' Ben asked as she sat down.

'Fine,' Harriet assured him. 'Everyone at home sends their love, and your mother has sent some of her damson jam for you.'

Ben groaned. 'I've got a shelf full of the stuff already. You'd think that after twenty-six years she'd know I don't like damson jam.'

'Perhaps she's trying to convert you. Which reminds me—she wants to know when she and your dad are going to get to meet Cindi!' Harriet laughed, but her laughter died on her lips as she studied Ben's haggard face.

'What's wrong?' she asked, her concern intensifying as he shook his head. 'Come on, Ben,' she cajoled, 'this is me—remember!'

She hadn't forgotten, even if Ben had, how he had helped and comforted her through the break up of her own first big romance during their first year at university.

'It's Cindi,' Ben admitted unhappily. 'We had a bit of row over the weekend. And it isn't the first one either. Harry, I just don't understand her,' he said vehemently as he swung around in his chair to look at her. 'I mean, one minute she's "let's move in together and start planning a future" and then the next she's saying, "I'm out with my friends and I don't want to know you." And all because…'

'Because what?' she pressed, but Ben shook his

head. Harriet sighed. Cindi, the girl Ben was dating, had recently joined the company too, although since they were working on different projects, and she herself had been away on holiday, Harriet hadn't had any opportunity to get to know her as yet. She knew that Cindi and Ben had been dating, and that they had fallen head over heels in love with one another.

'Everyone has lovers' tiffs, Ben.' She tried to comfort him. 'Perhaps give yourselves a chance to talk the problem through together…?'

'This isn't a tiff. She's being totally unreasonable and she knows it. And as for talking it through—!' His normally easygoing expression hardened. 'No way I am going to be given ultimatums about the way I live my life!'

Harriet could see that he genuinely believed he had a grievance, but she still tried to lighten his mood by teasing, 'What has she done? Told you all your old sports stuff has to go?'

When he didn't respond she looked worriedly at him and said quietly, 'Okay, so it's something serious and I'm out of order trying to joke about it, but you can be a stubborn so-and-so at times, and if it's a matter of giving a bit or losing someone special to you then—'

'It isn't as simple as that, Harry, and if she genuinely loved me she wouldn't need to make such bloody ridiculous conditions because she'd know…'

'She'd know what?' Harriet demanded, mystified.

For a minute she thought that Ben wasn't going to answer, and then, as though he couldn't help himself, he burst out furiously, 'She'd know that you're the closest thing I've got to a sister, as well as my best friend, and that no way do you feel any differently about me than I do about you. Hell, just because she's never had any close friends of the opposite sex doesn't mean that— And as for saying that you might secretly be in love with me—well, that's just plain ridiculous!'

It took Harriet several seconds to assimilate what Ben was telling her, but once she had, she protested immediately, 'She can't possibly think that! You must have misunderstood.'

'I wish!' Ben responded darkly.

'Look, Ben, let me have a word with her,' Harriet offered.

'No. No! It's no use. She won't believe you, Harry. And that's what's really getting to me. I've given her my word that I've been totally up front with her about us, but apparently my word isn't good enough.' His voice hardened. 'What she wants—what she says her friends have told her she should demand—is for me to prove to her that there's nothing going on between you and me by cutting you out of my life completely. She says if I loved her then I'd agree. She says she will not accept me having another woman in my life who means more to me than she does. And she says that if I don't accept her terms then it means that you *do* mean more! I've tried to make her understand—to see…to admit that she's being sexist and stupid, and that if she loved me she would accept my word that she's got it all wrong. After all, I know you a damn sight better than she does. You aren't secretly in love with me, are you?'

Harriet burst out laughing. 'No, I am not!' she assured him truthfully.

From where she stood it was easy for her to see

how and why the argument had escalated out of control, even if she did feel affronted by Cindi's assumption that she was the sort of person who would try to break up someone else's romance. Take two people who had fallen passionately in love but who did not know one another all that well, add a generous helping of female jealousy, a pinch of insecurity and a good measure of male pride, and what you had were all the ingredients for a very destructive explosion.

Right now Ben might have an angrily stubborn look in his eyes, but Harriet could see the pain he was trying to hide. Automatically she leaned forward and took hold of his hand, giving it a comforting squeeze.

On his way past the large room which housed his creative design team, Matt Cole came to an abrupt halt as he surveyed the intimacy of the way Harriet was leaning towards Ben and reaching for his hand, her eyes liquid with tender emotion.

Matt was thirty-six years old, the head of his own highly innovative and profitable company, and supposed to be possessed of a sharply astute brain—so why the hell had he not recognised what was happening to him the minute he had set eyes on Harriet and taken immediate and evasive action then?

Because he had believed then, in his arrogance, that he had more than enough power and control over his emotions to keep them in check, that was why. He had felt the immediate fierce surge of emotional and physical reaction to her and dismissed its importance, shrugging it and his own feelings aside, telling himself that it hardly mattered that he happened to find her attractive since he had a rule that he never mixed business with pleasure. And, since he had never previously had any problems in sticking to that rule, he hadn't thought it would pose any problems now.

But he had misjudged the strength of his own feelings. Big time. Very big time.

He was the only child of older parents. His mother had died shortly after his birth, while his father had died when he was in his first year at university, and so all along Matt had focused on his work as a means of providing him with the only kind of security he had told himself he needed.

Marriage and children were on his agenda—eventually. But falling passionately, mindlessly and helplessly in love, and having his whole world turned upside down were not!

But that was exactly what had happened. And, what was more, with every day that passed it was growing harder and harder for him to deal with his feelings.

He had tried to distance himself from Harriet, to cut himself off from what he felt by putting up a façade of cold indifference, but he might as well have tried to breathe without oxygen he acknowledged grimly.

Every day, several times a day, he found himself making some kind of excuse to be in the vicinity of her desk. Every day he watched with a jealousy that made him appalled at himself as she lavished on Ben the attention he longed to have her lavish on him!

He had tried everything, from telling himself he was behaving unprofessionally to telling himself he was behaving ridiculously, but nothing made the slightest difference to what he felt. What he felt right now was that he wanted to stride over to Harriet and take her in his arms and kiss her—if not senseless then at least into a state where she wanted him to the same extent that he wanted her, and to hell with the consequences! But even stronger than his desire to make love to her was his desire to shield and to protect her. To shield her from some of her colleagues' contemptuous and critical comments about her and to protect her from the consequences of her own behaviour.

It made no difference how often he told himself that as one of his employees she had no more right to his protection than any of the others, or that he had no right to want to protect her. He loved her, and he couldn't bear to hear what was being said about her. He found it hard to stand to one side and allow the inevitable to happen. Because everyone, it seemed, believed that sooner or later someone, if not Ben himself, was going to tell her to stop making a fool of herself by displaying so plainly her feelings for a man who obviously did not return them.

If an adult human being had to suffer unrequited love, then better by far that they suffer it in secret—as he was doing.

But what right did he have to interfere? Either as her employer or as the man who loved her?

Morally perhaps none! But emotionally… Matt exhaled sharply.

Helplessly he watched Harriet move even closer to Ben. It was a physical effort to stop himself from going over and separating them.

Didn't she know what a fool she was making of herself? Didn't she care? Didn't she realise that people were discussing her and her obvious love for Ben—a man who saw her only as a friend—behind her back?

Because if she didn't she damned well ought to!

It would take a much braver man than Ben himself to tell her though, Matt recognised, and her female colleages seemed to prefer to gossip about the situation rather than do anything about it. He had happened to be standing out of sight but well within earshot the previous week, when Cindi had been despairingly confiding in an older woman employee about a row she had had with Ben over his friendship with Harriet.

'He swears that she is nothing more to him than a friend,' Matt had heard her saying tearfully.

'Well, he may see their relationship that way, but it's obvious that she doesn't,' her companion had retorted darkly. 'Look at the way she's followed him here! Don't make the same mistake I did, Cindi,' she had warned her. 'My ex swore to me that his secretary meant nothing to him, but, as the little tart told me the day he left me for her, she wanted him and nothing was going to stop her having him. Some women are like that! And if you want my opinion Harriet is one of them! I mean, you've only got to see her with Ben. It's obvious how she feels about him. She spends every spare minute she can with him. Take it from me, she wants him—no matter what he might say or think!'

'Don't, please,' Cindi had protested. 'Ben says he loves me, but...'

'Then tell him to prove it! Tell him that you want her out of his life!'

But Harriet very plainly was *not* out of Ben's life, and had no intention of getting out of it.

Didn't she realise what people were saying? Didn't she care that Ben was actually seeing something else? Had she no pride, no sense of self-respect or self-worth? Hadn't it occurred to her to stop obsessing about Ben and find a man who loved and wanted her? Matt wondered angrily.

A man?

His mouth compressing, he wondered helplessly for the thousandth time why this had had to happen to him! It wasn't what he wanted, and it sure as hell wasn't what he needed! It felt as if his jealousy was burning a hole in his gut.

Cynically he reflected that a sitcom writer would have a field-day, if not a whole carnival with the situation!

Matt loves Harriet, who loves Ben, who loves Cindi, who loves Ben, who does not love Harriet, who does not love Matt, who does love her—with the kind of savage, self-destructive, all-consuming hunger that set all his inner emotional buttons on overdrive and melt-down every damned time he saw her. And it didn't help that every damned time he *did* see her she was draping herself on or around Ben!

And what in some ways was even worse was the fact that Matt knew that if he were Ben, business ethics and self-imposed rules or not, he'd have had her in his arms, his mouth on hers, faster than she could blink. He drew in a deep, shuddering breath and fought for self-control.

Ignobly and impossibly he had even at one stage contemplated firing her. But, even if the law hadn't prevented him from doing any such thing without a watertight reason, she was far too much of an asset to the business for it to lose her.

And that was just one of the more minor reasons why he loved her. Unlike Ben, who was a good, solid and cheerful worker, Harriet had brought a passion and flair to her role in the team that had infused the project she was working on with a new dynamism.

It wasn't that he hadn't tried to overcome his feelings for her; he had! In the past few months he had dated more women than he had done in the past few years. But none of them had so much as dragged his thoughts away from Harriet for as long as five seconds.

Her Matt-aware antennae for once not working efficiently, Harriet was oblivious to the fact that Matt could overhear her as she shook her head and told Ben firmly, 'We can't talk about this here.' Giving his hand another squeeze, she suggested, 'Why don't we have dinner together tonight? I've got loads to tell you about what's going on at home.'

Watching her, Matt felt as though someone was ripping his heart, muscle from muscle. He wanted to stride over to them, to take hold of Harriet and ask her if she realised what she was doing. And then what? Force her to back off and allow Ben and Cindi to get on with their lives—and their love?

He had no right to interfere, he warned himself harshly. But if he didn't then who would? And besides, a dangerously reasonable little voice inside him argued, didn't he have the right as an employer to want a workplace free of any emotional entanglements and dramas that would take his employees' attention away from their work?

* * *

Oblivious to what Matt was thinking, Harriet watched Ben. He looked so dejected that she felt desperately sorry for him, and wanted to do whatever she could to help. Cindi obviously loved Ben, and Harriet knew that Ben loved Cindi. She was amazed that Ben had even needed to ask her if she was secretly in love with him! How could she be when…? When what? When she was desperately afraid that she had fallen in love with Matt?

Matt! Automatically she lifted her head and looked towards the corridor which led to his office, her body stiffening and hot colour staining her skin as she saw him standing watching them.

Ben was a good looking young man, but he was just that—a young man. In no way did he compare in sheer male presence to Matthew Cole, who was pure lethal adult, and so fully charged with testosterone that no woman living could fail to be aware of him. Not that she didn't do her bit for her own sex by fiercely pretending that she was not. She *was* aware of him. All the time! But some days, sometimes—like right now—something went wrong and her protective shield failed to work properly. Sometimes just the sight of Matt was enough to set up a chain of reaction inside her body that resulted in butterflies in her tummy and a weakness in her legs. But that weakness was nowhere near as dangerous as the weakness in her emotions.

Because the truth was that Matt epitomised everything Harriet had ever dreamed about in a man. He was her childhood prince come to life; her knight in shining armour. He was her darkly disturbing, secret sensual-fantasymade man. He made her ache with feverish longing—and, far more dangerously, he made her dream impossible daydreams about love and happy ever afters, and at least four little Matts or Matildas calling her Mummy!

And no way was that ever going to happen! Matt didn't even like her, never mind love her. In fact sometimes when he was looking at her the way he was right now, his slate-grey eyes iced with permafrost and freezing her with the most intimidating glare of fury she had ever seen, she felt that he actively disliked her.

Her heart might be sinking, Harriet acknowledged, but her chin wasn't going to. Bravely she tilted it, and met his slicing scrutiny.

What was it about the thickness of his close-cropped dark hair that made her want to slide her fingers into it, to mould them against the curve of his well-shaped head, whilst one of his strong hands cupped her own, and that hard mouth softened with desire and…?

'Harriet, I'd like to see you in my office.'

The cold, clinical words brought her back to earth.

'You mean now?' she queried. She needed to keep her distance from him right now, not get even closer to him. Harriet had her pride—the same pride that had led to her refusing to give in to her first love's demand that she go to bed with him—and she was not going to join the ranks of Matt's lovelorn adorers.

'I mean now!' he agreed, in a clipped voice that made Ben give her a small shove.

'See you tonight, then,' he said.

Matt had already disappeared down the corridor, and as she followed him Harriet wondered feverishly what he wanted.

There had never been any open clashes between

them. How could there be when he was not just her immediate boss but the owner of the company as well? But there had been plenty of subtle indirect ones.

It wasn't so much Matt's antagonism towards her that sparked off the fiery pride that led to her spirited defiance but her own shocked stark inner awareness of just how vulnerable to him she was.

Apart from the brief catastrophe of her first foray into love Harriet had remained heart-whole, and that was the way she had intended to remain until she was well into her thirties and ready to settle down. And then she had seen Matt and her sensible plans had self-ignited after one incredulous look at him. Nor had it made any difference telling herself that no sensible and right-thinking woman would be so idiotic as to fall crazily in love with a man who obviously was never going to feel the same way about her.

Abruptly Harriet realised that she had reached Matt's office.

An inimical biting grey glance impaled her where she stood, leaving her feeling as though her every thought had been dissected and then rejected.

'Come in and close the door.'

Her heart was going crazy inside her chest. But it wasn't her erratic heartbeat that bothered her as she mentally cursed herself for leaving her jacket on her chair.

The state-of-the-art office had a climatically controlled temperature that made it totally unnecessary for her nipples to do some temperature-awareness testing of their own. But that was exactly what they were doing—pressing themselves against her clothes for the entire world to see, as though she was standing in an arctic wind.

Or sexually aroused. Well, she certainly knew which it was, and she could only hope that Matt did *not!*

Her nipples tightened so fiercely that she almost cried out in protest.

'Sit down.'

Woodenly, Harriet did so.

For once Matt had no carefully thought out plan of action mentally organised. He only knew that for her own sake Harriet needed to distance herself from Ben—both in her own emotions and in other people's eyes.

The intensity of his grim expression as he battled with his own private devils increased Harriet's apprehension. What on earth had she done?

'It's come to my attention that your…feelings for Ben are the subject of a great deal of office criticism and gossip.'

Harriet could feel the tips of her ears starting to burn hotly in mortified shock. Matt had swung his chair around so that she could only see his profile, but she was miserably and humiliating aware that he could still see how his words were affecting her.

Her whole face was burning now, with both anger and humiliation, as the full ramifications of his accusatory and demeaning statement sank in.

Immediately she rushed to defend herself, and to reject what he was saying. 'If you are referring to Cindi's ridiculous suggestion that I am secretly in love with Ben—'

'Secretly?' Matt stopped her sharply, turning to face

her. 'There was nothing secret about the touching little scene I just witnessed. Touching, that is, unless one happens to know the truth! And the entire company knows the truth, Harriet.' The look Matt gave her made her want to disappear!

Through stiff, shock-numbed lips Harriet managed to demand, 'And that truth is…?'

There was a look in her eyes that made Matt want to go to her and hold her, tell her that nothing and no one was going to be allowed to hurt her whilst he was there to prevent it, but he knew that he couldn't. He was doing this because he wanted to help her, not because he wanted to hurt her!

'That you are refusing to see that your love for Ben is not returned, that it never will be returned. The way you are pursuing him so obsessively, following him and clinging to him, is not only coming between him and Cindi, it's making you the object of other people's contempt as well.'

The cold, brutal words hit her like physical blows, and as from physical blows Harriet recoiled from them, whispering painfully, 'No, that isn't true.'

'It *is* true. Have you no pride? No self-respect?'

The blood receded swiftly from Harriet's face, leaving it creamily pale as shock and outrage filled her.

Cindi's assumption and Cindi's ultimatum had obviously not been confined merely to Ben! It was bad enough discovering that her colleagues shared Cindi's misinterpretation of her relationship with Ben, but to discover that Matt was not just privy to it but believed it as well filled her with blistering hot shame.

Valiantly she struggled to overcome her feelings and to explain. After all, no matter what her private feelings might be, Matt was her boss, and at this stage in her career she couldn't afford to earn any kind of black mark, still less be written off as some kind of obsessive who was trying to force herself on a man who didn't want her!

'I was just trying to tell Ben—'

'What?' Matt challenged her, striding from behind his desk and coming over to her. 'What were you trying to tell him? That he'd be better off with you? With your love?'

'No!'

'No? So what, then? Were you pleading with him to love *you?*'

'No! *No!*' Harriet denied fiercely, getting to her own feet to confront him and then wishing that she hadn't as she realised how close to him she was.

She wasn't a small woman, at five feet nine inches tall, but she was small-boned and slender, and Matt was well over six feet, with a physique which Ben had told her came from his days as captain of his university's rugby team.

How on earth had this happened? How could she possibly be in this sickeningly humiliating situation?

Matt could see the pain in her eyes. Part of him felt bitterly angry with her for what she was doing, but most of him simply wanted to hold her and comfort her. Her pain was his pain, and he hurt for her and with her.

It was simply to comfort her that he had put his hands on her and drawn her towards him. Nothing more!

Harriet stiffened as Matt's hands closed on her upper arms, knowing that right now she was far too emotionally frail to withstand something like this.

Ben was forgotten as though he had never existed. She tried to drag air into lungs compressed with shocked physical awareness.

Matt was touching her. Matt was looking down into her eyes with frowning bleakness.

She exhaled shakily.

He shouldn't have done this. He shouldn't have touched her, Matt recognised grimly. No matter how altruistic his original motivation and intention had been. Abruptly he released her.

As Matt thrust her away Harriet tensed, hating herself for the way she wanted—no, not just wanted, but ached and needed—to cling to him.

'Quite apart from anything else,' she could hear Matt telling her grimly, 'your behaviour is causing disruption and…and discord here in the office. And that is something I will not tolerate. We work together here, in very tight-knit teams, and every single member of those teams has been selected by me personally as a vital component of their particular unit. But if I thought it necessary for the greater good to replace one of those components then I would have no compunction whatsoever in doing so. Do you understand what I am saying?'

'Yes, you're threatening to sack me,' Harriet answered him briefly. 'But you've got it all wrong! And so has Cindi! I do love Ben, yes! But as a friend…as a brother, if you like. Not…not in the way that you are trying to imply!'

'You mean there's nothing sexual in your…your…?'

'Nothing,' Harriet emphasised fiercely, without letting him finish.

'No?' Matt gave her a cynical look that made her whole body burn with resentment. 'Then prove it,' he told her in a clipped voice.

Harriet exhaled noisily. 'And how exactly am I supposed to do that?'

'Well, you could start by making it obvious and public that you're very involved with.. dating someone else.'

'Dating someone else?' Harriet repeated blankly. 'Who?'

'Me!'

The colour came and went in Harriet's mobile face—and if she had but known it her shock only echoed his own, Matt acknowledged. What the hell did he think he was doing? Morally and in every other way there was he was totally out of order. He should make it clear immediately that he hadn't meant what he had said and that Harriet was to ignore it. *Immediately!*

Matt was suggesting that she pretend to want him? No pretence was necessary!

'You can't mean… Are you saying…? Oh, no, I couldn't do that. It's impossible… No. No way!' she told him a little breathlessly.

Her words didn't just sting Matt's pride raw, they blew a large hole in his good intentions as well as shattering them into nothing. A ruthless determination swept over him, swamping everything else.

'You've just said that you aren't in love with Ben— I'm giving you an opportunity to prove it.'

There was a small suspenseful pause.

'If you don't take it then I'll know that you are lying,' Matt finished coldly.

Harriet looked at him, wondering how on earth she had ever got into such a mess.

'No one will ever believe that you and I are dating.'

'Then it will be up to us to convince them, won't it?' Matt said smoothly. 'The choice is yours!'

'Some choice,' Harriet muttered, adding fiercely, 'Why are you doing this?'

Her throat felt raw, the backs of her eyes stung, and her chest hurt, as though she were about to come down with a heavy cold. Her physical reactions weren't caused by a physical virus, though, but an emotional one.

'I'm doing it to stop you causing disruption and discord in my business. Besides, I should have thought that if you genuinely don't love Ben, as you claim, then you'd jump at the chance to prove it—and to give Ben and Cindi a chance to find happiness together,' Matt reiterated curtly.

No way could he tell her that he was doing it purely and simply because he wanted any excuse to be with her…

'What was all that about?'

Harriet gave a nervous look over her shoulder as Ben came up to her at the water cooler.

'What…what do you mean?' she hedged.

'What did Matt want? You were in there for ages, and when you came out you looked…'

For a moment she was tempted to tell him, but before she could say anything she heard Matt saying smoothly behind her, 'Have you told Ben about us yet, darling?'

Harriet almost dropped the cup of water she was holding, but she suspected that the shock on her face was nothing to the stupefaction on Ben's as Matt came between them.

'Harry?' Ben questioned incredulously.

'You're trembling. I hope that's because of me,' Matt was murmuring against her ear as he relieved her of the paper cup she had all but crushed by sliding one hand around her waist to turn her towards him and removing the cup with the other.

Ben was positively goggling at them, his mouth half open and a look of total shock on his face.

'You mean, you two are…?' He shook his head.

'We certainly are,' Matt assured him calmly. 'In fact we very much are—aren't we, Harriet?'

The look he was giving her was practically a physical caress in itself, Harriet recognised weakly, and her wretched body was certainly responding to it as though it were.

Ben obviously hadn't missed the high octane sensuality of the smoky look Matt was giving her, because suddenly he started to frown—an expression that Harriet recognised all too well.

Ben was her friend, but he was also male, and as such he had always taken a very brotherly and protective attitude towards Harriet where other men were concerned. And right now he was looking at Matt as though he was a suspicious father about to demand to know Matt's intentions!

'You never said anything to me!' he accused Harriet sternly.

'I asked her not to,' Matt answered promptly for her.

Somehow the hand which had relieved her of the paper cup was now holding her own, his fingers sliding between hers in a manner so intimate that Harriet was having trouble breathing properly. Her skin tingled, and liquid pleasure shot up her arm like an injection of some kind of sensual drug that locked into her heart.

She had the strongest need not just to move closer to Matt's body, but also to press herself against him with wanton abandonment.

Wicked images of the two of them alone together somewhere very private filled her head in a dangerously explicit slide show. Matt perching on the edge of a desk, his legs open as he drew her to him to kiss her passionately, whilst her fingers explored the hard muscles of his thigh, her touch making him growl in protest and take her hand and place it on the swollen bulge of his erection. Whilst he was kissing her he would slowly unfasten her top and remove it. His hands would cup her breasts and savour their shape and feel as her tight, erect nipples flaunted their eager hunger for his touch… Abruptly Harriet called her thoughts to order as she heard, 'But now that things are serious between us it's different. I don't care who knows how I feel about Harriet!'

'Things are serious between you?' Ben's frown cleared, leaving him looking both relieved and happy.

CHAPTER TWO

'Harriet, I don't understand you! There's Matt telling me that things are serious between the two of you and you haven't said a word! Why not?'

'Er...well, until he called me into his office I didn't know that things were serious,' Harriet explained, mentally justifying her statement by reminding herself that it was the truth after all—if not in the way that Ben would interpret it.

'Well, once Cindi knows this she's going to—'

'Be very relieved,' Harriet finished firmly for him, adding, 'If you love her as much as I think you do, Ben, you won't make an issue of this silly mistake about me. After all, if she didn't love you she wouldn't care about my relationship with you, would she?'

'No... But...' He gave a small sigh. 'She had a few days' holiday to use and she's gone to see her parents—cooling off time, she called it.'

'Well, if I were you I'd be waiting for her when she comes back with something very romantic planned.'

'Yes. I'll do that.' He paused, and then said worriedly, 'Harry, this thing between you and Matt... Don't rush into...anything, will you? I mean, you haven't... He hasn't... And Matt is...'

Oh, yes! Matt most certainly was, Harriet agreed mentally as she told Ben lightly, 'You worry about your own love life, Ben, and leave me to worry about mine.'

Smiling at him, she leaned forward and kissed his cheek.

Within seconds the phone on her desk rang, and when Harriet picked up the receiver she heard Matt saying coldly, 'I've booked a table for us at the Riverside for nine p.m. I'll pick you up. And by the way, I thought I'd made it clear there's only one man you kiss from now on and it isn't Ben!'

Harriet wanted to tell him that there was no way she intended to have dinner with him, but he had already ended the call. Silently she replaced the receiver. Her head was whirling and her heart was pounding at the thought of what had happened.

Matt had asked her if she wanted people to believe that she was secretly in love with Ben, and of course she didn't. But the cure he was offering her was far, far more dangerous than the supposed disease!

And how ridiculous it was for him to go to the lengths of taking her out to dinner just to stop her seeing Ben, as she had planned. Her heart gave a funny little jerk as it threw itself against her ribcage. She acknowledged that there was a certain dangerous pleasure in the thought of Matt having the kind of feelings about her that would cause him to feel jealous of her being with another man. Not that he was ever likely to!

The Riverside was the area's most exclusive hotel, and was run by an ex-TV chef and his model wife. What on earth was she going to wear? And what on earth was she doing worrying about what she was going to wear when she had so much that was far more important to worry about?

Displacement therapy, that was what it was! And

nothing whatsoever to do with any wild and totally idiotic desire to have Matt take one look at her and wish that he was serious about her for real!

Matt stared out of the large window of his penthouse suite above the office block. He had bought the suite because it saved time to live and work in the same building, and he'd hired a turnkey designer to sort out the décor for him. The result was a state-of-the-art modern living space in which he constantly felt as though he was somehow a jarring and unnecessary presence, breaking up the place's austere and sterile symmetry of grey on grey, chrome, glass and granite.

Harriet would, of course, be fiercely contemptuous of it—and no doubt of him for living in it. He just somehow knew that she was an Aga and comfortable country house kind of woman. And somewhere deep down Matt suspected that a part of him was dangerously close to being an Aga and country house kind of man, with four children, who chose to work at home so that he could be with them…

Because of Harriet? Matt started to frown. Why the hell had he fallen in love with her? *How* the hell had he fallen in love with her? He'd only had to look at her to know what that red hair and passionate energy were going to mean! And that was without the complication of her blinkered fixation on a man who didn't want her. If he had any sense he would… He would what? Turn his back and walk away from her?

So why the hell was he sitting here reliving the feel of that thick silky waterfall of hair running through his fingers and the effect of those awesome green eyes looking up into his?

If he hadn't had the presence of mind to push her away there was no knowing what might have happened. No knowing? Matt derided himself savagely—he knew damn well what would have happened: what he had wanted to happen and where he had wanted to have it happen!

It had stunned Matt when a male business associate had commented enviously on his 'playboy' reputation, remarking on the number of women Matt was known to have dated. It had never occurred to him that the method he had chosen of trying to eliminate his feelings for Harriet would result in him gaining the reputation of a would-be stud! The truth about his supposed 'reputation' was that it was largely unfounded.

His recent succession of dinner dates had been just that—dinner dates! And by his choice! In fact he couldn't remember the last time…

Restlessly he got up and walked over to the large window with its view of the city.

Liar, he goaded himself mentally. Of course he could damn well remember. And he could remember too that halfway through dinner he had suddenly looked at his elegant blonde-haired companion and realised with a savage stab of anger that he was both totally unaroused by her and totally bored with her.

That had been the evening after he had interviewed Harriet for the job. His date had been none too pleased to be returned home instead of being taken to bed, and she had let him know it!

Matt frowned as he heard his intercom buzz.

Striding over to it, he flipped it on.

'Matt, it's Ben. I need to talk with you.'

Matt hesitated briefly before answering, 'Fine—come up, Ben.'

As he opened the door to him Matt could see the way Ben looked admiringly around the apartment.

'This is way cool, Matt,' he enthused. 'But Harry won't like it—' he began, then stopped, looking self-conscious.

'It's okay, Ben. I know this place isn't to Harriet's taste,' Matt offered, intending to reassure him, but to his surprise Ben suddenly started to scowl fiercely.

'Harriet's been up here, then, has she?' he demanded, looking pugnacious.

'We *are* dating,' Matt answered obliquely, an unfamiliar and unwanted sensation of having been wrong-footed suddenly hitting him.

Ben's current attitude was not exactly that of a young man who resented Harriet's emotional dependence on him and her taken off his hands at any cost.

'It's about Harry that I came to see you,' Ben told him determinedly, giving Matt the kind of look he last remembered receiving from the very protective father of the girl he had taken to his first school dance.

'I see. Would you like to sit down? Or is it going to be a short conversation?' Matt asked drily.

A tinge of colour darkened Ben's face, but his jaw was still set stubbornly. He had come up here for a purpose and he wasn't going to leave until he had a reassured himself on Harriet's behalf. She was his best friend, after all, and, knowing what he did about his own sex, he wanted to make sure she would be all right.

'Harry hasn't said much about how things got going

between the two of you…' he began. 'In fact, I wouldn't have thought she was your type. I've known her since we were kids, and she's my best friend.' Ben stopped, took a deep breath, then began again. 'You said you were serious about Harriet and I hope that you mean that, Matt, because Harry just isn't the type of woman who would let a man into her life in a personal sort of way if she didn't care a hell of a lot about him. She was pretty badly hurt by a rat of a guy when we were at university. Luckily she had the sense to listen to me when I warned her about him, so things never went too far, if you know what I mean. Of course I know it isn't anyone's business but their own how many partners a person has had, and I don't suppose I'd be all that pleased myself if I found I'd got a virgin on my hands…' Matt pressed on doggedly.

A virgin! Ben was trying to tell him that Harriet was a virgin?

Two vastly different emotions speared through Matt at the same time. One was a savage protective fury with Harriet for loving Ben to the extent that she did—ridiculously, in this day and age, she was saving herself for him—and the other was a fierce and disgraceful thrill of hot male hunting instinct. An assured and certain determination to ensure that he was the one who released Harriet from the sensual imprisonment of her virginity.

'So you see,' Ben was continuing, 'if your intentions towards her aren't honourable, so to speak, then it would be better—'

'Ben,' Matt interrupted him firmly, 'I can assure you that my intentions are very honourable.'

'You mean...commitment...? Marriage?' Ben questioned.

Matt's mouth compressed.

'Yes, I mean just that,' he agreed. He meant it, all right, he recognized—after all, he couldn't be any more emotionally committed to her than he was. She already occupied his thoughts 24/7, and as for marriage...

As for marriage! His heart lurched against his ribs and pain tore into him. If circumstances had been different, if Harriet had felt about him as he did about her, then of course he would be wanting marriage, Matt acknowledged grimly. And so, he damned well hoped, after what Ben had just told him, would she!

'You do? Oh, well, that's all right then!'

Beaming with delight, Ben got to his feet to shake Matt's hand. 'Great girl is Harry,' he assured him enthusiastically. 'Good sense of humour, great legs. Must say I was worried... I thought you might just be... Well, I thought I'd better warn you that Harriet isn't that sort of woman.'

No, she wasn't. And Matt decided grimly that he suspected he knew why!

'Thank you, Ben,' he said, dismissing his guest.

Half an hour later, when Harriet opened her door to Matt's knock, the great legs were in evidence but the sense of humour was not.

Not that Matt was in the best of moods himself. The fierce sexual elation he had felt at being told that Harriet was a virgin had given way to an equally fierce and savage fury that she should be idiotic enough to want to save herself for Ben. Ben who did not want her and who, quite plainly, was not right for her! It was, Matt had decided, just the kind of ill-judged, crazy thing a stubborn woman like her would do— saving the gift of herself as well as her love for just one man.

Of course if *he* had been the man…

Harriet took a step back in the hallway as she saw the way Matt was glaring at her. No doubt in his eyes she didn't come anywhere near matching the sophisticated elegance of the women he normally took out to dinner. Her dress was four years old, a simple basic black crêpe number which up until now she had always felt she looked quite good in. With it she was wearing her one pair of expensive shoes, high-heeled and, if she was honest, just a little bit uncomfortable.

'Do you live here alone?' Matt demanded, frowning as he looked up and down the narrow dark lane.

'Yes, I do,' Harriet confirmed. 'I shared with Ben at university, but—'

'Now he wants his own space?' Matt broke in, without allowing her to finish.

Angrily Harriet tilted her chin and told him firmly, 'Actually, I am the one who wanted my own space. And my own washing machine and my own bed!' she added pithily, remembering how much it had infuriated her to return from a visit somewhere, pre-Cindi, to find that one of Ben's mates had 'borrowed' her bed in her absence.

Matt's mouth compressed. When was she going to see sense and accept that Ben did not want her?

'If you're trying to convince me that you shared

Ben's bed you're wasting your time,' he told her angrily.

Immediately Harriet stepped back into the house, but as she reached for the door to turn and slam it Matt guessed what she was about to do and grabbed hold of her wrist.

'Look, why won't you face up to the truth? What is it about you that makes it so hard for you to accept that Ben doesn't want you?' he demanded brutally.

If she really had loved Ben the way Matt seemed to think she did his words would have been unbelievably hurtful and cruel, Harriet decided. 'What is it about *you* that makes you think you've got the right to tell me what to do?' she countered, trying to get her wrist back.

'I've told you what my motivation is,' Matt answered, refusing to release her.

'And I'm telling you that you are barking up the wrong tree. I do not love Ben other than as a friend!'

'How can you say that when—'

'When what?' Harriet challenged when Matt suddenly stopped speaking.

'When you can't string a sentence together without including his name in it,' Matt said evasively.

What the hell was happening to him? He had almost blurted out what Ben had told him.

'We'd better make tracks, otherwise we'll be late,' he added curtly.

Harriet glared at him. 'If you think I'm going to have dinner with you now—'

She gasped as Matt tugged on her wrist and closed the space between them.

'If you think that you aren't...' he retorted softly.

It must be the fact that she was not wearing a coat, coupled with the evening air, that was making her tremble so much, Harriet decided dizzily. But the truth was that it was the musky male scent of Matt's skin playing havoc with her senses, making her want to bury her face against him and breathe it and him into her. She wanted to burrow against his warmth, she wanted…

A shudder ripped through her, causing Matt to curse under his breath and drag her into his arms, holding her hard against his body as he lifted his hand to cup her face and take possession of her mouth.

Right now, more than anything else, he wanted to take her back into the house, carry her upstairs and remove every piece of clothing from her body so that he could show her just what a fool she was for wasting her time wanting Ben when she could have him. That scent she was wearing was driving him crazy, making him feel so damned horny…

Harriet moaned excitedly beneath the hot, thrilling thrust of his tongue. Her fingers dug into the hardness of his shoulders as pleasure exploded inside her like a firework, showering her with golden starbusts of erotic sensation. She could feel his hand in the thick softness of her hair, his thumb massaging the delicate over-sensitive spot just behind her ear and sending a hot zigzag of female arousal jolting right through her.

Just his touch was enough to activate the kind of ache inside her that she already knew would lead to a sleepless, wanting night.

She might, thanks to Ben's determined and some-times unwanted protection, be the oldest virgin in the whole city, but that did not mean that her body didn't already know how to respond to the sweet hotness of the pleasure that could possess and convulse it.

These last months working for Matt had shown her how easy it was for just the thought of him to activate that pleasure, and right now her over-stimulated senses were clamouring hungrily for the real thing.

'Why don't we forget dinner?'

Harriet blinked. How had that happened? How had she said the very words she had just been thinking but in Matt's voice?

Matt groaned inwardly as he realised how out of control he was getting. 'Forget I said that!' he told her tersely.

Forget *he* had said it?

'I suppose you thought I was someone else?' Harriet challenged him angrily.

'Just as you wish that I was someone else?' Matt demanded.

Whilst Harriet struggled to regain her composure Matt hurried them both out of her front door and locked it, handing her the keys before he guided her to his parked car.

Harriet was too engrossed in her own thoughts to object to his cavalier control of the situation, along with her door keys. She had wanted Matt to take her to bed! No, Harriet corrected herself. She had wanted to drag Matt upstairs and take him to bed, and she had nearly told him so!

'Look, there's no point in you giving me the silent disapproving treatment because I'm not Ben. Try facing up to reality!'

Harriet didn't trust herself to reply. She just shook her head in silent frustration.

* * *

'Good evening, sir, madam. Would you care for a drink in the bar first? Or would you prefer to go straight to your table?'

Matt looked questioningly at Harriet.

'Straight to the table, please,' she answered, ruefully aware that despite everything she was extremely hungry. And she was also extremely aware of the fact that they were being shown to what had to be one of the restaurant's very best tables, with a little almost private area all to itself. They could see out through the windows over the river and also around the restaurant, if they wished, and yet at the same time retain their own privacy.

Grimly she wondered how many other women Matt had brought here. An awful lot if the way the head waiter had recognised him was anything to go by, surely?

She had barely completed her chain of thought when Matt suddenly announced, 'I'm surprised that Henri remembered me—it's ages since I last ate here.'

Harriet almost choked on the delicious walnut roll she was eating.

'There wasn't really any need for you to do this, you know,' she said later, when they had given their order and been served with their food. 'After all, Ben isn't going to see us here!'

'Do you wish he could? Do you think it would make him jealous?'

Harriet exhaled fiercely down her nose and put down the glass of wine she had just picked up.

'For the last time, I am *not* in love with Ben. And having him around when I am out on a date is normally the last thing I would want.' When Matt frowned she told him fiercely, 'This may come as a shock to you, but the only way I love Ben is as a brother, and it's as a brother that he behaves when I date anyone—a very over-protective brother at times, and that isn't always what I want!' she added darkly.

She stopped as she realised how much the wine had loosened her tongue and just what she was in danger of saying and to whom!

'In answer to your question, I brought you here to save you from the temptation of going to see Ben,' Matt said curtly, before continuing, 'I don't need to ask why you don't want Ben treating you like a brother. You obviously want him to think of you as a potential lover, not a sister, and because he doesn't, you—'

'You are just misinterpreting what I said to suit your own ends,' Harriet objected angrily. 'That is not what I meant at all.'

They were glaring at one another like two opponents, their argument only brought to an end by the waiter coming to remove their plates for the next course.

CHAPTER THREE

HARRIET stiffened as she saw the look of appreciation and invitation the pretty girl behind the reception desk gave Matt as they left the restaurant. Yet another reason for keeping clear of him, she decided grimly. What woman in possession of all her senses wanted a man who attracted and encouraged the interest of virtually every female he came into contact with?

Not that Matt had encouraged the girl's acquisitive hungry look, Harriet was forced to concede as Matt strode past her obliviously. But that did not alter the fact that if he had done the girl would have leapt to seize the opportunity, Harriet acknowledged.

Courteously Matt placed his hand beneath her elbow to escort her across the car park, rather in the manner that her father adopted towards elderly female members of the family, she reflected darkly.

Her attention was momentarily distracted by the sight of a couple several yards away, wrapped in each other's arms and exchanging the most passionate of kisses as the woman fumbled to unlock the door of the car.

The pounding of Harriet's heart inside her chest was followed by an ache of longing that seemed to seep into every bit of her.

What would it be like to be loved and wanted by Matt like that? Well, whatever it was like she wasn't going to be the one to find out, she told herself sharply.

Matt frowned as he glanced down towards Harriet. She hadn't spoken since before they had left the restaurant—which was, he suspected, quite a record, since during the rest of the evening she had engaged in the kind of conversation that had left him reluctantly impressed by its range and depth. Matt wasn't used to his dates having as keen an interest in world affairs as he did himself, nor in them being so comfortable and informed in debating them.

Just listening to Harriet gave the words 'verbal foreplay' a whole new meaning, he decided ruefully. Certainly he had never expected that he would find anything erotic in a vigorous discussion about the merits of a home-based workforce. But then he found just about everything about Harriet erotic. In fact, she fascinated him, infuriated him, and just about occupied every one of his waking hours as well as a large percentage of his sleeping ones. And that meant...

Harriet glowered at Matt as he suddenly and for no reason at all stood still right in the middle of the car park.

The couple by the car were still kissing.

Matt followed the direction of her gaze and tugged grimly on her arm so that she had to look away.

'Stop thinking about it,' he said curtly. 'It's not going to happen!'

Harriet could feel her face starting to burn with guilt and chagrin. Had he really guessed so easily how much she had wished that she were the one being kissed so passionately, and by him?

'What makes you think I want it to?' she demanded defensively.

They had reached his car, and as he unlocked it

Matt gave her an oblique look. Her full lips were set in a constrained closed line and her green eyes were a mutinous jade.

He opened the passenger door for her, but as she stepped past him he encircled her with the car door and his body.

'Of course you want it to. You're in love, or you think you are. But Ben is not in love with you.'

Ben! Harriet went limp with relief and sagged against the car. Of course—he thought she was in love with Ben!

'But that doesn't stop you wanting to feel his mouth on yours, wanting to…'

The raw sound of Matt's voice jerked her into defensive anger.

If she had been in love with Ben his last words would not have done her any good at all. As it was they were making her want to look at Matt's own mouth as though she were magnetised by it! And not just look at it, she admitted longingly.

'Have you ever thought of writing sex scenes for films?' she asked him, with what she had intended to be sarcasm but which instead sounded more like breathless wonder, Harriet recognised in self-disgust as she scrambled into the car.

To her relief Matt refused to pick up her gauntlet, and started the car instead.

Half an hour later, as they drove through the down-at-heel area where she lived, Harriet could well imagine what Matt must be thinking. But she liked her small house, tucked in cosily with its neighbours, and she liked her long back garden even more.

As though he had read her mind Matt broke his

silence to announce tersely, 'This is a pretty rough area. Not one I would have thought safe for a woman living on her own.'

Yes, it was a bit of a rough area, and following an outbreak of violent incidents she felt increasingly worried about the fact that gangs of youths had begun to roam the local streets, and that if you possessed a car it was not considered wise to park it outside.

But the area still had a certain artisan quaintness about it, and—even more important to Harriet—her little house was affordable and within public transport distance of the office.

She also liked the fact that she had a local butcher and grocery shop, and that most of her elderly neighbours had been born and bred there and so were full of stories of how the area had once been. But now she was seeing it through Matt's eyes, and what she was seeing made her feel both angry and uncomfortable.

Outside a local take away a gang of youths were scuffling and exchanging obscenities. Harriet could see the look Matt was giving them.

She felt obliged to defend them. 'They're only young.'

'And that gives them licence to be foul mouthed?' Matt challenged her. 'Aren't your family concerned about the kind of area you're living in?' he demanded.

Mutinously Harriet turned away from him, pretending not to hear. The truth was that her parents had been dismayed when she had shown them her new home—but she had managed to talk them around.

One of the reasons she had returned home at the weekend had been to wave them off for her father's lecture tour of America. Since her brother and his family lived in New York, Harriet knew how much her parents were looking forward to their visit, and being able to spend some time with their grandchildren.

'Harriet…' Matt began ominously, and then stopped as he turned into her narrow street and they both saw the police car and the ambulance, lights flashing, outside her elderly neighbour's home.

Her own feelings forgotten, Harriet pressed her hand to her mouth in anxiety. Mrs Simmonds was in her late eighties, and had a fund of interesting stories about the past, but Harriet was aware that she had a weak heart and had taken to surreptitiously checking on the elderly lady every day in a way that meant that she did not hurt her pride.

'Oh, no!'

'What the—'

They both spoke at the same time, and Matt stopped his car.

'It's Mrs Simmonds,' Harriet told him shakily as they watched two burly ambulancemen carrying the old lady into the ambulance on a stretcher.

A police officer was already approaching the car.

'What's happened?' Matt asked.

'I'm Mrs Simmonds's neighbour,' Harriet told him, and got out to join Matt and the policeman. 'I know she has a weak heart…'

'Some young thugs broke into her house,' the policeman told them angrily. 'Ransacked the place, they did, and made so much noise that someone across the street rang us. We don't know yet how bad the old lady's injuries are. She's had a very nasty shock, so they're taking her into hospital to keep an eye on her for a couple of days.'

'Why would anyone break into her house? She doesn't have anything to steal,' Harriet protested, pale with alarm. 'She…'

The policeman gave her a pitying look. 'It will be a drug-related crime, miss. They get that desperate for it they'd rob their own grandmother—and often do—'

Harriet shuddered.

The ambulance was already drawing away, and the policeman turned to return to his own car and waiting colleague.

'Right—that's it,' Matt announced as soon as both vehicles had gone. 'No way are you staying here on your own! I'm going to give you two choices,' he told Harriet grimly. 'Either I stay here with you tonight or you come back to my place with me. I don't care which choice you make, but let's put it this way. I only have one bedroom!'

Harriet felt a jolt in her stomach as though someone had kicked her. One bedroom! Already her body was reacting to the sensual mental fantasy she was creating! What would Matt say if she told him she wanted the second option?

'I mean what I say, Harriet!' he said sternly, oblivious to the erotic meanderings of her wayward thoughts.

She wished! Oh, how she wished!

Her heart was bumping uncomfortably against her ribs—and not just because of the effect Matt was having on her.

Her own honesty compelled her to admit that the attack on her neighbour had shocked and frightened her. She was extremely apprehensive at the thought of spending the night alone, worrying that the attackers might decide to come back!

'I don't have much of an option, do I?' she asked Matt, saccharine-sweetly. 'But I warn you my spare room is very small and has a single bed. A very small single bed.'

'I'll live,' Matt answered laconically. 'Give me your keys.'

Idiotically she handed them to him, her heart giving a funny little skip beat at the intimacy such an action suggested. And then it gave a much stronger kick as Matt's hard, warm fingers closed around her own. Inside her head she had a sudden mental image of him enfolding her hand within his own and them sliding his fingers between hers, and inside her body she had an immediate and explicit surge of aching heat.

Hot-faced, she dragged away her hand and then berated herself mentally for being so vulnerable and weak-willed as Matt let them both into her small, cosy home.

And Harriet's home *was* cosy. As cosy as a small, neat and warm little nest. Her little front room was painted cream, to match the cream rugs on the polished floorboards, and Harriet had made the curtains herself, in a natural woven fabric. Her log-burning stove was her pride and joy, a bargain buy from a scrapyard, and the small terracotta linen-covered sofa had been cadged from her parents and reupholstered for her as a moving-in present.

Harriet could see Matt staring around the small room before following her into the kitchen, with its dining area in the conservatory addition.

Harriet had painted the cheap flat pack kitchen units

herself, after bullying Ben to help her assemble them, while her dining room furniture had been junk shop finds which she had patiently restored.

As he looked around the comfortable kitchen, with its cream painted units and earthy-toned décor, Matt acknowledged that it took far more than an expensive designer to create a home—and, moreover, whatever it did take Harriet had it in spades.

To Harriet, though, his silent inspection of her small home spoke of arrogance and even possibly contempt. After all, she had heard all about Matt's state-of-the-art expensive penthouse from Ben.

'You don't have to stay here,' she told him fiercely. 'It was your choice. Not mine. My home may not compare with yours—'

'No, it doesn't.' Matt stopped her grimly.

His rudeness momentarily silenced her.

What would Harriet say if he told her how much he had grown to detest the sterile bleakness of a place that not even the most charitable person could call a home?

Broodingly he roved around the kitchen whilst Harriet watched him resentfully. What was he doing? Trying to make the point that her small home made him feel confined?

'Look, there's really no need for you to stay here,' she said. 'I can always ring Ben and ask him to come over.'

Immediately Matt swung around. 'Oh, yes, you'd like to do that, wouldn't you? Like hell you will, though! Hasn't anything I've said to you sunk in? The whole purpose of this…this…'

'Farce?' Harriet supplied bitterly for him.

'This exercise,' Matt continued, ignoring her, 'is to put a barrier between you and Ben, not give you the excuse to invite him to share your bed!'

'He would not be sharing my bed!' Harriet protested, rushing into impetuous denial. 'When he stays here he always sleeps in his own room.'

'His own room?'

Harriet could understand the hard edge to Matt's voice, but not the white line of tightly reined in emotion around his mouth.

'I suppose you even sleep in the damn bed after he has gone, do you? Dreaming virginal dreams of sharing it with him?'

Now it was Harriet's skin that blanched as fury and shock poured through her in a thunderous fall of ice-cold disbelief.

Turning on her heel, she headed for the door. But Matt got there before her, barring her way with the arm he stretched across it. He felt as shocked by what he had said as Harriet looked, but it was impossible for him to recall the words now.

'Harriet, I'm sorry,' he apologised gruffly. 'I…I was out of order. I shouldn't have…'

Harriet wasn't sure she could trust herself to speak, so instead she put both her hands on his arm and pushed hard against it, to make him remove it from the doorway and let her walk away.

Which was a mistake.

A big mistake. As she discovered when, instead of giving way, his arm pushed hers back and then snapped around her along with its fellow, so that she was tightly bound against Matt's chest.

'Let go of me!'

Not only was her demand ineffectual, it was also muffled against Matt's body, Harriet recognised weakly.

'Not until you've let me apologise!'

Was he serious? Did he realise just how many apologies he now owed her?

'For what?' she asked him pithily, if somewhat breathlessly, and she tussled to put enough space between his flesh and her lips so that her own breath didn't come bouncing back to her off his skin and, by some alchemic means, taste of him! 'Insulting me or imprisoning me?'

'I shouldn't have made that comment about your virginity.'

Harriet went completely still, and then took a deep, shuddering breath.

As though he knew she was going to try and lie to him, Matt added quietly, 'Ben told me.'

'Ben?'

'He thought it was something I should know… Just in case my intentions towards you weren't serious. He may not love you as you want him to, but it's obvious that he feels a…a certain sense of…of responsibility towards you.'

Matt discovered that he was having to battle with himself to make that admission. It would have suited his purpose far better had he been able to point out to Harriet that Ben had no feelings for her of any kind.

But Harriet was barely aware of the last part of his speech. All her concentration was focused on those three appalling words—*Ben told me.*

Never had Harriet wished more that she were the fainting type. Deprived of the opportunity for such an escape, she contemplated the effectiveness of a long, piercing scream—but abandoned it as pointless.

Instead she took a deep breath and said heavily, carefully spacing out each word, 'Ben told you that I am a virgin?'

Did she realise how cute she looked, breathing heavily down her nose like that when she was angry? Matt wondered adoringly.

'He was trying to protect you!' Matt found himself defending Ben in a gesture of male solidarity, but then he saw the smouldering volcano of wrath that was burning in her furious gaze.

'Oh, yes, I'm sure he was,' Harriet burst out furiously. 'After all, he's been doing it ever since I hit puberty, when he told me that boys only wanted one thing! What is it about you men?' she demanded in a wearily aggrieved voice. 'Ben would run a mile if he found out that a girl he was dating was a virgin, but he expects me to…to feel grateful to him for preserving mine when… Oh, this is just too much!' she exclaimed. 'How could he do this to me? Doesn't he realise that if you and I were in lo— Er, I mean, if we were seeing one another you would have discovered for yourself long before now that I hadn't slept with anyone before?'

Discovered for himself? Long before now? Matt found that he was suddenly having a great deal of trouble breathing. To calm himself down he forced himself to play devil's advocate. 'Perhaps I'm so passionately in love with you that I'm prepared to wait?'

Harriet gave him a narrow-eyed look of open female contempt.

'Because I want to make our first time extra special for both of us...' he elaborated.

Hell, what was he saying that for? Matt cursed as his own body reacted immediately and openly to the intimate images his words were conjuring up.

Harriet could feel herself starting to tremble. No, not tremble. It was a small, delicious, erotic shudder of anticipatory pleasure that was galvanising her body, making her feel so sensuously boneless and weak that she couldn't move a single muscle to prise her eager flesh away from the hardness of Matt's body.

The hardness! Matt had an erection, and her body was savouring that knowledge as her hips ground hungrily against him.

A man could drown in the deep green pools of Harriet's gaze, Matt decided rawly, as his hands slid lower to lift her more tightly against him. His own gaze lowered from her eyes to her mouth, and all hell broke loose inside him.

Inside him—and somewhere upstairs inside the house, where the crash of splintering glass shocked through the silence.

'Wait here,' Matt commanded as he released her, but Harriet ignored him, following him as he took her stairs two at a time and then almost cannoning into him as he threw open the door to the small bedroom which overlooked the street. Harriet paled as she saw the broken window and the glass covering the bed and the floor.

Amongst the glass was a brick. Matt frowned and said, 'Ten to one this is the work of those louts who attacked your neighbour. There's no point in ringing the police at this time of night—we'll do that in the morning. You'd better pack a case.'

'What?' Harriet shook her head vehemently. 'Nothing is going to make me leave here. They might come back, and if the house is empty...'

'Nothing?' Matt queried meaningfully.

Harriet frowned in confusion, not following his train of thought.

She could see the impatient rise and fall of his chest as he breathed in and then exhaled.

'No way am I leaving you here on your own. The other bed is covered with shards of glass which means that if you opt to stay here then I shall be sharing your bed!'

Harriet dropped her gaze hurriedly. Ben was always telling her that she had give-away eyes, and she did not want Matt to see the little gleam in them that said her body was reacting to his threat more as though it had been a promise!

Of course it would be impossible for him to sleep on her small sofa; it was too small even for her!

'Don't worry, you and your virginity will be perfectly safe.' Matt deliberately injected an urbane, almost bored note into his voice.

Harriet swallowed hard on the small lump of disappointment clogging her throat. 'But you said that if...' Self-consciously she fell silent, leaving Matt to agree laconically.

'If I was passionately in love with you it would be different. Yes...' As Harriet turned away from him, intending to go and get something to clear up the mess, he added sardonically, 'I suppose you have some crazy idea of saving yourself for Ben?'

Harriet was too outraged to be cautious.

Turning around, she told him explosively, 'Absolutely not! I haven't any intention of saving myself for anyone! There are two reasons why I am still a virgin. One of them is Ben's wretched dogged persistence in behaving like a moralising big brother whenever any man gets near me. And the other is—'

'Yes?' Matt prodded politely 'The other is...?'

Unable to look at him, Harriet muttered, 'The other is that as yet I haven't found anyone I want...that is, someone who I... Oh, for goodness' sake,' she said in exasperation. 'None of this is any business of yours. Have I quizzed you about your virginity?'

Matt started to shake with laughter. For some reason her angry and grudging admission had made him feel extremely light-hearted. 'No, but since you have now raised the subject I am quite happy to tell you that I lost it on my eighteenth birthday to an older woman— she was all of twenty-one, and in the throes of a break up with her partner. Somehow I don't think I created a very good impression!' he added drily.

Not then, perhaps, Harriet reflected achingly, but since then she had no doubts whatsoever that there were any number of women who had some very special sensual memories of what it was like to share Matt's bed.

As she walked away Matt had to give his libido a severe talking to.

'Well, I think that's the worst of the glass cleared up, and that cardboard I've put over the window should hold up until the glazier gets here.'

Matt stretched and yawned whilst Harriet watched with a fixed, strained expression on her face.

It had taken Ben three months to assemble her kitchen units and put them in place. Three months of spending hours on end in the confinement of her kitchen with him, breathing in the air of his exertions, and yet not once, not one single time, had she felt as she did right now with the scent of Matt's working male body filling the space around her and her body reacting it as though to some kind of nuclear sexual turn-on. Bottle it and women would be aching with lust twenty-four hours a day. She certainly had been ever since she had met him!

'A king-size bed?'

Matt had not added the words 'for a virgin' but he might as well have done, Harriet thought as he came to an abrupt halt just inside the door of her bedroom.

'It was a present from my brother and my sister-in-law,' she told him coldly.

'Mmm... Think they might have been trying to tell you something?' Matt asked, quirking one eyebrow.

'Look, there's no need for you to keep harping on about my...about it. I don't know why on earth Ben had to tell you anyway,' Harriet seethed.

'I've already explained. He wanted to make sure I had honourable intentions towards you,' Matt answered her.

'Honourable intentions!'

Harriet's pretty white teeth snapped together in frustration.

Her bedroom echoed the natural colours and fabrics of the rest of the house, Matt recognised when he managed to drag his gaze away from her long enough to glance around it. The room was dominated by the large bed, with its cream throw, and also held a faint but to him very discernible echo of Harriet's scent— her own scent, not the pretty floral perfume she wore for work.

He smothered a small groan! How the hell was he going to sleep, with her lying beside him and the scent of her all around him, when his body ached so damned much for the feel of her, the taste of her, the sweet, erotic moaning cry of her as he…?

He dragged himself from the dangerous scenario he was mentally creating to hear Harriet saying in a businesslike manner, 'I think I've got a spare robe you can use…'

'Spare? You mean Ben's?' Matt challenged her brutally.

Harriet paled, but stood her ground. 'No, I do not mean Ben's. Actually, I bought it for my father to use. He and my mother stayed here and looked after the house for a few days whilst I was away on holiday last year.'

'Ah…'

Matt was tempted to apologise, to tell her that he was only goading her for her own good, so that she would realise the folly of clinging to an outworn fantasy of having a relationship with Ben and see for herself how much more she would enjoy having one with him!

But Harriet had her back to him and was pulling open a drawer to rummage inside it, muttering, 'It's in here somewhere…'

Matt held his breath as a small scrap of silk and

lace fell on the floor. A cream silk thong? With ribbon ties? His imagination was running riot and so was his arousal level. One tug of his teeth and those bows would be history! They would be history, but the soft female flesh they concealed would be his!

As she found the robe Harriet gave a sigh of relief and closed the drawer, only seeing the thong as she did so.

She was closer to it but Matt was faster, and to her outrage he dangled the small item of underwear from one finger in front of her.

'A present?' he said provocatively.

'Certainly not,' she told him primly. 'I bought it myself!'

Too late she recognised the trap he had set for her.

'Even virgins like pretty underwear,' she said crossly, pink-cheeked.

'This is not pretty underwear,' Matt informed her immediately. 'This, let me tell you, in every male lexicon there is, is classified as provocative and sexy!'

'Provocative and… Oh…!'

'Bra to match?' Matt questioned interestedly.

Harriet's bosom heaved and jiggled distractingly, causing Matt to pay it more attention than her answer.

Out of nowhere a surge of hot, driving male possessiveness overwhelmed him and he had a primitive urge to lock Harriet and her underwear away where no other man could see them. Preferably in a bedroom… His bedroom…

'Do you want to use the bathroom first?' he heard Harriet asking him frostily.

'First? You mean we aren't going to be using it

together?' he joked. 'It's ages since someone scrubbed my back for me!'

Harriet was exhausted. Her hormones didn't know where they were. They knew where they wanted her to be, though. Lying pinned to the bed beneath the hot and aroused weight of Matt's preferably naked body, whilst he…

It was just as well she still had those thermal pyjamas her great aunt had so kindly given her last Christmas. She could just imagine what Matt would have to say about her normal habit of sleeping in the nude!

CHAPTER FOUR

HARRIET huffed as she rolled over and into the bank of spare pillows she had insisted on placing down the middle of the bed between Matt and herself—after Matt had announced his intention of sleeping in the nude and had refused to change his mind.

'It's the way I always sleep,' he had told her dismissively.

It was also the way she always slept—but not on this occasion.

'Anyway, you're wearing enough for both of us,' he had added drily.

Harriet made a small sound of irritation as she tried to pull the itchy fabric away from her skin. She was too hot…too wide awake…and much, much too conscious of the man lying peacefully asleep in the bed beside her. Not that she could see him, with the pillows in between them, but if she pushed one of them down a little bit…

Matt was lying with his back to her, his dark head a blur on the white pillow, his bare arm thrown over the duvet, the rest of his body outlined beneath it.

Harriet made a small frustrated sound beneath her breath, released the pillow and rolled over onto her stomach.

But the damage was done and the mental image stored inside her head would not go away.

The trouble was that she was used to having the

whole of the large bed to herself to stretch out in, instead of being hedged in with pillows; that was what was keeping her awake! But Matt was fast asleep, so there was really no harm in removing the pillow barrier now, was there?

Stealthily Harriet removed the pillows and dropped them onto the floor at her own side of the bed.

Cautiously opening one eye, Matt watched her, hastily feigning sleep when she turned back towards him.

Now that Harriet had removed the barrier, nature could do the rest, he decided happily, and he rolled a little closer to the centre of the bed and felt it depress beneath his weight.

Bemusedly Harriet felt her body start to move…as though she were lying on a slope, she decided vaguely. Not that it mattered. Not really. Matt was fast asleep, after all, and she was wearing her pyjamas.

Matt wasn't wearing anything, though. And now he had turned around in his sleep. To Harriet's mortification, as she rolled into him he threw one bare leg over her and pinned her against the bed.

She tried to move, discreetly and silently, so as not to wake him, but for some reason the more she tried to ease herself away the heavier and more imprisoning the weight of his leg became.

Despairingly, she contemplated physically pushing him away, but just as she was about to touch him he muttered something in his sleep and she froze, alarmed that he might wake up.

Instead he muttered again, then lifted his arm and wrapped it around her.

She was trapped in the bed, imprisoned against him

and unable to do a single thing about it without waking him.

And she didn't want to do that!

So she might just as well succumb, then, mightn't she?

A fierce shudder of pleasure ran through her at the mere thought of sleeping wrapped in Matt's arms, her body pressed against the hot satin warmth of his skin.

If only she wasn't wearing Great-Aunt Madge's wretched pyjamas!

If only she might have the courage to reach out and make a leisurely exploration of the sensual feast of naked Matt now so temptingly within her reach.

It would be a crime to waste such an opportunity—especially when she had dreamed wantonly of it and of him virtually from the first night she had met him!

Unfortunately the fact that she couldn't move her arms without risking disturbing Matt meant that she had to be inventive in the way she indulged herself in her voyage of exploration. But happily she soon discovered that her lips and her tongue were avid and acutely sensitive sensory tools.

For the first time in his whole adult life Matt truly and fully understood the meaning of the phrase 'hoist with his own petard.' His subtle machinations had backfired—explosively—on him! He didn't dare so much as move a muscle. If he did…

A low male groan bubbled in his throat. Harriet wriggled uncomfortably in the itchy fabric of her pyjamas and yawned hugely. The events of the day were catching up on her. She yawned again and nestled closer to Matt, making a soft almost purring noise in the back of her throat.

*   *   *

At some point in the night she half woke up. Bewildered to find she was wrapped in something irritatingly itchy and unwanted, she pulled off her pyjamas and then curled back against Matt with a sigh of relief.

Matt woke up first, registered the soft silkiness of bare skin next to his own, and cursed beneath his breath as his body immediately reacted to it. His movement away from her woke Harriet, who pushed back the bedclothes sleepily.

Unable to stop himself, Matt let his hungry gaze drink in the sight of the soft full globes of her breasts. In the coolness of the morning air her nipples were erect and tipped with rose brown against the paleness of her skin. His hands ached to cup and mould them. When she felt his mouth on them would she arch back in eagerness, to give herself freely to him, her fingers locking in his hair as she urged him to take the tight peaks deeper into his mouth and suckle pleasure from them? Would she part her legs and offer him the soft triangle of curls at the apex of her thighs, urging him to stroke the mounded flesh they covered and then move lower, parting the neatly folded lips, sliding between them, slipping between them as her body swelled and moistened for him?

What the hell was he trying to do to himself? His erection was already so damned hard he didn't dare move.

'What have you done with my pyjamas?' Harriet demanded wrathfully as she grabbed the duvet and hauled it up to her chin.

'I haven't done anything with them!' Matt denied. 'You were the one who removed them!'

'What? No, I didn't,' Harriet protested hotly. 'I would never—' Abruptly she stopped suddenly as she had an unwanted flash of memory of itchy fabric and her desire to be rid of it.

'Harry, is that Matt's car outside—? Oh, whoops!'

They had both been so engrossed that neither of them had realised there had been a brief knock and the bedroom door had been pushed open by Ben!

As she saw him Harriet gave a small squeak and dived beneath the duvet, leaving Ben to go slightly red and look a little bit sheepish.

Matt said calmly, but with an unmistakable edge to his voice, 'Yes, it is my car, Ben. How did you get in, by the way?'

'I've got a key,' Ben told him easily, making a swift recovery as he responded to Matt's calmness, adding hopefully, 'I just thought I'd call 'round and see if I could use Harry's washing machine. Mine's broken, and I didn't fancy the laundrette.'

'Tell him he can use the machine, but I am not doing his ironing,' Harriet muttered from beneath the duvet.

'I've got a better idea, Ben,' Matt announced crisply. 'Why don't you go and buy yourself a new washing machine—you can send me the bill. And I will change Harriet's locks. In fact, if you give me a minute I'll come down with you now, see you out and relieve you of your key.'

Pleasant though Matt's voice was, Harriet could hear the steel in it.

The moment the two men had gone she escaped

from the bed and grabbed her robe, pulling it on and
making a dash for the bathroom.

When she had showered and dressed behind the
safety of the locked door Matt still hadn't returned. It
occurred to her that he might not be going to, that he
might simply have decided that it would be easier and
more tactful for him to leave without saying a formal
goodbye!

It was certainly a sensible means of bringing to an
end an episode which she suspected neither of them
would want to dwell on—although for very different
reasons.

Sensible or not, though, it was certainly having an
irritatingly irrational and unwanted lowering effect on
her spirits, Harriet admitted, as she tugged a brush
ruthlessly through her hair and reminded herself that
she had far important things to do than languish
about aching for a man who didn't want her.

There was the broken window to report, for a start,
and then the glass to get fixed. A small shiver ran
through her at the thought of her own vulnerability.

Taking a deep breath, she reminded herself that she
was a modern, independent woman and that it was
ridiculous of her to feel sorry for herself just because
Matt wasn't here to share such tedious practical chores
with her.

Opening the bedroom door, she stepped through it
and came to an abrupt halt, her eyes widening in disbelief as her gaze swivelled to the bed, where Matt
was lying propped up against a bank of pillows—the
same pillows she had thrown out last night. He was
wearing the robe she had bought for her father, and it
was so loosely tied that it was gaping open to reveal

an erotic baring of body hair. She ached to ruffle it with her fingertips and…

Hastily Harriet grabbed hold of her rebellious and far too dangerous thoughts, focusing instead on the wrath-provoking fact that Matt was not just lying back at ease on her bed but was also reading her paper, whilst next to him on the bed was a tray of tea and a plate of hot buttered toast. As she sniffed its warm, mouthwatering aroma Matt looked up from *her* paper to look briefly at her before raising one eyebrow.

'Why the rush to get dressed?'

'Why?' Harriet gave him an incredulous look. 'In case you've forgotten, Ben just walked in here and found us in bed together!'

Matt started to frown and put down the paper. 'So how is getting dressed now going to affect that? Ben knows that we're a couple.'

Just hearing Matt say in that firm, totally male voice the word 'couple'—as matter-of-factly as though it were the truth—was having the most disturbing effect on her. But it wasn't just Matt's voice that was making her yearn for his calm assertion to be the truth was it?

It *wasn't* the truth! And she needed to get a grip before she became totally lost in a fantasy that could only cause her heartache and anguish, Harriet told herself fiercely.

'What Ben knows is what you want him to know,' she told Matt fiercely. 'What I know is that this whole…mess has been created and caused by you because you will not accept that I have no romantic interest whatsoever in Ben.'

'If I don't believe it it's because your own actions

have made it obvious how you feel. And I'm not the only person to see that.'

'If you're talking about Cindi again—' Harriet exploded.

'Yes?' Matt invited her in a dangerous voice. 'What is it with you?' he demanded harshly when Harriet made no response, throwing aside the paper. 'Have you no pride, no self-respect? What will it take to make you recognise what you are doing to yourself?'

'Not you!' Harriet shot back at him furiously.

'If that's a challenge then let me tell you that I'm a man who never ever backs down from one,' Matt warned her softly.

There was a look in his eyes that was mesmerising her, Harriet decided. And a tightening spiral of mingled apprehension and female curiosity exploded inside her at the hint of dark warning in his voice.

Changing tack, she told him recklessly, 'You had no right to make Ben give you his key!'

Matt's mouth tightened, giving Harriet an opportunity to be both bemused and caught off guard by her own immediate desire to find out just how long it might take for someone to kiss the hardness out of his mouth and feel it soften to hungry passion. A small shudder ran through her at the thought of conducting such an experiment herself.

The effect her own thoughts was having on her was distracting her so much that she only just managed to hear Matt's crisp reply.

'On the contrary, I have every right not to want another man to have access to your home, your bed, and most especially to you.'

A weakening female longing ran through her. If

only those words were true! And thank heaven that she was not foolish enough to voice that wish!

'The only thing Ben wanted access to was to my washing machine,' she pointed out waspishly, adding, when Matt remained unmoved, 'You do realise that he's now going to think we really are lovers, and that we're…?'

'That we're what?'

'Ben knows I wouldn't go to bed with someone if I didn't…if I wasn't…'

Harriet compressed her lips. 'I think I should warn you that Ben has some pretty old-fashioned ideas about how…well, certain things. And now that he's seen us like this he's going to start asking all sorts of questions.'

'He already has,' Matt informed her nonchalantly. 'Which is why I've told him that we're getting married!'

Getting married!

Harriet couldn't believe her ears!

'Try to look on the bright side,' Matt encouraged her.

'What bright side?' Harriet croaked acerbically. 'How can there be a *bright side?*'

'Well, for one thing Ben isn't going to find it necessary to protect your virginity anymore, is he?'

'But I'm…' Harriet began, and then stopped, colour flooding her face as something in the way Matt was watching her made her heart start to race bumpily. 'This whole thing is crazy. I'm going downstairs to ring the police and a glazier,' she told him crossly.

'It wouldn't have worked, you know,' Matt said as she reached the door.

'What wouldn't have worked?' Harriet demanded.

'Saving yourself for Ben.'

Harriet had had enough. With her hand on the door she told him angrily, 'You are the one who came up with that scenario—not me! So far as I'm concerned my virginity is just an…an unwanted encumbrance, and personally I'd be only too happy to be rid of it. But of course there's no way you are going to believe that, is there? Because there's no way you would ever admit you are in the wrong! You just aren't going to believe it—whatever I say—or do! Not even if I went out and…and…and slept with the first man I could find!'

'Why go *out* to find one?'

Harriet's eyes rounded and she stared at him, not sure if she had misheard or misinterpreted his soft question.

'You mean, I should…you would…?' She stopped and shook her head as her voice became a small, breathless squeak.

Matt gave her a mocking look. 'See what happens when you make theatrical threats you can't carry through?' he taunted her.

'It wasn't a threat—' Harriet started to defend herself, but to her relief Matt's mobile phone started to ring, and as he reached out to answer it she made a swift exit from the bedroom.

Downstairs in the kitchen, as she waited for the kettle to boil, she closed her eyes and leaned against one of the kitchen units.

What if she had taken Matt up on his challenge? What if she had boldly told him that she wanted him to relieve her of her burdensome virginity? What if…?

But she knew that her feelings for Matt would never be satisfied by a clinical cold sex session, no matter how proficiently executed on Matt's part. And, worse than that, she knew that such an event could and would only leave her craving what she had been denied.

Instead of indulging herself in imagining them making love, what she really ought to be doing was worrying about the complications Matt had caused by pretending to Ben that they were getting married.

Matt's telephone call was from Ben, who wanted to tell him how much his washing machine was going to cost.

'Have you and Harry set a date for the big day yet, then?' Ben asked, once Matt had assured him that he meant what he had said about paying for the washing machine.

'We're working on it,' Matt answered, tongue in cheek.

After he had ended the call Matt started to frown. Did Harriet really think he had been deceived by her denial that she wasn't saving herself for Ben?

And as for that idiotic claim she had made—hadn't it occurred to her that he could have chosen to take her words at face value and put her in a position where…?

Where what? Where he would physically take her in his arms and then take her to bed and show her, share with her, so much pleasure that she would never want him to let her go? Where she would love him as he longed for her to do? As though he was the only man she ever could or would love, now and forever!

Matt's frown deepened. The intensity of the feelings she aroused in him still had the power to shock him.

Pushing aside his pain, Matt got off the bed and headed for the bathroom. Did Harriet not realise the risk she had taken? Didn't it occur to her how another man might react to the kind of challenge she had given him? He was beginning to think that for her own protection, and his sanity, he ought not to let her out of his sight!

CHAPTER FIVE

HARRIET had just finished speaking to the hospital to check on her elderly neighbour when Matt walked into the kitchen, and her concern for the old lady was in her eyes as she turned to him and said worriedly, 'Mrs Simmonds's injuries are more serious than they thought. She's fractured her hip and she's still in shock. The hospital says that it could be several weeks before she's well enough to come home. What kind of people would do a thing like that, Matt?' she demanded passionately. 'To a helpless elderly woman…'

'The kind who would do the same thing to a young woman who is equally helpless, even though she might be too damned stubborn to accept that!' Matt warned her grimly.

Harriet gave a little shudder.

'I'm going to ring the police to report the damage here last night, get someone 'round here to install a decent security system, and then—'

'You're going home?' Harriet suggested eagerly.

'And then we are going out shopping,' Matt told her with an unkind smile.

'Shopping?' Harriet queried uncertainly.

Matt leaned back against the wall and folded his arms across his chest 'Shopping! As of now, until I deem it safe for you to be here on your own, you and I will be sharing the same roof. That roof can be this one—although it could be damned uncomfortable with a team of workmen installing a security system—or it

74

can be mine. I don't care. But what I do care about is that when, as it will do, our relationship becomes public knowledge, you are wearing my engagement ring— here.'

As he finished speaking he took hold of her hand and tapped her ring finger meaningfully.

'What on earth for?' Harriet asked, once her body had stopped reacting to his touch and her emotions had stopped rioting at the thought of what it would be like if he really meant it. 'No one gets engaged these days just because they've spent a night together...'

'No, but they do when they're planning to get married.'

'But we aren't!'

'Ben thinks we are,' Matt reminded her. 'And I intend him to go on thinking that! There's no way out, Harriet,' he informed her.'I'm not letting you off the hook. You need to break out of this addiction you've developed—for your own sake as much as Ben's and Cindi's.'

'I am not addicted to Ben and I am most certainly not letting you buy me an engagement ring!' Harriet protested. 'Wearing it would make a...a travesty of...of...'

'What you mean is that you don't want Ben to see you wearing my ring. Why not? After all, he's already seen you in bed with me—'

'Exactly!' Harriet pounced triumphantly. 'He's seen me in bed with you, so why does he need to see me wearing an engagement ring?'

'*He* doesn't, but I think it would be better for you..and me—if other people did,' Matt replied obliquely.

'If I loved a man I wouldn't care who knew I had

spent the night with him,' Harriet told him passionately, even though a small voice inside her reminded
her that Ben would certainly mind, and would be all
too likely to assume his big brother role and tell Matt
so!

'Maybe not. But if he loved you with the same intensity, and if, like me, he was a certain old-fashioned
type of male, who wanted to tell the world how he felt
about you and how committed he was to you, he
might! In fact there's no might about it! He would!'

Harriet opened her mouth and then closed it again,
for once lost for any kind of comeback.

If she refused to go along with what Matt was planning, and if Ben then thought that she and Matt had
quarrelled and their 'relationship' was over, he'd be
fussing over her like a mother hen—just as he always
did when he thought she was upset or in trouble.
Harriet could well imagine what that would do to his
own relationship with Cindi, especially in view of the
ultimatum Cindi had already given him.

Sometimes in life a person had to put another person's feelings and needs before their own. This was
her time to do that for Ben, Harriet recognised. She
had already come between him and Cindi unintentionally; she certainly wasn't going to risk doing so a second time.

And what was an engagement ring anyway? Nothing
permanent or legally binding! If by wearing it she could
buy Ben and Cindi enough time to patch up their dif-
ferences and get their relationship on a sound enough
footing for Cindi to have complete trust in Ben's love
for her, then that was what she was going to have to do!
And besides, seeing her wearing Matt's ring should

surely also go a long way to making Cindi herself realise that Harriet wasn't romantically interested in Ben.

'So that's the ring sorted out,' she heard Matt declar-
ing. 'Now, you'd better pack enough stuff to last you
at least a week—I've decided it'll be much safer for
you to stay at my penthouse...'

'Your penthouse! But that's in our office block! I'm
not staying there!'

'Of course you are. What better way could there be
to reinforce the fact that we are now a couple?'

Wearing Matt's ring was one thing—moving into
his apartment was quite definitely another.

Harriet put up the fiercest fight and the best argument she could against them 'living together,' but in
the end Matt wore her down by the simple expedient
of steamrollering over every single point she made,
and she was forced to give in.

Her hands trembled as she packed her things, her
nerves jangled by the situation which had gone way
beyond her control.

Why on earth couldn't Matt have simply accepted
her assurance that she had no romantic interest in Ben?
Instead of involving them both in this increasingly
complicated and, for her at least, increasingly dangerous situation!

Miserably she acknowledged that his misjudgement
of her was going to expose her to far more emotional
danger than she felt equipped to handle—and if, as
she feared, she fell even more deeply in love with him
he would be the one to blame!

Yes, he would be the one to blame. But she would
be the one to pay, in sleepless nights and in a heart
and body that ached unbearably for him.

*   *   *

Matt broke his concentration on driving to turn his head and glance briefly at Harriet. She had not spoken a single word to him since they had got into his car, but he could almost smell the hot, slow burn of her angry resentment.

'This city is becoming too damned overcrowded,' he commented grimly as the intersection in front of them became gridlocked.

'That's why so many firms are encouraging their staff to work from home,' Harriet replied without thinking, and angry flags of colour flew in her cheeks when she realised that Matt had tricked her into breaking her mental vow to keep as much distance between them as she could by not talking to him.

'Well, it's an excellent option for some businesses,' he agreed.

'Including yours?' Harriet asked him.

'Maybe in time. I can certainly see that if I were to marry and have children then there would be a distinct appeal in it for me personally. With modern technology I could work from home myself quite easily, and therefore no doubt so too could my employees.'

The very sound of the word 'children' on his lips made Harriet's whole body ache. For them—for him—for the feel of him within her whilst his body and hers created the new life that would be their child.

The feeling that suddenly shook her was like nothing she had ever felt before—immediate, primitive, and possessive of her mate, of their child...of their love.

Unable to bear the intensity of her own emotions, she looked out of the car window and then frowned.

'Matt, where are we going? This isn't the way to the office,' she protested sharply.

'We aren't going to the office. We're going shopping. The engagement ring—remember?' Matt answered as he turned into a narrow street that fed into the car park of an exclusive shopping mall built around the city's most prestigious luxury hotel.

'We'll get the ring and then we'll have dinner here later, to celebrate.'

'Dinner here? We can't!' Harriet panicked. 'I'm not wearing the right clothes.'

Honesty almost compelled her to add that she did not even possess anything remotely suitable to wear at such an exclusive establishment, but before she could do so Matt was shaking his head, telling her, 'Don't worry. I'd like to change, too. I'll book a room and we can shower and change there before dinner.'

When he saw her expression he told her suavely, 'It will be expected. People are bound to ask questions. It would be a very unusual couple who did not celebrate their engagement.'

'We are a very unusual couple,' Harriet reminded him through gritted teeth. But Matt was already pulling into one of the exclusive spaces reserved for hotel guests and the car door was being opened for her, making it impossible for her to continue her argument.

'I've booked a table for dinner and a room,' Matt told Harriet carelessly ten minutes later, when he returned to her side in the elegant reception area.

'I can't believe you're making all this unnecessary fuss,' Harriet protested.

'If we were really getting engaged would you consider it an unnecessary fuss?' Matt asked her evenly.

'Of course not,' Harriet denied promptly. 'Every woman wants such a special occasion to be…special. Oh!' She gave Matt a glare of goaded anger in response to his infuriating expression. 'If I was really making that kind of commitment, a public dinner in an expensive hotel wouldn't be the way I would want to celebrate it,' she continued passionately.

'No? Then where would you want to celebrate it?' Matt asked her drily.

Looking away from him, Harriet said softly, 'Somewhere private, romantic…and special…where we could be alone.'

'Such as? A silken tent on desert sands?' Matt mocked her, watching her face as she shook her head.

Her eyes were brilliant with emotion, and behind the anger she was showing him the wildly passionate side of her character. There was a longing that softened her mouth and burned hotly in her eyes, and immediately his own body responded physically to it. So much so, in fact, that he had to turn slightly away from her and try to distract her.

'A remote cottage with open fires and soft rugs, perhaps?' he suggested softly. 'Where your lover could lay you down and cover your nakedness with his own whilst he watched the pleasure he was feeling reflect back to him from your eyes?'

As he spoke Matt's voice had deepened and developed a raw note to it that raised the tiny hairs on Harriet's arms. Deep inside her she felt a piercingly sharp ache.

'Or perhaps you'd like to lie back in a bath scented with rose petals whilst he slowly…?'

Any one of them, Harriet wanted to beg him frantically. Any or all of them—and now, right now…

He was doing it again, Matt warned himself. He was building images, emotions, dreams for himself which had no substance in reality.

But what if...?
What if nothing. He stopped himself sharply.

A little ruefully Harriet acknowledged that a pair of jeans, a tee shirt and a casual lightweight jacket, no matter how much the modern, acceptable and go-anywhere uniform they normally were, were hardly the kind of clothes she would have chosen to wear for an outing such as this one.

No! Had she and Matt really been going to choose her engagement ring, and then going on to celebrate their engagement, she would have wanted to be wearing...

Unbidden, an image appeared inside her head of the bow-tied briefs she had last seen dangling from Matt's fingers. As it just so happened the briefs were part of a matching set, and the bra that went with them tied provocatively at the front with satin ribbons...

Knowing they were going out on such a romantic and emotional mission, wouldn't she have wanted to dress in something suitably reflecting the day's mood and the reason for it?

But if Matt had been watching her dressing... watching whilst she tied those fragile bows...would they have got as far as leaving their bed, never mind their home?

The images that her over-excited mind were conjuring up brought a feverish flush to her face, and a shallow race to her heartbeat.

As Matt headed for the main exit from the hotel, Harriett discovered that she couldn't resist continuing with her private fantasy. Mentally she covered her breasts and the hard peaking of her nipples against the semi-transparent silk of her bra with a soft cashmere top. Cashmere always felt so sensuous to touch, and, if it was fine enough, when he looked at her Matt would be able to imagine the shape of her breasts, the way he had caressed them during their early-morning lovemaking.

Locked in a battle with her own recklessly wanton imaginings, Harriet froze as Matt suddenly reached out and took hold of her hand, lacing his fingers through hers, and then locking his grip on her when she tried to pull away.

'We're madly in love,' he told her when she gave him a mutinous look. 'Remember?'

'We're in the middle of a shopping mall,' Harriet protested. 'People don't—'

'No?' Matt stopped her. 'Look over there.'

Several yards away from them a couple were walking hand in hand together, obviously completely absorbed in one another. And not a particularly young couple either, Harriet noticed ruefully, as they stopped walking and the man bent to whisper something in the woman's ear. Immediately she turned a radiant face towards him and he moved closer, kissing her tenderly.

For some reason the small intimate scene made Harriet's eyes sting with tears.

'That's different,' she said to Matt fiercely. 'Anyone can see that they really do love one another.'

'You mean because he did this?' Matt challenged softly. And as Harriet turned automatically towards him he reached out with his free hand to cup her face, smoothing her skin with what had to be mock tender fingertips. Harriet could feel the warmth of his breath against her hair, the hard, sure maleness of his hand on her skin. A pulse was jumping frantically at the base of her throat, and her heart was racing to try and catch up with it.

No amount of will-power could stop her from turning her head towards him, green eyes clashing with molten grey. Harriet breathed in sharply and then exhaled on a jagged breath that parted her lips. She could almost feel the molten burn of Matt's gaze on her mouth as he slowly bent his head.

Silently they looked at one another. Her mouth had gone dry, and try as she might she could not drag her gaze away. A sensuous shudder shook her body, and as though it was the signal he had been waiting for Matt covered her mouth with his own.

Was she really making that small, almost incoherent sound of aching pleasure? Was she really turning into the curve of his arm, his body, virtually encouraging him to tighten the intimacy of his hold on her? Shockingly, the mere touch of his lips suddenly became a hard and demanding pressure, and the kiss of passion suddenly overtook convention as his feelings overwhelmed him. As hers were overwhelming her, Harriett admitted dizzily as she returned the hungry pressure of his mouth and longed for the stabbing thrust of his tongue against her own. She wanted to stay like this forever, to feel like this forever. She wanted...

Harriet moaned a small feline protest as Matt softened the kiss and released her mouth.

Reluctantly she opened her eyes and realised where she was and what she was doing.

Wordlessly she looked away from Matt, fighting back over-emotional tears.

Starkly Matt looked at her averted face. Who had

she been thinking of when she had returned his kiss with such fierce passion?

Did he really need to ask himself that question? he derided himself bitterly.

Grimly he tightened his grip on her hand, and then inclined his head in the direction of a small coffee-shop. 'Would you like a coffee?'

'What I'd like—' Harriet began through gritted teeth, and then stopped as the outfit displayed in a nearby shop window caught her eye.

A pretty dress, soft and floaty, in delicately patterned silk, it was so beautiful it made her catch her breath. It shrieked that special brand of expensive simplicity and it was just the exact shade of cream that suited her to perfection! In fact it embodied everything she had ever craved in a dressy outfit, right down to the delicate shoes teamed with it. She knew without having to go anywhere near the window that it would probably have the kind of price tag that ran into more than she spent on her wardrobe in a whole year. Even so a small yearning sigh escaped her lips as she had a momentary vision of herself wearing it, with Matt looking adoringly and hungrily at her, and…

Matt frowned as he watched her. There was a rapt, dreamy expression on her face as she stared at the dress in a shop several yards away. A fragile, almost flimsy sort of dress, which would float distractingly around those luscious legs of hers.

Matt's gaze became equally absorbed…

'Excuse me—are you going to go into the coffee-shop? Only, if you aren't…'

Harriet went pink as she realised that she and Matt were blocking the entrance to the café.

'I've just remembered there's a good wine bar right

'round the corner. It's almost lunchtime—we'd be better going there and having something to eat.'

Harriet barely had time to blink before she was being whisked around the corner and down another marble floored walkway into a stylish and very busy wine bar, where Matt somehow managed to get them a table.

They had just given their order when Matt suddenly frowned and stood up. 'I forgot. I need to go back to the cash dispenser. You wait here. I won't be a minute.'

The wine bar certainly had a very glitzy clientele, Harriet conceded as she sipped her drink and waited for their food and Matt's return. She didn't normally come into this part of the city, preferring to spend her spare time in its parks and galleries.

Matt was taking rather longer than she had expected, but fortunately so was their food. Typically, as soon as the waiter appeared with their order, she saw Matt shouldering his way through the crowd by the wine bar door.

'Sorry I was so long. There was a queue,' he informed her as he sat down.

CHAPTER SIX

'WE CAN'T go in here!'

Harriet held back as Matt reached out to ring the discreetly placed doorbell.

'Why not?' he demanded. 'It's a jewelers, isn't it?'

'It isn't just a jewellers,' Harriet hissed. 'It's *the* jewellers...' But it was too late; a smartly suited young woman was opening the door for them and they were being ushered inside.

Even the quiet hum of the air-conditioning sounded expensive, Harriet reflected as she breathed in air scented with just a hint of some discreet perfume.

'Good afternoon, sir, madam. How may we help you?'

'We would like an engagement ring,' Matt announced, squeezing Harriet's hand in warning, as though he had anticipated that she might argue with him.

'Ah... If you would care to come this way? We have a private room.'

The private room was bigger than her small living room, Harriet recognised as they were shown into their seats as carefully as though they were made of precious glass.

'Do you have something special in mind?' the assistant asked Harriet.

'Er...no... Just something simple and small,' Harriet replied uncomfortably.

Why on earth had Matt brought her in here? Even the teeniest chip of diamond they sold would cost the earth—she just knew it.

'My fiancée prefers simple designs,' she heard Matt saying suavely to the woman.

'Perhaps a single stone ring, then? I'll bring some to show you.'

When she came back and put down not a tray but a collection of boxes, each holding the kind of solitaire diamond ring that Harriet had only previously seen on the fingers of the mega-rich, she swallowed and blinked—and tried to keep her gaze averted from one particular ring, which glowed and shimmered and whispered a whole host of tempting things to her.

'I...I thought something smaller...' she said, her voice cracking. She looked down at the array in front of her and whispered, 'Something much smaller.'

The sales assistant's smile had started to dim, and Harriet could feel the grimness Matt was exuding.

'I like this one!' he announced peremptorily, his hand moving and unbelievably picking up the very ring Harriet had looked at.

'Ah.' The sales assistant's sigh was pure liquid approval.

Harriet couldn't help but agree as she looked at the oblong stone in its plain setting, so pure and white that the light dancing on it almost hurt her eyes.

'An excellent choice, if I may say so. And a beautiful stone. Perhaps madam would like to try it on? The band is a little on the small side, but naturally it can be sized to fit her.'

Harriet prayed with all her strength that the ring would be too tight, that Matt would be forced to pick something else more modest—because she knew he wouldn't want to leave the shop without a ring. But, even though she herself would have sworn that the ring would be too small for her, it slipped down her finger and settled there as snugly as though they had been made for one another.

'Perfect.' The sales assistant smiled.

'We'll have it,' Matt announced.

Ten minutes later, after a celebratory glass of champagne, they were leaving the shop—with the ring.

Harriet barely waited for the door to be closed behind them before turning to Matt and bursting out, 'I can't wear that ring!'

'Why not? Because Ben isn't the one who is giving it to you?' Matt shot back brusquely.

'No!' Harriet denied fiercely. 'It has nothing to do with that!'

'Then what has it to do with?' Matt enquired sharply.

'It's far too expensive.'

'Engagement rings are supposed to be expensive.'

'No!' Harriet corrected him emotionally. 'Engagement rings are supposed to be a token of love and commitment. If I ever do wear one, those are the yardsticks I shall measure it by...not...not its financial value. But then it's typical of men like you, Matt, that you should insist on picking something so expensive—a status symbol ring so that everyone can see how rich and powerful you are!'

Harriet knew that part of her furious outburst was fuelled by her own inner cocktail of volatile emotions. After all, she was in a false engagement to the man she had fought so hard to pretend she did not love, only to recognise instead how very, very much she did love him. It was an act which should have been filled with love and joy, but instead it had merely been a cold financial transaction, resulting in a physical ache deep inside, that gnawed unceasingly at her, and a growing resentment at being misjudged and condemned for a non-existent crime. For some reason Matt's purchase of the ring symbolised for her the combined pain of all of those feelings.

Perilously close to tears, she started to walk away, gasping in protest as Matt's hand shot out, his fingers curling around her wrist as he yanked her back towards him.

Her heart hit her ribs in one shocked beat when she saw how anger had turned his skin bone-white around the mouth, and frozen the grey of his eyes to silver.

'No, Harriet, what's typical of a man like me is that when I put my ring on the finger of the woman I love, I want the world to see that love reflected in it. And, more importantly, I want *her* to see that love, to know my love. To know that just as the ring is unique and beautiful, so to me is she. The purity of the stone reflects my belief in the purity of the love we share, untainted and unmarked by any past loves. I want her to see in its strength the strength of my love for her, and in its flashing fire the fierce heat of my passion for her. But more than anything else Harriet, I want her to look at the ring and know that what truly binds us to one another are bonds we ourselves have chosen—bonds that go way above and beyond any mere ring!'

Harriet couldn't bear to speak. She felt as though her emotions had been cut to ribbons and were now so painfully raw that she felt sick with the agony of them.

Knowing that one day Matt would love someone just as he had described to her, and that that woman would not be her, had opened a door for her on a whole new world of pain.

'Change the ring if you wish to do so,' Matt said tersely. 'It really doesn't matter to me.'

But it did matter, he acknowledged inwardly. He had seen how Harriet's gaze had been drawn to it, and crazily he had hoped…

'Let's get out of here,' he said curtly. 'I'll—' He started to frown as his mobile rang, and as she heard him talking Harriet recognised that his caller was one of his main clients.

'I've got to go into the office,' Matt told Harriet crisply when he had finished. 'Jardines need the Mortlake site package we did for them retailored urgently.'

'I'll come with you,' Harriet offered immediately. He frowned again, so she added, 'I worked on the original with Ben and Charlie.'

'Okay… We'll get a taxi—it will be quicker than getting the car,' Matt said, and he hurried her towards the exit.

'How much reworking do we have to do?' Harriet asked as he hailed a cab.

Jardines was a large accountancy firm and Matthew Cole Ltd was designing their new head office.

'Enough!' was Matt's unforthcoming reply as they got in the cab.

*   *   *

'Dammit, this isn't going to work!'

As she heard the frustration in Matt's voice Harriet got up from her own terminal and walked across to his office and peered over his shoulder at his computer screen.

'Look at this,' Matt told her grimly, drawing her attention to one particular detail. 'Jardines need this aspect, because it's one of their trademark fixtures, but because of the extra meeting rooms they've asked to have included it just isn't going to configure.'

Frowning, Harriet leaned closer, wholly absorbed in the complex problem on the screen. Her hair fell forward as she did so to brush against Matt's hand.

'I can see what you mean,' she agreed, every bit of her attention focused on the screen as she peered at it and then drew back slightly. 'I think—' she began, and then stopped.

'Yes?' Matt encouraged her.

Harriet shook her head. 'I don't know if it will work, but maybe if you moved the main block to here and streamlined the add-ons, then perhaps you could turn the signature piece at an angle…'

'Show me,' Matt commanded, moving back so that she could get closer to the screen.

Matt had already suspected that she was one of the most proficient and innovative lateral thinkers on his team, and now she was proving it to him.

Quickly Harriet slid into the chair he had vacated. She had worked like this with other people a hundred thousand times—two heads close together over the screen, two bodies sharing the same small space meant for one as they worked to resolve a problem—but that kind of proximity had never affected her like this before. Now it breached her professionalism and distracted her from what she was doing, she admitted, as a sharp frisson of hot awareness heightened the effect of the adrenaline already rushing through her veins and her brain worked overtime to solve the problem in front of them.

Working under pressure like this always excited and energised her, and she felt a surge of professional pleasure as she showed Matt what she meant.

Tensely Matt watched her, quickly picking up on what she was trying to do and moving even closer to work with her.

'Yes. Yes! That's it! Harriet, you've done it!' he exclaimed triumphantly. 'And if we take this out of here, and add it on here…'

Harriet's eyes widened appreciatively as Matt took up her thought process and ran with it, refining and honing it with skilled expertise.

'We've got it. Got it!' Matt exulted, standing up and drawing Harriet with him. 'Good thinking, Harriet!' he praised her, and then leaned forward and brushed her cheek with his lips in relieved appreciation.

'I'm glad I was able to help,' Harriet answered, her voice fading away as somehow her gaze became focused on his mouth and her heartbeat started to hammer.

She heard Matt mutter something under his breath, and in the next second she was in his arms, his mouth on hers.

Harriet heard herself moan as her lips parted and his tongue found hers. The high-voltage tension caused by the intensity at which they had been working must have caused Matt's sudden explosion of passion, Harriet decided dizzily, as his tongue plunged deeper and his hands dropped to her hips, pulling her into his body.

Her own body's swift recognition of his erection sent messages to her brain that had her wanting to explore it more intimately, to run her fingers over it, stroke it, savour it, feel the thick, full hardness of it naked beneath her touch.

A violent shudder racked her body and Matt groaned, his fingers kneading the rounded curves of her bottom, urging her even closer to him. The desk was only just behind her, and inside her head feverish images were already forming.

Matt moved his hand, cupping her breast gently, plucking the pouting tightness of her nipple through her top and making her moan eagerly into his kiss.

He pulled her top out of the way, fiercely and urgently, as though he was as out of control as she felt, Harriet recognised weakly when he pushed aside the fabric of her bra and then lowered his mouth to her breast.

A thrill of primitive female pleasure engulfed her as Matt tugged passionately on her nipple. Her hands reached to clasp his head against her body whilst her body arched in immediate eager response.

The office's muted hum was being overwhelmed by the unsteady sound of their ragged breathing and the hard suckle of Matt's mouth on her breast—an erotic overture that heightened Harriet's arousal and totally drowned any inner voice of caution as its siren call dragged her deeper and deeper into her need.

Outside, down below them, an ambulance siren suddenly wailed into clamouring life.

Immediately Matt released her and stepped back

from her, his reactions far, far faster than her own. Her body was aching tormentedly, still clamouring for his touch whilst she struggled to make her trembling hands restore order to her clothes.

'Harriet— Believe me, I never intended...' She could hear Matt speaking grimly, his obvious and immediate rejection of what had happened forcing her to follow his example—for the sake of her pride if nothing else.

'I... I...it doesn't matter. There's no need to make an issue of it,' she said quickly, mortified by the thought that he might start to question just why she had responded to him so immediately and so intensely. 'It wasn't important, Matt. Sometimes these things happen when you're working at high pressure.'

To her relief Matt had turned his back to her, and therefore he couldn't see just how much he had actually affected her.

'Do they indeed?' There was an odd inflection in his voice, but before Harriet could question it he was continuing almost brusquely, 'Look, it's gone six o'clock. I'll call you a cab and you can go back to the hotel and get ready for dinner. The table isn't booked until eight. That will give me time to send this stuff off to Jardines, then get changed here and meet you at the hotel.'

'Do we have to have dinner?' Harriet asked him warily.

'It's a damned sight safer option that staying here and finishing what we just started,' Matt answered her brutally. 'And let me warn you that right now, the way I'm feeling, it would be damnably easy to stand in for

Ben and play out your little fantasy for you, if that's
the way your mind is working.'

'No, it is not!' Harriet denied immediately, but her
face was burning. Inside her a voice was urging her
to give in to her real feelings and take what he was
offering without questioning the reasons for his offer,
no matter what the consequences!

For a moment she was almost tempted to tell him
that the only man who ever featured in her sexual fantasies was him, but somehow she managed to stop
herself.

'I'll call that taxi,' Matt said flatly.

As he walked away from her he was cursing himself
under his breath. If he didn't get some space between
them, and soon, he would be taking her up to the penthouse with him—if he could last out that far—and the
kind of sex they would be sharing would be hot and
immediate and dangerously soul-baring.

At least if he sent her straight to the hotel he would
be able to calm himself down. A cold shower might
be a good idea as well, he derided himself, as he felt
the almost painful ache of his straining erection.

What the hell was happening to him? The thought
of having sex here in the office would normally have
been more of a turn-off for him than a turn on!

He had booked a room, Matt had said, but this wasn't
a mere 'room,' it was a palatial suite! Round-eyed,
Harriet looked at the table the waiter had just wheeled
in and left: mouthwatering-looking canapés, strawberries dipped in chocolate, champagne on ice—a truly
romantic offering! Had someone told them they were
about to celebrate their 'engagement'?

Just thinking about it sent a surge of stomach churning mixed emotions racing through her. Her heart twisting, and on edge, Harriet walked through the bedroom. The business clothes she had in her case were hardly going to suit the occasion, were they? She hadn't packed her black dress, and—

Abruptly she came to a halt as she stared at the huge bed, and the glossy designer carrier bag on it.

There was a card pinned to the bag with her name on it in Matt's handwriting. Uncertainly she took it off and read it: *Hope I've got the right size.*

Frowning, Harriet withdrew the tissue-wrapped package from the carrier bag and opened it, her heart somersaulting with a mixture of disbelief, angry pride and a sharp pang of pure female delight, which she tried to subdue as she saw the dress she had admired earlier in the day.

What on earth—? How on earth—? It had to be mere chance, didn't it, that Matt had bought her this particular dress? His action had to have been motivated by his desire not to be shown up by her, didn't it?

That knowledge alone should have had her wrapping the dress up immediately and refusing to even look at it, never mind thinking about wearing it! And perhaps if it had been any other dress but this one she would have done just that. But as she shook it free of the tissue Harriet caught her breath. It was so perfect for her, and the right size as well. In other circumstances she would have loved wearing such a dress for her lover. Her lover... For Matt.

Emotion choked her.

She wasn't going to wear it, of course. She couldn't!

Not the dress or the little strappy shoes that went with it either.

And yet she was holding it up in front of her, and her heart gave a sharp pang as she recognised that she had been right. The dress was perfect for her.

And perfect for the occasion.

She had never owned a dress like this. Matt had never seen her wearing anything that declared so emphatically that this was a dress a woman wore for herself and for a man… Her man.

Wearing such a dress would be almost a declaration. An invitation. At least it would be for her.

And that would certainly be one way of proving to Matt that he was totally wrong about her feelings for Ben, a small inner voice told her recklessly. There was still a sharp sensual ache deep inside her body, and suddenly it became much fiercer, an ache that included longing and excitement as well as arousal.

She gave a small, reckless toss of her head.

Tonight she and Matt would be celebrating their engagement, and if she chose to take the situation he had created a step further, if she chose to take the fantasy a step further, and celebrate it in the most natural way of all for a woman in love to celebrate that love, then why shouldn't she do so? She was an adult, and answerable only to herself.

And, as today had shown, Matt wasn't immune to her—even if it was only sexual desire that aroused him.

Why shouldn't she claim this night as her own? Why shouldn't she claim Matt as her own, even if it was only for a few hours?

The audacity of her own thoughts shocked and excited her, feeding the everlasting flame of her love. Was it really such a dreadful thing for her to want to be with him in the most intimate way possible, the way nature had ordained for a woman to be with the man she loved? And she did so love Matt!

Harriet drew in a deep sigh and touched the delicate fabric tentatively. She didn't have much time to make up her mind. Matt would be here soon. She looked at the chilling champagne. Her heart was racing, her blood seething through her veins as though it was already filled with champagne bubbles. Perhaps if she were to have one glass—just to calm her nerves a little! It was only champagne after all! Quickly before she could change her mind she reached for one of the bottles and opened it neatly.

Pouring herself a glass, she took it into the bathroom with her, appreciatively admiring the extensive and very expensive range of toiletries. The hotel management were certainly thorough; there was even a sealed pack of condoms tucked discreetly into a basket of other personal requisites.

Half an hour later, she was just finishing her second glass of champagne and studying her reflection in the bedroom mirror, when the suite door opened and Matt strode in.

Her heart rocked on its axis and a rush of love surged through her. He had changed his casual clothes for the formality of a dark suit and a shirt and tie, and Harriet feasted her hungry gaze on him for as long as she dared.

When he saw her, Matt came to an abrupt halt.

'The dress was the right size, then?' he demanded almost brusquely.

'It fits perfectly,' Harriet answered softly. 'But you really shouldn't have bought it for me.'

'Think of it as a bonus,' he answered tensely. 'You deserve one after solving the Jardines problem for me.'

He didn't sound like a man who had just had a problem solved, Harriet decided, her own mood altering to match his when she saw the way he was frowning and felt the coldness emanating from him.

'I opened the champagne,' she said. 'Do you want a glass?'

His frown seemed to deepen.

'You were the one who said we had to behave as though we were genuinely celebrating our engagement,' Harriet reminded him, sensing his disapproval.

'In public,' Matt said harshly, immediately flicking back his cuff to look pointedly at his watch. 'Our table is booked for eight and it's almost that now.'

His hostility was flattening the bubbles of her own earlier excitement threatening to steamroller over the sharp thrill of delicious and wanton anticipation the champagne had nurtured. And not just the champagne, if she were honest. The intimacy they had shared earlier had left her sensually intoxicated and eager to continue from where they had left off, leading her into a dangerous world of fantasy. But Matt, it was plain, had totally dissociated himself from what had happened. She couldn't let go of her own dreams so easily, though. Her love was a fierce power, overwhelming her normal caution.

A small spurt of rebellious recklessness kicked dangerously to life inside her.

Lowering her lashes, she tried to hide what she was feeling, unaware of just how unintentionally seductive she looked as she reminded him, 'We're celebrating our engagement. Surely we're allowed to be a little bit late? After all, it's obvious from the champagne the hotel has left that they expect us to have our own private celebration…'

Matt witnessed her unexpected transformation from virgin into seductive vamp with a feeling in his gut that made him want to take hold of her and—

'How many glasses of that stuff did you say you've had?' he demanded, striding over and removing the bottle from the ice bucket.

'Only two,' Harriet told him defensively. 'Plus the one I poured for you!'

'Three glasses of champagne on an empty stomach?'

There was a look in his eyes that was irritated and then for a brief moment filled with something else— a hot, hungry maleness which he quickly leashed.

'I ate some of the canapés and chocolate strawberries,' Harriet assured him virtuously. 'You should try one, Matt, they're delicious,' she encouraged, picking one up and offering it to him.

When he shook his head, she held the chocolate-coated fruit to her own lips, licking the chocolate coating off with happy and uncalculated sensuality.

Matt closed his eyes.

He had deliberately delayed getting here, knowing that in his present vulnerable emotional and physical state he just could not trust himself to be alone with her. The last thing he was equipped to cope with was this. A Harriet transformed into the most unbelievably irresistible virgin turned vamp, and having an effect on him that made him want to strip that damnably erotic dress she was wearing from her body, pour what was left of her glass of champagne over her skin and lick it from her whilst it cascaded over her breasts and pooled in the hollow her belly before. And as for those strawberries…

He looked into her face and saw the soft, illuminated look in her eyes, the half-shy, half-bold way she was looking back at him. He took a step towards her. If she thought he was going to let her get away with looking at him like that, tormenting him like that… Any minute now she was going to end up on the bed, and he was—

Grimly he closed his eyes and took a deep breath, like a diver who'd just come up for air. She didn't know what she was doing—and she certainly didn't know how he felt, he reminded himself.

Refusing to look at her, he removed the ring box from his pocket.

'Look, get this damned thing on, and then we're going down to dinner. And you are not having any more champagne.'

Harriet tilted her chin.

'We are getting engaged. You have to put the ring on for me,' she told him, waggling her ring finger.

Three glasses of champagne and she was like this? He felt like a hormonal teenager, recognising for the very first time what the male hunting instinct was all about, Matt recognised grimly.

He was sorely tempted to tell her that if he went near her now he wouldn't be putting the ring on her finger, but taking the dress she was wearing off her body.

*   *   *

If Matt came over to her now, she was going to put her arms around his neck and kiss his mouth as she had been longing to do for what seemed like forever, Harriet decided dizzily, far more intoxicated by his presence than she would have been by any amount of champagne. And then she was going to tell him that there was no way she was going to get engaged to him unless he took her to bed first. And then if that didn't work she was going to—

Her gaze swivelled to the suite door as it suddenly rattled and two waiters came in, plainly not expecting to find them there.

'It's all right—you can take the trolley,' Matt said. 'We were just leaving...'

'But please leave the champagne...' Harriet called out, as Matt took hold of her arm and practically dragged her into the corridor.

Before they reached the lift he pushed the ring onto her finger, and all she could do as he bustled her inside it to join the other silent passengers was give him a reproachful glower.

'Have you ever made love in a lift?' she asked him conversationally, once it had stopped and they had got out.

Matt stared at her. Vintage champagne on an empty stomach was obviously a new experience for her.

'No, I haven't,' he told her tersely.

'Have you ever wished you had, though?' Harriet persisted.

'Not as much as I wish you had stopped at one glass of champagne,' Matt said through gritted teeth, and he almost marched her into the hotel's exclusive restaurant area.

Harriet produced another pout, and then became distracted as she caught sight of herself in the bank of mirrors that decorated the corridor.

'This dress is just so lovely,' she sighed. 'It makes me feel like a different person.'

'It's certainly making you behave like one,' Matt allowed drily. If he was honest, Matt knew that if circumstances had been different her unexpected transformation would have had him not just tenderly amused and protective, but more than ready to play the erotic game she had so innocently started.

The sight of Harriet with her inhibitions and her defences removed was proving to be a very dangerous and powerful aphrodisiac so far as he was concerned.

'We've just become engaged,' Harriet reminded him reprovingly. 'I'm supposed to be in love with you, remember?' She flashed her ring at him. 'And I just want you to know, Mr Cole,' she said breathily, mimicking Marilyn Monroe, 'that you are the sexiest man alive and I'd much rather be upstairs alone in the suite with you than down here in the restaurant.'

'Really? Rather than being with Ben?'

'Who's Ben?' Harriet asked him sweetly.

'I take it you won't be drinking any wine with your meal?' Matt asked Harriet drily as they studied their menus.

'No…I think I'd better stick with the champagne,' Harriet answered innocently, looking up enquiringly when she heard him make a muffled sound.

*   *   *

'Why don't you have another coffee?'

'I've already had three cups,' Harriet reminded Matt solemnly as the waiter lifted the coffee pot.

The restaurant was almost empty, and the bubbles of excitement singing in her veins had become a giddy fluttering of butterflies in her stomach as she contemplated what lay ahead.

In fact she was a little surprised that she hadn't had any second thoughts—or abandoned her reckless decision before she could put it into practice.

The truth was, though, that if anything her determination to return to the suite and somehow, by hook or by crook, ensure that tonight Matt became her lover had grown stronger during the evening rather than weaker.

The effects of the champagne she had drunk earlier might have worn off, but the effects of her love for Matt and the intimacy they had shared had not!

'I think they're waiting for us to leave,' she told Matt, ruefully indicating the hovering waiters.

'Yes. If you're sure you don't want any more coffee I'll take you up to the suite,' Matt accepted curtly.

As he escorted her out of the room Harriet turned towards him and whispered mischievously, 'Thank you for my beautiful ring, darling,' and then reached up and pressed a brief kiss to his mouth.

The minute he had seen her safely inside the suite he was going to leave her there alone, Matt decided grimly. She hadn't had any alcohol to drink over dinner, and surely the effects of that damned champagne should have worn off by now, but she had spent the entire evening openly flirting with him. As the lift doors opened and they stepped together into its empty intimacy he decided that he didn't know which he wanted to do the most—strangle her, or...

When he saw that she was looking at him with liquid-eyed expectant hopefulness, he took a deep breath and told himself that he must be imagining things. He made sure he stood well away from her.

The lift took them to their floor and he waited for her to step out. Harriet turned to him and told him reproachfully, 'You might at least have kissed me, Matt. Every woman has a right to be kissed in a lift once in her life—especially when she has just got engaged...'

Removing the suite key from his pocket, Matt unlocked the door and held it open.

Happily Harriet stepped inside, and turned to smile at him.

'Sleep well,' Matt told her dismissively. 'I'll give you a call in the morning.'

Harriet's eyes widened. 'You're leaving me here on my own?'

Matt could hear the disbelief in her voice. 'I might as well go back to the penthouse.'

'Matt!' she protested, unable to conceal her distress. But it was too late—he was already closing the door.

This couldn't be happening to her! He couldn't have left her! But he had.

Harriet blinked hard, swallowing the taste of her disappointment.

So much for her plans!

Matt reached the lift and pressed the bell.

He had done the right thing. He knew that. If he had stayed he could count on one hand the seconds before he would have had Harriet in his arms, showing her just what effect her behaviour towards him over dinner had had on him, and how dangerous it was to flirt with a man as much as she had flirted with him. Especially when that man was already so damned hungry for her that—

The lift arrived and the doors opened.

Matt got in and pressed the button.

Have you ever made love in a lift? What the hell kind of question was that? He closed his eyes and then opened then again as the lift reached the car park floor.

Disconsolately Harriet removed her precious dress and wandered into the bathroom. The whirlpool bath caught her attention and she heaved a small sigh.

She might as well enjoy some sinful self-indulgence, even if it was not the kind she had longed for.

Turning on the taps, she ran a bath and removed the rest of her clothes.

Matt reached into his pocket for his car keys, frowning as he realised that he had only both suite keys.

Now, why on earth had he done that? Or did he really need to ask himself?

Fate was a funny thing, he decided as he locked the car and started to retrace his steps.

Harriet didn't hear him enter the suite. In fact the first she knew of his presence was when he walked into the bathroom to find her lying back in the whirlpool bath, with only her head above the mass of bubbles which had already spilled over the sides of the tub.

'Matt,' she whispered weakly. 'I don't know what

I've done, but I think these bubbles are getting a bit out of control.'

'That's what happens when you play around with things you don't understand,' Matt heard himself answering thickly.

Did she have any idea what she was doing to him? As she tried to sit up foam clung to her skin and then slid from it, revealing the creamy swell of her breasts. 'I can't switch the whirlpool jet thingy off.'

'You'd better get out, then, and let me try.'

'It would be much easier if you got in,' Harriet told him softly. 'And much more fun!'

Matt stared at her, but although she flushed slightly she didn't look away from him.

'You do know what you're saying, don't you?' he demanded, before stressing, 'What you're inviting...?'

Mutely Harriet nodded her head, and then told him brightly, 'The hotel is awfully well-organised, Matt. They even provide condoms.' She stood up in the bath. 'Help me out, please.'

'I thought you wanted me to get in with you?' he reminded her huskily.

Matt closed his eyes, exasperated with himself for his own lack of self-control. What the hell was he doing? But it was too late to back out now. Harriet was looking at him, her eyes glowing and an expression of radiant expectancy on her face.

'Oh, Matt!' she whispered. 'I do want you to make love to me so very, very much. You will, won't you?'

CHAPTER SEVEN

HARRIET gave a small gasp as Matt lifted her body out of the bath. 'Your suit!' she protested. 'You'll be soaked... Mmm.'

If *he* didn't care about his suit, then she wasn't going to worry about it! Not when he was kissing her like this.

He should not be doing this, Matt warned himself. But somewhere deep down inside himself he knew that there was no way he could not. Some foolish, stubborn part of him refused to relinquish its passionate belief that if only he could show Harriet what real love—*his* love—was like, then she would recognise how much she wanted it, and him, and how little she wanted Ben.

Harriet hardly dared allow herself to believe what was happening. To believe that it was Matt who was holding her and kissing her. But her body had no time for such foolish hesitations. Her body was far, far too busy showing its appreciation of the sensual pleasure it was enjoying, and what was more it was demanding that Harriet threw every bit of her emotional and cerebral energy and concentration into actively participating!

And why should she not do so, when it was so very, very much what she wanted?

Eagerly she wrapped her arms around his neck and pressed her naked body as close to him as she could, returning the hard, demanding pressure of his mouth with a kiss of fevered longing. Delicately she ran the tip of her tongue along the line of his mouth, tracing it, probing its defences. She lifted her breasts and the urgent thrust of her body brought a sensually erotic friction to her nipples with each unchoreographed and instinctive movement it made.

Matt had always prided himself on his self-control, but now he realised that it had never previously been truly tested, that all other sensual intimacies had barely touched the surface of what uncontrollable need actually felt like. The feel of Harriet's tongue tip innocently mimicked and mirrored the most intimate kind of man-to-woman penetration; the hard points of her stiff nipples were hot stabs of pleasure burning against his skin with every writhing movement of her body. These were all guided-missile assaults on a defence mechanism which in the past had known little other than the equivalent of a mild attack with a handheld catapult.

Even the erection he could feel straining against his clothes had an unfamiliar dimension to it—not so much in size, or even intensity, but in something that went way beyond that. A sort of spiritually physical homing need, Matt recognised to his own grim shock.

So this was physical love. This savage, untameable hunger that would break down every barrier between them until they were perfectly united as one. This seeking, aching drive to complete himself within her.

What he felt was both primitive and spiritual. The most basic of man's desires and the most elevated, straining together to form an emotional and physical hunger that held him helpless in its grip.

Harriet could feel how aroused Matt was, and beneath the immediate kick of her sweetly pleasurable excitement she could feel the rhythmic pulse of her body's answering response.

Impatiently she tugged at his shirt, her skin starting to flush with betraying heat.

How long was he going to make her wait?'

Somehow her love-hungry thoughts had become achingly impatient words, whispered against Matt's mouth as she tried to steal the intimate kiss she was longing for.

And when he heard them Matt felt the last of his self-control being dragged away with them. He gripped her bare arms firmly and eased her away from his body, ignoring her small moaned protest. When she tried to reach out to him he tugged her hands down and held them carefully with one of his own, whilst he started to undress himself impatiently with the other.

'Wait…just wait,' he told her thickly, his molten grey gaze holding the dark liquid passion of jade.

When he tugged off his shirt he felt the shudder that jolted her through his own body, like an electric shock. Her already prominent nipples flared into irresistible dark-flushed temptation.

Harriet shuddered again when he looked at them, and somewhere inside his head the need to experience how she would react when he gave in to the craving to have her breasts inside his mouth struck him with such force that he had dropped to one knee and begun lapping at first one and then the other with fierce urgency before he could stop himself.

Her hands trapped behind her back, Matt's tongue

laving her exquisitively aroused nipples, Harriet shuddered more under the liquid surges of pleasure that ran through her.

Pulling her hands free of Matt's grip, she started to finish the task he had begun, tugging frantically at fabric and fastenings until she could feel the heat of his flesh beneath her hands.

The tug of his mouth on her breast drew a sharp, wild cry from her lips and she raked his flesh with her nails, unable to stop herself from reacting to the needs he was feeling.

She could feel it gathering swiftly inside her, like a fast-flooding river, channelled into the place where its intensity would set in motion a cataclysmically powerful reaction.

Fear spiked and shook her; the swift race might prove too fast to be properly harnessed. As though he sensed it too, Matt swept her up into his arms, kicking aside the tangle of his clothes, and carried her into the bedroom.

In its shadows Harriet could almost see the beat of his heart beneath the golden sheen of his skin. Wonderingly she raised her hand to it, her fingertips measuring each thudding, driving beat, knowing already with the most intense emotion and physical anticipation that soon that driving power would be replicated and intensified within her own body.

Matt could feel the strain on his own self-control as he placed Harriet on the bed. Things had gone too fast, and for him too far now, for the slow, gentle voyage he had intended.

Harriet lay on the bed and looked up at him. She was shockingly close to her orgasm...too close.

In her mind's eye she could see the foil wrapper of the condom she had secreted away in her handbag, which was within reach beside the bed.

A surge of explicit heat tightened sharply inside her. Deliberately and determinedly she opened her legs, and looked directly into Matt's face.

The dark tide of colour that surged through his face as his arousal strained towards her only heightened her own.

Boldly she touched her own body, biting down hard on her lip as she felt the immediate tense contraction, her gaze fixed fiercely on Matt's as he shuddered violently in response.

'Now, Matt… Oh, please, now—now…' Her words were lost, crushed beneath his mouth as his hands shaped her. She could feel the thick, hard throb of him against her thigh and her fingers reached blindly for him, discarding as they did so the foil wrapper she had been clutching.

Somewhere, outside himself and the ferocity of his driving need, Matt registered and recognised it, automatically responding to his own inbuilt set of unbroken rules.

Harriet, clinging to the edge of a place she couldn't bear to let herself be swept from, heard the brief rustle and felt the chilling emptiness of where he had been. But before she could think logically about what was happening Matt was holding her, kissing her, entering her as slowly and carefully as he could whilst his whole body shook under the unbearable burden of his own self-control. She exhaled a delicious moan of joyous pleasure as she realised that her fantasies were going to be more than fulfilled.

The brief feeling of pressure, the sudden stilling of Matt's body, were unwanted interruptions and delays. Instinctively she showed him this, moving fiercely and eagerly against him until he drove deeper and then more deeply still as she clung to him and urged him to take all that she wanted to give him, her body glorying in each new thrust.

Dear heaven, but she felt so good, so perfect, with her flesh enfolding him, holding him, gripping him. She moved deliberately against him, inciting him to plunge deeper.

Harriet could already feel her orgasm overwhelming her—tight, fierce bursts of sensation that echoed the pulse of life itself. She heard Matt shout out in exultation and the intensity increased to a frantic explosion of savagely powerful contractions that were a world away from anything she had previously experienced.

Held fast in Matt's arms, still trembling between each jagged breath, Harriet felt herself fall from the euphoric haven she had been inhabiting through doubt and shock into the cold, unwanted world of reality.

Matt was renowned for his astuteness. How long would it be before he guessed how she felt about him? And when he did what was going to happen?

Harriet suspected she already knew the answer to her own question.

She would suffer the misery and the humiliation of being told that Matt did not want her love—and, worse, she would probably be banished from his life! She couldn't bear to let that happen!

She must not let him guess how she really felt!

*　*　*

His chin resting on the top of Harriet's head, Matt blinked fiercely. No one, nothing, had ever touched his emotions so intensely as what he had just shared with Harriet. It was true that love gave the physical act of intimacy between two people an extra dimension that took it into another world. He felt awed, humbled, fiercely and passionately completed, and equally fiercely and passionately determined that he was never, ever going to let Harriet go.

Surely she must have shared some of those feelings?

All his adult life he had protected his own deepest emotions, but now he knew that he had to tell Harriet how he felt, that he had to beg her if necessary to let him wipe the slate clean so that they could begin again—two people who could together touch immortality through their shared love.

He took a deep breath and began, 'Harriet, why—?'

Immediately Harriet froze. It was happening already, the very thing she had dreaded. Matt was going to ask her why she had responded to him in the way she had, and then he was going to answer his own question by telling her that he knew she was in love with him.

She couldn't let that happen.

'I know what you're going to say, Matt.' She stopped him quickly. 'But you've got it all wrong. The only reason I made... I did what I did was because I couldn't think of any other way of convincing you that, contrary to your constant accusations, I am not saving myself for Ben.'

Her sharp, careless words hit Matt like blows, like acid-tipped arrows to his heart. He went completely still, and then moved away from her so brutally that Harriet felt as though he had physically pushed her away.

'Thank goodness you were quick-thinking enough to remember the condom,' she added chattily. 'It was a wonderful experience, Matt, and I got so carried away that I would have forgotten.'

There! That should take care of any thoughts he had of questioning the intensity of her response, Harriet decided fiercely.

She waited for Matt to respond, but instead he simply got out of the bed and walked silently into the bathroom, firmly closing the door.

A pain like no other she had ever experienced filled her. It was so intense, so immense, that she couldn't contain it. It felt as though it was weeping from her heart into her blood, seeping through her pores until every bit of her was saturated with it.

There was no escape from it and there never would be, Harriet acknowledged in anguish.

CHAPTER EIGHT

NUMBLY Harriet opened her fist and stared at the ring in the palm of her hand. Unable to bear its brilliance in the face of her own pain, she closed her hand again, so tightly that the stone dug into her skin.

She hadn't seen Matt for over a week. He had left the hotel after they had made love without saying a single word to her, and she had discovered when she had arrived at work in the morning that he had been called away on some urgent business.

She had received a terse text message from him, demanding: 'Wear the ring—I meant what I said'.

And of course she'd had to, for Ben's sake! And now it seemed that everyone knew that she and Matt were supposed to be engaged.

Now at last it was Friday, and she had decided it was the last day of her working life with Matt. If she couldn't endure the pain of her unwanted love when he wasn't there then how on earth was she going to bear it when he was?

The tears threatening to pour from her eyes were as sharply painful as the diamond cutting into her hand.

'Harry—there you are!'

She forced a smile at Ben came bounding up to her. 'How's Cindi?' she asked him.

'She's fine. We're both fine. In fact we're over the moon,' he confessed happily. 'She's finally accepted that she got it all wrong about you and me, and she's

taking me home with her to meet her family at the end
of the month. But first we're going to have a couple
of days away together, so that I can follow Matt's
example and pop the question! I love her so much,
Harry, but there's no way I could have accepted her
if she hadn't been understanding about you and our
friendship.'

Harriet's heart sank further with every word he ut-
tered. Everything Ben was saying confirmed what she
herself had feared. She suspected that if she and Matt
'broke up' now, it would do irreparable harm to Ben's
romance.

But of course the truth was that she and Matt had
nothing together to break up. She meant nothing to
him. Nothing at all!

Tears filled her eyes. Frantically she tried to blink
them away.

'Harry?' Ben queried, bewildered. 'What is it?
What's wrong? I thought you were happy.'

It was more than Harriet's savaged emotions could
stand. To her own humiliation and disbelief she discovered that she had stared to cry.

'Thank you, Ben. I will deal with this,' Matt announced from behind them.

Both of them swung around in shock, neither of
them having heard him come into the room.

'Oh, Matt. It's you! Good.' Ben looked relieved.
'Well, I'll take myself off and...'

'That won't be necessary,' Matt told him grimly.
'What Harriet and I have to say to one another is going
to be said in the privacy of my apartment, and not
here in the office!'

So far he hadn't so much as looked at her, never

mind addressed her directly, Harriet recognised, torn between a sweet, aching longing, unbearable pain, and total and absolute misery.

He was looking at her now, though, pinning her with that ice-grey look of his whilst he held open the office door and said coldly, 'Harriet?'

Reluctantly she started to walk towards him, preparing her verbal defensive attack as she did so.

And she didn't wait to reach him to launch it. 'There really isn't any point in this Matt,' she began, but to her shock he forestalled her, manacling her wrist with a hard, determined grip.

But it was still his touch, still his flesh on hers, and she was still oh, so achingly vulnerable to that.

Panic engulfed her like the cold, icy waters of a well she had fallen into and couldn't escape from.

'No! Let me go. You know—'

Immediately Matt swung around to face her.

He must have been working hard, she decided, because there was a sharper edge to his jaw, a leanness to his face, and the shadow of something in his eyes that suggested a hard, punishing week without proper meals or sleep.

'I know what? How hot you are in bed?' he taunted her savagely. 'Do you want me to tell Ben that? What we have to say to one another needs to be said in private—unless you want me to go into explicit detail in public,' he told her brutally.

Harriet felt herself sway as her body absorbed the shock of his open threat.

He hadn't had a single second's respite from thinking about her all week—which had defeated the whole

purpose of setting up a rigorous diary of appointments
to keep him out of the office, Matt acknowledged bitterly.

This morning, knowing he would be seeing her, he
had been forced to admit that his need to do so had
outstripped his pride by about one thousand to one.

He had even planned during his early-morning drive
back how he could use the fake engagement he had
created to build a very real intimacy between them—
the kind of intimacy which, whilst a form of purgatory
for him, would at least give him the opportunity to
find some way to win her love.

And then he had walked into the office—his office—to find her with Ben!

Matt didn't know how to contain the savagery of
his own pain. He told himself that he wasn't going to
say a word to her until they reached the penthouse,
but no sooner were they outside the room than he
found himself breaking his own rules.

'I don't care what you have to say about it, Harriet,
or how much you argue,' he told her harshly, 'our
engagement is still very much on, and will remain on.'

'You don't—'

'And what is more,' Matt continued thickly, 'if necessary it will be continued as far as marriage.'

'If necessary? What do you mean, if necessary?
How could it be necessary? I—'

'We had sex,' Matt told her. 'You could be carrying
my child.'

Matt's child.

Harriet felt her heart beat a sharply painful tattoo of
longing.

'No!' she whispered, shaking her head. Her mouth

had suddenly gone dry and she had to wet her lips with the tip of her tongue. 'That's not possible...you used a condom.'

Matt gave her a derisory look. 'That's no guarantee!'

What on earth had he started? The fierce mule kick his words had brought to his emotions had activated a response in his body that told him how much it was now wanting to ensure that his unfounded threat became an absolute certainty. A child; Harriet's body swelling with his child.

Harriet felt as though she was drowning in her own sickening panic.

'No. *No*. You can't make me. I *won't* marry you, Matt. Not even if I am pregnant. I...I couldn't bear it.'

Matt went perfectly still as he heard the emotional agony in her voice. His own emotion carved twin deep grooves of biting loss along either side of his mouth, but Harriet was too caught up in her feelings to notice. He marched towards the private lift that serviced his apartment, aware that Harriet was following him.

Savagely he pressed the button and the doors opened immediately.

'Don't do this to me, Matt,' she begged as she got in the lift with him and the doors shut behind them. 'I couldn't bear being married to you when I love you so much and you don't love me at all. In fact I think it would kill me.'

There was a sharp, tense silence, and then Matt asked very quietly, 'Would you like to repeat what you just said?'

Harriet closed her eyes and gulped in air.

'You heard me.'

'You love me so much…?' Matt prompted her.

'Yes,' she whispered in defeat.

'And I don't love you at all?'

Matt reached behind him for the 'stop' button and pressed it hard.

Harriet gasped in shock as the lift's abrupt halt threw her against him. No, not against him, she recognised dizzily, but into him—into his open arms, which wrapped tightly around her, whilst his mouth fastened hungrily on hers in a fierce claim of possession.

'Wrong!' Matt corrected her thickly against her mouth when he was finally able to release it. 'I do love you. I have loved you and I shall love you more deeply, more passionately, than I ever thought it was possible for me to love anyone.'

'You love me?' The miracle of hope began to edge into her voice.

Matt groaned and took her back in his arms, releasing the lift button as he did so.

He was still kissing her when the doors opened.

'Have we reached the penthouse?' Harriet asked dizzily.

Matt turned his head and glanced into the office behind them—to see his staff working very hard at not noticing their intimacy.

'Not exactly,' he answered.

Uncertainly Harriet turned her head.

'Matt, everyone can see us!' she whispered, pink-cheeked.

'Yes, they can,' he agreed, still holding her in his arms. Obviously he'd pressed 'stop' before the lift had started moving, and now the doors had opened automatically. 'And what they can see is that you are mine.'

'I never loved Ben the way you thought,' Harriet told him truthfully. 'I've never loved anyone the way I love you, Matt. It wasn't true what I said about…about going to bed with you to prove to you I wasn't saving myself for Ben either,' she added huskily. 'I wanted you like that the moment I saw you.' Her body shuddered in visible longing. 'In fact I think I fell in love with you the moment I saw you, but you were so…so cold towards me…'

'Was I? It must have been something to do with all those cold showers I kept on having to take,' he teased her, changing tack to ask, 'How do you feel about a June wedding?'

'June?' Dismay darkened her eyes. 'But it's already May, and that means waiting a whole year.

'I mean *this* June,' Matt corrected her softly, firmly closing the lift door.

'Where are we going now?' Harriet asked.

'To heaven,' he answered thickly, 'via the penthouse. Unless you really want to know what it's like to make love in a lift?'

'Oh, Matt it's the same suite!'

Harriet's eyes shone with love and a longing that made Matt's hands tremble slightly as he locked the suite door and turned to walk towards her.

'I wanted us to celebrate our true engagement here, where we both made our commitment to one another, even though then we didn't know we shared those feelings. Harriet, come here. I can't bear not having you in my arms a second longer.'

'What about the champagne?' Harriet protested. 'And the canapés and the chocolate coated strawberries…?'

'What's that look for?' she demanded, when Matt suddenly started to smile as he remembered what he had wanted to do that first night she had so innocently tormented him.

When he told her she blushed and laughed, and then whispered to him that she'd like to reciprocate but that she loved the taste of him so much she didn't want to dilute it with champagne.

'Harriet…' he groaned unevenly.

'I don't know how I'm going to bear sleeping without you for three whole days when we go home for the wedding,' Harriet said, tugging at his shirt buttons and nuzzling her lips against his skin.

'We'll be able to make up for it once we're on honeymoon,' Matt promised.

'Mmm…a whole month of just the two of us.' Harriet shuddered with eager pleasure, and then sighed happily as she succeeded in unfastening his shirt.

EPILOGUE

'OH, LOOK at the bride—isn't she beautiful?' the little girl called out in excitement as she stood on the pavement watching the bridal party arrive.

Harriet could see her father's proud smile as she walked towards the church on his arm.

It was a perfect June day, and the ivory silk gown she and her mother had chosen together moved softly in the warm summer air.

Her brother and his wife and children had flown over from America for the occasion, and behind her she could hear Ben speaking sternly to her small niece and nephew, reminding them of their important duties as flower girl and page boy.

A smile curled Harriet's mouth.

She knew it was unusual for her to have a male supporter as part of the bridal party, but Ben was her best friend and Matt had totally agreed with her wish to honour that friendship by asking Ben to be her supporter and Cindi to be her bridesmaid.

'Of course you will have to wear pink,' Harriet had told Ben gravely.

'Over my dead body.' Ben had refused point-blank—until he had realised she had been teasing him.

The church doors opened and Harriet stepped from the sunlight into the porch. The organ music swelled and Harriet walked as slowly as she could down the aisle on her father's arm—when in reality she wanted to run to Matt as fast as she could.

Around her the pews were filled with family and friends, but Harriet was oblivious to everyone but Matt. Matt was now her family, her friend, her all and her everything.

Unconventionally he was standing facing her, watching her draw closer to him, and when she reached him they looked at one another, sharing an intimate moment of silent commitment and promise.

The familiar words of the marriage service began. 'Dearly beloved...'

Matt was hers; for now and forever.

Liz Fielding started writing at the age of twelve, when she won a writing competition at school. After that early success there was quite a gap – during which she was busy working in Africa and the Middle East, getting married and having children – before her first book was published in 1992. Now readers worldwide fall in love with her irresistible heroes, adore her independent minded heroines. Visit Liz's website for news and extracts of upcoming books at www.lizfielding.com

Look out for Liz Fielding's next feel-good read:
HER WISH-LIST BRIDEGROOM
on sale February 2005 in Tender Romance™!

THE TEMP AND THE TYCOON

by
Liz Fielding

CHAPTER ONE

'WAIT for me!'

Talie Calhoun sprinted across the marble lobby of the Radcliffe Tower as the lift doors began to close. The occupant of the lift obliged by holding the doors, and she beamed a grateful smile in his direction.

'Thank you so much! It's my first day and I am sooo late,' she said, all in a rush as she checked her wristwatch and let out a tiny wail of anguish before looking up at her fellow passenger. Nothing unusual there. Looking up was what she did, mostly. Her grandmother had warned her. If she didn't eat up her spinach and crusts she wouldn't grow tall and her hair wouldn't curl.

One out of two to granny.

Oh, good grief. It was just her luck that the man was a serious babe magnet. Slate grey eyes, cheekbones to die for, a mouth that you just knew would melt your bones. If you were in the market to have your bones melted, that was. In short, the kind of man that you wouldn't want to meet unless your make-up was perfect, your clothes elegant—but sexy—and your hair totally in control. Instead, she was pink in the face, dishevelled and flustered. She wasn't even going to think about her hair…

'That's not good, is it?' she said, offering a smile. But if she'd been hoping for reassurance, she was out of luck.

'It does suggest a certain lack of enthusiasm,' he replied coolly.

Would it have hurt the wretch to smile?

'Which floor?' he enquired.

'Oh…' She consulted the card she was holding. 'Thirty-two, please.' Then, as her knight errant pressed the button for her floor, 'It's not true, you know,' she said. 'I am *incredibly* enthusiastic.'

He lifted his left eyebrow no more than a millimetre. It expressed a world-weary lack of belief that she found totally galling.

'No, honestly!' she protested. Then, 'But you're probably right. This may be the shortest temp job in the entire history of temping.'

'If it was important, maybe you should have set your alarm a little earlier.' Her outraged response to this calumny was still a fledgling thought when he said, 'Who are you going to work for?'

'The Finance Director.'

'Then you *are* in trouble.'

A twinge of unease tightened her stomach. She couldn't be that unlucky…

'Look, it wasn't my fault. My alarm was set for six o'clock. I was *almost* here an hour ago.'

'I should perhaps warn you that the Finance Director never accepts ''almost'' as good enough.'

'Please… Tell me that you're not him…'

'No. You're safe for another couple of minutes.' His smile was definitely worth waiting for. Tiny creases appeared at the corners of his mouth and eyes to demonstrate that, although it was more ironic than ha-ha-ha, it was the genuine article.

'Whew!' she said, flapping her hand as if to cool

her cheeks—actually, it wasn't wholly pretence. 'That would have been a really bad start.'

'Late is bad enough. Have you got a good excuse prepared? Delay on the Underground is a favourite, I believe.'

'With good reason,' she declared. 'But it wasn't anything that simple. I wish it was.'

The eyebrow did its job again, inviting her to elaborate. Or maybe in disbelief… 'Look, it's just me, okay? I seem to have this fatal attraction for calamity, mayhem and misadventure. Today it was some poor man having a seizure down in the Underground.'

'That's a reason for him being late, not you,' he pointed out.

'Yes, but I will get *involved*.'

'Oh. I see.'

For a moment she suspected that he was laughing at her. No, his mouth was perfectly straight…

She dragged her gaze from the kind of lower lip that sent a rush of hormones to her brain.

'He'd, um, collapsed on the platform. People were walking right past him. I suppose they thought he'd been taking drugs or something. It wasn't exactly a rerun of *While You Were Sleeping*—'

'I'm sorry?'

'The movie? Where the girl rescues the guy when he falls onto the track and then everyone thinks she's his fiancée…' She stopped. Clearly he hadn't a clue what she was talking about. 'Obviously I couldn't just leave him there.'

'Obviously,' he said. And then he did smile. Really smile. He was clearly killing himself with the effort not to laugh out loud.

Why did men *always* do that?

Because she was only five foot three in her thickest socks and twenty pounds overweight, according to some stupid height/weight chart in one of her aunt's slimming magazines?

Why was it that only tall, thin people were taken seriously?

'You find that funny?' she demanded.

'No! No, absolutely not,' he said, rapidly losing the smile. 'You weren't afraid?' Then, 'I suspect that's why none of those people stopped.'

'Of course it was, but he was sick. He needed help. I grabbed the nearest person and wouldn't let go until the poor woman got out her mobile phone and called for an ambulance. Then I did what I could to make him comfortable. Of course it took the paramedics forever to get through the rush hour traffic, and then I had to stay and explain what had happened, what I'd done.'

'Is he going to be all right?'

Okay. He'd smiled at the wrong moment, but he had asked the right question...

'I think so. He was a bit dazed, but he seemed to have pretty much recovered by the time I finally got away.' The lift stopped, the doors slid back. 'Uh-oh. This is my floor. Well, thanks for holding the lift.'

'Anytime. Just yell,' he said, and then he smiled again. And her bones...melted.

Oh, good grief. She'd yelled... In the hallowed precincts of the Radcliffe Tower...

'I only do that in an emergency,' she said, again wishing she was six inches taller so that people would take her seriously.

She was tired of men smiling indulgently at her. Not that she could have done anything about it if they were gazing at her with undiluted passion. But even so. A girl needed a morale boost once in a while.

'Keep your fingers crossed for me.'

'I will,' he said, then spoiled the effect by saying, 'But I doubt that will be necessary. I suspect you could talk your way out of anything.'

Jude Radcliffe was still smiling as he walked into his own suite of offices on the top floor of the tower. Catching his PA's startled expression, he straightened his face and said, 'Call Mike Garrett, will you, please, Heather? Tell him I'd appreciate it if he didn't give his temp a hard time about being late. She dealt with a medical emergency on the Underground on her way to work.'

'Good heavens. Was it serious?' Then, with a frown, 'What were you doing on the Underground?'

'I suspect it was dramatic, rather than life-threatening, and I wasn't involved. I just rode up in the lift with the woman.'

'You seem to have covered a lot of ground in a short time. What's her name?' she asked, picking up the telephone.

'She never stopped talking long enough for me to ask her.'

'Obviously she had no idea who you were.'

'I doubt that it would have made any difference.'

'Really? Well, good for her. Description?'

'How many temps do you think they'll have arriving late in Finance?' he said, suddenly regretting the impulse to get involved. 'She's small, with hair like an exploding mattress.'

'What colour mattress?'

'Blonde.'

'Ah.'

Ah? What did 'ah' mean? He refused to ask.

'Keep an eye on her, will you? See how she does. If we've got a suitable permanent opening we might consider her. If she's interested.' Realising that Heather was looking at him with a speculative little smile, he said, 'The woman stopped to help a total stranger when everyone else walked by. People like that are rare.'

'If she was telling the truth. It must have occurred to you that she might simply have been lying in wait for you to arrive with this heart-touching story well prepared?'

That he hadn't—not for one minute—was disturbing. It was usually his first thought, and his last one, too. 'Anything is possible,' he replied, and, in an attempt to discourage any foolish ideas that might be lingering in Heather's normally intelligent head, 'Which is the reason I asked you to keep an eye on her.'

'Right. Of course it is. And which is most important, Jude? Her skills or her social conscience?'

At which point he knew that he was being teased. That his PA thought he'd been snagged by some eye candy with an above average IQ who'd taken the trouble to use more than her looks as bait. And that, for once in a long while, he'd fallen for it.

'You've been working for me too long to ask that,' he said, deciding that enough was enough. 'When you've spoken to Mike, bring in the New York file. I want to fine-tune the details before I leave for Scotland.'

Talie enjoyed working for the Radcliffe Group. The job was demanding, but she relished the opportunity to stretch herself. So much of her time in the last couple of years had been lived within the confines of her home; the chance to get out into the workplace, talk to some people who knew nothing about her, do ordinary stuff for a couple of weeks, was her version of respite.

Even if it meant having to cope with her aunt's attempts to get her involved in a slimming regime.

Her only disappointment was that she hadn't met her knight errant of the lift again. She'd hoped to thank him properly. She would put him right about Mike Garrett, too. Mike had been *totally* understanding about why she was late that first morning, was an absolute sweetheart to work for, and she sincerely wished she had more than just the one week standing in as holiday cover for his secretary.

Unlike the eponymous owner of the Tower.

Jude Radcliffe, according to her new colleagues, who'd whisked her off to their favourite lunchtime watering hole and wasted no time at all in filling her in on just how lucky she was not to have been assigned to the top floor, was a total bastard to work for.

She might have dismissed this as pique that their personal billionaire, although apparently sex-on-legs and unaccountably unattached, was totally oblivious to their charms. However, a couple of the other senior secretaries who'd worked for him when his PA was away shuddered so convincingly at the memory that she knew it had to be true.

His PA was considered to be something of a dragon, too, although she'd seemed pleasant enough when she'd stopped at Talie's desk later in the week to ask if Mike was free, taking the time to ask how Talie was settling in, make sure she'd found her way around, ask what her plans were, suggest she leave her CV with Human Resources.

Since Jude was away the week she worked for his company she didn't have the opportunity to check him out for herself. Apparently his idea of a holiday was walking in the Scottish Highlands—shock, horror, face-pulling all around. It didn't sound that terrible to Talie, but she didn't say so. She was a temp, and her opinion didn't count. She was just there to listen. But it was clear the rest of his employees felt the least he could do was indulge himself in a lavish lifestyle and give them something to gossip about over the skinny latte. And when they looked at her, expecting her to agree that the man was a disappointment all around, she did her best to hide her amusement and agreed with them.

'Natalie! I can hear the phone!'

She was already halfway down the stairs before her mother called out. Phone calls early in the morning or late at night always meant bad news and she snatched it up. 'Yes?'

'Talie? Talie Calhoun? This is Heather Lester. From the Radcliffe Group? We spoke—'

'I remember,' she said. 'I'm sorry if I snapped, but I was—'

'Asleep. I'm the one who should apologise, for disturbing you in the middle of the night. I do know how unsettling late-night phone calls can be. Unfortunately I've got a bit of a crisis and it wouldn't wait until morning.'

About to explain that she hadn't been asleep, Talie said, 'Oh.' Then, 'What kind of crisis?'

'Before I go into details, can I just ask if you have a valid passport?'

'Well, yes.' She had once had a life and holidays abroad, like ordinary people.

'Well, that's the first hurdle. The thing is, I'm supposed to be flying to New York with Mr Radcliffe tomorrow morning—actually, it's this morning now— but my daughter has gone into labour two weeks early and her husband is away, so she needs me.'

'And you need someone to take your place?'

'At zero notice.'

'And you're asking me?' Talie caught her breath. 'To go to New York?' With the total bastard?

'My choice is limited. There aren't too many secretaries who can take shorthand verbatim. And Mike spoke very highly of you.'

'He did? Gosh, how kind of him. I'd give him a reference as a great boss anytime.'

'That speaks volumes in itself. He'd rather type his own reports than cope with incompetence. However, I'd be lying if I said he was as difficult as Jude. I wouldn't want you to get the impression that this trip will be a holiday. It'll be damned hard work.'

Yes, but it would be damned hard work in New York!

She hugged the excitement close to her chest and

said, 'Well, of course. I don't imagine Mr Radcliffe takes his secretary away with him purely for decoration,' she said. And then clapped her hand over her mouth as she realised how that must sound. 'Oh, crumbs. I didn't mean—'

'It's okay, Talie. I know exactly what you meant. The other thing I have to impress on you is the need for total discretion.'

'I always assumed that was the first requirement of the job, Mrs Lester. But if you're concerned, then maybe you should send someone you know.'

'It's Heather. And I'm asking you. Yes or no? Will you go?'

Reality beckoned.

'I'd absolutely love to, but the thing is I've already got another temp job lined up and I can't let them down—'

'I've already spoken to the agency. They will re-arrange the booking if you are willing to take this assignment.'

In the middle of the night?

Apparently sensing her disbelief, Heather said, 'I'm a personal friend of the manager. Who speaks very highly of you, I might add.'

'Oh, I see. Well, if you're sure. I mean, surely there's someone else at the office…' She stopped, remembering how the other women at the office spoke about Jude Radcliffe. 'Who can do shorthand,' she finally managed.

Heather laughed. 'Not like you, Talie. You'll have my undying gratitude if you'll take this on.'

And clearly the undying gratitude of the right-hand woman to Jude Radcliffe was something well worth having. In the unlikely event that she would ever be able to take on a full time job.

Assuming that all objections were disposed of, Heather went on, 'A car will pick you up at nine-thirty to take you to the airport. The driver will have everything you need in a carry-on bag, including some notes I made in case something like this happened.'

'Heavens, that was lucky.'

'Not lucky. It's called forward planning. Babies have a habit of doing their own thing. You'll have my laptop, too, and there's everything you'll need on that. Jude's been away, so I'm sure he'll want to work on the plane. Have you got a notebook handy?'

Heather spent ten minutes or so briefing her before rushing back to her daughter. Talie replaced the receiver and sat on the bottom of the stairs for a moment, staring down at the pages of shorthand notes she'd taken down, utterly stupefied by the speed at which events had overtaken her.

She needed to move. She needed to pack...

'Who was that?' Her mother's voice finally filtered through the disbelief that something so amazing could have happened to her. 'Who could be so thoughtless, calling at this time of night?'

She stirred, went back upstairs to her mother's room. 'It's okay, Mum, it was work. A special temping job has come up and I'm going to have to go away for a few days—'

'Away? Where? I can't—'

'You'll be fine,' she said, firmly putting a stop to her mother's panicky reaction. 'Karen is here until the end of the month, remember? And I'll ring you every day.' She decided it would be wiser not to mention exactly where she'd be phoning from... 'I bought some videos for you today,' she said, changing the subject. 'A couple of old Doris Day movies.'

'Really?' Her mother brightened momentarily. Then, 'If only your father were here.'

'I know, Mum. I know.' She brushed the hair back from her mother's forehead and kissed her. 'You go back to sleep. I'll bring you some breakfast before I leave tomorrow.'

'Heather? I've been trying to get you all morning. What's this damn nonsense about you not coming to New York? I'm at the airport and the flight has already been called.'

'I'm sorry, Jude. I did try and get you last night, but I could only get your answering machine and it ran out before I could explain—'

'And then you switched off your phone.'

'I can't have it on in the hospital.'

'Hospital! What hospital? What's happened?'

'Nothing to worry about. It's just my daughter. She's gone into labour early and she's having a bit of a torrid time, poor darling. They're considering a Caesar—'

'And you're a surgeon?' He didn't wait for an answer. 'Stop fooling around and get to the airport. You can buy the baby something special at Tiffany's—'

'Talie can take shorthand as fast I can, and she's fully briefed. I promise, you won't even miss me.'

Talie? Who the devil was Talie?

'Your daughter's got a partner, hasn't she? She doesn't need you to hold her hand—'

'Jude, I have to go.'

'I refuse to cope with some stranger. I want you. Here. Now!'

'She's not a stranger!' Then, 'Isn't she there? The car was supposed to have picked her up at nine-thirty.'

At that moment the automatic doors slid back, and as Jude Radcliffe caught sight of an unmistakable mop of blonde hair that even under restraint looked in danger of exploding he stopped listening. It was the pocket-sized blonde bombshell from the lift. She was pushing a trolley laden with a mountainous heap of luggage and talking to an elderly woman who was searching her handbag in a totally distracted manner.

'Heather,' he said, 'you're fired.'

And he cut the connection.

Talie, looking around desperately for someone in uniform to grab and ask for help, suddenly found herself confronted by her knight errant, freed from the armour of navy pinstripe and looking totally gorgeous in a grey cashmere sweater that exactly matched his eyes.

'Good heavens, are you going to New York, too? How brilliant! I thought I was going to be on my own with Jude Radcliffe, and everyone says he's a total...'

She stopped. The girls in the office might well be right, but it occurred to her that saying the first thing that came into her head might not be wise since, knight errant or not, he had to be one of Jude Radcliffe's famously bright young men. And, ignoring that enticing left eyebrow, which was inviting her to continue, she turned quickly to the elderly lady she'd rescued as she'd struggled with her trolley.

'This is Kitty,' she said. 'She's going to visit her

new grandson in New Zealand. At least she would be if she could find her ticket.'

'It's all right, dear. I've found it. It was stuck between my book and my box of tissues.'

Talie breathed a huge sigh of relief as the woman finally produced the folder from the depths of her bag. 'I'll just take her to find her queue and then I'll be right back.'

'You're going nowhere. Our flight has already been called. You should have been here an hour ago.'

'I know, but there was an accident in the tunnel,' she said, a touch less brightly as it occurred to her that her knight might be dressed casually for travelling, but his expression was as unyielding as granite. Typical. Just when she could do with a smile or two to allay nerves that were stretched to breaking point, she finally got 'serious.'

'And you had to give first aid?' he enquired.

'Not this time,' she said, and, assuming he was teasing her, began to relax and smiled up at him. She was on her own with the smiling, she discovered. Losing her own rapidly, she said, 'I'll only be a minute—'

'You're not listening to me, Talie,' he said, in a tone that stopped her in her tracks.

'Oh, you know my name?'

'It's not a name. It's the word that goes in front of "ho."'

'It's short for Natalie,' she replied, refusing to allow him to rile her, furious with herself for being foolish enough to daydream for a whole week about riding in the lift again with him. 'The alternative is Nat,' she said. 'Which would you choose?'

There was a pause that lasted a heartbeat, no more.

'Talie what?'

'Calhoun,' she said, certain that she'd won a very small victory. But, refusing to fall into the trap of smiling again, she offered him her hand in her most businesslike manner. 'I'm standing in for Heather on this trip. Her daughter has—'

'I know what her daughter has done,' he said, taking her hand and clasping it in his, holding it a touch more firmly than was quite comfortable. Rather more 'You're not going anywhere' than 'How d'you do?' 'And I hope they run out of gas and air.'

'That's not very nice. I'm sure she didn't do it deliberately.' Then, seeing from his expression that she wasn't doing herself any favours, she said, 'I'm sorry, you have me at a disadvantage. You know my name, but I don't know yours.'

He didn't immediately fill the void, but instead gave her a look that took in her entire appearance, from the top of her embarrassing hair, via the comfortable trouser suit—it had been a toss-up between style and comfort and, taking into consideration the fact that she'd be sitting in it for seven hours, she'd gone for comfort—to her lowest heels. Right now she wished she'd gone for style, four-inch heels and to hell with practicality...

At that moment Kitty stopped fussing with her bag and looked up. 'Good Lord, aren't you Jude Radcliffe?' she said. 'I bought shares in your company after I saw you on TV. You were so charming when that nasty interviewer was rude to you...'

'Charm is all a matter of perspective. From Miss Calhoun's point of view I'm a total...' And that enticing left eyebrow invited her to fill in the blank.

The word that slipped from her lips wasn't the one she'd heard applied to him. But it was near enough.

CHAPTER TWO

'WELL,' Talie said, since she had to say something. 'Now we *both* know that I'm just as good at talking myself into trouble as out of it.'

It earned her a smile of sorts. The kind that said 'Now I've got you...' And she began to see how, while the 'sex-on-legs' tag fitted him to a *T*, he might not be the kind of man you'd want to work for.

Not that she anticipated having that particular problem for very long.

'Can you wait until I find out where Kitty needs to go before you sack me?' she asked.

'You're not getting off that lightly.' He snagged a passing female in a uniform with a glance—something she had signally failed to do with any number of glances—and said, 'Lady Milward is having trouble finding her check-in desk. Will you please take care of her?'

And then he really smiled. The full-scale, hundred-and-fifty-watt variety. The girl was putty by the time he'd reached sixty watts—if he'd looked at her like that Talie would have been putty—and she briefly considered a lecture on energy saving. Then decided she was in enough trouble...

'Have a good trip, Kitty,' he said, turning to the old lady and offering his hand. 'I hope to see you at the next shareholders' meeting.'

'You know her?' Talie demanded, having rescued

her own luggage from Kitty's trolley before it was whisked away.

'When she said she was a shareholder I looked at her luggage label. You were suckered, Talie Calhoun. But I don't suppose you're the first person she's fooled with that helpless dithering act. It's by getting other people to do their dirty work for them for nothing that her kind got rich in the first place.'

'I don't care how much money she has,' Talie said, outraged. 'She needed help; I gave it.' And, since she had nothing to lose, 'What's made you so cynical?'

'Experience. Make a note to send her an invitation to the cocktail party.'

A note? As in, like his personal assistant? And suddenly his 'You're not getting off that lightly,' made sense. Sacking her would be too kind. She was going to have to work for him and suffer.

In New York, she reminded herself. In New York.

'Which cocktail party?' she asked.

'The one we hold for shareholders after the Annual General Meeting.'

'Right.' She made a move to dig out her notebook.

'A mental note. We have to check in before they close the flight.'

He picked up the cheap-and-cheerful holdall that had seen her through her student days but which looked embarrassingly scruffy next to the wheel-on laptop bag that Heather had sent with the car, and placed it beside his own equally worn leather holdall.

The thing about buying quality, she thought, was that it matured with age. The scuffs lent it character. Unlike cheap-and-cheerful which, once past its cheerful stage, just looked—well, cheap.

'Passport.' He held out his hand for it as they reached the first-class check-in desk.

He had good hands. Large enough to be comforting, with long fingers and the kind of broad-tipped thumb that... Well, never mind what the thumb suggested to her overheated imagination.

But you could tell a lot from a man by looking at his hands.

His lied.

She handed over her passport and tickets. The clerk already had all the details of the change of passenger in her computer, so there was no delay, and it occurred to her that, for a woman distracted by the difficulties of her daughter's labour, Heather had done an amazing job of handling the details so that Jude Radcliffe's life would proceed as smoothly as if she was there herself.

It was scarcely surprising that he was irritated to discover that instead of perfection he'd been lumbered with her. Maybe she was being a little harsh. Stifling a yawn, she made a silent vow not to do anything to annoy him further as she and the wheel-on laptop bag put in the occasional hop and skip in an attempt to keep pace with him as he strode towards the boarding gate, making no concession to the fact that her legs were at least a foot shorter than his.

She revised her earlier regret about her shoes, too.

In four-inch heels she'd never have made it.

She also vowed to keep her mouth shut. Not speak unless she was spoken to.

It wasn't easy. Her student travelling had been done using the cross-Channel ferry and backpacking across Europe, which she'd loved. Her one and only experience of flying was cattle-class on a package tour charter flight, and she'd hated every minute of it.

But this was different, and despite her apprehension—she refused to admit to the flutter of anxiety that until now she'd been too distracted to notice—she looked about her, eager to enthuse about the size of the seats, the amount of space each passenger had and the neat little individual television screens. She always talked too much when she was nervous.

Biting her lower lip to keep her mouth shut, she explored her space, picking up the entertainment programme. 'We get a choice of films?' she asked, forgetting her vow of silence in her astonishment.

'Other people might. You are here to work.'

For seven solid hours?

'Of course. I was merely making an observation,' she said crisply, and, restricting her enthusiasm to the business at hand, she opened the laptop bag. 'This is the note that Heather sent you, Mr Radcliffe,' she said, handing him an envelope. 'To explain about me.'

'I know all about you,' he said, without enthusiasm. 'You watch romantic films, attract trouble and are always late.'

This was definitely a moment for silence.

Satisfied, he said, 'And you will call me Jude.'

'Oh, but I couldn't!'

Well, that didn't last long…

'Try,' Jude insisted, trying very hard to keep his temper. Why on earth had Heather picked this woman as her stand-in? It was bad enough that he'd found himself constantly distracted by the memory of those few seconds they'd spent together in the lift, wasting time he'd allocated to thinking about the direction in which he should take the company during the next five years.

Instead of planning corporate strategy he'd been thinking about her ridiculous hair. That totally infectious smile…

He needed someone he could trust on this trip, and Heather was the one who'd suggested that this girl might have been putting on an act, for heaven's sake. That her story had been just that. A story to snag his attention.

Except he'd just seen her in action. If she was that good an actress she was wasting her time in an office. But somehow the fact that her compassion, her enthusiasm for life, wasn't an act disturbed him far more. He was more comfortable with guile. Understood it. Knew how to handle it.

He took a slow breath. He was stuck with her and they'd both have to live with it.

'I may be a bastard,' he said. 'Although my mother might take issue with you on that. And I certainly don't suffer fools in any shape or form in my organisation. But Heather calls me Jude and so will you.' Then, in case she was under any misapprehension that he was being friendly—he was deeply regretting his uncharacteristic impulse to hold the lift for her— 'That way I won't be constantly reminded of her absence every time you speak.'

And, without waiting for her to reply, he opened the envelope and took out a single folded sheet of paper. The note was brief and to the point.

Jude, I know you're going to be furious that I've had to miss this trip, but you know you're going to have to get used to working without me in the near future. I gave you a year to find a replacement and time is running out. And, no, I didn't do this deliberately. Even you must realise that I can't control the arrival of an impatient baby.

Just don't take it out on Talie. It's not her fault. Mike raved about her. She takes shorthand verbatim, and I took the trouble to check out her story about the incident on the Underground last week. Unlikely as it may seem, your little blonde was telling the truth.

I know—she's almost too good to be true. But I'm sure a week working for you will bring out any hidden flaws. If you behave yourself, you might even be able to persuade her to take you on full time. Heather.

He glanced down at the girl sitting beside him. 'Heather suggests you're almost too good to be true. Shall we see if she's right?'

'What?'

It was just as well her eyes were blue or he'd be forced to compare them with a startled doe's.

What an appallingly banal thought.

At least she'd made an effort to get her hair under control, stuffing it up into some kind of knot on the top of her head that was not so much a bun, more a cottage loaf. Even as he congratulated himself a curl sprang free, refusing to be confined by anything so feeble as a hairpin.

Realising that she was still staring up at him like a startled blue-eyed—and there really was no other word for it—doe, he said, 'If you'd like to get out your notebook some time before we arrive in New York, maybe I can find out if you're as good as Mike and Heather claim you are,' he prompted.

'But we haven't even taken off...' She caught her bottom lip between her teeth, presumably to prevent the rest of the sentence from escaping and thus provoking further sarcasm.

And that irritated him, too. He felt like being seriously—

'Would you fasten your seat-belts, please?' a stewardess said as she walked through the cabin, checking that everything was properly stowed. 'We'll be taking off shortly.'

Talie, it seemed, had a firm grasp of the priorities and got out her notebook before she fastened her seatbelt, made a note of the time and date, wrote something else in shorthand—probably what she wanted to say out loud but thought it wiser not to—and then turned to him, her pencil poised and waiting.

'Whenever you're ready,' she said. 'Jude.'

He dragged his attention from her hair, which was slowly unravelling, and began to dictate a series of notes on the ideas he'd had during his solitary days walking in the Scottish Highlands. The ones that didn't involve the dimple that appeared for no reason at all every now and then at the corner of her mouth.

The plane backed slowly away from the gate before taxiing to the runway. There was a long pause as they waited for clearance and, glancing across to ensure that she was keeping up with him, he noticed that the knuckles of the hand gripping her pencil were bone-white.

She was nervous? This girl who, without a second thought, leapt to the aid of total strangers in distress?

As he hesitated, she glanced up at him. It wasn't only her knuckles that were white, he realised, and as the engine noise grew and the plane began to speed down the runway he stepped up the speed at which he was dictating in an effort to distract her.

It might have worked, too, but when a day started out badly, it invariably kept going that way, and as they lifted off something crashed loose in the galley behind them. A woman in the aisle seat opposite them gave a startled scream and Talie jumped so violently that she would undoubtedly have left her seat if she hadn't been strapped in. As it was, her notebook and pencil took off on a flight of their own, and the pins which had been struggling manfully with gravity to hold up her hair gave up the effort and the cottage loaf exploded.

'Are we going to die?' she whispered.

'Yes,' he said, reaching out and taking her hand. 'But not today.'

He really was a bastard, Talie decided, as her heart rate slowly returned to normal. How could she ever have imagined for one minute that he was friendly? Charming? Totally scrummy, actually.

She had practically haunted the lifts of the Radcliffe Tower in her lunchtimes, hoping to run into him again. Knowing that she was being stupid. Just how stupid she couldn't possibly have imagined.

Okay. She'd give him the killer good looks—even if he was using those slate eyes to freeze her to her seat—and she was right about his hands. They were strong and capable and very good for holding on to when you thought your last moment had come.

Admittedly he'd lost the smooth, boyish look of the average pop idol, and settled into that look men achieved around their mid to late thirties and hung on to until the muscles started to sag a little around the jaw, when they were so old that it didn't matter. When he smiled he didn't look anywhere near old enough to be the ill-tempered tycoon described by her colleagues.

Unable to rescue her notebook until the seat-belt sign went off, Talie remained absolutely still, trying to ignore the warmth of his palm pressed against hers, the way his long fingers curled reassuringly around her hand. Instead she closed her eyes and re-ran their encounter in the lift, trying to work out how she could have got it so wrong.

He'd seemed friendly enough, but then she hadn't given him much of a chance to be anything else, prattling on about being late. He probably wouldn't have spoken to her at all under normal circumstances. Most of his staff probably wouldn't have dared say anything beyond good morning.

None of them would have yelled at him to hold the lift. They'd rather have been late.

And he wasn't being funny when he said she could talk her way out of anything, she realised belatedly. He was being sarcastic.

The seat-belt sign pinged off, but before she could move, reclaim her notepad, he had released her hand and picked it up for her.

'Have you stopped shaking sufficiently to carry on?'

he asked, handing it to her. 'Or do you require a medicinal brandy?'

'If I had a medicinal brandy that would be the end of my working day,' she said. 'Not the beginning of it.'

She looked around for her pencil, but it had rolled away under a seat somewhere, and since she wasn't about to crawl around on her hands and knees looking for it she took a new one from her bag. Then, suspecting that she might need more than one, she swiftly anchored her hair back into place and stuck some spares into the resulting bird's nest, so that she wouldn't have to cut him off in full flow.

'Whenever you're ready,' she said. Then, when he didn't immediately begin, she glanced up at him and realised that he was staring at her hair. For just a moment she thought he was going to make some seriously cutting remark.

Maybe she was mistaken. Or maybe he'd wisely thought better of it. Because after a moment he sat back, closed his eyes and continued pouring his thoughts out at a rate that kept her fully occupied for some time.

Her attention briefly wandered when an infant whose mother was deeply engrossed in the film she was watching caught her eye and with a giggle tossed a drinking cup in her direction, hoping for a playmate.

Any other time she'd have been there...

The cup rolled away down the aisle and the child started to cry. Talie found it really, really hard to stay put when every instinct was urging her to leap up and retrieve it. Instead she took a deep breath and, as she turned the page, hit the buzzer to attract the attention of the stewardess.

'Good decision,' Jude said.

She'd written it down before she realised that it was a comment rather than dictation. Clearly his eyes weren't as firmly closed as she'd imagined.

The flight passed without further incident. She typed up the notes Jude had dictated until the laptop battery beeped a warning that it was about to go flat. But if she thought all she had to do was hit 'save' and then relax for the rest of the flight, she was mistaken.

Jude stopped working on some figures, took a special adapter from his own laptop bag and leaned across her to plug it into the power outlet of the aircraft— obviously concerned that she'd do fatal damage to the aircraft electronics if he left her to do it herself.

He might be an unmitigated bastard as a boss, but he did have gorgeous hair, she thought with an envious sigh as she got an unexpected close-up. Dark as bitter chocolate, perfectly cut so that every silky strand knew its place. Even the lick that momentarily slid across his forehead needed no encouragement to return to order.

She tucked a stray curl behind her ear and comforted herself with the thought that good hair wasn't everything.

Kindness was much more important.

He refused all offers of tea, coffee, even lunch when it arrived, and, taking only water, kept working. She had no idea if he expected her to follow his example, but enough was enough. He might be able to function on fresh air, but she needed a substantial amount of calories if she was going to keep up this level of out-

put. She made a mental note to stock up on an emergency supply of chocolate at the first confectionery
outlet she passed.

After the stewardess had removed her tray, he began
again. This time dictating notes for an after-dinner
speech he was going to make to some business group,
stopping just before her right hand began to scream
for mercy.

She began to wonder if Heather's daughter had really gone into early labour. She might just have decided that she could do with a break, and could always
say it had been a false alarm...

Mentally slapping herself for having such evil
thoughts, she applied herself to the keyboard, and was
taken by surprise when the Captain announced that
they would shortly be arriving at JFK.

'I don't believe it! A yellow cab!'

Jude glanced across the road to where a constant
stream of cabs was picking up new arrivals. 'No,
you're right. It's yellow.' Then, spotting his driver
climbing out of a waiting limo, he said, 'This is our
car.'

He ignored her disappointment that they weren't going to drive into Manhattan in one of New York's
landmark institutions. It wasn't his business to fulfil
her tourist fantasies.

'Barney, Heather couldn't come this trip. Talie is
standing in for her, so you'll need to liaise with her
about when you'll be needed.'

'Pleased to know you, Talie,' Barney said, with a
wide smile. 'First time in New York?'

'Yes,' she said, beaming back. 'I can't wait to see the city.'

'Well, you climb in and buckle up now, while I take care of those bags, and we'll have you there in no time.'

She kept her notebook and the briefing file with her, and since, apart from the yellow cabs, the airport surroundings offered nothing more to interest her, she glanced through the crowded schedule for the trip. 'You have a meeting with your U.S. team at four o'clock.' Then, with a frown, 'That is so weird. We've already had four o'clock once today. I guess that's jet lag.'

'You would only have had four o'clock once if you'd changed your watch to New York time as soon as we took off.'

'Er—when?' she asked.

He didn't bother pretending to misunderstand her. 'You found time for lunch,' he pointed out. And she'd found time to re-pin her hair, too. His concentration had been ruined by the constant threat of a second detonation of hairpins. But their landing had been incident free and her curls had remained firmly anchored. He dragged his gaze from them with some difficulty. 'And you've no need to worry about jet lag. I promise you won't have any time to suffer from that.'

'Well, that's a relief. I was worried there...' Her mouth twitched, as if she was trying very hard to control a smile. 'Just for a minute.'

Humour? Well, fine. They'd see how long she could keep that up.

'And I don't have a meeting at four o'clock,' he pointed out. '*We* have a meeting a four o'clock.'

'You want me to take notes?' If she'd thought about it she would have assumed the New York office would supply someone to do that. In fact she didn't understand why the New York office couldn't supply him with all the secretarial support he needed.

'I'm not taking you along as a fashion accessory. Somehow I don't see pencils in the hair catching on in—'

But he could see that he'd lost her, and he turned to see what she was looking at.

It was, of course, the Manhattan skyline, hazy and golden in the early-afternoon sunshine. Right ahead of them the Empire State Building towered over the city, and a little away to the left the sun was striking off the polished art deco roof of the Chrysler Building.

It was the hackneyed subject of a thousand picture postcards, and he'd seen it so many times that it had lost any power to hold him, but Talie Calhoun was clearly entranced. She gave a little sigh of pure pleasure and said, 'I can't believe I'm actually looking at the Empire State Building. Going to the top is number one on my list of things to do while I'm here.'

'If you want to be a tourist, Talie,' he said, irritated that he'd lost her attention to a cliché, 'you're going to have to book a package holiday and do it on your own time. While you're here with me I'll want you available twenty-four/seven.'

Those blue eyes flashed back at him, and for a moment he thought she was going to give him an argument. Remind him that all he could demand of her was an eight-hour day—and he'd already had that and more.

Common sense won, although a mutinous lower lip trembled with outrage, fighting a fierce rearguard battle as she tried to clamp it tight against its more restrained upper partner.

He was almost sorry. He would have given a lot to know exactly what she was thinking right at that moment.

But then he'd have had to fire her, too.

CHAPTER THREE

TALIE clenched her jaw to keep her mouth from saying what was in her mind. She was professional. She could be cool. She knew that working on an overseas trip was not a nine-to-five deal. But she also knew that there was no way he was going to keep her occupied for every minute, day and night.

Even Jude Radcliffe had to sleep.

She would get to the top of the Empire State Building even if it was the only item she achieved on her wish list. She'd get someone to take a photograph of her while she was there, too. Then she'd send him a copy when they were safely home in London and leave him to wonder how she'd found the time.

But in the meantime she would be good. And since he had finally stopped issuing orders and pouring out dictation—it was likely that even *his* brain needed some down time in order to fill up with more words— she sat very still and enjoyed the rest of the ride into Upper Manhattan. She was thrilled by it all, even the worn-out buildings that skirted all big cities, and was finally rewarded with tantalising glimpses of narrow streets with pretty sidewalks that could have come straight from any Woody Allen movie.

She just about managed to bottle up her astonishment that the roads were so narrow. Or was it just the height of the buildings that made them appear that way? And she barely let out a squeak as she caught her first sight of Central Park, with the horse-drawn buggies lined up to give romantic rides through the park. It was so frustrating not to be able to share her enthusiasm with Jude.

'Was that on your list, too?'

Obviously it had been enough of a squeak to alert him to further 'tourist' ambitions.

'Sorry?' She tried to appear absolutely cool, as if she had no idea what Jude was talking about. It clearly wasn't working, so before that wretched eyebrow could go into overdrive she said, 'Oh, you mean a buggy ride in the park? No. It wouldn't be much fun doing it on my own.'

'No,' he said, after a moment. 'I don't suppose it would.' Then, as the car slowed to a halt in front of their hotel. 'Okay, you've got twenty minutes to freshen up before we leave.'

'Do you want me to deal with the check-in formalities?' she asked, as the bellman took their bags and summoned a lift.

'It isn't necessary. I keep a permanent suite here. It's less bother than an apartment.'

'Of course it is,' she said. And didn't even try to keep the irony from her voice. His payback came when he used a swipe key to open the door, then stood back to let her go ahead of him.

Her mouth didn't actually drop open, but only because she was already so deep in jaw-drop mode at finding herself in such surroundings that she had it tightly clamped shut for safety.

His suite had all the extravagant trappings she had ever seen in the movies she watched day after day with her mother. The luxurious furniture, a carpet that seemed to swallow her feet, flowers and fruit...

It even had its own little kitchen. And, less enticingly, the latest office technology set up in a mini-office.

But the stunning view of Central Park from her bedroom window cancelled out this reminder that she was here to work. Not that she had much time to linger over the view.

It didn't matter. Nothing and no one—not even Jude Radcliffe—could wipe the huge grin that was riveted to her face as she dived into the shower.

She was in New York!

'Have you ever considered doing something with your hair?' Jude enquired as they drove downtown. Her quick shower had reduced it to a mass of corkscrew curls that not even the toughest pin could hold down.

'What kind of something?' she enquired, looking up at him with an innocent look that he didn't believe in for a moment. He was beginning to get the measure of Talie Calhoun.

'Something involving the use of sharp scissors?' he offered.

'It has been tried,' she said, not unkindly, but as if explaining something to a fool. 'My hair, as you can imagine, was a trial to my mother, and once—after breaking yet another comb—she hacked it short with her dressmaking shears. It gave a whole new meaning to the description ''poodle cut.'''

He suspected he was supposed to laugh. Instead he found himself confronted by the pitiable image of a very small Talie, with her hair chopped off in uneven chunks, and wished he had kept his mouth shut.

'I had something a little more professional in mind,' he said, rather more gently.

'An expensive poodle cut?' she responded, not letting him off that easily.

'Okay,' he said, deciding to get the apology over and done with. 'Point taken. I shouldn't have—'

'I did briefly consider going for broke with a Number One,' she continued, as if he hadn't spoken. 'But the problem then would be that I'd be stuck with it forever, because I would never willingly go through the nightmare stage of growing it out.' Then, 'Of course, if you have any other suggestions I'd be happy to hear them. In the meantime, look on the bright side. If I wear it loose I can't park my pencils in it.'

For once in his life he couldn't think of a thing to say. His mistake had been to break every rule in his own handbook for dealing with people and get involved. He didn't even bother to try again with the apology. She'd matched him and then some, and he spent the rest of the journey with his mouth firmly closed while his mind—which had far more important things to concern it—wasted precious time wondering what on earth she was doing temping when she was not only hard-working, but smart enough to put him in his place without raising a sweat.

She seemed to have the same effect on everyone else when she walked into the boardroom and half a dozen of the least impressionable men he knew temporarily lost the power of speech.

'Gentlemen, this is Talie Calhoun. Heather is busy becoming a grandmother, and Talie is standing in for her on this trip.' About to say that they should give her every assistance, he realised it was unnecessary. He was more likely to be trampled in the crush as his staff overcame their initial shocked surprise and vied to shake her hand, offer her coffee, carry her bag.

He firmly resisted the foolish urge to beat them off, instead leaving them to introduce themselves while his lawyer updated him on the latest situation with the company they were planning to take over.

Talie had expected Jude to call the meeting to order, but since he was otherwise occupied she just smiled and enjoyed being the centre of attention while it lasted.

'Did you have a good flight, Talie?' a tall, tanned god-like figure asked, after he'd introduced himself.

'I didn't notice,' she said. 'I was working.'

'Any flight you don't notice is good flight,' another man said. Tall—they were all so damned tall she'd get a crick in her neck from looking up—dark and with the inbred confidence of a male who only had to smile to get what he wanted. 'Hi, I'm Marcus Wade.'

'How d'you do, Mr Wade?' she replied politely, taking the hand he offered.

'Marcus,' he said, not shaking her hand, just holding it.

'Oh, wow. I love that accent. Say something else,' said a voice behind her.

She turned her head—short of wrenching her hand from Marcus she had no other option—and smiled at a third, younger man. 'How now brown cow?' she offered, her consonants crisp, her diphthongs BBC-perfect. He pretended to swoon and she laughed.

'Is this your first visit to New York?' This from a

drool-worthy Brad Pitt look-alike. Make that all so tall *and* good-looking, she thought. They all looked so…wholesome. Except Marcus Wade. He had that bad-boy look that gave the mothers of impressionable girls the shivers. Fortunately, she was no longer a girl, and she'd never been that easily impressed. At least not until a recent ride in a lift. And that had proved how dangerous first impressions could be…

'Yes. It's amazing. I still can't believe I'm here.'

'Well, that's wonderful. You've got it all to see for the first time. The Statue of Liberty, Central Park, Times Square—'

'The first thing you have to do is take a boat trip around the harbour,' someone else pitched in.

'And a bus tour—'

'Actually, I don't think I'm going to have time—'

'Sunday brunch at Katz's is a must. You are going to be here over the weekend, aren't you? I'd be happy to take you.' This from Marcus, reclaiming her attention. And now he wasn't smiling; he was totally serious. As if this was the most important thing in the entire world at that moment. She was good and didn't laugh. Instead she said, 'That's really very sweet of you, but—'

'Sweet! She said "sweet"…priceless!'

Marcus didn't seem to think it was priceless. He just glowered at the man who thought it was…

'But we're leaving on Thursday morning,' she finished.

'But you'll have time to see a show?' the B.P. look-alike, sensing an opportunity, immediately leapt in. 'You *have* to see a show—'

Jude found himself distracted by the knot of eager

young men clustered around Talie and glanced across, intending to call the meeting to order. Instead he caught a glimpse of her and forgot what he was about to say.

She'd abandoned the shapeless trouser suit and flat shoes for a charcoal-grey suit that skimmed her old-fashioned hourglass figure, high heels that drew attention to a pair of the classiest ankles he'd ever seen, and her hair was lit up like a halo by a bright ray of sun striking in through the window.

'—and the Empire State after dark. That's a must. We'll do it tonight, Talie. Dinner first, after the meeting, and then I'll take you for a ride to the top of the world—'

'Not this evening, Marcus,' he said abruptly. 'Talie has a prior engagement with a computer, and I'm sure you'll have plenty to occupy you, too.'

'You don't let her eat?'

Jude found himself being challenged by one of his brightest young men—not, as he'd anticipated, for power, but for the attention of a girl. He would soon learn to choose his battles with more care. Save his big moves for something that mattered.

There was always another girl.

'It was Jude who worked through lunch today, not me,' Talie said, glancing at her hand so pointedly that Marcus could do nothing but surrender it. 'Can I get anyone coffee before we start? Jude?'

Burying his annoyance that she'd leapt, quite unnecessarily, to his defence, he said, 'No. Let's get on.' He indicated that she should sit beside him, and then tried to forget about her as they began to thrash out the details of strategy for the following week.

It wasn't easy.

It was impossible to be unaware of the fact that whenever he spoke he had a rapt audience. Maybe it was unswerving interest in the business at hand, but he had the uncomfortable feeling that it was Talie's presence beside him that fixed their attention. He'd never had to compete with a bunch of testosterone-driven young executives for Heather's attention. Or with her for theirs, he thought, as he glanced down at Talie to ensure that she wasn't flagging and caught her exchanging a smile with someone.

But then Heather was about to become a grand-mother, he reminded himself as they finally broke for sandwiches and coffee. Talie was swamped with offers of help as she poured and served, although he noticed that Marcus was doing a pretty good job of keeping all comers at bay, blocking their moves with his foot-baller's shoulders as he whispered something in her ear.

He'd been Jude's first choice to run the New York office. Unstoppable when he wanted something, his charm disguising the essential ruthless edge.

Talie threw back her head as she laughed at some-thing he'd said, at which point Jude stopped congrat-ulating himself and abruptly called the meeting back to order.

'What are you doing about dinner, Jude?' Marcus said, as the meeting finally broke up. 'I can call that Italian restaurant you like and see if they can give us a table.'

'If you think your day is done, Marcus, by all means go out and enjoy yourself,' he said, not fooled for a minute by this apparently casual invitation. There was only one person Marcus wanted to have dinner with, and if he couldn't extract her from Jude's side then he was confident enough of his power to charm to invite the whole group along. 'We are less fortunate. Talie has notes to type up, and I have plenty to keep me busy, so we'll have to make do with Room Service tonight.'

'That was terribly cruel,' she said, as they made their way out of the building.

'Cruel?'

'What you did to Marcus. He'll carry on working all night, now.'

'I've no doubt that's what he'll tell me he did,' he said. 'But I'm prepared to bet that it won't be more than half an hour before he's on his way to some classy little restaurant.' He resisted the temptation to add that he wouldn't be alone. It would make too much of nothing. It would suggest it mattered.

'Lucky him,' Talie said.

'You're hungry?'

She glanced up at him, and for a moment he thought she was going to say something important. She clearly had second thoughts, because she just shook her head. 'To be honest, I think I've gone past food. I'd rather just get on with typing up the minutes and then go to bed. I am allowed to sleep?'

'If you don't want to eat, I suggest you do just that.'

She didn't say a word, but her look spoke volumes.

'You'll be wide awake at three o'clock,' he said. 'You can catch up then.'

'You're all heart,' she said, climbing into the back of the limo.

'Hearts are for losers, Talie. There are no dividends

for being soft. The only thing you can rely on in this world is money,' he said. 'The deal.'

'Nobody can be that cynical,' she said.

He didn't bother to argue, and when, a few minutes after she'd retired, apparently too tired to keep her eyes open, he heard the phone ring in her room just once before it was snatched up, he decided that cynicism served him very well.

CHAPTER FOUR

'TALIE, will you call Room Service—?'

Jude's heart had lifted in anticipation of her bright presence, hard at work transcribing the notes of the meeting while the printer busily churned out all the stuff she'd typed up on the plane. But the printer was quiet, the laptop closed and, far from sitting at the desk working, his secretary was notable only by her absence.

'Talie?'

It was after seven a.m. He'd relied on the time difference to have him awake long before now—but then he hadn't gone to bed until the early hours. Talie didn't have that excuse, and when there was no answer from her room he rapped sharply on her door to rouse her, then took a bottle of water from the fridge. When, after he'd taken a long draught, there was still no sound of movement from her bedroom, he knocked again before opening the door.

There was no sound because she wasn't there, which was disturbing enough. But what rocked him back was the fact that her bed looked as if it hadn't been slept in.

He didn't know what made him angrier. That Marcus had been wasting time lusting after her when he should have been concentrating on the job in hand. Or that Talie had been stupid enough to fall for his smooth act.

Her only desire might have been to see the world from the top of New York's best-known building, but anyone could have seen that he had something much more intimate in mind.

The phone in his own bedroom interrupted his black fury and he snatched it up. 'Yes!'

'This is Vince from Security, Mr Radcliffe. We have…a situation.'

Talie. It could only be Talie… 'What kind of a situation?'

'Well, sir, we're holding a young lady here who's asked for a key to your suite. She says she's your PA, and while obviously she's lying—we all know Mrs Lester—I thought perhaps I should check with you. Before I take it any further.'

The delicacy with which this was put left him in no doubt what the man was thinking, and he was sorely tempted to leave Talie Calhoun to cool her heels for a while in Security. If nothing else, it would make him feel better. And teach her not to try and creep back in undetected after a night on the tiles.

Unfortunately he didn't have the time for that, but she could sweat it out for a few more minutes.

'I'll come down, Vince.'

And, replacing the receiver, he pulled on his sweats. While Little Miss Tourist was typing herself back into his good books he'd put in some time at the hotel gym.

'This is totally outrageous!'

He heard her before he opened the door.

'Please, ma'am, stay calm…'

'Calm! Have you any idea how I felt, being escorted from Reception into the security office with everyone looking at me as if I was some kind of crook, or a hotel thief, or a…a…a professional lady?' Her voice exploded on the final category.

'Now, ma'am, there's no need to get angry. We'll get this sorted—'

'You think this is angry?' she demanded.

She was standing in the middle of the security office, confronting three of the hotel's security officers, all of whom towered over her, and she wasn't giving an inch.

'This isn't angry. This is mildly irritated—'

'Talie? What's the problem?'

She turned at the sound of his voice. 'Jude. Thank goodness. What the devil took you so long?' For a moment the fierceness in her voice wobbled, betraying her fear, and he wanted to just reach out and hold her. Tell her it was okay… But before he could move she rallied. 'Why didn't you just tell him that it was okay? When he phoned?' She indicated the older of the men.

'I was coming down anyway, so I thought it would be better to reassure Vince in person.'

As he had anticipated, she had discarded the business suit, but she wasn't wearing some sexy little number with which to ensnare his young protégé. Instead she was dressed in a thin grey T-shirt that clung enticingly to her curves and a pair of cut-off jogging pants that displayed a disturbing amount of smooth, tanned leg.

And her hair—it was always the hair that dominated her appearance—was tumbling out of the band she'd used to tie it back and sticking damply to her face.

'Forget Vince! All you had to say was, ''If she's short, mouthy and has bad hair she's okay,''' she said, hands on hips as she turned and he became the target of her fury.

He was finding it difficult to stop himself from laughing, but knew she'd never forgive him if he did that, so he said, 'Vince, may I introduce Miss Talie Calhoun, who's standing in for Mrs Lester this week?' And then he did smile. 'She's okay. Could you sort out a swipe card for her, please?'

'Yes, sir.'

And suddenly no one seemed to find it necessary to hang around. Once they were on their own, he turned back to Talie.

'A *professional* lady?' he prompted.

Her cheeks, already pink, flushed a darker shade. Clearly the same impetuosity that had her leaping to the rescue of the halt and confused drove her tongue.

'I really don't think you need have worried on that score,' he said.

She instantly rallied. 'I was over-ambitious, you think?'

A strand of hair was corkscrewing wildly over her left eye. She blew it away but it fell back and, quite unable to stop himself, he reached out and tucked it behind her ear, holding it there.

'I think I'll pass on that one.' Then, realising that he was at risk of crossing a very dangerous line, he took a step back and, moving swiftly on, said, 'Where the devil have you been?'

She regarded him as if he was insane, before looking down at her clothes in a gesture that suggested he figure it out for himself. Then, presumably in case he was terminally thick, she said, 'I've been for a run.'

All night?

'On your own?' he asked, suddenly a lot more concerned for her safety than her morals.

'Is there some law against it?' Then, 'Look, I finally gave up trying to sleep at about four, typed up your notes and printed them out, and then I just wanted some fresh air—okay?'

'You've done *everything?*'

'You did say—'

'I know what I said. I didn't actually mean it.'

'Didn't you? Oh.'

She lifted her shoulders in something that wasn't quite a shrug but conveyed the same message. Why would she have doubted that he'd meant exactly what he said?

'I'm sorry. I'm so used to working with Heather—'

'No, it's okay. You were right. I was wide awake, and it was pointless just lying there waiting for the sun to come up.'

'So you typed up the minutes and then went for a run in Central Park?'

'In company with dozens of other people, so you needn't worry about me behaving like a "tourist,"' she said, making quote marks with her fingers. 'I was behaving like a gen-yoo-ine New Yorker.' Then, eyeing his sweats, 'If you'd woken up in time you could have come with me. Did you take a sleeping pill or something? I knocked as loudly as I could—'

'Why didn't you take the swipe card? It was on the desk.'

'I did, but I put it in my bum bag with my camera and I think the battery might have corrupted the magnetic strip. When I couldn't rouse you, I came back down here for a new one. Which is when I was "invited" to step into the security office.'

The manager himself returned, with two fresh swipe card keys. 'My apologies for the confusion, Mr Radcliffe,' he said. 'Mrs Lester telephoned to let us know you'd both be arriving yesterday. No one informed us that there had been a change of plan—'

'Amazing. I thought the woman was infallible,' Talie muttered.

'.. and naturally the reception clerk chose caution.'

'Of course, Mr Luis. It is entirely our fault—'

'Don't do that! Don't apologise to him. I'm the one who was treated like something untouchable,' Talie said, clearly believing—with some justification—that any apology should be offered to her. 'I have no doubt everyone would have been a lot politer if I'd been wearing designer running shoes that cost more money than I get paid for an entire week's work,' she said. Then, sweetly, 'Of course if I'd been a real crook I could have afforded them.'

'I'm sure everyone will treat you with the utmost respect in future,' Jude said, placing his hand firmly on her back and easing her through the door. Then, when there was a safe distance between it and them, 'You do realise that you have given me more trouble in two days than Heather has given me in ten years?'

She looked surprised—with good reason, since most of the disturbance was in his mind—and opened her mouth as if about to challenge him, before obviously thinking better of it. Instead she took a deep breath and said, 'This time the trouble really wasn't my fault.'

'I know, but the guy was just doing his job,' he said unsympathetically. 'Get over it.'

'Right,' she said, and, after another deep breath, 'Absolutely. I'll go back and apologise when I'm cleaned up.' Then, as they reached the lifts, 'I really am sorry I embarrassed you, but I was scared I was going to be thrown into a police cell.'

'I'd have bailed you out,' he promised. 'Eventually.'

She grinned. 'Yes, okay. I'm catching on. You're not as bad as everyone says...' Then, swiftly changing the subject, 'Honestly—look at me.' Her snit over as quickly as it had blown up, a smile tugged at the corner of her mouth, that elusive dimple tempting him to see things from her point of view. 'What did the wretched man think I was going to do to you?'

He looked. And felt an overwhelming urge to grin right back.

'I can't imagine,' he lied, overwhelmed with images of any manner of things she might do to him.

And he rapidly lost any desire to laugh.

'Here's your key,' he said, as he summoned a lift for her. 'Don't keep this one with your camera.' Despite himself, he was unable to resist calling her on her insistence that she was behaving like a local. 'Do you usually take it with you when you go for a run?'

'Absolutely,' she replied, all wide-eyed innocence. 'Doesn't everyone?' Then, with a grin, 'All right, it's a fair cop. I was being a total tourist, but I wanted some snaps of yellow cabs and skyscrapers, and that bridge where the old lady lived in the movie *Home Alone*—the Christmas one. And the place where everyone goes ice skating in the winter.'

'And which movie did you see that in?'

'*Serendipity*...' Then, 'Oh, you are sooo smart, Jude Radcliffe,' she said, laughing. 'They're not for me. I wanted them for my mother.'

'Of course you did.'

'No, honestly...' And while the smile was still fixed in place, and would have fooled the casual observer into believing she was the happiest girl alive, her eyes were no longer joining in. 'She's the movie fan. I didn't know if I'd get another chance to take pictures.'

'You're a bright woman. I have no doubt you'll find a way to get exactly what you want. I'll be in the gym for the next thirty minutes or so, if anyone is desperate to get hold of me,' he said as the lift arrived, glad of an excuse to walk away. He didn't want to know what had evoked those shadows. All he was interested in was that she did her job.

'A run outside in the fresh air would do you more good,' she called after him, holding the lift door.

'But this way I can watch CNN and get the latest stock prices at the same time.'

'That's got to be a recipe for a heart attack. Do you want me to order breakfast for you?'

On the point of asking her to have some freshly squeezed orange juice sent up, he found himself saying, 'We're in New York, Talie. Don't you know that gen-yoo-ine New Yorkers go out for breakfast?'

'Do they? How bizarre.'

'This from the woman who snaps as she jogs?'

'I'm a sad female with an incurable tourist habit, Jude. Get over it,' she said, claiming the last word for herself as the lift doors closed.

But at least the sparkle was back in her eyes.

CHAPTER FIVE

'SO, WHAT do you do apart from watch films, Talie?'

They'd walked to a small café where she had proceeded to wipe out all the good she'd done with her early-morning exercise by completely letting herself go and ordering crisp bacon, scrambled eggs and pancakes with maple syrup. And a side order of blueberries.

'Blueberries are really good for your eyesight,' she'd assured Jude. Not that he'd said anything. But that eyebrow...

'In that case better make that everything for two,' he'd told the waitress who'd brought their coffee and orange juice. Then, when she didn't leap in to fill the silence as she usually did, he'd asked her what she did besides watch films.

'Run,' she offered, suddenly wishing she'd just acted on her own initiative and ordered Room Service for both of them. Back in the suite he would have been concentrating on work. And so would she. They could have sniped at one another happily enough, without time to be distracted by personal details. But the buzz that had surged through her when he'd suggested going out to breakfast had nothing to do with the opportunity to behave like a New Yorker. She'd wanted him to notice her...

Dangerous.

No. Worse than dangerous. Stupid.

'Okay, you run…what else do you do?' he persisted.

She stopped toying with her spoon.

'I like to cook,' she said—that was safe. She looked up, faced him. 'And I do a little needlework.'

'Needlework?'

He didn't sound convinced. Maybe that had been pushing the bounds of credibility a little too far.

'I once started a sampler,' she assured him. 'It was for my Brownie needlework badge…'

He was supposed to laugh. He didn't. Instead he continued to regard her intently, as if he'd suddenly realised that she was a person, with thoughts and feelings. She'd felt a lot safer when he was being an irritable bastard. She could ignore that…

'Well, that's covered your hobbies. What about your life?'

'Oh, I *see*.' He wanted to know about her life. That was more difficult, because she didn't actually have a *life*—not the way he meant it, anyway. 'You want to know who I sleep with.'

He regarded her for a moment, but she had absolutely no idea what he was thinking, which was disconcerting. Few people could hide their thoughts so completely. He would be a formidable adversary, she thought, feeling quite sorry for the people who would be facing him across the boardroom table, fighting for their company.

'Actually, I was simply passing the time until the heart attack breakfast arrives.' Then, with a small but unmistakably dismissive gesture, he said, 'It's called having a conversation.'

For once she regretted that her own personal drawbridge was quite so well-oiled. Regretted the conversation they might have had. Found it harder than usual to paint on the bright smile as she said, 'You don't have to be polite, Jude. I assumed this would be a working breakfast and brought my notebook with me.'

'Then you assumed wrong. This is just breakfast.'

'Oh,' she said, for a moment flummoxed. She'd anticipated eggs and dictation. 'Well, excellent. That means I can ask you to take a photograph of me with the pancakes and maple syrup.'

'Why on earth would you want a photograph of you eating breakfast?'

'Oh, please! Not eating it. Just looking at it.'

'Looking at your breakfast?' he persisted.

'It's a memory, Jude, that's all. I'll show my mother the picture, and then I'll tell her how everything tasted and how the waitress sounded and how rude you were and how rude I was, and of course she won't believe me—because, after all, who would?—and I'll grin and she'll say, "How lovely." And, "I wish I could have been there." And I'll say, "Pack your bags. I'll take you." And then she'll say, "Don't be silly..."' She stopped abruptly. Then, because he didn't say anything, and the silence desperately needed filling with inconsequential, meaningless chatter, 'Haven't you ever done that? Made a memory to share with someone?'

'Not my mother,' he said.

On the point of his asking her if she would be sharing it with anyone else the waitress returned with their breakfast, and Talie instantly engaged her in conversation. If he'd been a sensitive soul he'd have thought she was doing it to avoid talking to him, but her interest seemed genuine enough. That was Talie. What you saw was what you got. Even ordering a box of doughnuts to take out was an adventure to her. Should she have sprinkles, or jelly, or apple? He resisted the impulse to ask what she was going to do with them.

'So, we've established that you have a mother,' he persisted, when he'd finally reclaimed her attention. 'Is that the sum total of your family?'

'I have a younger brother, Liam. He's reading law at Edinburgh. You've just been to Scotland, haven't you? Walking?'

'I take a few days occasionally. To get away from people, telephones. The silence helps me to think.'

'About ways to make even more money?'

'You have a problem with that?'

'Surrounded by so much beauty…' she offered.

'There's nothing ugly about money. It's the lack of it that makes life difficult. A lot of people depend on me to pay their mortgages, keep their families fed and clothed.'

'You worry about them?'

'You're surprised?'

She shook her head. 'I'm sorry. No. I just hadn't considered it that way before. As a responsibility.'

'It's one I chose. I could sell up, walk away—but then what would I do with the rest of my life?'

'There are always new challenges.'

'That's why I need to think.'

'I didn't mean new ways to make money.'

She was very good at redirection, he thought. Steering the conversation away from topics she didn't want to talk about, pointing it back at him. Given the opportunity, most people would rather talk about themselves. Unfortunately for her, he wasn't most people.

Unfortunately for him, neither was she.

'Give me your camera and I'll take that picture now, so that your mother can see just what a gannet you are.'

'You think she doesn't already know that?' She took a small digital camera from her bag and said, 'You just look there to compose the picture and then press that button.'

'I think I can probably manage that.' He framed her in the small screen and for a moment felt the charge of her enthusiasm, her exuberance, coming straight at him. But there was something else, too, underlying the brightness. Something that if it wasn't so ridiculous he might have thought was loneliness. 'Smile…' he said, quite unnecessarily, pushing the unexpected tug of long-buried emotions firmly away. Then, 'Hold it for one more…'

He checked the pictures to make sure they were as flattering as a photograph of someone beaming over the breakfast could be, flicking through the ones she'd taken earlier at the same time. Yellow cabs, the stars and stripes hanging from a building, a mounted policeman, one of the Central Park buggies, views of the park itself. She had a good eye for a picture. A real pleasure in the new.

He envied her that. He couldn't remember the last time he'd gone somewhere he hadn't been a hundred times before. Seen something that had made him wish he had a camera so that he could capture the moment.

Even in Scotland it hadn't been the scenery that refreshed him. Just the silence.

'What about you, Talie?' he asked, returning her camera.

'What about me?'

'What do you think about?'

'''...*when the full moon is shining in...and the lamp is dying out...?*'''

'When you're sitting on the bus going to work was more what I had in mind. But if you're in a philosophical mood I'll indulge you.'

She didn't immediately respond, and he had the feeling that he had somehow missed his cue to change the subject. That she hadn't anticipated indulgence. 'On the other hand,' he said, picking up her discomfort, 'if that's just a polite way of saying ''mind your own business...'''

'If you were being intrusive I wouldn't pussyfoot around. I'd tell you straight out.'

'Would you?'

Once again she was uncharacteristically silent.

How hard would he have to push before she ran out of those clever little diversionary tactics and got to the point where she was left with no choice but to talk or tell him to do just that?

Not that he needed to push. All he had to do was pick up a phone and he'd have her life history at his command. Where she lived. Where she went to school, college, her grades, everywhere she'd ever worked, every man she'd ever kissed. Perversely, he wanted her to trust him enough to tell him the important things herself. Especially why someone with her drive and skill—and a quick look through the work she'd produced before she left for her run was enough to demonstrate that she had both, in abundance—was working as a temp at an age when most educated women were already settled in a career, getting around to raising a family.

Why hadn't she mentioned sharing her memories with her father? Or any other man, for that matter.

But who was he to complain? He wasn't into sharing confidences either. All he needed to know was that she could do the job, and she'd already demonstrated that.

'Eat your breakfast, Talie,' he said. 'We haven't got all morning.'

'Of course. Time and take-overs wait for no man.'

They spent the rest of the morning dealing with e-mails from London before the UK office closed for the day, then refining the after-dinner speech he was to give that night. Then Talie summoned the car to take them downtown for a working lunch with the lawyers.

She was working hard to smother a yawn as she gathered her notebook, checked her supply of pencils, and it occurred to him that she'd already put in a ten-hour day.

'I don't need you on this one,' he lied.

'Really?' Then, 'You're only saying that because you don't want me snoring through the meeting.'

'You snore?'

'You doubt it?'

He wasn't going there.

'Take a nap, Talie.'

'A nap? You think a nap will do it? I feel like going to bed and not getting up until tomorrow morning,' she said. 'In fact, I might do just that. You won't need me this evening, will you?'

'You're not planning on sleeping,' he said. 'You think you can get in some sightseeing while I'm putting my reputation on the line in front of five hundred bankers and stockbrokers.' He hadn't forgotten that late night phone call. Marcus knew Jude would be fully occupied this evening.

'There's no fooling you, is there?'

'And no point trying to. Besides, you're wrong about tonight. You don't think I'm going to sit through one of those boring business dinners without some prospect of entertainment, do you?'

'I'm sorry? Entertainment? Why would you need entertainment when you can talk about money all night?'

Which would teach him not to be smart mouthed at her expense.

'I'm sorry, Jude, on this occasion you are going to have to manage without your clown. Your totally efficient PA covered most things, but she didn't mention dress-up clothes and I haven't got anything remotely suitable to wear.'

He'd offended her, he realised. And for once she wasn't bothering to hide it behind a smile.

Maybe he'd meant to. She was much too distracting to be a PA. She could be the best in the business, but there was no way he was going to give her the job.

He found himself thinking about her instead of giving his full attention to the problem at hand. Found himself watching her quick, sure movements as she took notes, as her fingers flew over the keyboard without once looking at it. Seeing the bright intelligence that needed no second telling, no explanations... Waiting for the delighted smile that broke out at the

slightest provocation. Catching the distant look that
came into her eyes when she thought no one was
looking.

She was getting under his skin, and he didn't allow
that. But he wasn't giving Marcus the opportunity to
get under hers.

'Clothes are not a problem,' he said. 'Buy something and charge it to me.'

Talie was feeling just the smallest bit miffed. She'd
worked her socks off for Jude Radcliffe, producing
immaculate work when anyone in their right mind
would have been asleep.

She was entitled to an evening off.

But, no. He wanted company at the dinner tonight.
She didn't object to that. If he'd said, Would you like
to come? It's going to be about as much fun as watching paint dry and I'd really welcome the company of
someone who makes me laugh…she wouldn't have
turned him down.

How often did you get to have dinner with a millionaire, for heaven's sake? And not an old, crumpled
one, but a tall, slate-eyed hunk of a millionaire who
should, by rights, have a six-foot supermodel on his
arm.

But she wasn't being asked. She was being commanded to dress up and provide him with 'entertainment.' And, unlike the rest of the guests, she didn't
even have the keynote speech to look forward to. She
already knew it practically by heart.

As if that wasn't bad enough, instead of taking a
well-earned nap so that she wouldn't look like death

by eight o'clock, she was going to have to shop for a dress. And she hadn't the first idea where to go.

Barney could have told her, but he'd taken Jude to his meeting. She could phone Heather. Maybe find out if *she* went along to these things. She should probably do that anyway and find out how things had gone with the baby. Jude would probably want to send flowers…

All she got was a message on the answering machine, telling her that the new arrival was a girl and everyone was doing well. Well, obviously she wouldn't be at home, but taking care of her daughter.

She would have left a message to say that they were doing pretty well in New York, too, but the tape was already full.

That left the hotel manager. She wasn't exactly thrilled at the prospect of asking the man for help, but the alternative was worse.

'Miss Calhoun,' he said, remembering her name without prompting, all smiles now he knew who she was. 'Please come through to the office.' And, when she was comfortably seated, 'How can I help you?'

'I'm looking for advice, Mr Luis. I joined Mr Radcliffe at very short notice, and now I discover he expects me to partner him at a business dinner this evening. Unfortunately I didn't pack anything suitable to wear.' She didn't actually possess anything remotely suitable to wear for partnering a millionaire— even as entertainment. 'I don't have a lot of time,' she said, 'and to be honest I don't even know where to begin.'

'If it's a business dinner I'd advise black.'

'The female equivalent of the dinner jacket? Isn't that a bit obvious?'

'On the contrary. On this kind of occasion "obvious" would be *not* wearing black. You need something elegant and understated,' he said, then regarded her, as if having trouble ratifying that description with reality.

'You don't think I can do understated?'

'On the contrary, Miss Calhoun. Having seen you reduce my security officers to quivering wrecks, I'm certain you can do anything you put your mind to.'

They were quivering wrecks!

'I did apologise.'

'I know. And you took them a box of doughnuts, too. They would probably die for you now.'

'Really—that won't be necessary.'

'Let us hope so. Now, if you'll just let me make one phone call...'

Within minutes he had arranged for her to see a personal shopper at a seriously up-market department store, and for her purchases to be charged to Jude Radcliffe's account with the hotel.

'If you have any problems, just call me,' he said, giving her his card.

'Thank you, Mr Luis.'

'It's my pleasure, Miss Calhoun. Is there anything else I can do for you?'

'Well, if "understated" is the order of the day, I should probably have my hair put in restraints.'

'There's a salon in the hotel. I'll let them know you'll need some time later in the afternoon. Just go along there when you're ready.'

The store was near enough to walk to, and by the time she'd arrived her Personal Shopper, who was tall, scarily elegant and understated to the point of invisibility, had a selection of dresses, shoes and accessories waiting for her to try on.

Understatement could grow on her, Talie decided, flicking through a dozen or so exquisitely cut black dresses.

Although one wouldn't want to overdo it.

'Jude?'

He was having a bad meeting. It wasn't that anything was going wrong; on the contrary, everything was going precisely to plan. His invitation to speak at the annual bankers' dinner had been the perfect cover for his trip to the U.S., and there hadn't been the slightest hint of the proposed take-over in the press on either side of the Atlantic.

He was, however, finding it difficult to give his undivided attention to the agenda.

Guilt, unexpectedly, was nagging at him. Heaven alone knew what had possessed him to insist Talie accompany him to the dinner. He would never have asked Heather to join him, and if he had she'd have known he was joking. Except that this time he hadn't been...

'Jude?'

He realised that Marcus was waiting for a response from him and was forced to mentally scroll back through the previous conversation before he could provide it.

CHAPTER SIX

TALIE slept through her facial and manicure, and still had time for an hour with a cucumber compress over her eyes before the telephone rang to wake her with the alarm call she'd booked.

She replaced the receiver, then lay back against the pillow, a hand over her stomach to quiet the little thrill of anticipation that fluttered through her. Buffed, polished, and with the most expensive dress she'd ever possessed hanging in the wardrobe, she had long forgotten her irritation at having to forgo an evening sightseeing.

She didn't even care that Jude hadn't thought it necessary to ask, rather than command.

She was excited, she realised. And just a bit nervous. The way she'd used to feel before going out on a big date. She could just about remember how that felt. Not that she'd ever been out on a date with a man like Jude Radcliffe.

She wasn't now, she reminded herself, firmly rejecting all thoughts of the way he'd held her hand when she was gibbering unattractively with nervousness as their flight left the ground, the touch of his fingers against her cheek as he'd tucked a stray curl behind her ear.

It wasn't personal. Her hair annoyed him, that was all. Hell, it annoyed her...

This was just a work thing. Obviously Jude needed someone along to take care of his speech, hand it to him at the appropriate moment…

No. That wasn't it. He was more than capable of taking care of his own speech. She couldn't think why he needed her with him, but being seen in the company of one of the world's most powerful businessmen was undoubtedly going to be the highlight of her year.

Probably her entire decade, the way things were going.

What it was going to be for him, she wasn't sure, but he undoubtedly had some good reason for wanting her there, and she doubted that it had anything to do with 'entertainment.'

If it was, he was going to be disappointed. She was going to be his Girl Friday. Supportive, discreet, doing absolutely nothing to draw attention to herself. Doing absolutely nothing that would give his eyebrow an excuse to get excited.

This was a once-in-a-lifetime Cinderella moment, and she wasn't going to do a thing to wreck it. She was going to be the perfect young businesswoman. Make him eat his 'entertainment' if it killed her.

She glanced at her watch. Plenty of time. And she smiled as she imagined his face as she walked into the room. Stunned by the elegant and understated perfection of her dress. Bowled over by her sleek new hairstyle.

'Talie…' He'd murmur her name on little more than a breath as he reached for her hand, whispered her name again, as if he could hardly believe his eyes as he bent to kiss her cheek and she caught the subtle scent of an Alpha male for once lost for words.

'Talie, you look...'

'Talie!'

She sat up with a start.

'Talie, are you ready?'

What? Ready? She looked at her watch.

Oh, sugar... She'd gone straight back to sleep.

'Ten minutes,' she mumbled, tumbling off the bed, trying to get her mouth to cooperate with her brain and her feet to go in the same direction as she scrambled for the bathroom.

Oh, good grief! Ten minutes wasn't long enough to be stunning. Ten minutes was barely long enough to be herself. She groaned. That would teach her to go daydreaming about laying waste to tall, dark and handsome millionaires.

And even if he did fall at her feet she'd just have to tell him to get up again. This Cinderella wasn't in the market for a prince—Charming or otherwise.

It was just as well that she hadn't planned on a leisurely shower—the steam would have reduced her carefully straightened hair to ringlets—since all she had time for was the shortest sponge down in history. With cold water.

And since, for once, she didn't have to do anything to her hair except flatten it with a brush where it was sticking up after she'd slept on it, she had absolutely loads of time to spend on her make-up—three whole minutes, in fact—before she slipped into the slither of silk crêpe that had probably cost more per square inch than anything she'd ever worn. Or was ever likely to.

Fortunately, since 'understated' people didn't discuss the price of anything, she'd never know exactly how much. And by the time the bill arrived on Jude's desk she'd be ancient history.

Ditto her new shoes and evening bag.

Jude was on the telephone when the door behind him opened, and he glanced at his wristwatch. Ten minutes dead. The girl was good, he thought, turning around. And he discovered to his surprise that breathing was not the simple, automatic thing that he'd always imagined it to be.

'Jude…?' The voice in his ear demanded a response. 'Are you there?'

'Yes—sorry, someone just came in…' And for the second time that day he found himself having to re-run a conversation before he could respond. Except that on this occasion his mind was a total blank. 'Let's talk about this tomorrow, Mike,' he said. 'I'm on my way out.'

'I'm sorry,' Talie said, with a tiny gesture towards the phone as he replaced the receiver. 'I didn't mean to disturb you.'

Didn't she? Then why the devil was she wearing a dress clearly designed for the purpose of disturbing any man with half a red blood cell? Although how just one bare shoulder, one bare arm, could be so… provocative was beyond him.

It wasn't as if the dress was tight. Or clinging. On the contrary, it skimmed her figure, merely hinting at the curves he knew it concealed. Maybe that was it. Concealment. And the counterpoint of creamy white skin against unrelieved black.

After his remark about 'entertainment' he'd steeled himself for something outrageous in scarlet. With frills. He knew he deserved it.

Subtle, he discovered, could be far more deadly. If he'd wanted her to cause a distraction he'd got everything he could have wished for.

Of course it didn't help that as she walked towards him the curved hem parted to the thigh to offer a glimpse of strappy shoe with a heel high enough to be used as a lethal weapon, a slender ankle, and just enough shapely leg to lay waste any banker whose arteries were not in tiptop condition.

His own heart was pounding uncomfortably, and he was familiar with her legs. He'd had a close up of them that morning, when she was wearing her running shorts.

Less, he decided, was definitely more.

She stopped. The skirt became still. Discreet. And he managed to drag his gaze back to her face.

'What the hell have you done with your hair?' he asked. He had to say something, and, on balance, her hair seemed safest. Gone were the wild curls. It was hanging sleek and straight to her shoulders, with just the tiniest lift at the ends.

He'd asked for it. And he discovered that he hated it.

'Nothing. I—and when I say I, I do, of course, mean you—paid a hairdresser a vast amount of money to iron it straight. I'm afraid you've had a rather expensive afternoon all 'round. But there it is.' And she gave a little shrug that offered him another glimpse of her ankle. 'High-quality entertainment doesn't come cheap.'

'We should be leaving,' he said.

'I'm ready.' Then, 'Don't forget your speech.' She picked up the stack of prompt cards from the desk and handed them to him. She used the sleeveless arm—it didn't even have a bracelet to make it look less naked—and taking them from her fingers felt like sin.

He slipped them into his pocket before opening the door and standing well back to allow her to precede him. He couldn't think of a thing to say as they rode down together in the lift, and Talie, for once silent, didn't help him out. But as they made their way through the lobby he couldn't miss the ripple of turning heads, the murmur of interest as, placing himself carefully on her sleeved side, he guided her to the door.

It was opened by Mr Luis himself, with the smallest bow to Talie.

But it was left to Barney to say what everyone was thinking.

'Wow, Talie. Great dress. You look fabulous.'

'Thank you, Barney,' she said, smiling at him as she ducked her head, her hair swinging forward as she climbed into the back of the car.

He should have said it, he knew, but it was too late. Anything he said now was simply going to echo the quiet nod from the hotel manager, Barney's natural spontaneity.

And look second-hand.

He was stuck with a throw-away line about 'entertainment.'

'Mr Radcliffe…'

He paused at the entrance to the hotel where the dinner was being held and their arrival was met by a barrage of flashes from photographers taking pictures for the financial papers.

'Okay?' he asked, glancing down at Talie.

'Oh, yes. Just a bit surprised. I didn't expect the celebrity treatment.'

'Why not? You look like a star.'

Maybe that was the way to do it. Just say what you were thinking—without thinking about it. How long had it been since he'd done that?

He discovered he could pinpoint the exact day, hour, minute…

It was perhaps as well that they were instantly swept up by the reception committee and he didn't have to follow up his remark with the usual crushing put-down. Instead he could much more safely introduce her to their host.

So much for dreaming, Talie thought as she was offered a glass of champagne. One brief glance and a 'What the hell have you done with your hair…?' She was beginning to think the girls in the Finance Department at the Radcliffe Tower were right. The man was a total…

'Is this your first visit to New York, Talie?'

The men were older, more powerful, but the questions, the exclamations over her accent, the invitations were the same. Unfortunately the only man she wanted to invite her to go sightseeing had other things on his mind. When Jude was asked by one of the party if he could spare her to sit by him at dinner, so that they could 'talk about London,' he was too busy talking about his favourite subject to do more than glance up and frown, as if he'd forgotten all about her, before, after a momentary pause during which she thought he was going to decline—she was there for *his* 'entertainment' after all—he nodded.

She bottled up her disappointment, hiding it beneath a smile, hoping she looked as if he'd done her a favour.

As if he'd notice.

Cool, elegant, sophisticated, she reminded herself, and once they were seated she turned to the man who'd sought out her company. 'So, when were you last in London, Carson?' she asked, doing her best to ignore Jude. He didn't seem to be having any trouble ignoring her.

Carson needed little prompting to talk about himself, and she gave him her full attention for a while before turning to the man on her left and sitting through an almost identical conversation. Getting on first name terms with millionaires was getting to be a habit, but it wasn't so difficult. They were just like other men.

Most of them.

Jude hoped that putting some distance between him and Talie would help. It didn't. Instead of having her next to him where, though he'd be assaulted by her voice, her scent, the certainty that every man's eye was upon her, he wouldn't have to look at her, he was now sitting opposite her and forced to watch every move, every smile, every laugh as she captivated the men sitting around her.

She wasn't just a runaway chatterbox, he discovered. She knew how to listen, and it wasn't only young, impressionable men who vied for her attention.

Old, impressionable men were equally Talie-struck.

He couldn't even justify his irritation by pretending that she was flirting outrageously with them. She wasn't. She didn't need to flirt. All she had to do was smile and they were at her feet—and once again falling over themselves to provide a personalised tour of the city.

'Carson, I allowed you the pleasure of Talie's company over dinner, but don't push your luck,' he warned.

'You can't blame an old man for trying.'

'It's becoming an epidemic. Men all over New York take one look at Talie and instantly decide they must take her "sightseeing." It never happens when I bring Heather with me.'

'Heather is a lovely woman. I promise next time she comes to New York I'll take her wherever she'd like to go.' The old man grinned. 'But only if I get Talie tomorrow.'

'Really, I don't have time for sightseeing, Carson,' she said quickly. 'I'm here to work.'

'You must have some time to yourself. Just because Jude thinks the world revolves around the office doesn't mean you have to subscribe to the same philosophy. All work and no play—'

'Makes a man dull, but rich,' Jude cut in. 'Spare me your homespun philosophy, Carson, especially since you've never adhered to it yourself. How many wives have given up on you?'

'Four.'

'I thought it was five.'

Carson appeared to think about it. 'You're right. Five. But given sufficient incentive a man can change.'

'In this case he isn't going to get the chance. Didn't Talie tell you that I'm taking her on a night-time tour of the city just as soon as we leave here?' He turned to her. 'Tell him, Talie.'

'That's right. Beginning with a visit to the top of the Empire State Building,' she responded without hesitation, smiling across the table at him. Familiar with the entire range of her smiles by now, he was not fooled for a minute. She was not in the least bit amused. 'It's so much more romantic at night. Isn't that right, Jude?' she prompted.

Romantic? Oh, good grief…

'That remains to be seen,' he replied. 'I believe the forecast is for rain.'

CHAPTER SEVEN

TALIE was not impressed.

'What was that all about?' she demanded as they left the hotel, the minute his speech was over, the applause still ringing in their ears.

'What didn't you understand? I thought you had a pretty sound grasp of economics,' he replied, as Barney opened the limo door for her to climb in.

'For a woman?'

'Don't be petty, Talie. It doesn't suit you.'

'No. Sorry. Anyway, I wasn't talking about the speech, as well you know. I already knew that by heart.'

Not entirely true. She knew the words by heart, but he'd put life, passion into them, given them power and meaning. And humour. He'd had them all laughing at the stories with which he'd interspersed his hard-news message on the economy. It had been a world away from reading the words off a computer screen or the prompt cards she'd prepared—and which he'd barely glanced at.

He'd engaged with his audience on a personal level that had surprised and warmed her. She'd felt, somehow, that he was talking directly to her. And she suspected that everyone else in the room had felt the same way.

'It was excellent, by the way.'

'I'd say I'm flattered, although I sense a lurking "but…"'

'If there is it's a butt with two ts,' she said. 'There was no need for you to butt into my conversation with Carson. I wasn't about to spill the beans—tell him I was too busy to go sightseeing because my boss needed me to hold his hand while he takes over yet another company.' Then, when he didn't rise to this provocation, 'Even though he did offer to take me on a boat ride around Manhattan.'

'You need someone to take you to the pier? Buy your ticket? I thought you were a modern woman who didn't need a man to hold her hand.'

'I don't. Carson was offering to take me in his yacht.'

'Really? I thought wife number five had got that in the divorce settlement.'

'Don't be petty, Jude.'

'No. I'm sorry to have spoiled your fun.'

'I didn't want to go with him,' she declared furiously. 'I'm not cross because you interfered with my social life. We both know that I don't have time to go pleasure cruising. But if you didn't think I could be trusted to keep my mouth shut why did you take me with you tonight?'

'It never occurred to me that you'd talk about my business dealings over the dinner table, Talie. Heather chose you. I trust her judgement.'

Slightly mollified, she said, 'Well, good. But you're lucky I'm not the kind of girl to hold a man to the promise of a good time.'

'Are you telling me you're too tired?' he asked.

'What?' Then, 'No, but you didn't mean it…'

'I never say anything I don't mean. Give us your New York By Night Special, Barney. Starting at 350 Fifth Avenue. Talie wants to take a long ride in an elevator.'

'Yes, sir!'

'You did mean it?' she said, her heart picking up a beat as he slid onto the seat beside her.

He shrugged, drawing attention to the kind of shoulders that would have looked more at home on an athlete than a businessman. She'd been trying to ignore them all evening. Trying to ignore him the way he'd been ignoring her. The amount of attention she'd paid him, it was scarcely any wonder that Carson had thought it was his lucky night...

'I was looking for a believable excuse to leave early,' he said. 'Before the heavy talking starts. You gave me one.'

'So that's why you took me along.' She gestured back towards the hotel as the car pulled away from the kerb. 'They all think ''sightseeing'' is a euphemism for the shortest route to the bedroom.'

'I don't suppose for a minute any of them thought I'd brought you to New York for your shorthand skills, Talie. Not in that dress.'

'What's wrong with the dress?' she demanded. 'I went for elegant and understated, which was a good deal more than you deserved. I could have gone for seriously ''entertaining,''' she reminded him, making little quote marks with her fingers. 'With a hemline up to here and a neckline down to here and—'

'And caused a riot?'

'Men are so shallow,' she said, trying very hard not to smile.

'Are we? So, who do you sleep with?'

Which would teach her to try and be smart with a man who'd forgotten more about manipulating conversation than she'd ever known. Teach her to use a cheap trick to stop the conversation when it was getting too personal. Jude had simply stored it away, using it back at her after he'd slipped beneath her defences with a compliment. But she rallied gamely.

'Do I have to be sleeping with anyone? It isn't compulsory, as far as I know.'

'I've seen the effect you have on the average male libido—' she didn't miss the 'average,' something they both knew he was not '—so unless all the men in London are blind or idiots, it follows that you must be beating them off in droves.'

'I wish. It's just the English accent exciting the locals. It doesn't have the same effect at home. And I think you lend me a little of your glamour, Jude. You must have noticed that a girl arriving in the wake of a millionaire becomes instantly more interesting.'

'So the answer is no one?'

This time he wasn't going to allow himself to be diverted, and confined with him in the rear of a limousine there was no escape—short of doing what she'd said she'd do and telling him to mind his own business. Which would put a swift end to the evening. Something that she didn't want. And not just because he'd promised her that long ride in a lift.

Why was it that 'no one' sounded so lame? It wasn't as if it was from lack of offers. It was her choice, and Jude didn't care one way or the other. He was just satisfying his curiosity. Demonstrating his power.

It didn't matter, she told herself.

Oh, but it did. Somehow admitting that the only male who ever spent the night beneath her duvet these days was Harry, the little stray black and white cat who'd invited himself in and made himself at home, was not the image she was hoping to project in her sexy black dress. A girl had her pride.

She could, of course, invent an intense and adoring lover, but it was late, and she knew she wouldn't remember what she'd said in the morning. And she'd already left it far too long to be convincing.

'It's late, Jude. If we're going to do "conversation," can we stick to simple stuff? I need a full eight hours' sleep before I can deal with advanced level.'

'If you need time to think about it, Talie, don't stress yourself. I can work it out for myself.'

Now she felt like a fool. She should have owned up to the cat...and the teddy. Her turn to shrug. 'Okay, I'll admit it. I'm a sad old bag who's on the shelf.'

'There are several things wrong with that statement, but they'll have to wait.' And, while she was still trying to work that one out, 'We've arrived,' he said. 'Do you want to do this, or would you rather go to bed?'

Startled, she turned to look at him. In the darkness of the limousine his eyes gleamed dangerously, and every cell in her body responded with shocking immediacy. 'Go to bed?' she repeated.

Oh, great, Talie. Come and out and say it, why don't you? After all, you're only his temporary secretary, and everyone already assumes you're sleeping with him. Why not give yourself a real treat? You know you want to...

'And put in a bid for the eight hours' sleep.'

'Oh...' For once entirely lost for words, she turned

and glanced out of the car window. Then, as she saw the address—understated and elegant in art deco script—she said it again. 'Oh... Wow!' At least she didn't have to pretend enthusiasm in an attempt to hide her blushes. 'We're really here.'

'I'll take that as a vote for the ride in a lift.'

Jude climbed out and offered her his hand. Taking it, she allowed him to lead her into the entrance, but dug her heels in when he walked straight past the exquisite 1930s lift lobby.

'Where are we going?'

'I'm afraid the paying public don't get to use that area. Three and a half million people a year require something a little more hard-wearing. We go down here.'

'We do?' Then, seeing the signs, 'We have to queue?'

'I'm afraid so. Although it's late, so hopefully not for long.'

There was a photographer waiting to snap arrivals in front of a backdrop of the building.

'You don't have to buy if you don't like it,' he said, when Talie hesitated.

'Oh, right.'

'You want me to take you together?'

'No.' She quickly detached herself from Jude before he took the initiative and did it for her. 'Just me.'

'Number eleven. You can pick it up on the way out,' he said.

'It wasn't like this in *Sleepless in Seattle*,' Talie said as Jude headed towards the window to pay. For once she had to think of something to say to fill the void, rather than just letting the words spill out.

'You should get out more. This is real life, not a movie, Talie.' He took her by the arm and led her towards the lifts. 'At least it's fairly quiet. At midday this place is heaving.'

'I see. Obviously you've been here before. Despite the fervent protestations to the contrary, it would seem that you're not entirely immune to sightseeing.'

'No, I've done my share. But after a while it all gets to look the same, so now I just concentrate on business.'

'You're just a cynical old man who's seen it all. Maybe you should wait in the car. Or go back to the hotel and work on a deal. I can get a taxi back to the hotel. I haven't been in a yellow cab yet and it would give me a chance to tick it off my to-do list.'

It occurred to her that she was beginning to sound crabby—unrequited lust had that effect on her—and she shut her mouth.

'You'll need someone to take a photograph of you at the top to prove you've been there, won't you?' He took the small bag she was carrying from her. 'Or are you going to pretend that you didn't bring your camera with you, just to prove me wrong?'

'You are such a know-all,' she declared, snatching it back before he could look.

'Not at all. The enthusiastic tourist never travels without her camera—or how would she remember everything she's seen?'

'I'll never forget what I've seen. The photographs aren't for me—'

'I know. They're for your mother. I'm beginning to wish you'd brought her with you. She could have taken her own photographs while you concentrated on work.'

She stared at him. She was entitled to be a little crabby. He was the man of her dreams as well as being the boss from hell. It was a very bad combination. But this outing was his idea, so what was *his* problem?

Then the lift arrived and she let the bad feelings go, taking a deep breath as she stepped inside.

As they joined the dozen or so other people who'd been waiting, and rode up in unnatural silence, Jude was unable to take his eyes off her. Wide-eyed and holding her breath, she watched the floor numbers being counted in tens as the high-speed lift sped them to the top, and despite himself he found her excitement infectious.

A second lift took them the last few floors, and he pushed open the door to the viewing platform, holding it wide so that she had an uninterrupted view of the city lit up before them.

'Oh.' She took a step down, then another. 'Oh, my goodness, it's so beautiful,' she said, her voice catching in her throat. Then she looked back up at him. 'Thank you, Jude.'

'Don't waste your time thanking me,' he said, his own voice catching just a little as her hair whipped across her face in the breeze. 'Go and take your pictures.'

He followed as she walked slowly around the viewing deck, stopping from time to time to exclaim at some spectacular sight…a bridge, a building she recognised, a name.

'Hey, there's Macy's! Right down there, below us.'

He looked down, then at her. 'Yes. So?'

'It's *Macy's*. The department store.'

'It's too late to go shopping.'

'No…it's on 34th Street,' she said, as if that should mean something to him.

'This has something to do with a movie, doesn't it?'

She stared at him. 'I can't believe you haven't seen *Miracle on…*' She stopped. 'No, I'm not wasting another breath talking to an old cynic like you. I doubt you ever believed in Santa Claus.'

'I am not old,' he protested, putting twenty-five cents in the binoculars for her so that she could look at the distant lights. 'I'm like the street. Thirty-four. In my prime.'

'Really?' She looked through the glasses, moving them until she found something that caught her attention. 'Cynicism is sooo aging.'

'You see wrinkles? Grey hair?' he demanded.

'That's just time showing, not age. Age isn't anything to do with muscle tone. It's in the mind.'

'Are you suggesting that I have a grey, sagging mind?' Then, when she actually looked as if she was giving it some thought, 'Hesitate one second more and you're fired.'

'You can't fire me. The enthusiastic tycoon needs his Girl Friday to keep track of his thoughts. However grey.' Then she smiled. 'Fortunately the condition is not incurable. Do want to take a look at the Statue of Liberty?' she asked, standing back and offering him the glasses.

'I've seen it, thanks.'

She tutted, catching her hair and tucking it behind her ear before taking another look for herself. 'On the other hand, some cases are beyond help.'

'Oh, I see. That was a test?'

'The view is always new, Jude.'

'Really? And what bumper sticker did you read that on?'

She didn't answer, just stepped back, shivered a little as she looked around, and rubbed her arms. He took off his jacket and slipped it around her shoulders, pulling it close in front of her. As she looked up to thank him he saw the lights of Manhattan reflected in her eyes and discovered that she was right. Even the most familiar scene in the world could take on a totally new dimension if he took the trouble to look.

'Is that it?' he said, fighting down the urge to kiss her that had been dogging him ever since she'd looked up at him in his own lift. 'Have you finally run out of snappy little homilies?'

'You have to *want* to be rescued, Jude.'

Rescued?

'I'm not lost.'

'You're just in denial. What you need is a twelve-step plan to recover your sense of wonder.'

'Wonder?' Was that what he saw in her eyes? The excitement that seemed to radiate from her and light up any room? 'Okay, I'll let that pass on the grounds that you're suffering from jet lag.'

'Step one is admitting you have a problem.'

'The only problem I have is you, Talie Calhoun. Give me your camera and I'll take a photograph of you.'

For a moment the image in her eyes seemed to shimmer, then she lowered her lashes as she opened her bag to take out her camera and the image was gone. By the time she looked up her smile seemed to have lost its natural sparkle and become mechanical.

'Talie—'

'Do you want me to take a photograph of the two of you together?'

Before Talie could say it wasn't necessary Jude had handed the camera to the kindly woman who'd offered. 'That would be great. Thank you.'

And, after glancing down, he scooped Talie under his arm and lined her up for the shot. 'If we stand here,' he said, 'you'll be able to tell your mother that Macy's is right behind us.'

She muttered something under her breath that he didn't quite catch—wasn't meant to catch. He thought it wiser not to ask her to repeat it.

'One more to be sure?' the woman asked.

'Thank you,' Talie said, sliding out from under his arm and reclaiming the camera immediately the woman had taken the second photograph, tucking it straight into her bag without looking at them.

'A pleasure. You two have a nice evening.'

'Shall we take a rain check on the rest of the tour, Jude?' Talie said, turning to him. 'It's getting late and we've got a busy day tomorrow.'

He glanced back at the city, sparkling with light, colour, and felt an odd reluctance to leave. But Talie was already heading towards the exit and he followed her, catching her in time to open the door.

'You're tired?'

'I'll survive. At least I will if I don't wake up at three o'clock again.'

'If you do, give me a knock and we could have a crack at some of that advanced conversation. The wee

small hours of the morning are supposed to be con-
ducive to the spilling of secrets.'

'Who said I have secrets?'

'Everyone has secrets, Talie, and you're already
privy to a lot of mine.'

'Business secrets don't count.'

'No?'

'No.' She managed a grin. 'So if we're going to
share pre-dawn confidences you're going to have to
be prepared to trade.'

CHAPTER EIGHT

TALIE opened her eyes and thought for a moment that she'd overslept. Then she picked up her watch and fell back against the pillows. Four o'clock. A marginal improvement on the previous night, but not by much, and while her head was telling her to close her eyes and go back to sleep her body was wide awake, eager to leap out of bed and go for an early-morning run.

That was the trouble with habits, they died hard, but there hadn't been a lot to stay in bed for in the last couple of years, and lying there feeling sorry for herself hadn't been an attractive option.

She hadn't even given it more than a passing thought for quite some time—there was no use pining over what you couldn't have—until she'd been blindsided by a good looking stranger in a lift and had found herself remembering just what she'd been missing.

She turned over, buried her head under the pillow and tried to block out the promptings of a body kept on short rations for too long—a body suddenly confronted with all the temptations in the sweet shop window and demanding gratification.

There had been a moment, the space of one slow heartbeat, when Jude had put his jacket around her and she'd been certain that he was about to make an unforgettable memory just for her, up there on top of the world—the kind that no camera could compete with. But a kiss wouldn't have been enough.

And anything more would have been impossible.

It didn't stop her thinking about it, though.

She could have done with a pile of work to attack and fill the empty hours until dawn. She didn't even have a book or a magazine to distract her. She might have been a bit slow to work out who he was, but once she'd got the picture she'd understood that asking him to wait while she grabbed the latest bestseller as they flashed through the airport shopping mall would not go down at all well.

She turned the pillow over to the cool side, lay very still, and used basic relaxation techniques to make her limbs go heavy, doing her best to ignore the time-to-get-up insistence of a body used to routine. It was no good. All that happened was that she was relaxed and wide awake.

She eased herself into a sitting position, picked up the phone and dialled home, where it was a civilised nine o'clock in the morning. Her aunt answered.

'Talie? What time is it with you?'

'Don't ask. I can't sleep and it's too early to get up. Can you call me back for a chat?' she begged—she'd given her aunt her number at the hotel so that she wouldn't have to pay for her calls home at hotel rates—and snatched the phone back up the minute it began to ring.

Jude, unable to sleep, heard the brief ring of the phone and glanced at his watch. It was just past four. An odd time for a phone call—unless it was from home. And, concerned that it might be bad news, he flung back the covers and pulled on a robe before crossing the sitting room to Talie's room.

He tapped. The low murmur of her voice stopped, then she said, 'Yes?'

Taking that as an invitation, he opened the door.

Talie was sitting propped up against a pile of pillows in the huge bed, her eyes dark and lustrous in a dim circle of light from the bedside lamp. Her hair had given up on the expensive styling and curled back into its natural ringlets and she was wearing what looked like a baggy T-shirt with a cartoon kangaroo printed on the front.

As an essay in seduction it should have been a disaster. His body was quick to tell him that it was anything but. He'd never seen a woman looking so appealing, so desirable, so sexy…

'What is it, Jude?' she demanded.

Jerked out of the fantasy his mind was weaving, he said, 'I heard the phone. Is anything wrong?'

'No. I couldn't sleep, so I asked my aunt to call me for a chat.'

'Hang up. Talk to me; it's cheaper.'

'You're not paying for the call,' she objected.

'All the more reason to do as I say and stop squandering your hard earned money. I'll go and make a cup of tea,' he said.

And he tore himself away before he forgot himself…and the fact that she worked for him. Busying himself filling the kettle, finding the tea bags, he tried not to think of how it would feel to have her warm body curled up against him, her hair soft beneath his hand…

'I'm sorry I disturbed you—'

He fumbled a mug as he dropped a tea bag into it, juggling with it until he finally managed to set it straight on the counter before he looked around.

'That's a bad case of nerves,' she said, going through the cupboards. 'You really should try to get more sleep.'

The kangaroo had been hidden beneath one of the thick white bathrobes provided by the hotel, and she looked as soft and cuddly as a teddy bear and ten times more appealing. She found what she was looking for—a teapot—and when she straightened they were standing very close.

She smelled of clean sheets, soap and warm skin. Innocent scents that stirred him in a way that the most expensive perfume never could. And unless he moved she was going to have to squeeze by him.

He didn't move.

For a moment the only thing that moved in the kitchen was his heart, beating as if he'd been hitting the treadmill in the basement gym instead of lying in bed for the last few hours.

She was so still that for a moment he thought she must be able to read his mind. Then she handed him the pot and said, 'Warm this, will you? If we're going to have tea it might as well be a decent cup.'

'Yes, ma'am.' His voice was throaty, his hand not quite steady as he poured in some water from the kettle, then swished it around before tipping it into the sink. 'So, you ring home and ask them to call you back?' he said stupidly.

It would explain the phone calls—although they must be keeping somewhat extended hours back home.

Her aunt?

'It's a lot cheaper than paying inflated hotel rates,' she said.

'I wouldn't expect you to pay for your calls home,' he said, angry with himself for not having thought to tell her so. 'Besides, the lines to the suite are private. Nothing to do with the hotel. Call whenever you want to.'

'Thank you. That's very kind.'

'No, it's totally selfish. I want your entire attention on the job, not worrying about what's going on at home. And you didn't disturb me. I was awake.'

She fished the tea bags out of the mugs and, taking the teapot from him, dropped them in before pouring on boiling water. 'Milk or lemon?'

'Milk.'

She raised her eyebrows. 'You've got the fridge.'

Obviously she wasn't prepared to squeeze by and get it herself.

Pity. There was something so intimate about sharing a kitchen in the middle of the night. The air was pregnant with possibilities. Loaded with risk.

He was no stranger to financial risk, but it was so long since he'd played roulette with his emotions that he'd forgotten the urgency, the complete abandonment of all sense—the single-minded need to plunge into danger.

She carefully poured the tea.

He topped it up with milk.

'Thanks,' she said, reaching for a mug.

Forestalling her before she could take it up and escape back to the safety of her bedroom, he picked up both of them. 'Let's go and sit down.'

'There must be a better way to do this,' she said,

curling up in the armchair. It was a big armchair, but the message was plain. She was determined to keep her distance. So he took the sofa.

'Better way to do what?'

'Travel.' She took a sip of tea. 'They knew how to do it in the old days. Six days of luxury on an ocean liner. And no jet lag.'

'There's no reason why we shouldn't do that next time.' *We? Next time?* Where had that come from? He didn't actually care, he decided. The idea was intensely appealing. 'Ease ourselves gradually into the change of time zone by an hour a day. Arrive fresh and completely in tune with our surroundings.'

'Six days? Can you spare that much time?' she asked, refusing to pick up on the 'we.'

'I could give up walking in the Highlands. I imagine I would think just as well walking around the deck.'

'Well, obviously the scenery doesn't mean a thing to you, but you fly to New York a lot oftener than you take those breaks. I've seen your diary,' she said, when he raised his eyebrows. 'And I doubt you'd find an Atlantic crossing anywhere near as peaceful. There are all those cocktail parties, for a start.' She tapped her hand to her mouth in a parody of a bored yawn. 'The daily intake of dry martinis would lay waste to at least a zillion brain cells.'

He laughed. 'Would that be so bad? Since I only use them to think about money?'

'You might want to use them for something else one day.'

'What *is* your problem with money?'

'I don't have a problem with it. As you say, your staff have mortgages to pay, shoes to buy for their children. I'm glad you take your responsibilities seriously. I just think that there comes a time in a man's life when he should stop giving his entire attention to making the stuff and start thinking about how to use it.'

'For the good of mankind?'

'What else is it for?'

Caught without a slick answer, he said, 'Shall we get back to the important business of crossing the Atlantic without jet lag?'

'If you insist.' She shrugged, but he was sure she hadn't finished with that one. 'Where were we? Oh, right. The nightly cocktail party—followed, of course, by dinner at the Captain's table—'

'You think we'd get an invitation?'

'I don't know about "we." This has nothing to do with me. But a man with a whole building named after him could expect nothing less,' she declared.

'To be strictly accurate, it was named after my father.'

'He built it?'

'No. He died in an industrial accident when I was four years old. I built it and named it for him. The John Radcliffe Tower.'

'I'm sorry, I didn't know.'

'It's on the foundation stone. I'll show you when we get back.'

'Oh, but—'

'Do you think there would be deck games?' he prompted, refusing to allow her to spoil the fantasy by reminding him of the grinding poverty he'd come from. Or that she wouldn't be there when they got back.

'I should imagine so.' She pulled a face. Then, 'Don't they have shooting contests? Using those clay things? Very noisy.'

'They're big boats. We could find somewhere quiet. Sit out on the deck and watch the waves go by.'

'This is the Atlantic we're talking about, Jude. Force five gales and waves as big as... Well, I don't know how big they are, but they're bound to be really big.'

'You seem to know all about it.'

'I read a travel brochure once.'

'One that mentioned force five gales?'

'Well, no. It just said something about the boat being fitted with stabilisers and I read between the lines. I mean, why would a boat need stabilisers if there weren't big waves?'

'You didn't book a cruise, I take it?'

'It wasn't for me...' She shook her head. 'Look, I promise you, a man who's seen everything and done everything would be bored witless in six minutes, let alone six days. I mean, the Atlantic looks the same all the way across.'

'I'm willing to make the sacrifice if you are.'

'Aren't you forgetting something? I'm just a temp. Heather Lester is your secretary. She's a fine woman. The perfect PA.'

He wasn't forgetting a thing.

'Perfect, but no longer a fixture. She's been talking about retiring as soon as I can find someone to replace her. In fact she gave me twelve months' notice. It'll soon be up.'

'Have you found anyone?'

'I haven't been looking. I was counting on her

changing her mind. Now I suspect that she's done it for me. And she's chosen you.'

'Then she's going to be stuck with you for a while longer. I can't take on that kind of commitment. Did I tell you that her daughter had a little girl, by the way? Would you like me to send flowers? I would have done it, but I didn't know her daughter's married name. Or address.'

'Congratulations, Talie.'

A small frown creased the smooth skin between her brows.

'You managed to stay with the same conversation for all of fifteen minutes. Of course it was all pure fantasy. No real life stuff to send you running for cover. But the minute it got personal you changed the subject.'

'No, honestly—'

'Why can't you take on the kind of commitment that working for me would entail?'

There was a long pause. She looked into the mug of tea she was holding, as if that would offer her an escape.

'I'm sure Heather knows,' he prompted. 'She wouldn't have considered sending you on this trip unless she'd already thoroughly checked you out. Something I know she's done. She even checked out your story about the incident on the Underground.'

'That's outrageous! Why would I have lied about that?' Then, as her quick brain answered her own question, a flush stole across her cheeks. 'Oh. I see. You thought I'd made it up to impress you. That I was coming on to you.'

'Actually, no. But Heather has worked for me a long

time. She's very protective. And somewhat cynical. She saw me through a very bad patch when I was confronted with the fact that a woman I'd trusted, loved, was passing insider information to her brother to play the stock market. Using me to get advance knowledge of mergers and take-overs to buy up shares that they knew would rise fast once the news became public.'

'That's serious, isn't it?'

'If I'd been implicated I could have gone to jail.'

'Did they? Go to jail.'

'No. I didn't believe it. I was so certain that I said I'd prove it, and I set a trap. A bogus take-over of a dummy company. I took a report home in my brief-case—something I'd done a hundred times before—setting out my plans to take it over.'

She didn't say anything, but he saw the question in her eyes.

'When someone started buying huge blocks of shares I confronted her. They took off—disappeared one step ahead of the police. He wasn't her brother, of course.'

'But that's…'

Words apparently failed her, but he wouldn't have been human not to feel warmed by her look of compassion. He refused to let her shift all the blame.

'She couldn't have deceived me if I'd been paying attention, Talie. I was careless. Took her apparent adoration as nothing less my due. I was, after all, the brilliant Jude Radcliffe. She saw that weakness in me and exploited it.'

'All you were guilty of was trusting someone you

loved. That's when you lost the wonder, isn't it? When "the deal" became the only thing you believed in?'

'I took a ride to the top of the Empire State with you.'

'Only because you had your arm twisted. You'd seen it all before.'

'I thought I had, but I saw something new tonight,' he said.

'Oh? And what was that?'

'I'll tell you if you'll stop avoiding my question. Why can't you take on the kind of commitment that working for me would entail?'

'It's nothing,' she said, far too quickly, and for once not quite prepared to meet his eyes. 'Family commitments, that's all.'

'If it's nothing, why won't you talk about it?' he persisted.

That caught her attention, but her eyes were like those of a startled creature caught in car headlights.

She held the stare for another ten seconds before breaking free. Then, with a shrug, she said, 'We don't—Calhouns. Talk.'

He might have offered her an argument about that, but he refused to take the bait and let her off the hook. Refused to say anything that would give her another chance to run away down some other conversational back alley.

For a moment she actually looked panic stricken. Then she groaned, dropping her face into her hands, and before he could think he was on his knees in front of her, taking her hands, forcing her to look at him.

'I trusted you, Talie. Trust me. Talk to me. Tell me what's wrong.'

She shook her head. 'Nothing. It's nothing. I've just realised that I'm just like her, that's all.'

'Who?'

'My mother. That's what she used to do. She was so good at changing the subject that you wouldn't notice. Get too close and she was off, rattling away about nothing. She had it down to a fine art. And if you got a bit insistent about going out for the day, or asked wasn't it time she had a holiday, she'd divert you with some article she'd read in a magazine. She read so many magazines—'

'Talie…'

She held up one hand to stop him. 'It's okay. I'm not doing that. Just trying to explain.'

'Take your time. Here. Come on.' And he reached out, gathered her in his arm so that she slithered down beside him.

After a deep breath, she said, 'My mother isn't well, Jude. I take care of her most of the time. Every few months Karen, her younger sister, comes and gives me a break so that I get a week or two out of the house.'

He didn't understand what distressed her so much about that. Or the fact that she'd found it so hard to tell him.

'You take a temporary job?' he prompted. 'Instead of taking a holiday?'

'I don't need a holiday. I need to be in the real world for a little while. To pretend that I've got an ordinary life.'

Instead of staying at home with a sick mother, watching sentimental movies. And he felt his blood run cold as he remembered telling her that she should get out more.

CHAPTER NINE

'Is it terminal?' Jude asked.

Talie shook her head. 'No. Terminal illness is something that people understand, sympathise with. My mother has agoraphobia. And since my father died there have been bouts of depression, too. Those why-don't-you-just-snap-out-of-it syndromes that irritate people who have no idea of the reality.'

'They are illnesses every bit as real, every bit as debilitating as any other disease.'

She smiled briefly at his understanding.

'Obviously it had been there for a long time, but Liam was away on a gap year in Australia, and I'd moved in with the man I assumed in that careless way of the young was going to be the till-death-do-us-part love of my life. It was only when my dad died that we discovered how bad it was. If I'd been home more, if I'd actually listened, stopped to think, take some notice…' She looked across at him. 'But your parents are always there, aren't they? Boring, grey people who don't do much and who you never think of as having feelings. Neither of them were the sort of people to talk about feelings.'

'Do you know what triggered it?'

'Apparently she lost a baby. Her first child. She had an emergency Caesarean but he had something wrong with his heart and didn't survive. I didn't know about it until after my dad died and everything fell apart.'

'I see.'

'Do you?' She looked up at him then. 'Everything was different then—brushed under the carpet as if it had never happened. No one ever talked about it. Not family. Not friends. She never had a chance to grieve. She was just encouraged to have another baby, as if that was all she needed. As if I could ever replace the one that was lost.'

'I'm so sorry.'

She managed a smile. 'More than you wanted to know, right?'

Wrong. He wanted to know everything.

'It's okay,' she went on, before he could reassure her. 'Really. At least we don't have to worry about money. Dad had that covered. He dealt with his own grief by working so hard that he dropped dead with a massive heart attack when he was fifty-two. But then Mum wouldn't go out, or away on holiday, so what else was he to do?'

'Talie—'

He had his arm around her, but it wasn't enough. He wanted to wrap her up in his arms, hold her, tell her that he would make everything right for her.

'I was so stupid,' she said, looking up at him, her eyes clouded with a sadness that tugged at a heart he'd put into cold storage years ago. The pain he was feeling had to be the return of warmth, love... 'I never caught on. She always had some excuse not to go out, some really convincing reason why she couldn't come and visit me in the new flat *this* week. And of course I was so busy with my own life that I let her get away with it.'

'Don't—'

'I was always trying to tempt her with brochures for exotic holidays, but she used to say that she couldn't leave her garden, or that Dad was too busy. And because he didn't deny it—protecting her because she didn't want us to know that she was a prisoner in her own home—I used to blame him.'

'And now you're blaming yourself.'

'Well, it's ironic, isn't it? I'm always leaping up to help total strangers, but when my mother needed me, my father needed me—'

'It's not your fault.' He had to convince her of that. 'Look at me, Talie.' She raised her lashes and looked at him with those amazing blue eyes that had held him prisoner since she'd first looked up at him in the lift and he'd have done anything to convince her. 'There's help out there. All kinds of help—'

'There were drugs for the depression. Once we realised that she needed help. But getting her to leave the safety of the house is different. She has to want that, and until she's ready to take that step I have to be there for her. She's mentally very fragile, Jude.' She briefly covered his hand with hers, then pulled away from him, sat up. 'I know you're trying to help, but you must see that even if you wanted me to work for you it just wouldn't be possible.'

'This isn't about me, it's about you. Your mother isn't the only one who needs help.'

'You think I'm the one who needs counselling?'

He didn't know what he meant—for once in his life he felt utterly helpless.

'I think you need to stop bottling it up. And you need to get out of the house or you'll become trapped there, just like your mother.'

'No, I'm out all the time. I do the shopping. Take a run every morning.'

'On your own?' And, when she didn't deny it, 'What about the theatre? Dinner with friends? Dates? Something as simple as a trip to the cinema to see the latest movie instead of an old video at home.'

That she didn't answer was answer enough.

'Maybe you're the one who needs a twelve-step programme, angel. To get a life.'

'I guess I deserved that,' she said. 'But I still can't work for you.'

'No?' He didn't give a hoot about that, he had no intention of offering her a job, but he wasn't going to turn down any lever to prise her free. He sympathised with her mother, but his concern was for Talie. 'So, will you tell Heather that she's got to put her plans for full time grandmotherhood on hold, or shall I?'

'You'll find someone, Jude.' She caught a yawn. 'Oh, now I'm sleepy,' she said with a smile. 'Just as it's getting light.'

'It's still very early. You might manage an hour or two.'

'Yes, well, I suppose it's worth a try. Thanks for listening.'

He stood up, pulled her to her feet. 'Anytime,' he said.

She picked up their mugs, took them through to the kitchen. He heard the tap run as she rinsed them out. About to tell her to leave it, that the maid would see to it, he remembered her bed—and realised she'd made it herself. And he knew that was how she filled her days. With endless small, repetitive jobs to stop herself from going mad.

A moment or two later her door closed quietly as she returned to her room. He should try to sleep, too. But he didn't move. The only reason she'd told him about her mother, he realised, was because she'd had that momentary glimpse of reality, a sudden fear that she was becoming like her, and he was glad he'd pushed. She needed to recognise the danger.

But that wasn't why he'd done it. He'd wanted to know her, know her secrets. He'd wanted her to trust him, and she had.

So what did he do now?

Talie woke to the faint sound of traffic in the street below. Despite the yawn, she had been certain the dredging up of painful truths would have kept her awake, but she must have fallen asleep as soon as her head touched the pillow.

She checked the time. It was still early and, rolling out of bed, she dressed quickly, hoping to get out of the suite before Jude stirred, keen to avoid him after the pathetic way she'd spilled out her problems.

More than he'd wanted to know—more than any man wanted to know, as she'd discovered for herself the hard way. Unluckily for him he'd caught her in that low ebb of even the most optimistic heart, which came in the darkest hours of the night, when the tunnel seemed endless and there was no light to show a way out.

He'd have done better to have joined her in bed. That way they'd both have had a good time. For a moment when he'd opened her door, just stood there looking at her, she'd thought…hoped…

Obviously she needed a cold shower, she decided,

shaking her head to rid it of such nonsense and tugging on her shorts. She hadn't been in such close quarters with a man since she'd had to choose between her mother and the man she'd been in love with.

Had never wanted to be.

Fortunately for her, in these days of sexual harassment in the workplace charges no man was going to take that kind of risk with a girl who worked for him.

Listening to her sob story had to be safer.

He was a good listener.

And he was right. It had helped to talk. She'd slipped into a dull acceptance of the situation. When she got home she would try again to get her mother to see someone. And if she wouldn't—well, she might take his advice and seek counselling herself. Someone to talk to who wasn't involved, someone detached. Maybe Jude Radcliffe would volunteer...

She pulled the lace of her running shoe so tight that it snapped.

Taking a deep breath, she concentrated on re-threading it, and when that was done she pulled her hair into a band to keep it off her face and eased open the door to the sitting room.

Jude, stripped and ready for action in cut-offs and a T-shirt, glanced pointedly at his wristwatch as he rose from the armchair. 'I was beginning to think I was going to have to come and throw cold water over you.'

Cold water. Good idea.

'Let's go,' he said.

'I'm sorry? Go where?'

'I'm taking your advice—abandoning CNN and the

Dow Jones Index for fresh air.' He tossed her a bottle of water and opened the door. 'Last one to Bow Bridge buys breakfast,' he said as he summoned the lift.

She tried to think of something sensible to say. More importantly to find the breath to say it with.

'You have got to be joking.'

Oh, that was good...

'Joking? Why would you think that? I'm here—'

She shook her head as she stepped into the lift. 'Not about coming with me. About a race to the bridge. Let's face it,' she began again, attempting to make herself clear, 'your legs...'

Her mouth dried as she found herself staring at them.

'What's the matter with my legs?'

Nothing. Not one thing. They were actually just about the most perfect legs she'd ever seen on a man.

'Mmm?'

Recollecting herself, she looked up. He was regarding her intently, and she wondered how on earth she'd ever thought his eyes were like slate. They were the dark blue-grey of storm clouds, swirling with danger, but always with the promise that the sun would break through in a shower of silver light. Last night she'd seen it for herself, and she knew that the mask he wore in the office was not the true man. That he blamed himself for making a mistake, for a lapse of judgement, and had shut himself away from the risk of repeating it.

'Talie?'

'What? Oh, they're, um, very...long. They give you an unfair advantage.'

'Not from where I'm standing. To win I'd have to

pass you, and deprive myself of the pleasure of looking at yours.'

He should be smiling if he was teasing…

'Should you be saying something like that to your secretary?'

'My secretary would never appear in public wearing cut-offs and a cropped T-shirt that exposes several inches of bare midriff.' And he did that thing with the eyebrow again.

Just when she was getting her breath back and her heart rate under control.

'If I'd known you were going to join me, Jude, neither would I.' Then, as the lift doors opened, she said, 'See you at the bridge.' And she took off, not even having to pause at the door, since a grinning porter leapt to open it for her. The street was quiet and she crossed it without looking back, determined to make him work to keep up with her if it killed her.

And it very nearly did.

'It looks like breakfast's on me,' he said, leaning against the parapet of the bridge as he tipped up his water bottle.

She was fit, she ran every morning, but she'd pushed herself to the limit and was bent from the waist, hands on her knees, trying to ignore the fact that he wasn't even breathing heavily.

'Rubbish,' she gasped, looking up at him. 'You could have taken me any time.'

'Why would I want to do that when I was having such a good time?'

This was definitely a moment for cold water, and she took a long draught from the bottle. She'd have tipped the rest over him, but her need was greater so she poured it over her head and face.

'Come on—you'd better keep moving.'

Obviously this was a good idea, but she didn't bother to say so, saving her breath for running, setting off at a brisk pace. She was immediately jerked back as Jude grabbed a handful of T-shirt.

'Slow down,' he said. 'Take time to enjoy the view.'

'Enjoy the view?' And she stopped, turned to him, placed her hand on his forehead before shaking her head. 'Extraordinary. I was sure you must be suffering from a fever. It must be lack of sleep. You'd better put off your take-over plans; the opposition will run rings around you in this mood.'

'I'm not going to give them the chance. Did you bring your camera today?'

Oh, right. Slow on the uptake, or what? He was feeling guilty for being so mean about sightseeing. Because she never got out of the house. This was his attempt at being *nice* to her.

'Look, if this is about last night there's absolutely no need for you—'

'Did you?'

'—to do this. I wasn't asking for your pity and I don't want it.'

'Who said anything about pity? I was simply offering you a photo opportunity,' he said.

Now she just felt stupid.

'I'm not denying that I admire your kindness, and your loyalty to your mother, Talie, but there are a lot of people in worse predicaments than you.'

Really stupid.

'Well, I'm glad we cleared that up. But, thanks, I took photographs yesterday.'

'But none of them had you in them,' he pointed out. 'Your mother would enjoy them a lot more if she could see you having a good time.'

She knew he was right, but she still left her camera undisturbed in the little bag she wore buckled around her waist. Any photographs of her would be an enduring memory of the man who'd taken them, and some memories it was wiser not to build.

'Jude, I'm here to work, as you have constantly reminded me. And I came out to run. If you want to walk back, I'll see you later.' She didn't wait for him to make a decision but set off briskly and didn't look back.

She knew he was keeping pace with her, her skin was crackling with the tension that seemed to snap between them, but even so she jumped when his hand came over her head to push the door open and hold it for her when she reached the hotel.

'Thank you.' Then, in the lift, attempting to be businesslike, 'What time do you want Barney to pick us up, Jude?'

'We don't need Barney today.'

'We don't? But—'

'I called Marcus last night and asked him to handle today's negotiations. I have something more important to do.'

'You're kidding me? What the heck could be more important than a take-over you've been planning for months?'

'A visit to the Statue of Liberty. A walk through Greenwich Village. Lunch in Little Italy. Maybe an art gallery—' He glanced at her. 'What else do you have on your list?'

'List?'

'You said the Empire State Building was at the top of your list…'

'Jude, get real. You didn't bring me to New York to go sightseeing. You've got to be there today,' she said, a touch desperately. 'It's important—'

'No. Life is important. That's just business. Marcus can handle it. So, what are we going to do first?'

'How about getting a grip on reality—?'

'That's exactly what I am doing. Besides, it's years since I've taken time out to look at the city.'

'Jude—' she began, knowing that she should protest.

He didn't look at her, just reached out and took her hand in a silencing gesture. Then, briskly, 'I'll give you twenty minutes to get ready. Wear comfortable shoes.'

'Hold it, mister!'

Confronted by this suddenly fierce little bombshell, legs astride, arms akimbo, Jude was sorely tempted to laugh. He'd felt like that a lot since Talie erupted into his life. It was the kind of feeling a man could get used to. But he managed to contain himself.

'What's the problem?'

For a moment he could see the battle between what she knew she should say and what she wanted to say going on inside her head. Then she said, 'Comfortable shoes? You are going to make me *walk* around New York?'

'Not everywhere. I thought we'd take the subway, just a couple of stops, so that you could say you've done it. We don't want to waste too much time underground when we could be on a bus seeing the sights. I might even hail a yellow cab, if you behave yourself.'

'Why? Why are you doing this for me?'

He could have told her then. The temptation was there. But it wasn't the right time. It was too soon. She wouldn't believe he was serious. He could hardly believe it himself.

'For you? This isn't for you, Talie Calhoun. This is for me. Step one on that twelve-step programme you advocated, remember? I'm searching for my sense of wonder,' he said.

This wasn't entirely true. His sense of wonder might have been hibernating, buried under a pile of paper, hiding away behind the barrier of an abrupt, repelling manner from any risk that it might take another beating—a barrier that had crumpled when Talie Calhoun bounded into his lift a couple of weeks ago—but it was wide awake now, and hungry.

'As my secretary, it's your duty to help me find it.'

She didn't move.

'In return I'll show you the city. I'll even take photographs of you having lunch, if you like.'

'Twenty minutes?'

'Fifteen, now. You've wasted five of them talking.'

CHAPTER TEN

THEY began by squashing into a subway train full of
office workers heading downtown. Jude had intended
to get off after a couple of stops, but he was enjoying
the excuse to put his arm around her, protect her with
his body from the crush too much to surrender it, and
they stayed on until they were forced to change at
Washington Square, where they stopped for breakfast.

'This is Greenwich Village, right?'

'Right,' he confirmed. 'You have a movie memory
you want to share?'

'I don't spend my entire life watching movies.'
And, before he could ask her what she did do, she
jumped in with, 'What about you? I know a multi-
millionaire's work is never done, but there must be
more to life than—'

'Money?'

'Work.'

'I keep busy.' She grinned. 'What?' She shook her
head. 'No, come on. If you've got something to say,
spit it out.'

'It just occurred to me that we're as sad as one
another. You're so caught up in business that you've
stopped seeing anything beyond the end of your desk.
I'm caught up in my poor mother's fear of the outside
world. We don't have a life between us.'

'I'd already worked that out for myself. That's why

235

we're sitting here over a leisurely breakfast overlooking the park, instead of closeted in a lawyer's office.'

'Well. Good.'

'Very good.'

They took a bus the rest of the way to Battery Park, bought tickets for the boat, and stood at the stern watching the Manhattan skyline retreat as they headed for Liberty Island. They bought a guidebook and walked around the statue, informing each other of the more amazing statistics until rain forced them to dive for cover in the gift shop.

Talie picked out a postcard to send to her brother, some key-rings to give to neighbours, then, spotting some green foam sponge 'Liberty' ray headbands, she said, 'Oh, my gosh, I have to have one of those for my god-daughter.'

'God-daughter? You have a god-daughter?'

'I'm getting to an age where my friends have children.' She grinned. 'Some of them are even thinking of getting married.'

'What happened to the till-death-do-us-part guy?' Jude asked.

And this time there was no hesitation, no change-the-subject conversational sidestep. 'Mark didn't bargain on my mother being part of the package.'

'Terrific.'

'It's okay. I didn't like his mother either.' Then, because he didn't say anything, 'No, you're right, Jude. It wasn't okay. It hurt like hell. But what was I going to do?'

'There's been no one else since?' Her turn to be silent. 'Just because your mother doesn't go out, it doesn't mean you can't, Talie.'

'No, but she always has to come first. Men can't deal with that.' She looked out. 'I think it's stopped raining.'

'Great. Time for one more photograph before we move on.' And he fitted the 'ray' headdress around her curls and handed her a bottle of cola. 'Hold that up.'

'I can't!'

'That little kid over there is doing it.'

'He's five years old!' But she did it anyway, because she wanted to see him grin again, to forget for a moment that it was just…a moment in time. That tomorrow they would fly home and her adventure would be over. 'I can't believe I let you talk me into that,' she said, as they walked back to the boat.

'It'll make your mother laugh.'

'Yes, it will. Thank you.'

Jude stuck his arm out for her to hook hers around it. 'Okay—next stop, Ellis Island.'

They stayed longer than they'd meant to, looking at the piles of luggage, the photographs. Reading the names. Listening to the echoes of history.

'Hungry?' he asked, as they boarded the boat back to Manhattan. She nodded. 'Italian, Chinese…?'

'American. A deli sandwich. I have to have pastrami on rye.'

'You do?'

'It's on the list,' she said, looking up with something that started as a grin but faded into something intense, unreadable, and Jude felt such a jolt of longing that it almost took his breath away. In the midst of the crowded, noisy boat they were for a moment locked

in a bubble of silence. A place where words were re-
dundant. A place where no one could intrude.

He reached up, touched her cheek with his knuckles,
and then, when she didn't pull away, opened his hand
and laid his palm against its softness.

She swayed into him as the boat began to move,
and he put his hand to her waist to steady her. Holding
her close. Asking all kinds of questions with his eyes,
his hands, his body.

Then a child stumbled over a bag and fell at her
feet and any answers were blown away.

Or maybe the speed with which she moved to pick
up the boy, smile at him before he could even think
of crying, was all the answer he needed.

'I'm so sorry,' his mother apologised to both of
them, as if aware that her son had broken into a
charmed moment.

'Don't be,' Jude said. 'He's a lovely boy.' He
turned to lean on the rail. 'We're nearly there,' he said,
glancing sideways at Talie.

'Yes.'

Nearly. But she would need time. It was okay.
There was no rush. Talie was special. Well worth waiting for. And as they left the park he hailed a yellow
cab, and took a photograph of her getting into it before
telling the driver to take them to Katz's Deli for pastrami on whatever kind of bread she wanted.

They didn't speak on the way there, but the cab
driver filled the silence with a running commentary on
the sights they passed, on the mayor, on the impossi-
bility of the traffic. And when Jude took her hand she
didn't pull away.

But when they had their food and were settled at a

table she was still unnaturally quiet, picking at her
food instead of tucking in. He said, 'Is there a problem?' She glanced at him. 'You're quiet. Is sightseeing
losing it's thrill? Or is it me?'

'You?' She smiled. 'No, Jude. You've been great.'
And she said it with sufficient conviction to give him
the kind of warm, fuzzy feeling that he'd been avoiding for so long. 'Sorry. I was miles away. What did
you want to talk about?'

'Nothing. Silence is good.'

'A relief, I should think. I know I talk too much. I
engage complete strangers in conversation at the bus
stop or the supermarket checkout, given the slightest
encouragement.'

'You even talk to strange men in lifts.'

She grinned. 'I'm incorrigible.'

'I'm glad. If you hadn't talked to me I wouldn't
have told Heather about you, and she wouldn't have
checked you out and chosen you to come to New
York.'

'And you'd be sitting in a boring meeting instead
of having lunch with me.'

He doubted the meeting was boring, but he was content with the choice he'd made. More than content.

'So, how are you feeling? On the wonder scale?'
she asked brightly, making a determined effort to
shake off whatever melancholy dogged her.

'Is that between one and ten?'

'There is nothing so cut and dried about wonder,
Jude. It goes to infinity and beyond.'

'Does it? I thought that was Superman.'

'Actually, it's Buzz Lightyear,' she admitted. '*Toy*

Story and *Toy Story 2*. Great movies…' She stopped. 'I'll eat my lunch now.'

But he caught her hand as she reached for the fork. 'The answer to your question is infinity,' he said.

For a moment she looked confused. Then she blushed.

And then he knew, without doubt, that he was in love. He knew that because what he felt was more than an urgent and overwhelming desire to possess her. To make love to her. It was a desire to protect her. To cherish her. To know that he could tease her and have her look at him like that fifty years from now.

What he said was, 'So, what do you want to do this afternoon? An art gallery, Radio City, the Metropolitan Museum of Art?'

'It's too nice to be indoors.'

'We could take a boat out on the lake in Central Park. Ride on the carousel. Or just lie on the grass, eating ice cream and looking at the sky.' Then, 'Or all of the above.'

'Hey, I'm impressed. You catch on fast.'

'You can't go home without eating ice cream. It's a national institution.'

'You won't get an argument from me.'

'Then I'll take that as a yes. But first we have to choose a gift for Heather's granddaughter. Any ideas?'

'Well, silver is traditional. A baby bracelet?'

'If you wanted to take a look around Tiffany's you just had to say so, Talie. Just don't ask for breakfast.'

'I really would like to take a look around Tiffany's,' she said.

Her reward for admitting it was a silver key-ring with a red enamelled apple fob. It came in its own turquoise suede drawstring bag, which was put inside a turquoise box, which was put inside a little turquoise carrier bag with 'Tiffany & Co' in discreet black lettering.

'I feel like Audrey Hepburn,' Talie said, as Jude handed the bag to her. 'Apart from the hair, obviously—'

'I love your hair. Every ridiculous curl of it,' he interrupted, sparking a dangerous warmth that spread from the vicinity of her waist to leave her feeling oddly weak at the knees. He caught her arm as they buckled.

'—and the little black dress,' she finished.

'You've got a little black dress,' he said, and his voice wasn't entirely steady either, she noticed.

'So I have.' She'd known that dress was special the moment she'd slipped it over her head. She'd been disappointed with his first reaction to it, but it had got her to the top of the Empire State Building. A dress that could do that—

'Wear it this evening and we'll round off the evening with dinner somewhere very special.'

They spent the afternoon in the park, laughing and talking. Not about movies, or business, but about themselves. Pretending for a few hours that anything was possible. And later Barney drove them across the Brooklyn Bridge to a floating restaurant, where they had dinner with all the lights of Manhattan shining in the darkness.

'It's been a lovely day, Jude. I'll never forget it,' Talie said.

He reached across the table, took her hand. 'It's not quite over. There's one more thing we have to do.'

'Jude—' she began, but her voice broke on his name.

'A buggy ride?' he said. 'For two?'

After a day in which they'd seemed never to stopped talking they were finally silent, with only the clipping sound of the horse's hooves as she took her own sweet time on her stately ride around the park.

It wasn't an awkward silence, but the quiet that came at the end of a perfect day, when you had your arm around the woman you were falling in love with, her head tucked against your shoulder, the scent of her hair, her skin, stealing your mind.

'Talie?'

She lifted her head from his shoulder to look up at him.

'On that wonder scale of yours...I've just decided that infinity is nowhere near high enough to describe the day I've had. I'm upgrading my assessment to "beyond."'

She smiled. 'But that doesn't leave you with anywhere to go. It's like saying it can't get any better than this.'

'You're telling me it can?'

Talie understood what he was asking, but last night's fantasy thoughts about him climbing into bed with her and them both having a good time with no strings attached had been just that. A fantasy. She wanted it every bit as much as he did, but she wasn't built that way. So, instead of the invitation to show him how much better it could be that he undoubtedly expected, she said, 'You have to believe that or what's the point?'

He took her hand, raised it to his lips and kissed it. 'I believe,' he said. And then, cradling her cheek in the palm of his hand, he bent to kiss her.

He didn't rush at it. Well, she knew the measure of the man. She'd spent three days with him. Watched him working. Heard him talking to his staff, his peers. He knew how to plan, knew not to barge in and take what he wanted, but to make surrender seem like a victory.

As he touched his lips to the delicate skin at her temple she discovered that she'd been holding her breath, waiting, wanting this… He moved to her eyelids, touching each of them with butterfly-soft kisses, and she heard herself utter a little give-away sigh. He brushed her cheek, lingered at the spot where a dimple refused to accept that she was grown up and go away. And then his lips touched her mouth with the gentlest of kisses, asking, *Do you want this? Is this too much? Show me…*

Not only did she want it, Talie knew that this was the kiss she'd been waiting for all her life.

Perfect. Pure. Beyond.

And that was why she pulled back. Not because she didn't want to spend the night with him. But because she wanted it too much.

'Jude—'

'Shhh.' He touched her cheek with his fingers, then said, 'It's over.'

For a moment she thought he was talking about them, and felt the sharpest stab of pain. Maybe he was, or maybe he just meant that the buggy had come to a stop. But she shivered anyway as he climbed down from the buggy, feeling chilled without his warmth at her side. Then he turned and held out his hand to help her down, tucking her arm under his as they crossed the road to the hotel, where they rode in silence up to their suite.

'Jude—' She tried again to explain.

But he slipped the key through the lock and pushed open the door. 'Goodnight, Talie. Sleep well.'

She paused on the threshold, wanting to tell him how much the day had meant to her, how much she wished she could respond to the demands of her body, the desperate urging of her heart to show him just how much he meant to her in the only way a woman truly could.

'Don't,' he said sharply. Then, more gently, 'I'll see you in the morning.'

She stood under the shower, the first cold one of her entire life, running it until her teeth chattered. Then she pulled on the baggy T-shirt she slept in, huddled up under the covers and, with the prospect of sleep about as likely as icicles in hell, switched on the television and surfed through the channels, looking for a movie…

Jude didn't hang about in the hope that she'd change her mind. He didn't want her to change her mind. He wanted her so sure, so certain, that nothing would stop her…

He stripped off and stood under the shower until he was numb with cold. It made no difference. One kiss. He'd allowed himself one kiss, and now he was burning up, throbbing for a woman in a way he hadn't in years. But not just for any woman. Only Talie would answer his need, and she'd wanted it, too.

He'd seen it in her eyes, liquid and dark. Felt it in the way her body had softened against him as he'd kissed her. Heard it in her voice, the soft sigh, the unconscious groan of frustration as she'd pulled away from the temptation he'd offered. But she respected herself too much to take easy pleasure for one night. And why would she imagine it would be anything more?

But it wasn't just for a night.

They'd spent the afternoon talking about the past. The events that had moulded them, made them what they were. She knew more about him than even his own mother, because that was how it was when you met someone you wanted to spend the rest of your life with. She'd changed his world, changed him, and he had to tell her. She had to know...

He threw on a robe, wrenching open the door, and like some kind of miracle she was there, standing in her bedroom doorway. Hair damp, kangaroo T-shirt on inside out...

'You didn't tell me,' she said. 'You said you saw something new. Last night, when we were at the top of the Empire State Building. You said you'd tell me if I stopped avoiding your question...'

'I saw the city as I'd never seen it before. Reflected in your eyes. Turned 'round. Like my life.' He reached out a hand to her. 'Tell me what you dream about, Talie—"*when the full moon is shining in...and the lamp is dying out...*"'

'A moment like this,' she said, grasping his hand. Holding it. 'A moment of pure magic.'

'You're cold,' he said.

'Warm me.' He held her then. Put his arms around her as he'd longed to do all week and held her close, and she said, 'Love me, Jude. Just for tonight, make all my dreams come true.'

Dreams don't come true without a lot of hard work. Nothing important, truly life-changing, is ever achieved without effort.

'Stand still, Talie. These buttons are so small.'

She *was* standing still; it was her mother's fingers that were shaking, and they both knew that. But one by one the buttons were fastened, and then she slipped into the loose-fitting ivory velvet coat.

'Lovely, dear. You look absolutely lovely.'

'And so do you.'

Her mother was wearing a coat and hat in a heavy deep blue silk that matched her eyes. Not that you could see much of her face. The hat was huge. It was still difficult for her to go out without somewhere to hide, to cut out the threatening spaces when she felt overwhelmed by them. But she'd been given a goal— a big enough reason to confront her fears, seek help. A reason to step outside the boundaries of her house, the safety of the walled garden at the rear.

Jude had been brilliant. Patient beyond words. Never pushing her. But never letting her slip back either. He'd sit and watch old movies with her, but afterwards he'd insist on walking her around the garden, always knowledgeably suggesting some new shrub that would do well and she should look at when she felt like a visit to the garden centre. Considering he lived in a riverside apartment, with nothing more horticulturally challenging than a balcony, he must have put in some serious homework on that front.

In fact, Jude could do no wrong in her mother's eyes.

Talie had tried to get her mother interested in joining a support group on the internet, but he'd bought her a computer of her own and signed her up to a group for people with similar problems. Not just agoraphobia, but women who'd had stillborn babies. People who could offer help in taking the small steps back into life. People who'd been there and could say with confidence, 'You can do it.' Because they'd done it themselves.

And, because Jude had done it, her mother had made the effort.

He'd talked to her about the wedding, too. Never letting her forget that it was going to happen. Involving her in plans for the service. Asking her to choose hymns. Seeking her advice about flowers.

Not that Talie had said she'd marry him. In fact she'd turned him down flat. But of course he just wouldn't take no for an answer. He'd treated the problem exactly like any other take-over bid, and had had no intention of letting go until he had got what he wanted.

And how could you fight a man like that?

A man who came to see you every day, no matter how busy he was, no matter how often you told him to stay away.

Who held your mother's hand as he coaxed her down a canvas tunnel he'd had erected from the front door to the gate and into the rear of a car with specially tinted windows and took them both to see the newest chick-flick.

Who bought a house with a wing for your mother and then asked her to help him find the perfect house-keeper. Someone who would always be there.

Who conspired with your mother and your aunt to whisk you off to New York for a long weekend, re-fusing to leave Tiffany's until you'd chosen not only an engagement ring, but a wedding ring, too.

Who could resist such a man?

He knew how to plan, knew how to take his time, knew how to make surrender seem like a victory. And, sooner rather than later, her mother had surrendered and promised that on her wedding day she would give her daughter away.

The tunnel to the gate was no longer a temporary can-vas shield but a delicately arched pergola, that would one day be dripping with wisteria, but for her wedding day it was woven with winter evergreens, bright ber-ries, and ribbons that matched the pretty tartan dresses of her bridesmaids.

And if it was her brother, Liam, and Talie who sup-ported their mother to the car, rather than the other way around, that was okay. She was getting there. Stronger day by day.

Jude turned and stood even before the vicar had given the signal—before the organist began to play, before Talie started towards him, a vision in a softly draped full-length coat of ivory velvet, open over a simple matching dress. Her hair, her lovely hair, was threaded with ivy and berries and tiny roses, her eyes a pure, true blue.

And as she walked on her mother's arm towards him those eyes never left him, until her mother placed her hand in his and took a step back.

'Dearly beloved…' the vicar began, and Jude closed his fingers over hers so that she knew he would never let her go as they turned together to face the future as a family.

Hannah Bernard always knew what she wanted to be when she grew up – a psychologist. After spending an eternity in university, studying towards that goal, she took one look at her hard-earned diploma and thought: Nah. I'd rather be a writer. She has no kids to brag about, no pets to complain about, and only one husband, who any day now will break down and agree to adopt a kitten.

Look out for the next book from Hannah Bernard:
THE DATING RESOLUTION
On sale November 2004, in Tender Romance™.

THE FIANCÉ DEAL

by

Hannah Bernard

CHAPTER ONE

LOU had a big family. And all her family members were currently staring at him. Parents, brothers, sisters-in-law—it rather felt as if he was on the wrong side of the witness stand for once. Not the most comfortable feeling in the world.

David was having second thoughts. Impulsiveness often paid off in court when he had to rely on instinct to get him through a tricky situation. It didn't work nearly as well with other people's families, and it was beginning to dawn on him that he should have employed a brain cell or two before deciding, What the hell? and jumping on the next plane. Discounting the frequent flyer miles, this had turned out to be a rather expensive joke, and now he was beginning to fear the Wrath of Lou. She would be here soon—and there would be hell to pay.

But he hadn't been able to resist. Lou's mom had sounded so thrilled on the phone, talking to her daughter's "fiancé" at last. He didn't know—yet—why Lou had been telling her family he was her boyfriend, when they were nothing more than co-workers, but some wicked impulse had prompted him to accept Mrs. Henderson's invitation to join Lou and the rest of her family for a weekend. Lou would be arriving straight from a week-long business trip.

"It's perfect timing!" Lou's mother had whispered, as if her daughter would overhear the conversation.

"You won't have seen each other for a week; she'll be so pleased to have you here." Her voice had lost its spark. "After what that man did to her... Well, let's just say I'm so pleased she's moved on. I was so glad to hear she was seeing someone again."

What man? What had he done to Lou? He had restrained himself from asking. As Lou's boyfriend, he probably should know—and even if he didn't, this sounded like something Lou should tell him—tell her *boyfriend*—herself. If it was any of his business. Which, in his case, it wasn't.

"Do you work together on a daily basis?" one of Lou's brothers, Neil, now asked. Yup, David was definitely on trial here.

"Not directly—we are on the same team, but most of our tasks are separate. We do attend meetings together every week, but other than that we work separately."

"But you see each other every day at work." Lou's sister-in-law sighed. "That's romantic." She poked her husband with an elbow. "Isn't it? Imagine if we could work together all day."

"Uhum," Neil responded, but tempered the noncommittal response with a smile. They were relative newlyweds, David had learned. Only married a year.

He could see a lot of Louise in her family. She had her mother's dark brown eyes, and shared her vibrant auburn hair color with two of her brothers. He suspected they all shared a stubborn streak too.

"You still have separate apartments, don't you?" another brother asked. "I think she needs to get out of that neighborhood. She has to be able to afford something better."

Their questions were becoming increasingly hard to field. Especially as he hadn't talked to Lou yet, and had no way of correlating their stories. The less said, the better—or this house of cards would come crashing down before Lou even got here. He faked a smothered yawn, and it had the desired effect.

"You're exhausted," Mrs. Henderson said sympathetically. "And you're still on New York time, so no wonder. I'll show you to Louise's room."

David murmured his thanks, said goodbye to the assorted family members, and followed his "mother-in-law" up the stairs. Louise's room? Did that mean they would be sharing a room? If so, this family was a lot more liberal than his own was.

"Here it is," Mrs. Henderson said, opening a door and gesturing for him to enter. "It hasn't been changed much since Louise lived here. She's never said so, but I think she likes coming back to it. Kind of like going back to her childhood."

It was a girl's room, no doubt about that.

"Where will Louise…?"

"Oh, you can stay together. No problem," Mrs. Henderson said, her smile somewhat embarrassed. "When two people have been together as long as you have, it's hopelessly old-fashioned to put you in separate rooms." She lit a small lamp on the desk under the window. "We may be country folks, but we *are* living in the twenty-first century after all."

He wasn't quite sure what to say. This would not improve Lou's temper. "Thank you," he said lamely, and Mrs. Henderson smiled, pointed out the bathroom at the end of the hall, and closed the door. He threw his duffel bag in a corner and himself on the bed. He stared up at the ceiling, chuckling as he realized he was feeling like a little boy waiting for an inevitable punishment. Lou would be here soon—and *then* he'd be in deep trouble.

They didn't know each other very well outside of work, but he was familiar with the steel of her temper. It served her well in court—and he was only grateful he'd never been opposite her in that arena. It was quite enough to have her as a rival for that promotion they were both angling for.

He sat up. What was he doing here, staring at Lou's junior high school class picture, when he could be in New York, working hard at inching ahead of her in their little race?

"David," he told himself. "Next time *think,* will you?"

Too late for that. He was also just about bursting with curiosity. Why had she told her family they were seeing each other? That mystery was intriguing—and even, in a way, flattering. He grinned, thinking about Lou's possible reactions to finding him here. She'd be mortified, of course, that he'd found out her little lie. Furious, too, that he'd decided to come out here and embarrass her. But she'd be mortified first. And—she couldn't tell her family the truth. Not now.

She *needed* him.

He could probably use that to his advantage. After all, *she* was the one who'd started this. Yup, he was nothing but an innocent pawn in her game.

Now all he had to do was figure out a way to prevent an immediate checkmate as soon as the queen entered the room.

He grinned. Attack really *was* the best defense, wasn't it?

Louise stopped the car outside her family's ranch and closed her eyes as she switched off the ignition. She started to pull the key out, but thought better of it. She could leave it behind. Here, it was safe. Wyoming was a long way from New York.

It had been a long day. A long week. In fact, the whole year had stretched almost into forever, but business trips always took extra out of her, and this one had taken an entire week—a tense week, of endless meetings and sleepless hotel nights. It was good to be home. Really home, not in the tiny New York apartment she'd lived in for three years but had never had time to really make her own.

It had been a while. Somehow time had slipped by. Over a year had passed since she'd seen her parents or brothers. The family reunion had been on the table for six months now, and through bribes, flattery and occasional blackmail she'd managed to slip enough tasks on her colleagues' desks to get a couple of days off—a long weekend.

She'd better make the most of it. If she got the promotion she was after life would become even more hectic. If such a thing were possible.

The silence as she got out of the rental car was astonishing. So was the murk of the sky above, punctured with the stars she never saw anymore. She was a city girl now, Lou acknowledged with regret as she paused with the trunk of the car open, staring up at her long-lost friend Orion. Her own night sky was the color of smog, and her ears were used to filtering out traffic sounds, music blaring from nearby apartments, police sirens and neighbors fighting. She'd all but forgotten what real silence felt like, and the twinkling of billions of stars above felt like magic.

But, unfamiliar or not, her city girl's heart still called this home.

Almost all the windows in the house were darkened. As they should be, past midnight. Looking up to her bedroom window, she saw a tiny light. There was also light in the kitchen window, and a curtain had moved when she'd pulled up in the driveway. She smiled as she let herself in through the unlocked front door. Mom had waited up for her. Of course she had. There would be hot cocoa in the kitchen. Her bed would be made with her favorite orange and yellow bedsheets, and there would be flowers in a vase and a glass of water on the nightstand.

No one in the world pampered like Mom.

"Louise!" Her mother's whisper was like a shout in the deafening silence. "About time, love! You must be exhausted." The hug was familiar, the smell of cinnamon too. Lou leaned into her mother's arms. Home. She was really here. New York seemed very far away—and, for now, good riddance. "It's so good to see you finally, love." Mrs. Henderson frowned, looking her up and down. "You're thinner. I knew you would be. But never mind—I have a plan to fatten you up."

Lou swallowed—there was a lump in her throat. She hadn't realized how much she'd missed them. Her family. The house. Everything. "Hi, Mom. I'm so glad to be here." She sighed, pushing her wheeled suitcase toward the wall, out of the way. "I'm sorry you had to wait up so long. There was chaos at the airport, and a mix-up at the car rental, or I would have been here sooner.''

Her mom reached out to tuck a lock of hair behind her ear. A familiar gesture Lou had all but forgotten. ''Well, I'm just glad you still know the way home, Louise. Come to the kitchen for a while and sit down. Aren't you hungry?''

''Not really. I ate on the plane.''

''How about hot cocoa and a tiny piece of chocolate cake?''

How could she resist that? ''Sounds lovely, Mom.''

Everything was the same in the kitchen. Familiar and warm. *Home.* Well—*almost* everything was the same. Lou stared at the dining area, then rubbed her eyes, hoping jet lag was messing with her eyesight. ''New furniture!''

''Yes, we got it before last Christmas. Didn't I tell you?''

''No.'' She slid into one of the new chairs and frowned. They felt all wrong. ''What did you do with the old chairs? And the table?'' She'd known every scratch on that table. She'd caused her fair share of them. Was it now gone?

''Don't worry, they're still in the family. Hailey and Ed took them.''

''Oh. Good.''

Her mom chuckled at the unconvinced tone in her voice. ''You kids are so conservative when it comes to our furniture, but then you're always complaining about us never changing anything.'' She put a plate of chocolate cake in front of Lou, and a steaming mug of cocoa.

"Yeah, we're weird that way, aren't we?" Lou picked up her fork and dug into the cake, reminding herself that this was not the time or place to count calories. Plenty of time for that once she was back in the real world. The real world, however, did not provide Mom's chocolate cake.

Her mother sat opposite her and chatted softly about her brothers, the grandchildren, her father, the farm. And Lou drank it all in. She heard it all on the phone, of course—she called her mother at least every other week—but it wasn't the same.

At least her mother wasn't asking about David. Yet. She would—and so would the others—but postponement of that interrogation was welcome. It was a headache. A self-inflicted one. But one that was becoming more and more complicated as time wore on.

It was probably time to put an end to it and find a new solution to that particular problem, she realized with a sigh. It had been nice while it lasted. Peace and quiet, freedom from the irritation of endless questions about her nonexistent love life, and, not the least, freedom from that irrational sense of guilt over causing her family worry.

Mom's chocolate cake was delicious. Her hot cocoa was delicious. Jazz played softly on the radio and Lou felt it was only yesterday that she'd knelt on a chair by the counter, carefully cutting out Christmas shapes in cookie dough. She flew up from the chair and suddenly enveloped her mother in a tight hug, tears in her eyes. "Oh, Mom, I missed home!"

Mrs. Henderson returned her hug, then started on a familiar refrain. "You should come home more often, Louise. It's not really that far, or expensive. We'll be glad to chip in if you can't afford the trip, you know that.''

"I can afford it. You're right. I should.'' She sat back down and picked up her fork. "Life is just so…busy." She liked it that way—but there were drawbacks.

"I know, love." Mom smothered a yawn, and Lou felt its twin sneak up on her.

"We should go to bed; it's late."

"Yes." Her mother's smile widened, and a twinkle appeared in her eye. "There's something you should know before you head upstairs, darling."

"Oh?" What now? Her bedroom was changed into a library? Her orange sheets had been changed for blue ones?

She didn't like changes. Not at home. Everything was supposed to stay the same here. Forever. She didn't expect it to, but that was how her heart insisted it *should* be.

"Yes. We have a surprise for you. In your room upstairs."

Lou stifled a sigh. A surprise. They'd painted her old room. Replaced her stuffed animals with porcelain statuettes. Knocked down a wall or two. They should; they had every right to—it wasn't *her* room anymore, and hadn't been for a long time—but it was hard to work up enthusiasm. She liked soppy nostalgia. "Yeah?"

Mrs. Henderson smiled, leaning back in pleasure. "David."

Lou's stomach plunged, and her fork clattered on the plate before she could stuff the last morsel of chocolate cake in her mouth. *Don't panic,* she told herself.

You don't know what this is about yet. "Yes? What about…David?"

Her mother's smile was smug and self-satisfied. "Your fiancé is upstairs in your room."

"What?"

"He's upstairs," she repeated. "He arrived this evening."

"How could he…? Why didn't I…?"

"It looked like you'd never get around to introducing us, so I took matters into my own hands. I called the office in New York while you were in Los Angeles and invited him."

"No. He can't be here." Lou shook her head, brain frozen in utter denial. She also had a strong urge to stuff the chocolate cake in her mother's face, but fear took precedence. This couldn't be happening. It simply couldn't. "David can't be here. It's impossible. He's in New York."

"He's here." Her mother nodded, still beaming. "He arrived just before dinner. He was very tired, poor man, and went early to bed, but I like him." She glanced at her watch. "He's probably asleep already."

"David is…" The light in her window. David. *Oh, God.*

"Upstairs. In your room. Be careful, dear, don't wake him up. He looked exhausted. We could hardly keep up a conversation with him over dinner, which was a shame—there was so much I wanted to ask him."

Lou stood up and carefully put her plate and glass in the dishwasher. How could David be here? How could David possibly be here? Her mother needed a good talking to. She couldn't *do* this kind of thing.

She couldn't just make one long-distance phone call and ruin Lou's life.

Oh, God, what now? Did everybody back at the firm know? Had David told them? Why had he come? Was this one big joke her colleagues were playing on her? Was her reputation in ruins? Could she kiss that promotion goodbye?

"Dear? Everything okay?"

Lou turned around, a fixed smile on her face, straining her facial muscles. "Everything's great, Mom. I'm home, and it's wonderful."

"And your David is here."

Lou nodded. "And...my David is here." She almost choked on the words. Still grimly smiling, she grabbed her suitcase. "I guess I'll go to bed now, Mom. I'll see you in the morning."

"Goodnight, love."

Lou fidgeted outside her bedroom, stomach churning in apprehension, until she could hear her mother beginning to mount the steps. Then there was no choice anymore. She had to go inside. Face David—for better or worse.

She opened the door carefully, remembering the squeak it always gave when opened wide, and slipped in sideways and quietly shut the door.

The room was almost dark, with just one tiny lamp lit in a corner, on top of her desk by the window. The light she'd seen from outside. She took a moment to get used to the darkness.

Maybe he was asleep. She couldn't figure out if that would be good or bad. On the one hand that would mean postponing explanations—and perhaps she would have come up with something brilliant by tomorrow. But on the other hand getting things over with would be a relief. Not to mention getting it straight from David just what he had in mind. She needed to know how he had ended up here—what the hell he was doing here in the first place.

He was there. No movement betrayed him, but when her eyes got used to the darkness she could see him. He was sitting at her old desk, where the small lamp was lit. Papers were piled all over it, his stylus brandished over his handheld computer. And he was staring at her with a look she only associated with fiascos at work—hers or his.

He was really here. And he wasn't looking happy about it. Her courage took one look at his face and escaped, squealing in panic, trying to find a rock to burrow under.

"Hi," she whispered. It wasn't meant to be a whisper. It just came out that way.

David didn't respond. He just kept staring at her. Then he leaned forward and his head fell on the desk with a small thud in a gesture that said more than a thousand shouted obscenities.

CHAPTER TWO

AT LEAST he wasn't laughing. Which probably meant he was here on his own, not on a let's-humiliate-Lou mission on behalf of their colleagues. Not that David seemed the malicious type, but she was now prepared for anything. She sort of felt she deserved it.

What had she been thinking?

Lou took a deep breath. "I'm sorry," she whispered, shrugging helplessly. The soft apology vanished in the shadows, and David didn't respond. She walked closer and repeated the apology.

She didn't know all the whys and hows, but David was here. She'd been using him—and he'd finally found out. Sorry was the only thing she could say, now that she'd landed him in this ridiculous situation, but the words didn't seem nearly enough, echoing empty in the small room.

David seemed to agree, as he did not respond, sitting slumped on her old office chair, his forehead resting on her desk. She couldn't see his face, and he wasn't speaking.

Of course he had every right to be furious. She couldn't blame him. But why was he here? Why had he come? Why hadn't he just told her mom there had been a mistake?

The silence stretched for several minutes, grating on her ears, before she tried again. "I'm really sorry, David. Believe me, I never meant…I didn't know—I didn't suspect this would happen. I got the shock of my life when my mother told me you were here. How did this happen?''

It was funny, she tried to convince herself, as David still didn't move so much as one eyelash. Maybe not today, or tomorrow, or even Sunday, but next week, when they were back in New York, back to daily life, he'd see the humor in this. He might even forgive her. Someday. They'd share a joke about this.

Right.

David wasn't answering her question. She tried for a weak chuckle. ''In a way it's funny, you know. We'll laugh about this someday.''

That finally got a response. He raised his head slowly, just enough to impale her with those eyes. In the dark, she couldn't see the color, but she could imagine the laser blue flame. His eyes were his most striking feature. She'd noticed that the first time she saw him.

''Funny?'' His voice was strangled, probably by shock. He shook his head slowly. ''Yeah, *Louise,* it's hilarious, isn't it?''

Dammit. Wrong approach. She reverted to the apologies. Safer, although it was out of character for her. She didn't like to be in the wrong—she liked apologizing even less. ''I'm sorry.''

David's head hit the table again and he groaned. His voice was familiar as it reached toward her in the dimly lit room—but it too, was different out here. He belonged at the office, or beside her in court, or arguing with her over a conference table. He did not belong here, in her childhood bedroom. ''I can't believe I'm here,'' he said. ''It's unreal.''

That was what she'd been thinking too.

How were they going to get out of this mess? But at least he was talking now. A step in the right direction. Or at least a step in *some* direction. She wasn't sure if in their current position a right direction even existed.

"Did you tell anybody about this?" she asked. She had to know. She'd handed David an opportunity on a plate. If this got out, it would no doubt mean a big black warning sign across her employee file—might even put an end to her ambitions of ever making partner at the firm. She couldn't afford a scandal. Her heart started pounding, her palms sweating just at the thought. She'd already had a close call once. It couldn't happen again.

Then why had she opened herself up like this? Stupid, *stupid.*

"Tell someone? Like who?"

Who did he think he meant? "Somebody at the office, of course. *Anybody* at the office. Felix, Johnny, Samantha... Did you tell *anyone?*"

"Of course I didn't tell them." He sounded offended that she'd even asked, but his answer was a huge relief. Even if she was exaggerating, even if something like this wouldn't affect her future, she did have a reputation to maintain and an image that couldn't stand the ridicule that would inevitably follow if they found out about this.

"Thank you," she whispered.

"Don't worry. I'll find a way for you to pay me back, *Louise.* I promise."

Fine. Fine. She'd pay up—no problem. If only he'd stop calling her by her full name. She never used her first name in New York. She was either Lou or Ms. Henderson. Never Louise. "You're a good sport, David," she said hesitantly, ready to shut up if that was what he preferred. Tonight, she would tiptoe around him. She never tiptoed around anybody, certainly not around her colleagues, but for what she was putting him through now he deserved no less.

She pulled a second chair out and sat down opposite him. His gaze followed her, and the tension slowly left her as she read no malice there. Maybe this was a salvageable situation after all. "From what Mom says, it looks like you fooled her. And if you fooled her, the rest of them would have been no problem. I'm impressed."

"I didn't have a choice, did I?" he murmured, eyes closed again. "I had to fool them."

Of course he'd had a choice. Although now was probably not the best time to point that out. He could have refused to participate in the mess she'd signed him up for without his permission. He could have outed her as a liar to her entire family. He could have told the entire story to their colleagues for a good laugh, perhaps even increased the chance that *he'd* be the one to get that promotion instead of someone hysterical and pathetic enough to lie to her family about having a boyfriend.

Stop overreacting, Lou!

But he hadn't taken advantage of the situation, and she was hopelessly in his debt now. She had some serious groveling to do. "I appreciate it, David."

He didn't answer, just opened one eye and stared at her again, until she started to squirm. This was *so* embarrassing! Then he finally straightened up, looking around her old room with a resigned look. He shook his head. "Your parents are pretty open-minded."

"Not exactly how I would describe them," she replied, confused. "Why do you say that?"

David gestured around. "Putting us together in your room."

"Oh." She hadn't even realized that in her panic over having to face David alone and explain everything. "Oh, no. I'll take the floor, David. No problem. This is all my fault." Yeah. She deserved a sleepless night on a hardwood floor. She deserved worse than that for being this stupid. How could she have imagined she'd get away with it for so long? "I think my old sleeping bag is at the back of the closet. I'll be fine on the floor."

"You're staying in the bed," he growled, giving her a grim look. "What kind of a gentleman would I be if I let my fiancée sleep on the floor?"

"It's out of the question, David. I couldn't let you take the floor after all you're doing for me."

"I'm not sleeping on the floor either, *Louise*. As your parents have noticed, there is plenty of room for two in that bed. And that's where we'll both be staying."

"But—"

"Don't argue. We need our sleep tonight. Lot of people to lie to tomorrow, remember?"

Gulp.

She swallowed her impulse to snipe back. Not now. She had *a lot* of serious groveling to do, and for tonight she'd be meek and apologetic. No other choice. Then, when the weekend was over, she'd start work on repairing their professional relationship. It could be done—maybe. After all, in a few months she'd be either his boss or his subordinate. And even if one of them left the company she might be meeting him in the courtroom all their professional life. Since a memory wipe wasn't an option, it was imperative to get out of this with some dignity intact.

"I'll just go brush my teeth," she muttered. She grabbed her toiletries and fled to the bathroom, grateful for a reprieve.

"What were you thinking?" she asked the pale, stricken face in the mirror, then tried to put that question out of her mind. There was no point in blaming herself for that error of judgment. There was no erasing what had happened—now she just had to get through this without any major bloodshed.

She hurried with her task of getting ready for bed, some corner of her mind convinced that the sooner she got to bed and fell asleep, the sooner all this would be revealed as a bizarre nightmare. She'd wake up alone, and David would remain where he belonged— at the office, half a continent away.

As she opened the door to the bedroom again David brushed past her without speaking, the bathroom door shutting decisively behind him.

What was the hurry? She'd escaped to the bathroom to get a few moments of peace, fully expecting the third degree as soon as she got back. But now David didn't want to talk. He didn't want to know *why* her family thought they were a couple? That made her feel even worse. She'd expected an interrogation, a chance to explain her reasons—make him see that at the time everything had been rational. This *had* made sense— and he'd never been supposed to find out.

She groaned as she climbed into bed and pulled the duvet up to her chin. They'd have to talk—and they'd have to do it tonight. There wouldn't be any privacy tomorrow. They'd have to talk about this—she'd have to explain.

But she was feeling too nervous to raise the subject. At work, David angry was a formidable sight. He tended to emit an almost visible aura of fury, masked in calm politeness. And her guilt was escalating by the minute now that she was over the initial shock and had had time to think about it.

David returned, flipped off the light without speaking, and started to undress.

"What are you doing?" she squeaked. He wasn't getting naked, was he? Sharing a bed was bad enough.

David paused. She couldn't see him looking at her, but she could imagine the look he was giving her.

"Sorry," she muttered, feeling rather foolish. She had a feeling she'd be feeling foolish for quite a while, and she didn't like it one bit. "Never mind. Forget it."

"I'm not sleeping with my clothes on, *Louise*. Live with it."

"Yeah. Of course. Sorry." He'd see the humor in this later, she told herself. She turned her back to him, and a moment later felt him get into bed. He settled on his back and she squirmed further away, giving him the lion's share of the duvet.

Well? Talk?

Tomorrow. Maybe they'd both be in a better state to discuss this tomorrow morning. They'd wake up early and talk—it was probably better that way.

"Goodnight," she said timidly, and got a barely

audible grunt in return. She breathed in and out twenty times, her mind agitated as she tried to think of a way to make amends. Was he still angry? She hated to go to sleep angry. It was something her grandmother had felt strongly about, and she'd been raised always to make peace before going to bed.

She inched on to her back, careful not to move too close to him. She cast around in her mind for a safe opening for the conversation. "Would you prefer this side of the bed?" she whispered. "No problem. I don't mind which side I'm on. If you're used to—"

"Just go to sleep, Lou."

At least he was calling her by her nickname again. His use of Louise—a name nobody ever used in New York—had twisted the knife. It had felt sardonic, as if he were making fun of her. She felt marginally better, and even allowed herself to turn her head toward him and send a small smile to his hard profile in the darkness. "Okay. Night."

It wasn't that easy. Just the fact of having ended up in bed with David was disturbing to her nerves, and the events of the day didn't help—or the fact that they really did need to talk, to plan the weekend ahead. Hypothetical conversations kept running through her mind as she tried to anticipate David's questions and how she could answer them without looking too bad.

The bed was way too small. Even though she had inched toward the very edge of the mattress she could feel the heat of him beside her. And there was only one duvet. Plenty big enough for two people cuddling together, but barely so when they were trying to stay as far apart as the narrow bed allowed.

Intermittently, moonlight spilled in through the window through the cover of clouds. Every few minutes it became bright enough to see that David's eyes were just as open and wide-awake as hers as he stared up at the ceiling.

"Stop squirming, Lou," he said suddenly. "Go to sleep."

"Easier said than done," she muttered.

"We're in this, and there's no way out. Worrying about tomorrow won't help."

"As I said, easier—"

"Just close your eyes, pretend you're back in New York and none of this has happened, and sleep. You'll need your energy tomorrow."

There was silence for a while, until she noticed his eyes were still open. He wasn't taking his own advice. "You're not falling asleep either."

He turned on his side to look at her, and the sound of his body moving against the covers felt strangely intimate. "I have my script for tomorrow to memorize, don't I? Loving fiancée, future son-in-law and brother-in-law, brand new uncle. All sorts of roles."

Sarcasm. David's weapon of choice. She opened her mouth to say she was sorry once again, but thought better of it. He already knew she was as sorry as she could possibly be—why didn't he just get over it? She wasn't forcing him to go along with this. It was his choice, and if he was going through with it anyway he could just as well do it with good humor, couldn't he?

"It's not that dramatic, David. All you have to do is be yourself—within certain parameters. If we get any difficult questions—well, I'm sure we can squirm out of them. We'll just try to stick together, not contradict one another and it'll be fine. We'll be fine.''

Why had he come? What the hell was he doing here? She was dying to ask, but was almost afraid to. What if he said he'd felt sorry for her after learning about her pitiful lie? She'd rather be the laughing stock of the whole office than an object of pity.

''We'll be fine,'' she repeated. Maybe if she said it often enough it would come true.

He didn't answer and she turned away, determined to close her eyes and wait for sleep to pay a visit.

The house creaked. A car passed along the distant road that ran by the ranch. She counted two hundred and ninety-six of her father's sheep in her head and marveled at the heat a man's body could bring to a bed. Even with half a foot between them he was much better than a hot water bottle.

''Two years, eh?'' David's voice was thoughtful, and slightly astonished.

She turned her head to look at him. His gaze was fixed on the ceiling, his eyes glinting in the darkness. He looked different from the man she was used to working with. Of course he did. She'd never shared anything more intimate than a fountain pen with that man—certainly not a bed.

''Two years, what?''

''Two years that you've been lying about me being your boyfriend.''

Uh-oh. ''Has it really been that long?''

He nodded. ''So your mother told me, during those endless three hours I spent here before you decided to show up. And it was just last Christmas that I popped the question, wasn't it?''

Funny, with all this heat emanating from her face she really should be lighting up the room. Humiliation—mankind's untapped source of energy. How could she have been stupid enough to take her lie so far? She sighed. She'd gotten cocky. It had been so easy, and been such a load off her shoulders not to have her family worried about her anymore. She'd assumed she could end it whenever there was a danger signal.

But there hadn't been one. Just a head-on collision without warning.

"By the way," he added. "You should probably know this—your mother asked, and I told her we might start thinking about children in three or four years. It's not time yet, but we want at least two. A boy and a girl. A third one is a possibility. But of course only after we're married."

This was too much. She slapped the mattress with the flat of her hand, annoyance cutting through her embarrassment. "David, cut the sarcasm. I know you want to torture me, and I probably deserve it, but I'm exhausted now. Can we save this for tomorrow?"

"We could, Louise, but since we both seem to be suffering from trauma-induced insomnia we might as well do it now. There are things I need to know. There are things you need to know."

"You were never meant to find out."

"That's pretty obvious, or you would have briefed me before allowing your mother to invite me here."

"It was all a huge accident, David. I didn't do it on purpose."

He finally turned his head towards her, his gaze no

less penetrating despite the darkness. "Tell me, Lou. Tell me the details of this *accident*."

Boy, this was humiliating. What was he thinking? She prayed he wasn't thinking she'd done this because she was secretly in love with him. Anything other than that. "It was a survival strategy. And it worked—for two years it has worked fine, and you need never have known."

"*Survival* strategy?"

"You spent the evening with them, David. You've seen what they're like."

"Your folks? Yes. Loving, cheerful, rather loud. Very proud of you."

"And hopelessly overprotective," she added.

David nodded. "I'll grant you that. I did get the third degree this evening. I don't think your brothers like me very much."

"I didn't get a moment's peace after I moved to New York. They were always worried." Especially after what had happened at her first workplace, of course. She knew her mom had been surprised that she had again become involved with a colleague. Surprised—but relieved that she'd moved on.

"Natural. I'm not sure where you live, but your family says your neighborhood is rough. Living alone in such a neighborhood, in that city—they have every reason to worry about you."

"Natural, yes. Intolerable, *yes*. It was driving me nuts. Then one day I was talking with Mom, and she was going on and on about how I had to be careful, how she worried if she called and I wasn't home." She shook her head and sighed deeply at the thought. "And somehow, *somehow,* I told her I was seeing someone, so I was perfectly safe even if I wasn't home late in the evening when she called.''

"I see.''

"Exactly. She was so happy, and the constant questioning stopped entirely for several weeks. It sort of snowballed from there…''

"And why me? Why did I get the honor of being chosen as your fake fiancé?''

She shrugged. "Accident. You were standing there in the hallway outside my office when I first told Mom about my so-called boyfriend. You and Felix. She asked me to describe him and… well…I sort of used you as a template.''

"Template?'' David frowned. "I am a template?''

"Whatever. Call it what you want. I stole your looks for my fictional boyfriend, okay? Blue eyes, dark brown hair…'' Her phrasing had been somewhat more flattering, and had included a few sighs and gushes that hadn't been too hard to fake, but there was no need for him to know that. "You know…no big deal. Could have been anyone. You were just a random choice since you were standing right there.''

"I see. So Felix could just as well be the lucky groom-to-be?''

She chuckled weakly. "Hardly. You were obviously the better catch.''

"A *catch?* What am I? A trout?''

Her sudden giggles echoed from the walls of the quiet room and she covered her mouth with her hand. "Sorry.''

"It's just so…absurd,'' he said, the tone of his voice conveying the absurdity better than his words. "What normal person would do something like this?

What normal person would lie to their family, make up a boyfriend? Make up the details of an engagement, for God's sake? It's ridiculous!''

"Obviously I'm not a normal person,'' Lou snapped. Why did he have to go on and on about this?

"Your parents knew a lot about me,'' he rumbled. "In fact, it sounded like they knew just about everything about me.''

She shrugged. "I told you—you were my template. They kept asking about you. I mean, they kept asking about my boyfriend. What he looked like, what he did for a living—all sorts of things… Well, I had to keep things consistent, so since I had started with describing you I just kept to your statistics. Easier. Less risk of forgetting details or giving conflicting information.''

"And you gave them my name too?''

"I shouldn't have done that,'' she murmured. "That was a huge mistake. But I did give them a false last name.''

"Taylor instead of Tyler? Hardly perfect camouflage. When your mother called, she asked for David Taylor—and the receptionist immediately asked if she didn't mean David Tyler.''

"As I said, it was a mistake.''

"There are quite a few mistakes, aren't there?''

Why couldn't he let this rest? It couldn't really get much worse, could it? So why was he rubbing it in? Lou swallowed another biting retort. Later. She was being appreciative of his help now. "Yes. I'm very grateful, David.'' She reached toward him and touched his shoulder in an instinctive apologetic gesture. It was warm and smooth to the touch. She snatched her hand back. "I'm…''

"Sorry?" he supplied.

"You know I am. I'm not saying that again."

David turned on his side to face her, arm tucked under his head, eyes glinting in the dark. "You know—I don't get it, Lou. You're always so organized, always thinking ahead, so cool and calm and collected. You must have had a plan. About the future. Did you think you could carry on like this forever?"

"No," she said, trying not to sound too miserable. "But it was going so great. They were off my back and didn't worry about me. And at any time, if they started to demand meeting you, I could just tell them we'd broken up. I never imagined they'd go behind my back and contact you—if that had ever crossed my mind I would never have done this."

David made the mistake of chuckling, and a certain glint in his eyes raised her hackles. When he smiled, her suspicions bloomed. He wasn't as shocked and upset as he'd seemed to be, was he? "Why didn't you call me?" she asked guardedly. What *was* he doing here? "I had my cell phone. You could have called me as soon as Mom called you and we'd have straightened this out instantly."

"You mean, you'd have had to 'fess up to your parents?"

"I don't know. 'Fess up, lie to them that we'd broken up—anything." She frowned in the darkness. "Why didn't you call me? Or put my parents off? There's something not right about this."

"I would have got you in trouble."

"Not necessarily. You could have told my parents that you couldn't make it, and then just let me deal with them. There was no need for you to actually come out here.''

''Are you implying I have an ulterior motive?''

She sat up, certain now. ''I *know* you have an ulterior motive!''

David was biting his lip, and the faint lines on his forehead cleared as he started laughing. ''Okay, I confess. After I understood what was going on I had this burning curiosity to see how you would squirm out of this.''

''Aha! So it wasn't all noble self-sacrifice after all?''

''No.'' He was chuckling and she wanted to hit him with something. Unfortunately, the only thing within reach was a pillow, and she didn't think it would be smart to engage David in a pillow fight. Instead she tried for an icy tone.

''Enjoying yourself so far?''

His teeth glinted in the moonlight. ''Pretty much. Especially as I think that under the current circumstances you may be willing to give me what I want.''

She glowered at him, but it probably didn't do much good in the faint light. ''What do you mean?''

''Come on, Lou. Don't pretend you don't know what I'm talking about.''

''You mean you want—?'' She shook her head fiercely as she realized what he was asking. Of course. What else? ''No way. *No way!*''

''You owe me. Are you saying this weekend isn't worth it to you?''

She took a deep breath and held it for a while, staring down at him. ''David, the Ricardo case is *mine!*''

''It's only yours by accident. You know that. We

both worked hard at landing that account, and the case could just as well have been mine. I want it.''

She pressed her lips together as she thought it over. His full cooperation in return for the Ricardo case?

It was probably a fair price, she conceded reluctantly. She didn't like it—but, after all, everything had a price, and she'd always believed in settling her debts. She lay back down and stared up at the ceiling. "Okay. Done. You get the Ricardo case.''

David made a small sound of satisfaction. "Great. Nice doing business with you, Louise.''

"Don't gloat.'' She was feeling better now. Not a lot, but a bit. At least she'd paid up and no longer had to grovel. "Did you have this planned from the beginning? Did you decide to come just to steal one of my biggest cases?''

"No. Regrettably, I'm not that devious. It didn't occur to me until about ten minutes ago.''

"Then why did you come?''

"What—you don't believe I'm just a nice guy and wanted to help you out?''

"I'll ignore that. The real reason you're here…?''

David was grinning again. "Well, you know what they say. Keep your friends close…''

"And your enemies closer,'' she finished with a sinking heart. "I see. I'm the enemy.''

"Nah. Not an enemy.''

"As good as. You know as well as I do that one of us is going to get that promotion. And only one of us.''

"May the better person win.''

She shook her head. "I still don't understand why

you'd bother. What did you hope to gain by coming here?''

"It was just an impulse," he said. "I didn't have an evil agenda. I was just curious about what in the world was going on, and if it helped me to understand my future subordinate…''

"Future boss," she corrected.

He laughed. "One or the other—than that was all the better.''

"Terrific. Now this is team building?''

He was still laughing. "Yeah. All we need are paintball guns.''

Work didn't matter too much at the moment. As long as he promised not to spoil this weekend for her family, she could deal with work issues later. If she played her cards right he'd soon be begging for her help with the Ricardo case. It wasn't as straightforward as he seemed to think.

"But you're going to play along with my folks, right? No funny stuff—nothing that could arouse suspicion? Promise?''

"Of course. I'm not going to give anything away, Lou. I'm not a bad guy—honest. Plus, I've already been paid for my services.''

He was teasing her again. But fine. "Okay. Good. Then let's focus on this weekend. What will we do? How do we get out of this?''

"I don't know what you had in mind, but if it was up to me we'd play along for now, the best we can," he answered shortly. "Bluff our way through it.''

"Then what?''

"Then we forget all about this, and after a while you can tell everybody we've broken up. Simple.''

"Simple," she repeated. "Yes. Simple." It really was that simple, wasn't it? She felt herself relax for the first time since her mother had mentioned David's name. This might work out after all. "Right," she breathed, and turned on her side to hug her pillow. "Goodnight."

"Goodnight, Lou."

Moonlight flittered in and out of the room for a small eternity.

"I still can't sleep," she said, almost soundlessly.

"Me either. Guess we're too tense from all the excitement."

"Maybe we should do something."

"Like what?"

"I don't know. Play cards? I hate playing cards, but anything is better than just lying here unable to sleep." She slapped her pillow, feeling frustrated. "Maybe the problem is that it's just so weird for us to be in bed together."

"If the platonic aspect is what's bothering you we could always have sex."

She was sitting up before she'd realized she'd ordered her muscles to move. *"What?"*

A sound emerged from David, and Lou was torn between relief and indignation when she identified it as a chuckle. "Kidding, Lou. I'm kidding. Not one of my best, I admit, but still a joke. Did you really think I was serious?"

"Of course not." She lay back down and stole a bit more of the duvet. He no longer deserved all of it. "This is just my standard preprogrammed response to any offers of sex."

David gave a surprised chuckle, twisting his head

to look at her. She refused to acknowledge it, and stared up at the ceiling instead. "Are you serious?" he asked.

"No," she said, biting her tongue. How could she have said that? How could she have given her rival personal ammunition like that?

"You *are.* You have some sexual hang-up. That's why you always turn down dates."

"I do not," she retorted, irritated and embarrassed at how interesting he seemed to find this discovery, and praying he'd let it go and forget all about it. This wasn't something she'd tell her colleagues about. Hell, it wasn't even something she talked to her *friends* about.

No such luck. David turned on his side, bracing his head on his hand. "Yes, you do. This is interesting. Something to pass the time. Tell me about it. I can keep a secret."

"No."

"Come on," he cajoled. "I'm your boyfriend, remember? I need to know these things."

"Don't be silly, David."

"I promise not to tell anyone at the office. Well— not more than one or two of the guys, at most."

"Oh, shut up."

"Maybe it'll help to talk about it. Maybe all you need is a male perspective."

"Let me guess—then you're going to offer to show me how it should be done?"

"Well…if you ask nicely…"

His voice was teasing, but she wasn't in the mood to be teased. "Stop it, David. If you're giving me a choice between playing cards and talking about my sex life, I'll take the cards, thank you."

"Not nearly as much fun," he muttered, falling on his back. "Spoilsport. Fine. Let's just return to our regularly scheduled insomnia, then."

CHAPTER THREE

No. She hadn't climbed on top of him while asleep. That couldn't have happened. She wasn't used to being in bed with a man—she certainly wouldn't climb on top of one when forced to share a bed with him. It just couldn't happen.

But here she was, her leg thrown over his thighs and half her torso on top of his. Not to mention her face tucked into his neck. She was breathing in pure David.

It had to be *his* fault.

And…his hand—yes, it was somewhere it definitely shouldn't be. But it was difficult to blame him for that. He was the one innocently sleeping; she was the one who'd draped herself over him and still had her hand buried in his hair. Later she'd wonder just how this had happened. Now there were more urgent things to think about.

Like—how to escape without waking him?

"Morning." His voice rumbled in her ear, and the dilemma was solved as she flew off him and nearly tumbled to the floor. He caught her around the waist and pulled her to safety.

"Morning," she croaked, running her hands through her hair, pushing it away from her face.

Innocently sleeping? With his hand on her butt?

She looked at him with suspicion. David, in return,

was looking at her with a strange look that she couldn't quite interpret. "What?"

"Nothing. You just look different than usual."

She made a face. "I'm wearing pajamas, not a business suit, and my hair is a mess." She touched her cheek where it felt hot from having rested against his chin. "And since we somehow got tangled together I've probably got whisker burns on my face instead of makeup. Of course I look different."

David rubbed his stubble. "Yeah. Sorry. I'll shave before we go to bed tonight."

Before we go to bed tonight?

He expected to wake up with her on top of him again? Yeah, as if that would happen.

"No need," she snapped. "I'll get a spare mattress for tonight. We won't have to share a bed again."

"What a shame," David drawled. "I could get used to this."

Her gaze was drawn to his face. She wasn't the only one who looked different. His eyes looked darker with the stubble complementing them, and he looked decidedly sexy.

Sexy?

She hadn't really thought that, had she? David was a colleague. Of course she wasn't blind—but she didn't go around thinking he was sexy. Such thoughts would do nothing but distract her at work.

But there was just something about the way his hair stuck up, and the way his eyes were still unfocused and sleepy…

He sat up and stretched, and the room warmed considerably. He should wear pajamas. He definitely should wear pajamas. She should point that out to his Secret Santa next Christmas.

Yes, it was time to get out of this bed, out of this room and take a shower.

"I guess we should talk before we go downstairs," David said. "Is there anything I should know?"

"Lots," she said with feeling. "I could write a book."

He grabbed his watch off the nightstand and put it on. "You've got ten minutes to work for that Pulitzer."

"You were kidding, weren't you, about having told my parents we were planning on two or three children? You didn't really tell them that, did you?"

"Yup, I did." He didn't look sorry either. Instead he looked rather satisfied, as if he'd known just how deep a hole he was digging for her in return for the pit she'd pushed him into.

"Revenge, was it?"

"Betcha."

He looked so self-satisfied that she had to bite her lip to keep from laughing. Why would she laugh now, when she was about to go downstairs and face her family with a fake fiancé—who'd just promised them 2.5 grandchildren—in tow?

"We'll go home with a couple of pairs of booties, then," she warned him.

"No problem. I'll use them for my cat. Pink booties for the front paws, blue ones for the hind paws. The poor thing is neutered, so it's only fitting."

"You've got a cat?"

"Yep."

"I didn't know that."

"I know you didn't know that."

"How?"

"Your parents didn't know that little detail, but it looked like they knew everything else about me that you know."

Lou groaned. This was looking really pathetic, wasn't it? "I can explain."

To her surprise, David patted her shoulder soothingly. "It's okay, Louise. You explained last night. Don't worry about it. Now that I've thought about it, I'm okay with posing as your boyfriend for a couple of days. It's fine."

"It's not fine."

"We're in this together. We'll make it. Don't worry."

Lou grabbed her clothes. She'd get dressed in the bathroom after her shower. "This is going to get so complicated if we're really going to fool them. I mean, we'll have to look like we're in love."

"Cool. Do I call you darling or honey or sweet-cakes?"

"*Louise* is bad enough, thank you. This isn't that easy, David! We'll have to convince them we've been together for two years. People who've been together for two years know each other inside and out. With a kind of familiarity we don't have." She braced her knuckles on the windowsill and stared out, cursing. "We're going to slip up. I just know it."

"We'll improvise. Don't worry. It'll be fun. Want to practice some kissing?"

"Fun?" She twisted away from the window to look at him. "David, it will not be *fun*. It will be hard work.

Exhausting. And I'm going to feel like a liar and a fake."

He raised an eyebrow and she looked away, pushed both hands through her tangled hair. "Yeah, yeah, I know. I've been a liar and a fake for two years. But not face-to-face." She groaned. "I could never lie to my mother when I was a kid. What happened?"

"You grew up?"

Lou shook her head with a weak chuckle. "Yeah. That's probably it. I grew up to be a liar."

"You're an excellent liar, Louise. You've got them all fooled. I'm impressed."

"Are you going to be calling me Louise from now on?"

"Yes."

"I've never liked that name."

"I like it. Sounds very feminine and sweet."

"That's precisely why I don't like it."

An eyebrow rose. "Sounds like you've got issues, *Louise*. Does this relate to your confession from last night?"

"Oh, shut up," she muttered, and grabbed her toiletries. She would not be discussing her *issues* with David of all people. "I'm hitting the shower."

Lou yawned as she entered the kitchen. The shower had been refreshing, but it hadn't made up for her lack of sleep recently. Not only last night, but for the past weeks too. She never slept well in hotels. Sleep had always come easy back here—but then she'd always slept alone.

"Trouble sleeping, love?" Mom threw her a dish

towel. "The plates are still in the dishwasher. Would you get them on the table while I flip the pancakes?"

"Sure. Morning," she muttered, starting to set the table.

"How's David?" her mother asked. "He seemed so tired last night."

Lou tried to clear her mind in preparation for the inevitable questioning. "He's fine. After all, he got a lot more sleep than we did. He's taking a shower, then he'll be right down."

"Good." Mrs. Henderson hesitated. "You know, I was going to give him his own room, but your brothers persuaded me otherwise. They said it would be ridiculous to stick the two of you in separate rooms after you've been together for two years." Her mother grinned awkwardly. "We decided they were right. I suppose we have to go with the times. Marriage is more like an afterthought these days, isn't it?"

"Oh, Mom, it's fine. Separate rooms would have been fine." Her spirits lifted as a thought occurred to her. "In fact, if you're more comfortable putting David up in the guest room that would be more than fine with us."

Her mother smiled, reaching up in a cupboard for more dishes. "Oh, I don't know, dear. I wouldn't be that happy if someone tried to separate me and your father overnight."

Damn. "I'm not sure. Teddy bears are a hell of a lot less trouble than men," Lou muttered.

"Sorry, honey, I didn't hear you. What did you say?"

"Oh, nothing." She wasn't about to admit to the oversized yellow plush duck that had taken up permanent residence in her bed. Her mother thought she'd given up stuffed animals at the age of ten. "Mom, how did you arrange all this? Getting David here?"

"We have our connections," her mother evaded, trying to look mysterious. "It was about time. Two years and we hadn't even met your mystery man." There was slight reproach in her mother's voice, and Lou concentrated on her task of aligning knives and forks.

"You manipulated us, you know," she said, without too much feeling. Better to save her energy for the big issues. "Mom, you know I don't like it when people try to control my life. I'm a grown-up now, remember?"

Mrs. Henderson brushed the hair away from her face and kissed her cheek. "I wouldn't dream of trying to control your life, my little grown-up. I just want a tiny glimpse of it."

Lou rolled her eyes. "Right."

"Overprotection is a mother's job. Live with it. And after what *that man* did to you—"

"Mom!"

"Yes, yes, we're not talking about him. Hopefully never again. My point is we want to know the man in your life. David seems very nice. I like him."

"Yeah. He's nice." For a given value of "nice," she supposed that was true.

"He even seemed shocked when I put you in a room together. I suppose his own parents aren't as open-minded as we are." Now there was pride in her tone, and Lou felt like groaning. There didn't seem to be the slightest chance of getting David his own room. "Have you met his family yet?"

"No. Not yet."

"Shame. But that's what the city does to people. Severs all family ties. Where does his family live?"

"Ahhh… Dammit, I can never remember the name of that town."

"Louise!"

"Just ask him." She shrugged. "We don't talk much about our families. We work together—so we mostly talk about work."

"You must know where David grew up, at least. Are they still there, or did they move away?"

Her mind was blank. As she groped for an answer that would make sense David walked in, his hair damp from the shower and dressed more casually than she'd ever seen him. He looked great. "Morning," he said with a smile, then put his arm around her shoulders and kissed her temple. *What?* "It's so peaceful out here. I could have slept forever."

"I was just asking Louise where you're from, David," her mother said. "We'd really like to meet your parents soon. Where are they?"

"Ah—they're…they live in Florida."

Her mother looked disappointed. "So far away. That's a shame."

"Isn't it?"

"But at least we'll get to meet them at your wedding."

Lou reached up in a cupboard, noisily grabbing glasses and banging them on the counter.

Mrs. Henderson seemed to get the picture, and even sent an apologetic glance. David, however, did *not* get the picture. "Plenty of time to plan the wedding, Mom—can I call you Mom?"

Or perhaps, Lou thought fuming, he got it just fine.

"Of course," her mother said, taken aback for a second, but then smiling in pleasure.

Lou took advantage when her back was turned and glared at David. "No, he can't!"

"Louise, I think it's lovely that he wants to call me Mom…"

"No! No way. There is no marriage here. He can call you Mom when he's your son-in-law. Not before."

David snagged her for another kiss on the temple. "She's a bit old-fashioned in some respects, isn't she?" he said, his arm over her shoulder, affectionately squeezing. She pulled away and opened a cupboard, pretending to search for something. Did he have to smell so good on top of everything else?

"Was she this bossy when she was a little girl?" David asked her mother, and was rewarded by a chuckle and an embarrassing anecdote.

He was really not going to make this easy for her, was he?

Her brothers had arrived. So much was obvious by the children's yelling outside the house. Lou grinned with pleasure, rushing to meet them. She saw the children rarely, and she missed them. They grew up so fast. She'd made sure her brothers regularly e-mailed photos of them, so she would at least recognize them when she saw them again, but it wasn't the same.

David kept up his little drama over the entire meal. On the upside, his behavior had everybody convinced. On the downside, it was playing havoc with her nerves. Every casual touch, every intimate smile— how was she going to tolerate this for an entire weekend? They wouldn't be going home until Monday evening. Monday seemed like a lifetime away.

After brunch, she made a "work-related" excuse to the others and dragged David out of the room, out of the house and into the backyard. Once there, she strode with him to the edge of the yard, where a wire fence closed the domestic garden off from the farm animals. It was quite a walk, but she needed the distance if she was to scream at him properly. Noise carried easily out here.

"David, what the hell are you doing?" she yelled as loud as she dared. "Are you trying to make this even worse than it is?"

There was a teasing glint in his eyes that made her want to push him into the pile of manure on the other side of the fence. "What's wrong? I'm playing the role you put me in."

"You're playing it a bit *too* well! I did not tell you to kiss me or hug me, or talk about our wedding, or ask you to call my mother Mom, or tell everybody how many children we're planning on! And what do you think you're doing, asking Mom what I was like as a child? Are you going to be looking through my baby pictures next?"

David was grinning. He was actually *grinning*. "Relax, Lou. It's all part of my role. We're not going to be very convincing if I keep my distance and act like I'm never going to see them—or you—again."

"But—"

"I'm just acting like a normal loving fiancé would."

He was right. Wasn't he? Why was she screaming at him? She couldn't remember just at the moment.

The fact was that he was impossible, and he kept grinning, and he looked gorgeous, and she couldn't get it out of her mind how sexy he had looked this morning and how good he had smelled when he'd hugged her in the kitchen.

She turned away from him to stare over her parents' land. This wasn't good. Not good at all. In fact, they were rapidly approaching a disaster situation.

Fortunately, she'd brought a large supply of antacids.

David had discovered he liked the look of Lou in casual dress. She'd changed before his eyes. He was seeing a side of her she never showed at the office. She seemed younger, softer—playful as she dealt with her bratty nieces and nephews, amused though weary of her mother's constant questions about him and their relationship, and her deep affection for her family kept reminding him of his own family. He'd call his parents when he got back home. His mother's birthday was coming up soon. He should go home. It had been far too long for him too.

Lou was staring out into the fields. Her profile showed a clenched jaw and a tightly drawn eyebrow. She was tense—and probably angry. Almost as tense as she'd been last evening when she'd entered the bedroom. "Relax, Louise," he told her. "Keep this up and you're going to give yourself an ulcer. It's not worth it."

"Correction, David. *You're* going to give me an ulcer."

He spread out his arms in a gesture of innocence. "What did *I* do?"

She looked at him. Her eyes were huge, filled with something he hoped wasn't misery. That would take the fun out of this entire thing. "What happens when we get back, David? How will this affect our working relationship?"

"It won't."

A spark started glowing in her eyes and she straightened up, the country-girl image fading to be replaced with an aggressive self-assurance. "I'm going to get that promotion, you know."

"You don't say?"

"I've worked for it, I deserve it, and I'm going to get it."

He grinned. "Me too. See? We have a common goal."

She scowled. "How will you feel about me being your boss?"

He crossed his arms. She wasn't the only one who could be aggressive and self-confident. "That's not going to happen."

Lou looked back out over the fields, her shoulders sagging a bit. "Will you use this situation to gain an advantage?"

"No."

"Why not?"

"Because that would be cheating—and I don't cheat."

"You know as well as I do that back there the jungle law is in full effect. It's all about the survival of the fittest. It doesn't matter how you get ahead, only that you do. No matter how many people you tread on to get there."

"Is that what you believe?"

She shook her head. "No. I don't believe the end justifies the means. A handicap in our profession, but I can't help it."

"Don't worry. I didn't come here to win our race by stomping you into the ground."

She was vulnerable, he realized. More vulnerable than he'd ever guessed from working with her. The self-confidence that radiated from her was only skin-deep. Underneath that exterior was a woman none of them knew.

A woman he found himself wanting to get to know. "You don't trust me, do you?" he asked.

She shook her head. "It doesn't matter." She sighed. "I'll just have to wait and see what happens when we get back." She gestured out into the fields. "I don't suppose I can chain you to a fence or leave you inside one of the pens?"

"And tell your father to release me only after you've secured that position?"

A reluctant grin started blooming on her face. "My thoughts exactly."

"How about this? We'll do it the old-fashioned way. Fair and square." He held out a hand. "Deal?"

"Fair and square—here, and when we get back?"

"Yep."

She hesitated only for a moment before taking his hand. It was cold, but her grip was firm. "Deal," she said, pulling her hand back much too soon.

Somehow the weekend passed without any major mishaps. Despite David's presence she managed to achieve some quality time with her parents and brothers, and got to know her little nieces and nephews

anew. She'd been heartbroken—and terribly guilty—
to find out that the little ones barely remembered her
except as a name in a birthday card. In their minds
she was the distant aunt who sent the big presents, and
they had looked at her with huge eyes, both shy and
curious. The shyness had slowly evaporated—but they
would be quick to forget her again.

She *definitely* needed to come home more often.

David fit in. She wasn't sure how he managed to,
but he acted as if he'd been her fiancé forever, and did
an excellent job at dodging difficult questions without
it being too obvious. Everybody was fooled—and they
seemed to like him, too.

Her mood lightened as soon as they passed the halfway mark—Sunday afternoon. A day and a half down;
another day and a half to go. They might actually get
away with this!

Monday evening, her parents insisted on driving
them to the airport, where her father made good his
threat to throw a small tantrum at the ticket counter to
get them seats together. Lou hid behind a column and
grimaced. "That's my dad."

"I think he's quite right," Mrs. Henderson said,
standing straighter in defense of her husband. "Of
course you should go home together. It shouldn't be
that much trouble to change the tickets—if the airline
would only show a little human courtesy instead of
relying blindly on rules and regulations and red tape."

"Well, I believe Dad has forced them to display
human courtesy," Lou said, grimacing as she gestured
toward her father, who had just turned around grinning, holding up two boarding passes. "He actually
did it," she said in disbelief.

"Of course I did it," her father said, thrusting the passes in her hand. "There you go. You get to hold your man's hand during takeoff—and you've got your dad to thank for it!"

Lou chuckled as they hugged her parents goodbye. She was approaching ecstatic. They were going to get away with this! It was almost too good to be true, and as she settled in her window seat the relief was overwhelming. They'd done it. Amazing.

Except—she still had one last discussion with David to get through. She intended to get started on some serious conversation as soon as their plane was in the air. This wasn't over. Not quite.

She rested back in her seat and stared out the window as they lifted off. Then they were above the clouds and the view was cut off.

Time to talk.

"David?"

"Hmm?"

His answer sounded as if he was barely conscious. She glanced to her side to find him engrossed in a report. "David?" she repeated, patting his arm to get his attention over the loud whine of the engines. "We need to talk."

He looked up. "Yeah?"

She took the report out of his hands and tucked it in the magazine holder in the seat in front of him. A smile started in his eyes, and then reached his lips. "You're looking serious, Louise."

"You're not going to tell anybody about this, are you?"

"About the weekend?"

She nodded.

David cocked his head, studying her carefully. "I hadn't thought about it, but that panicked look in your eyes tells me I'd better not."

"Right. You can't."

"Why? Notwithstanding that it makes a great story, this whole thing might be easier if they're in on the joke. In case your parents call us at the office, or something. Everything will be smoother if they play along."

"In on the *joke?*"

He looked absolutely clueless. "Yes."

She took a deep breath. "This is not a joke, David! Don't you see? If word got out that I'd been lying about you being my boyfriend—I'd look like a fool." She *was* a fool, in this particular case, but that wasn't the issue here. "In no time we'd have rumors circling, and they would make me look like a lovesick idiot."

"Lovesick idiot?" He was obviously fighting a chuckle. "You as a lovesick idiot—I can't quite get that picture into my head, I'm afraid. Can you demonstrate?"

Lou shook her head impatiently. The flight was only a few hours. Probably not nearly enough time to get through to David if he wasn't going to cooperate. "You *know* what people would think."

"I'm afraid I don't."

"Well, think! What would *you* think if word got out that I'd told my family I was engaged to Felix or Johnny?"

"That you had terrible taste in men."

Okay. She'd have to spell it out to him. Well, what was one more humiliation in the grand scheme of things? "What they would think is that I've been pining over you from afar, and finally my imagination got the better of me and I started thinking we were really together and I've been telling people about it, believing my fantasies were true…"

David's eyebrows rose higher as her monologue continued, and by the time she was finished he'd started laughing. "Lou, now you *are* letting your imagination get the better of you. Nobody's going to think you're delusional. They'll understand. Hell, they'll think you're brilliant for having thought of this solution. After all, most of us have mothers we'd like off our backs."

"I'm serious, David. Promise me you won't tell anyone. If this gets out…"

David shrugged. "Sure. If it means that much to you, I won't breathe a word."

"No one," she stressed. "If you tell just one person, the secret is out. Promise you won't tell anyone."

"I promise. No one will find out."

"One more thing…"

"Yes?"

"You can't call me Louise."

"Aww, come on! I like calling you Louise!"

"I mean it. Nobody up there calls me Louise. You can't. It will look suspicious."

"Louise—nobody will even notice."

"You can't call me Louise!" she insisted.

"Fine. Fine. But," he added, pulling at his report until it sprang away from the magazine holder, "you owe me big time. You know that, don't you?"

Lou groaned. "Yes. I owe you."

He grinned at her sideways as he opened the folder.

"Especially if I ever need someone to pose as my girlfriend. You'll do it no questions asked?"

"Yes."

"Even if it means you have to kiss me?"

"David!"

He looked injured. "Hey, I pretended to be your beloved for an entire weekend, and I didn't even get a kiss."

Lou rolled her eyes and made a big show out of digging for the news magazine she'd bought at the airport. "Yeah, like that would be a big treat."

"The guys would love to hear I got to kiss you."

How very high school. Though admittedly, half the department seemed to be stuck at that particular developmental level. "I see—you want a trophy kiss? And you'd *tell* them? You kiss and tell?"

"No." He sighed, and settled down to concentrate on his reading. "Of course not. I didn't kiss and I won't tell."

There were fresh tulips on Lou's desk when she arrived at work in the morning. She stared at them, puzzled, as she put down her briefcase and absently straightened the overflowing stack in her inbox. Who could have sent her flowers? Why?

"Congratulations!" Samantha hugged her. "Welcome back!" She waved a hand at the flowers. "We all pitched in. I can't believe you guys hid this from us for so long! Nobody ever noticed you so much as sneaking glances at each other. Unbelievable."

This couldn't be what it sounded like. It was impossible. "What?" she croaked, in an attempt to get something more coherent out of Samantha.

"Actually, you two deserve tar and feathers," Felix drawled from the doorway, grinning. "But congratulations anyway. I don't know how you pulled this off for two years."

Things were becoming clear. And her knees were becoming weak. She collapsed in her chair, brain cells madly colliding as she tried to figure a way out of this. "How did you find out?"

"Your mother called last week, just after David had left," Samantha said. "Some last-minute message, so we gave her his cell phone number. She told us."

Mom. She should have guessed her mother was somehow involved.

Samantha kept prattling. "I almost couldn't believe it. I mean, okay, seeing each other behind our backs is one thing, but you're actually *engaged!* To *David!* I'd never have guessed in a million years. I can't believe how well you guys hid it." Samantha grabbed Lou's left hand, then the right one. She started frowning. "Where's your ring? You can start wearing it to work now. We all know. There's no need to hide it anymore."

"I see," she said weakly.

Samantha shooed Felix out of the room and came to sit on the corner of Lou's desk. "Why on earth were you hiding your relationship anyway? I've been trying to fix you up with guys for over a year! I would have saved myself the effort if I'd known you were already taken. Now I know why you never looked at another guy!"

"We thought it could be…awkward," she muttered. David. She needed to get a hold of David. *Now.* "You know. Working together. A lot of companies don't like their staff to get romantically involved. You know. Against policy.''

''Rubbish. As long as you're not boss and employee it's fine.''

Right. And neither the engagement nor their current employment status as equals would last too long—she hoped. ''Do you know if David is in yet?''

''No. Haven't seen him. Missing him already?''

Lou mustered up enough strength for a weak grin. Did she have David's cell phone number? She started to ask Samantha, but bit her tongue just in time. She was David's fiancée. She should know his phone number. It should be item one on her speed dial. Samantha left with one more wink, and Lou bent over her desk, trying to slow down her heartbeat. David would be here soon. They'd figure something out. She wasn't sure *what*—but something.

A few minutes later Lou was staring at her screen, without the slightest idea what was on it, when the door burst open and David strode in, finally looking properly frazzled. Seeing him that wild-eyed was a rather satisfying feeling. He was also back in a suit and tie, and he looked like a different man from the one she'd gotten to know over the weekend. The effect was rather disorienting. Getting things back to normal might take more of an effort than she'd anticipated.

''Morning, David,'' she managed to say more or less normally, and he closed the door securely behind him. For a moment he stood with his back to her, then twisted around. ''They all know! I mean, they *think* they know!''

Lou gestured at her flowers. ''You don't say?''

''You got flowers?'' David sat on the edge of her

desk and snorted. He grabbed her pencil mug and started fiddling with the contents in fast, nervous movements. "What I get is a full office of grins and wolf whistles."

"Idiots with teenage minds," Lou muttered. "Do you get a prize for thawing the ice lady?"

An eyebrow rose. "You know about that?"

"Of course. I work hard at living up to my stupid clichéd nickname. Really, they could have come up with something more original, don't you think?"

"They're just jealous because they've all been dying to take you out."

Was that gloating in his voice? "Right. Now they think I turned them down because of our relationship. Makes their little egos all better."

"Why *did* you turn them down? Because of your *issues?*"

She glowered at him. Why couldn't he forget her stupid slip of the tongue? "Yes, that's an important question. We absolutely must discuss that. We don't have anything more urgent on our plates today, do we?"

Her sarcasm never worked on him. "Don't you like men?"

"You mean as a species?"

David grinned. "Yeah."

"Despite their many shortcomings, I like men just fine."

"Just as long as they keep their distance? You need therapy. I'm much cheaper than NY shrinks, you know."

He was one clever remark away from ending up with a wastepaper basket over his head. "Stop it,

David. I don't need therapy. I'm fine. I'm great! And please keep your voice down," she added in a slightly less aggressive voice. "Don't talk about this at the office. You never know who's listening. Especially now." She glanced at the door. "I bet we've got several ears squashed to that door right now. So, not here—ever."

"No problem. Where do you want to talk about it?"

"David!"

"You can trust me. I told you—I'm good at keeping secrets."

"Thank you," she said, with just the right tone of irony. "For your information, I do date—though it's been a while now. My icy reputation is greatly exaggerated. I don't date a lot because I'm busy, and I never date colleagues because that's just not a good idea and can lead to consequences more serious and longer-lasting than a broken heart." She paused for breath. "Happy?"

"Not particularly."

"Well, I don't care. Drag your mind out of my personal life and concentrate. What are we going to do about this?"

David shrugged. "Tell them the truth?"

She groaned and rested her head in her hands. "No. We can't do that. You know we can't. I'm going to look like a total idiot if we tell them."

"We don't have to tell them the whole truth. We could always tell them your mother misunderstood something," David said doubtfully.

"From what I understand, there was no room for misunderstanding. Samantha wants to know where my ring is."

"Now I have to buy you a ring?" He grinned. "Fine. We'll stop by at Tiffany's after work and get you a diamond."

"You are so not funny, David."

"Then why are you grinning?"

"I'm not."

"Sure you are. I saw the corners of your mouth move."

"It's not a *grin*. I'm having an uncontrollable twitch caused by overwhelming anxiety. A full-blown panic attack may be imminent."

"I see. Well, what do *you* think we should do? It is *your* problem, after all."

"It looks to me like it just turned into *our* problem, David."

"Okay." He stole her chair, sat down and made himself comfortable with his feet on top of her desk. He grabbed one of her pens and rolled it between his palms. "How about this—we use the same plan as for your parents. We'll play along for a while, then break up."

It was the easiest solution. And they could synchronize it, tell her parents at the same time, which would prevent a similar occurrence in the future. Lou rolled her shoulders, trying to force herself to relax. Maybe there was an easy way out after all. "You're right. That's the logical way out. It should be easy, right?"

David grimaced. "Easy? I'm not sure about that part."

"Sure. It's not like we have to act any differently. People aren't expecting us to be all lovey-dovey at work. Nothing has to change. Nothing at all." She smiled in relief. "This will work out fine. We don't have to pretend anything for their benefit, and in a few weeks or months we'll have an amicable friendly break-up and everything will be just like before. We won't have to actually *do* anything.''

David's eyes were alight with a teasing sparkle that was becoming familiar. ''Nothing? Aw... Does that mean we won't be having any lunchtime quickies on your desk?''

''David!''

''Come on! Where is your sense of humor? Wouldn't it be fun? I'd meet you in the hallway, call 'Your office or mine?' ''

Louise lowered her voice, trying to make it ominous and threatening. ''David...''

It didn't work. He continued relentlessly. ''We would spend our lunch hour mundanely reviewing some files, then muss up each other's hair and clothes ever so slightly, and leave the office with huge smiles on our faces.''

''I don't think so.''

''We'd shock the entire floor. We might even make the Christmas Yearly news sheet. Think about the rumors we'd start!''

He seemed to actually be waiting for an answer, so she gave him one. ''No.''

David threw her globe-shaped pencil sharpener up in the air, and failed to catch it. It crashed on the edge of her desk, spilling shavings on the carpeted floor. He didn't notice the mess, but as she picked up the two pieces of the globe and fitted them together again he finally got out of her chair and headed for the door.

''It would be so much fun!'' he said wistfully as he opened the door.

Lou stared at the pencil shavings he'd just trodden into the carpet. ''You're going to get us fired,'' she groaned.

CHAPTER FOUR

A WHOLE month passed and, surprisingly enough, David was on his best behavior. Their fifteen minutes of fame were over, and nobody treated them any differently for being a couple. In fact, everything was almost like before.

Except for her heart's annoying tendency to pick up speed whenever they were alone together, a teasing glint in David's eyes whenever they met—and, of course, Samantha's regular question in an increasingly disapproving tone: "*Still* no ring?"

"Uh…no more than last week, Samantha." Lou shook a pen at her assistant. "Stop asking. I told you—I'm not getting a ring. I don't want one. Honest. I've never liked wearing rings and I see no reason to start wearing one now."

Samantha shook her head, frowning in disapproval. "You can't be engaged without a ring! That's not a real engagement!"

"Engagements are about an emotional commitment two people make to spend their lives together. It is *not* about wearing a rock on your finger."

"The rock is not optional," Samantha stated. "If you've got some kind of objection to wearing rings, you could have it on a chain around you neck. You have to have a ring. I don't believe David agrees to this. He's never seemed this cheap—"

"David is not cheap!" She had to stand up for

her fiancé, make-believe or not, right? It was a fian-cée's duty.

"Or this superficial! I can't believe it." Samantha shook her head in emphasis. "Every *real* man wants his fiancée to wear his ring."

"Whether she wants to or not?" Lou inquired mildly.

Samantha grabbed the papers from Lou's outbox, destined for her own inbox, and clutched them to her chest. "Yes, whether she wants to or not." With a shrug she turned toward the door. "Obviously you're a lost cause. Maybe I should talk directly to David about this. I can't believe he agrees!"

Why did everybody think it was perfectly natural to meddle in her personal life? "Why not just take it up at a Friday meeting?" she called after Samantha. "Discuss it openly among the twenty-eight of us? Hey, or perhaps we could ask the board to rule on it? We'll make corporate history. 'Livingstone's Great Ring Debate.'"

The phone rang, and Samantha sent her a hurt glance from the doorway before vanishing with her burdens—real and imagined. Lou sighed as she picked up the phone. "Lou Henderson," she answered absently, one hand cradling the phone and the other picking out letters on the keyboard. Work kept piling up—and it was now more important than ever to keep up with it. Her superiors would be keeping a close eye on her work now that a promotion was imminent within the next year or so.

"Hi! I'm Helen, David's sister. So nice to hear your voice at last!"

Lou dropped the phone. It bounced off the keyboard

and from there onto the floor. She swore as she picked it warily up with two fingers, pulse already up in the stratosphere. *What now?* "Hello?" she said, with an awful sense of foreboding. But it couldn't be. David's office number only differed from hers by one digit. This had to be a wrong number. "Who did you say this was?"

"Helen. I'm David's sister—he must have mentioned me."

"Of course." No. "Helen—David's sister." Dammit. "Nice to meet you. I mean—hear from you." She closed her eyes and prayed for a second before adding, "Shall I put you through to David?"

"No, absolutely not!" Helen laughed. "He thinks big sisters have been put on the earth to torture him, and he probably wouldn't approve of me cold-calling you like this. But I just had to."

Oh, God. How had David's sister found out? How much had she found out? What the hell was going on? Lou held the phone between her ear and shoulder, in a position that would probably cause her neck to cramp, and frantically typed out an instant message to David on her computer.

Come over here!!! Now!!! Emergency!!!!!!

David would understand the multiple exclamation marks had to mean she was hanging onto the end of her rope by only one claw.

He'd better.

"Mom and Dad told me about you yesterday, after David called, and I just had to call."

Mom and Dad? After David called? Fingers trembling, Lou slammed a second message through the keyboard.

%% $% &%*(!!!!!!!!!! I'm going to bury you alive under a mountain of file cabinets!!!! My office NOW!!!!!!*

"I see," she managed to mumble, voice more or less under control.

"We have to meet, don't you agree? Will you be able to make it to the big birthday bash? David wasn't sure yesterday, but said he'd ask you. Mom would be ecstatic."

Birthday bash? What was going on? *And where the hell was David?*

Just as she was about to mumble apologies to Helen, claim an emergency—anything just to get rid of her while she tarred and feathered David—the object of her fury, ambled into her office, holding a file. He obviously hadn't been to his computer yet to see her messages, or he wouldn't be so relaxed.

"David is here now," she said with relief, while sending David a glare that should have scorched his tie off. All it did was cause his eyebrows to raise. "I'll just get him for you. Hang on."

She thrust the phone at David and turned her back to him as he greeted his sister. Dammit! She started pacing the floor, hands crossed on her chest and a frown so deep on her face she could feel her facial muscles settling in a permanent groove. Perfect. On top of everything else, David was giving her wrinkles.

David glanced at her occasionally while he chatted with his sister, and should have looked terrified when he finally put down the phone. Instead he was wearing a "gotcha" grin.

"Helen says—"

"You told them about us!" she interrupted, jabbing a finger in the air to emphasize her point. "I mean, you lied to them, too!"

David shrugged. "You said you owed me a favor."

"This is way beyond doing you a favor!"

"Why? It's exactly the same thing I did for you! And remember, I specifically asked if that included pretending to be my girlfriend if I ever needed you to, and you said yes."

"I thought you meant going to a party with you or something! Not involving your entire family in the same lie as mine." She groaned. "Didn't you learn anything from my mistake?"

David perched on the edge of the desk and she pushed at the floor with her foot until her chair rolled a few inches away. He still seemed to exude electricity whenever they were close together. It was highly disturbing—not to mention distracting, and a bit frightening. She wasn't used to this, and it scared her that she couldn't control her own reactions to him.

"What's the problem, Lou? You deal with your family, I deal with mine. I help you—you help me."

"It didn't cross your mind to warn me before telling people about this—before giving them my phone number, for God's sake?"

"For once, I'm innocent. I didn't give them your phone number. But Helen has her sources. And, well—yes, it did occur to me to tell you before. I rejected the idea."

"And—*why* did you do that?"

He grinned and reached out to pat her knee. "Knowing you, you'd probably have found some way to squirm out of it, and I didn't want you to do that." He winked at her, and she could have brained him with her Eiffel Tower paperweight. "I know how you hate to break promises, so I decided not to give you the chance. See? I *am* a nice guy."

She was fuming by now, mad enough to stand up and start pacing around the room. Especially as it had occurred to her that this had been his plan all along. "This is why you were okay with everything, isn't it? Back at the farm? You were already planning this, weren't you?"

David winced. "Really, Louise, how cunning do you think I am?" He grinned. "I don't think even I'm smart enough to pull off such a complicated evil scheme. It would take a devious genius."

"Oh, you're devious all right! You weren't doing me a favor at all! You'd already decided to use this for your own purpose! This suits you just fine!"

"Well, yes. It does. My parents are off my back. You, of all people, should know what a relief that is. I need to go home for my mother's sixtieth birthday soon—and for once I won't be set up with half the women in the county. It'll be great."

"David…?"

"Yes?"

Lou sat back down. She leaned back in her chair and took a deep calming breath as she rubbed her temples. "Admit it, you're just doing this to pay me back!"

There was a knock on the door, then Felix stuck his head in the doorway. "Lovers' quarrel?"

"No!" Lou snapped at their boss.

At the same moment David drawled, "Lucky me, huh?"

Felix grinned and held out a pile of papers. "Try to keep the fighting to off-hours. But I'll leave you to it. And this is for you, David."

"Aw, come on," David complained. "More paperwork?"

"Stop complaining. It's in your job description. I checked."

David shook his head. "More of this and I'll jump ship," he threatened with a mock sulk. "You know the guys on floor seventeen keep trying to headhunt me."

Felix shrugged. "We've got an ice maker and they don't. I'm not worried—at least not in the summer."

"You have a point," David conceded. "Anyway," he continued, when Felix was gone, "the thing is, Mom's sixtieth birthday is next weekend. And you're coming with me, like it or not."

"Really?"

He nodded. "Yup. You made a promise and it's time to pay the piper. You can't bail out on me now."

"It didn't occur to you to check with me first—even if just to see if I had other plans for the weekend? I do have a life outside the office, you know."

"I thought I'd risk it," he said affably. "*Do* you have plans?"

Lou wanted to tell him that, yes, she did have plans. She was tied up all weekend scrubbing the bathroom tiles and did not have time to play his girlfriend. But her inborn sense of fair play didn't allow her. David was manipulating her, and he might have an ulterior motive, but he *had* been a good sport when she'd involved him in her long-term lie—and it wasn't as if *he'd* been given any advance warning. She didn't even want to imagine what most of the other guys at the office would have done in his place. She did owe him.

That didn't mean she had to be happy about it.

Or that he'd escape paying up.

"You'll have to pay, then."

"What are you talking about? *You* owe *me.*"

"Well—I paid up in full last time, didn't I? It's your turn."

He almost turned pale, and she had to bite her lip to keep from cackling. "No," he said, shaking his head. "I'm not giving you the Ricardo case back. Not now. I clocked over thirty hours on it this week alone."

"You're not the only one who spent time on that case."

"Come on! You're not playing fair."

"I'm playing precisely as fair as you did."

"I've sweated over this one! You can have one of my other cases. How about Harlan & Stock?"

"No. It's Ricardo or nothing. Your call." She shrugged and pulled up a random paper to look at. "I really don't care if you accept the deal or not, but it's the only one on the table."

David brow was heavy, but a tiny grin was pulling at his mouth even as he crossed his arms on his chest and shook his head. "You drive a hard bargain, Louise."

"Take it or leave it."

He held out his hand. "Fine. Done."

"Then we're even? Okay? No more little schemes?

We break up by the end of the month, and then all this will be over.''

"Okay." He lifted her hand to his lips, but she yanked it away before he could kiss it.

"Don't be silly. Now, get out of my office before I change my mind."

"You're cute when you're bossy," he said affectionately as he headed for the door. "Saturday morning, nine o'clock."

"What?"

"Our plane. It leaves at nine o'clock next Saturday morning."

She tapped her foot and clenched her hand around a pencil. "Do you mean to say you were so sure I'd agree that you already booked the tickets?"

"Yup."

She sighed. Terrific. Not only was she gullible and a compulsive liar—she was predictable too.

CHAPTER FIVE

"YOU'RE still mad, aren't you? You weaseled the case out of me, and you're still mad."

What was the holdup? Why didn't the pilot start the engines so she'd get a few hours of peace—if not quiet? She'd no interest in conversation with David. Her nerves were frazzled enough already. There would be enough of that when they got to his parents' place.

"Gee, what tipped you off?"

"You're reading the *Wall Street Journal.*"

"So?"

"You never read the *Wall Street Journal.*"

"I'm broadening my horizons."

"I see." David tapped his fingers on his knee, then started rummaging in his briefcase until Lou looked up from the paper and sent him a stare.

"Do you have a problem, David?"

David smiled with the joy and smug satisfaction of a toddler who's gotten his mother's attention by scribbling graffiti on brand-new wallpaper. He held up his handheld computer. "No, I'm fine. Got my Palm Pilot. It's got games."

"Excellent," she said icily.

"By the way, do you have any idea why Samantha isn't talking to me?"

"Ah, that."

"Yes. What have you been telling her?"

"Nothing. She thinks you're either cheap or unromantic not to have bought me a ring."

"Unromantic? Cheap?" David sounded outraged. "She used to have a crush on me, you know. You're letting her think I'm a total loser?"

"It's not my fault! I've told her it's not you, it's me, that I don't want a stupid ring. But she says that it doesn't matter, you should still have bought me one." Lou took a deep breath. "She also informs me regularly that the fact that you haven't bought me a ring, whether I want you to or not, indicates a flaw in your personality, not to mention suggests that you may be chronically unable to form a complete commitment, and I might want to reevaluate the substance of our relationship and the direction it's taking."

"That's it?" David prompted when she paused for breath again.

"And she knows the name of a very good therapist."

"Ouch."

"Yup. Ouch."

"I guess I should count my blessings that I'm getting the silent treatment."

"I don't know. Your reputation is in ruins." She flipped a page of the *Wall Street Journal.* "Now, be a good little boy and play a computer game."

He chuckled. "Yes ma'am."

After the long plane trip came a long car drive, and it was six o'clock by the time they finally arrived at David's parents' home. They'd been expected for dinner, and the house seemed full of people. David's parents greeted her enthusiastically, as did his two sisters and their flock of toddlers. It was all terribly confusing.

As she was whisked into the kitchen for a girl-chat with David's sisters and mother, Lou couldn't help but think back on David getting that phone call from her mother, unprepared, then arriving at her parents' farm to be interrogated by her parents and siblings, and keeping up the pretence all along—for her sake. It had been quite heroic of him.

Of course it wasn't heroic at all to spring his mother and sisters on her without warning, so it probably all came out even in the end. David had handled her family just fine—she'd be able to deal with his family just as well.

No problem.

"To tell you the truth, we've been a bit worried about David," one of his sisters confided. "To be absolutely honest, Helen and I were beginning to worry that he was gay. Not that it would be a big problem—I mean, if you're gay you're gay—but to be still in the closet at his age…"

"David? Gay?"

Kathleen shrugged. "So many men are these days," she said morosely. "I'm speaking from experience. Find a single man in his thirties and he's gay. Maybe there's a new craze."

Lou almost spurted out her tea. "A gay craze?"

"Probably not," Kathleen allowed with a smile. "But anyway, with him living in New York…never talking about a steady girlfriend, never bringing one home…we started wondering. Not Mom and Dad, of course. It would never cross their minds." She shifted, moving closer into a conspiratorial position. "But why in the world did he keep you a secret from us for two years?"

Lou shrugged. "We're not living together or anything. We wanted to keep things private. You know— in case it went wrong. So few relationships last these days, don't they? Especially for busy career people like us."

"Oh." Kathleen sighed. "So that means you two are pretty sure this is it, now, doesn't it?"

Uh-oh. How had she managed to dig that hole and jump into it? "Well…" There was only one response. "Uh, yes."

"Weren't you interested in meeting his folks before now?"

"Of course. But you are so far away, and we're always busy, and there was plenty of time…"

"Have you talked about a date? Do you suppose it will be this year?"

"What date?"

Kathleen laughed. "For the wedding, of course! Mom and Dad are really hoping you choose to get married here. The local church. But don't let them push you," she added. "Not at all. You should do this your way. If you want to get married while tandem skydiving in Central Park, go right ahead. Don't let us manipulate you. It should be your day."

Yikes. "Well…"

"But, just so you know, the church is lovely. It's tiny and old, but in excellent condition, and everything smells of tradition and promises. It has this wonderful hand-carved altar that dates back to 1815. It would be an unforgettable wedding."

"I..."

Kathleen held up her hands. "Sorry, I'm pushing. Forget I said anything. Sometimes I remind myself too much of my mother."

"What's wrong with your mother?" Mrs. Tyler said from the doorway, pulling gently on her daughter's ponytail as she entered the room. "You're not frightening the future mother of my grandchildren away, are you?"

"Mom! *You're* going to terrify her! Don't you have enough grandchildren to spoil?"

"Never enough," Mrs. Tyler said, with a grin that reminded Lou of her own mother.

Lou escaped to the backyard when most of the family had gone to bed. She didn't feel sleepy, despite the long day of traveling, and she had a lot to think about. With all the lies hanging over her head, the house felt almost claustrophobic.

The yard wasn't big, but neat, and there was a bench under a tree—perfect for sitting and pondering the meaning of existence. She sat down on the wooden bench and enjoyed the silence of the evening—a blessing after the nonstop chattering of the past few hours.

She was feeling guilty. Yeah, *now* she was feeling guilty. She hadn't felt so guilty about lying to her own family because they deserved it, dammit. They'd brought it upon themselves with all their demands and questions and overprotective phone calls. But David's mother was so proud of her only son, and so happy that he had finally found true love. She groaned and pulled her feet up on the bench, hugging her legs to her chest.

She sat like that for a long time before there was the sound of soft footsteps through the grass, and when she looked up David was sitting down beside her.

"Hi," he said, smiling. "I couldn't find you anywhere. Everything okay?"

She shook her head. "I'm dying of guilt."

"What for?"

"Your mother. Your sisters. I didn't think this would be so bad—I thought I'd just be paying you back for the favor you did to me, but... David, they're talking about weddings and babies!"

"Just like your folks did."

"That was different. There was a good reason. You don't have a reason. You're just doing this to pay me back, aren't you? Your family is the victim in this."

"I'm sure they'll recover."

Lou stared at him through the dim glow from the porch light. The lighting painted shadows over his face and he looked different, almost dangerous for a moment. Then he tilted his head and grinned at her, and she recognized him again "Why are you doing this, David? I mean, really? Don't tell me it's to avoid being set up on a reunion with your old high school girlfriends."

"The opportunity presented itself," he drawled. "I'm already your boyfriend in the eyes of most of the people we know, and whenever I come home I am under constant attack about when I'm going to bring a woman with me. When life hands you a lemon..."

"Newsflash, David. I am not a lemon! And your *lemonade* is causing a lot of problems. It's not just your mother, although I feel for her, I'm going crazy here myself."

"You mean my mother's talk about our future? Been there, done that, remember? You'll live."

"David, your mother is talking about grandchildren!"

"I know. She's been talking about grandchildren since I turned twenty-one. Did she show you the rocking horse?"

"What rocking horse?"

"Never mind. It'll be tomorrow's treat."

Lou whimpered. "I can't believe it. What do I tell her?"

"I don't care. Anything you'd like. Do you want kids?"

"That is not the issue here. Why in the world are you asking me that? I'm not going to disappoint your mother by promising her grandchildren we're not going to have, David! I can't believe you're suggesting that."

"Fine. Tell her it's none of her business, then. She can take it. I've been doing it since I turned eighteen and was officially no longer her business."

"Children never stop being their parents' business." She groaned. "At least I'm getting my own room. The silver lining."

"It's right next to mine. You can sneak in whenever you're lonely."

"I don't think so."

"Are you sure? I have a Spiderman pillow. You can share it."

In spite of herself she started to giggle. "No. Really?"

"Yup. Mom thinks I'm nostalgic for my childhood.

So whenever I come home I sleep on a Spiderman pillow.''

It was silent for a while, and the evening grew chilly, and the temptation to lean towards him, to have his arm over her shoulders to draw her close to share his warmth grew stronger. It was a physical pull that had nothing to do with common sense, and she resisted it.

"You've got a great family," she told him.

"Yeah. So do you."

Love warmed her heart as she thought about her parents and brothers. "Yes. We're lucky, aren't we? I miss my folks. I should go home more often."

"Time seems to pass faster in the big city, doesn't it?"

"Yeah. And the kids grow up without you noticing. My niece—she's nine years old. I think I've been giving her presents more suited for kindergarten children."

"Yeah. I'm not sure I realized my nephews were walking yet, and they'll be entering kindergarten soon."

They sighed in unison.

"And the old people," David said after a silence. "My grandparents. I saw them three years ago, and they were playing Frisbee with their great-grandchildren. My mom just told me my grandmother can hardly walk at all anymore. She's using a walker."

"I'm sorry."

"I should go home more often."

They shared a sad smile of mutual understanding.

"You know, they may be right. It may be time to start thinking about having kids."

Lou started laughing. And once she'd started she couldn't stop. "What?" David asked, bemused.

"Oh, Lord, both our parents would kill to hear us say that, David. Anyway, *you* don't have anything to worry about. You'll be able to have children into your seventies."

"I'd like to have *grandchildren* in my seventies."

"You want kids?"

"I hadn't thought about it before. It was something for 'later.' But when I think about it, I suppose I do… And I'm not sure the timing is ever going to be right. What about you?"

"About the same, I think." She changed the subject. Something had been sneaking up on her. David hadn't been totally honest with her. "What is the real reason you brought me here?"

"What do you mean, the real reason?"

"You have a hidden agenda. Again."

"I told you—to get peace from the women in my family. If I'd come alone my sisters would have set me up with half the women in the county."

She straightened up and dealt her trump card. "Exactly. Tell me this, David—what's wrong with being set up with half the women in the county?"

He just looked at her blankly and she shook her head with impatience. "I'm not buying it. We've worked together long enough for me to know that you *like* being chased by women."

David stared at her for a moment, looking crestfallen. "Oh. I do, don't I? You've got a point there."

"Right. Well? Why are you doing this? What's the real reason?"

"Hmm. Maybe I don't want to be chased by women

anymore.'' He leaned forward and grinned at her. ''That ever cross your mind? Maybe I just want to be chased by you.''

''Oh, really?''

''It's true. Do you think I've been flirting with you for a year just for kicks? I'd almost given up trying to get you to notice me.''

Notice him? Oh, she'd noticed him all right. She'd noticed those twinkling blue eyes the moment they'd first shaken hands.

''And then you threw this wonderful opportunity at me,'' he continued, and winked. ''You couldn't have expected me to pass that up, could you?''

Dammit all to hell. She couldn't deal with this. She didn't want to deal with this—not with the way he made her feel: confused, excited—on edge. And far, far too intrigued.

Hadn't she learned anything by now? Wasn't one huge mistake enough? She wasn't overreacting, just trying to learn from her mistakes. No—not all men were bastards. Yes—getting involved with a colleague was a mistake. Even if he wasn't a bastard.

Even if he quite possibly believed she was worth sacrificing the Ricardo case for.

She took a deep breath. ''Well, *yes!* I did expect you to pass that up.''

David clutched his heart theatrically. ''Rejected again.''

''Grow up!''

''I'm fully grown, Louise.''

She had to keep talking, keep arguing, or she'd say the wrong thing. Do the wrong thing. She was far too attracted, far too tempted to let things happen, to allow him closer, to give in to the almost irresistible urge to relearn what his hair felt like under her fingers. It hadn't been hard before—but now, seeing the light of interest in his eyes, sensing the tension snapping tight between them— Aw, hell!

She shook her head, breaking eye contact, and pointed upwards. Anything to change the subject. "See? You never see that in the city, do you?"

For several minutes they just looked at the stars, silent. Then David's voice broke through her concentration. "When we get back to the city, why don't we give it a go?"

"Give what a go?"

"You and me. For real."

He was serious about this—and she couldn't figure out how it made her feel. "You're kidding," she said weakly.

"No, I'm not. Why not give it a try? Let's see if this relationship of ours can stand reality. How about it?"

She shook her head and punched his shoulder with a fist, trying to turn his question into a joke. "Well, for one thing I think you are drunk on small town air."

"Why not? It could work."

"David, you don't want to date me. You really don't. Believe me, you don't."

"I do."

"No, you don't."

"Why?"

How many reasons did he want? "We work together. You know it isn't a good idea."

"There's no official policy…"

"You know we're competing for a promotion, David!"

"We can find a way."

"No."

"Why?" He held up a hand when she opened her mouth to repeat her objections. "Apart from the work issues, give me one good reason."

"I'm—we're just not matched. It wouldn't work."

"Not matched?" David frowned, then grinned. "Do you mean the I-don't-like-sex part? No problem. We'll work on that part."

"Very funny." Lou stood up from the bench and instead flopped down onto the grass. Better keep her distance from David in this mood.

"I'm serious. Seriously serious."

She propped her heavy head on her hands and groaned. "I think I'm getting a headache."

"Already?"

He always made her laugh; she had to give him that. "Oh, shut up."

"Really, Lou. I mean it. Why not?"

"You're being absurd."

"Why? We're compatible. We share a sense of humor, we've always liked spending time together. Sounds like a perfectly logical idea to me."

"That sort of thing isn't a cerebral *logical* decision, David! If two people want to get involved it happens of its own accord. It can happen gradually or suddenly, through an attraction, not because they decide that, hey, it would be a logical idea!"

David cackled. "Exactly! I knew it, Louise! You're a romantic after all."

She found herself blushing, and heard her voice get

defensive although there was no reason for it to. "Of course I am a romantic. I believe there's a special someone for everyone out there."

David leaned towards her until he was half off the bench. She leaned away. He leaned closer. She made a feeble attempt to escape, but fell on her back in the fragrant grass. He followed, bracing himself on his elbows at either side of her head. "Okay. Then let me be your special someone, Lou."

She stared at him. He was hard to resist when he whispered such a tempting offer in that sexy voice. Why was he so hard to resist?

Necessary to resist. She remembered her late nights at the office and her will resolved. Maybe, maybe if David were someone else, if he wasn't a colleague and a rival, she'd give it a chance, but her career meant everything to her. There was too much at risk. Not only her heart—but her job too. She might be willing to risk one—but not both on the same gamble. Not again. "No."

"Say yes. Give it a try."

"No."

David shook his head, frowning. He shifted until he could reach up and touch her lower lip with a finger. "You're doing this all wrong. 'Yes' starts with your tongue against the roof of your mouth." He pressed inwards, parting her lips until his thumb brushed the tip of her tongue. "And then you end with a sort of hissing sound. Like a snake. Sssssss."

"David…" she tried to say, but it was hard with his finger on his lips. In a sudden fit, a mixture of exasperation and regret—and something else, something *primitive*—she was tempted to bite it.

"What you're saying is 'no'—a word made up of completely different sounds, starting with the tongue against the upper palate. Now, try the yes again."

His face was just a few inches away and she couldn't break eye contact—it was impossible. She could feel his breath fan her cheek, his chest touch her shoulder. Their position felt intimate, and his finger against her lips should have felt invasive—but it didn't. Just alien and exciting at once, his nearness alone responsible for an army of goose bumps running up and down her back.

"Don't do this, David," she whispered. "I'm close to having a nervous breakdown and you're not helping. I can't think when you're like this—and there is no way, no way, I'm dating a co-worker ever again."

"Again?"

"Never mind."

"When are you going to tell me that story?"

"Never."

He digested that. "I see. Can I kiss you, then?"

"No!"

He sighed and moved away. "Dammit. I knew I shouldn't have asked first. That's it. No more gentleman crap. You have been warned."

Lou sat up. Being horizontal around David would just get her in trouble, especially if he'd decided not to be a gentleman anymore. "Maybe we should go inside and get some sleep. Big act to keep up tomorrow."

"Yeah. By the way, my parents love you," David said. "So do my sisters. Has Mom mentioned the village church yet?"

"No, but Kathleen did. Or Helen. Maybe both of them."

"The hand-carved altar from 1813?"

"1815."

"I stand corrected."

"They thought you were gay."

"What?"

"Your sisters. They wondered if the explanation of your seeming lack of girlfriends was that you were gay."

David swore. "Isn't that typical?"

"Your sister told me the junior prom dress story. Thinking back, they thought that might have been a hint."

"I was just a baby," David growled. "You can't hold that against me."

"Mmm. That's right. Just a baby. Six years old and already a cross-dresser."

"Watch it, Louise," he warned her. "Don't push it."

"I'm so afraid," she muttered, but when she looked at him and saw him reaching for her with a glint in his eyes she remembered he was a fallen gentleman. She jumped to her feet, even as temptation told her to stay. She'd never been fond of taking risks. "I'm off to bed," she called over her shoulder. "See you tomorrow."

She got a very ungentlemanly grunt in response.

CHAPTER SIX

THE birthday party for David's mother was loud and chaotic, and filled with people Lou didn't know, all of whom wanted to meet her. She was grateful for David's presence at her side—he seemed to realize how insecure she was in this role and tried never to let her out of sight. He was always there the moment she was in trouble with a question.

He was a good liar, she noticed with some chagrin. What did that say about his personality?

Well, he was a lawyer, after all. They both were. That might account for the mountain of lies they were building together.

When most of the guests were gone, and the siblings and their spouses had cleaned up, David took her hand. She'd intended to leave for her bedroom upstairs, but he pulled her toward the back door. "Where are we going?" she protested.

"I want to show you a secret."

"A secret? What kind of a secret?"

"Wait and see."

They were already at the back of the property, and David grinned at her as he ducked under a low branch and dragged her with him. Suddenly it seemed they were inside a forest.

"It's just like a real forest, isn't it?" David whispered, as if reading her mind. He kept walking and she followed behind. "You'd never guess you were in the middle of a town."

The trees whispered in the night and faint moonlight filtered down. David kept walking, until suddenly he knelt down by a tree, pushing some low branches out of the way. "See?" He gestured for her to kneel beside him.

"I'm not dressed for this," Lou objected.

He held out a hand. "Live a little, Louise! I'll pay for the dry cleaning."

Reluctantly, Lou knelt down beside him and looked. He *would* be paying that dry-cleaning bill. "I don't see anything."

"There's a hole under the roots of the tree, a big one—well, at least it seemed big when I was ten. It's almost like a cave. It was my secret hideaway when I was a kid." He crawled forward and vanished under the branches, and then his hand reappeared. "Come on…"

She opened her mouth to tell him she wasn't really dressed for reliving childhood adventures, and dry-cleaning might not do the trick if she was going to be crawling around under trees. But then she took his hand anyway.

He was right. The "cave" was big enough for the two of them to sit on a mattress of pine needles, and she could imagine young David making his home here. It smelled of earth and rotten leaves, of childhood secrets and boyish happiness.

"Once I fell asleep here," he whispered. "The police were searching for me by the time I woke up."

Lou chuckled. "I've heard that story. Your mother

told me. The time David got lost in the smallest forest in the world.''

''I didn't want to tell them about my hideaway. So I just said I'd gotten lost. I was teased for years, but it was worth it. This is all mine.''

She tried to get comfortable, but it really was impossible. David saw her squirming and reached out. ''Here. Sit against me.'' He pulled her close until her back was against his front. He rested his head on top of hers. ''Isn't this cozy?''

Cozy? Yes. But did she want to get cozy with David? No! Nevertheless she was allowing him to draw her against him, allowing him to put his arms around her as if there was so much more between them. She was even relaxing into him and enjoying it far, far too much.

This wasn't smart. She was sending him mixed messages and it wasn't fair either. Not fair—and, with some men, dangerous. She shuddered and squeezed her eyes shut to push away the memory, rid herself of the nasty kind of goose bumps. David wasn't like that. He wasn't.

And, because he wasn't, the nasty memories vanished as soon as he took her hand and squeezed it.

''Is this where you brought your high school girlfriends?'' she asked. She'd get up in just a minute. As soon as he stopped nuzzling her hair.

''Jealous?''

''Terribly.''

He chuckled. ''No. No girlfriends. Ever. This was a true secret. Nobody else ever came here. Not even my best friends.''

''Why did you bring me here, then?''

"Because you told me your secret. Accidentally, I'll grant you that, but fair is fair."

"I see."

"And I also brought you here because, even though I never wanted to bring anyone to my secret place, I always fantasized about making out here."

"Oh, Lord."

David shifted, and just as she'd mastered enough energy to stand up his hands went to her shoulders, his thumbs gently rubbing the muscles she hadn't known were so tense. "So, want to make out?"

She was alone with him in a secret hideaway where nobody would be able to find them. But there was no inkling of fear, just nervous excitement and a frantic need to remind herself that it wasn't a good idea to get involved with him. This was the guy she hoped to beat in a frantic race for promotion in a cutthroat industry where almost every nasty trick was considered fair. What was she doing with him here?

"You're impossible," she said, but her tone was weak and unconvincing and they both knew it.

"Dare you," he whispered, and his voice was in sweet symphony with the brushing of wind through the branches above. "Give us a chance. See what happens. What do you have to lose?"

What, indeed? She'd always subscribed to the "better safe than sorry" philosophy, but lately the logic behind that, once so clear and irrefutable, had began to blur. "I'm not going to be goaded into something."

"Why? What are you afraid of?"

"David, you know all the reasons why it's not a good idea. I've repeated them often enough."

"So what? Ignore your reasons and let it happen."

"Why...?"

"It's not a big deal, Louise. Go out with me. Just once, for starters. You can always dump me if you don't like it."

She turned her head in an attempt to look at him icily, but it somehow failed when his face was only inches away. "Can't you just consider yourself dumped already?"

"No." He laughed, and with a familiar pang her attention was drawn to the tiny lines at the corners of his eyes, the way his mouth curved, and the white glint of his teeth.

"Why?" she asked. "Why are you doing this?"

"Because you're cute."

She scowled. "I'm not *cute*. I'm grumpy and bad-tempered and neurotic. Didn't you notice?"

"Sure. But you're also cute." He bent his head, nuzzling her shoulder, and she could smell him—a scent she associated with their nights together at her parents' house. Her heart picked up speed. "I think we could have something special if you'd just open your cage for a minute."

"Open my cage?"

"Yes. And let me inside. Then you can close it again. No problem. It'll be nice and cozy. Just the two of us and the steel bars."

She took a deep breath. "David, sometimes I can't decide if you're some sort of a postmodern poet, or just nuts."

David smiled at her, and continued to dig into her personal life with a casual, conversational tone. He stopped rubbing her shoulders, and instead his arm went around her, lying over her chest as his head rested on her hair. And she still hadn't moved away. Pathetic. She had only herself to blame. "Talk to me. Tell me about *that man.*"

He was using her mother's inflection. Had they talked about this? Oh, God, what had her mother said? "No, thank you."

"Okay. Your rule about not dating co-workers—about not dating *me*—is it because you were once burned?"

"You could say that, I guess. But it's not the only reason. There are a million perfectly logical reasons why it's not a good idea."

He waited. "Tell me about him."

Oh, why not? Maybe he'd leave her alone if he heard the whole story. Or was it the darkness that had this effect on her, making her want to spill her guts? "I was naïve and stupid—childish, I guess you could say. Straight off the farm—and at my first real job." She grimaced. "From farm life to a pool filled with sharks with full bottom drawers of antacids and stimulating prescription drugs. It was a surreal switch."

She was silent for a while, going over the long-past events in her head, then David's low voice broke into his concentration. "What happened?"

She shrugged. "Nothing much. There was this guy. 'That man.' He let me do most of his job for him. Took all the credit and additionally made me look bad because I was so besotted that I neglected my own job to do his."

She could almost hear David digest that and come up with, So? Why had she started this? Did she really want to tell him this whole sordid story? "Were you together long?" he asked at last.

"No. A very short time. My blinders started falling off as soon as we got actually involved. Then, just a couple of weeks later, I finally found out he was married. He got furious when I confronted him. Said I should have known that from the start. And when I told him to go to hell he got violent."

David's hands stopped rubbing her shoulders and held still. "Violent? Do you mean physically violent?"

She took a deep breath and shrugged to hide her flickering emotions. It had been a while since she'd thought back on that time. It was a closed door to her—but there was still a mess inside.

"Lou? Did he hurt you?"

She brought a hand to her face and rubbed her forehead with the back of the hand. She looked to her right, into nothing. "Yes. But I was lucky. We were at the office after hours. Nobody was there, so screaming wouldn't have done me any good, but then the phone rang in one of the offices and he let go of me for a second. I managed to run away before much happened. I just had a few bruises." She noticed David's hand was clenched in a fist, resting on her shoulder, and she touched the back of his hand. "It was a long time ago. Don't feel sorry for me. I'm long over it."

"I'm not feeling sorry for you. I'm just wondering what his address is and if you're going to post bail for me when I kill him," David said calmly.

She almost smiled. "I appreciate the thought, but he's not worth the bother or the prison sentence. I was lucky. I got away."

"What happened then? Did you quit your job?"

"No. I had planned to ask for a transfer, but it was already too late. He'd smeared me with enough dirt so that I was asked to resign—or else be fired."

"What?" David swore loudly. "Why didn't you press charges and get *him* thrown out of there?"

"My word against his. I wouldn't have had a chance. I did go to the emergency room and have a report made on my injuries, just in case, but I knew there was no point in pursuing it."

David was a lawyer. He knew the statistics as well as she did. "Yes. You're right. It would have been tricky, even with your bruises."

"Not worth the agony of going through the process and having it dragged through the courts—possibly the media, since he was a big shot in the area. Anyway, that brought me to Livingstone's with a strict rule—no involvement with colleagues."

"That guy was a creep! What difference did it make that he was a colleague? That's completely beside the point!"

"Don't you understand? I vowed I'd never risk both my heart and my job at the same time. And up until now everything's been going great at Livingstone's. Even with my ice-lady reputation."

"Uh-oh," David said when he saw the look in her eyes. "You mean until I came along and messed up your neat life?"

"Yes."

"You know that jerk is not representative of all men, don't you?"

"Yes, David. I'm not afraid of men. Why are you so insistent that I am?"

"Because you haven't let anybody close since that bastard, have you? Nobody—not only colleagues."

"No."

"Why?"

She shrugged. "It's not like it's a big deal. I'm just very happy with my life the way it is. Honest. I don't feel I'm missing out on anything."

"How long ago was this?"

"A couple of years."

"You've been at Livingstone's three years."

"Okay, almost four years."

"That's a long time. Isn't it time you gave one of us a chance?"

She grimaced. "Sure. Probably someday. At the moment it's not all that tempting to go through a barrelful of bad apples just on the chance that there's a good one at the bottom."

David blinked. "On behalf of my gender, I should probably be offended by that analogy."

"You're blowing this out of proportion. It's not like I'm determined to be a spinster. If I ever meet a guy that I can imagine spending my life with, it will be fine."

"I see. And this dream guy of yours, what's he like?"

"None of your business."

"Does he wear a halo?"

"What are you trying to say?"

"I think you may have your ideal man up on a pedestal so high that you don't even know what he looks like anymore. That's convenient, isn't it? You don't have to expose yourself to failure again—or to abuse. You're safe. Safe and alone."

"And your solution to my 'problem' is sleeping around?"

"I never said that."

She leaned back against a tree root, looking up into the "roof." She was probably all covered in spiderwebs, but she didn't much care anymore. "Then what the heck are you suggesting?"

David touched her arm, curled his hand around it gently, then lifted it so her hand rested on his shoulder and her body turned towards him. His eyes were dark shadows in the evening dusk filtering down into their hideaway, yet burning with intensity. Why did they always do that? He touched her cheek and somehow she felt herself relax into his touch. "That you sleep with *me,* of course."

His tone was light. She rolled her eyes and pulled back a fraction. His hand tightened on hers and he wouldn't let go. She didn't struggle—it always felt far too good to be close to him. "Talk about an ego the size of the solar system. No, thank you. I'll pass."

"That's a shame," David said regretfully. "Are you sure?"

"David, stop it. This is none of your business."

He kissed her once, quickly, softly, so fast that she didn't know until it was over. "You kind of made it my business when you selected me to be your boyfriend, you know."

"I'm sorry. I'm so sorry—and because of what this has done to *me,* not you. But you're paying me back in full, aren't you? I'm here, posing as your girlfriend. What more do you want from me?"

"A kiss."

"What?"

"I really, really want to kiss you, Lou."

Oh, God. His voice was low and sexy, and his eyes were dark and seductive. "Why?"

"Well…" He cocked his head to the side, pretending to think deeply on the subject. "Perhaps because you're grumpy and bad-tempered? I've always had a weakness for that."

She shook her head. "Don't complicate this, David. It's already complicated enough."

"Exactly. One kiss isn't going to make it any worse."

"Yes, it will!"

"Why? Got a problem with kissing too? Or is it just the more involved stuff?"

She bit her lip. "Please don't make fun of me."

"I'm not." The grin vanished off his face. "I'm sorry, Lou, I really didn't mean to make fun of you. It's just my nature to turn everything into a joke."

"I know. It's one of the things I…like about you."

His gaze dropped to her lips and she started to panic. He couldn't kiss her. She didn't trust herself if he did. Something might happen. Something—out of control. "No, David! Don't you dare!"

"Dare what?"

"Kiss me…" Her voice lowered to a whisper. "Don't kiss me, David."

"Why not?"

"I don't want you to."

"Liar." He leaned over her, his face so close that his hair fell forwards to brush her forehead. "'Fess up, Lou. You do want me to kiss you. You really, really want me to."

"No."

"Yes. And I'm not going to do it until you admit it."

Lou frowned. He was on his side, leaning over her, so close that she was stuck between him and the tree root, his leg over one of hers. It should have felt claustrophobic, but it didn't. "Good. Get off me, then."

His mouth—damned tempting mouth—curved in a grin and he moved even closer. "Are you sure you want me to?"

No. "Yes, dammit." She squeezed a hand between them and shoved at his chest. "You're acting like a caveman." *And I like it.* God, that was embarrassing.

"Okay." He sat up straight and sighed. "No kiss. Happy now?"

"Very much. Thank you."

"Not at all wondering what it would've been like?"

"You've got an inflated ego, David." She refused to meet his eyes and started crawling out of the hideaway. Childish games were not for her. She'd paid her debt to David. It was time to get back to the city, back to work, and put this behind them.

CHAPTER SEVEN

THE Monday meetings were becoming a challenge. This morning David's gaze seemed to follow her every move, and once, in the middle of in impassioned speech, she caught him staring at her lips with such a look of utter concentration that she started stuttering and then choked when sipping on the water Felix handed to her. She sent David an angry glare when she thought the others wouldn't be looking, but he just raised his eyebrows, looking innocent once again.

"David, would you meet me in my office?" she said calmly as the meeting came to an end. "I'd like to consult with you on something."

David nodded, and followed her down the hall in silence. She shut her door firmly, and pointed him to a chair, then sat down in a position of authority at her desk.

"This won't do," she told him. "This can't go on. We can't work together like this."

"What are you talking about?"

"What do you think I'm talking about? You can't look at me like you did in that meeting. It throws me completely off balance. I looked like an idiot."

"Look at you like what?"

"You know what," she said hotly. "Don't pretend you don't. Ten minutes ago you were looking at me like...like... Well, you obviously weren't paying *any* attention to the case we were discussing!"

David squeezed his eyes shut for a moment, then laughed. "Dammit, Lou, you caught me."

"You can't do it anymore."

He still wasn't looking repentant. "I don't have much control over my thoughts where you're concerned."

Lou stood up and turned away from him to stare out the window. Then she twisted back. "David— please try to act normal around me. Just like we used to. This is too difficult."

"Don't you ever think about me?"

She halted. "What do you mean?"

"Don't you ever look at me over that conference table and think about us together? About that kiss we missed out on in my hideaway? About how it felt to wake up tangled together?"

"Yes," she confessed in a low tone. "Maybe that's the problem. Nothing happened, so we obsess about it. We'll get over it."

She realized her mistake too late as David sprang up and walked toward her, his steps purposeful. She stood up, bracing herself for another argument, but there was none. He didn't even pause before he put his hands on the wall at either side of her head, and kissed her.

As kisses went, it wasn't spectacular, she tried to tell herself. Just short and sweet and simple, right? Nevertheless the short contact had made her dizzy. Then he just stood there, his nose almost touching hers, and said nothing while her entire insides quivered in anticipation of something more.

She wasn't getting over this, was she?

"Well?" he challenged her. "It's over and done with. Was it as terrible as you thought?"

"I never thought it would be terrible."

"Then what, Lou? What did you think it would be?"

Frightening. Opening inviting doors that she didn't want to step through. Stealing a piece of her heart. Yes, he'd done all that already.

"Okay," she said, taking a deep breath. "We got that over with. Can we get back to the matter at hand now?"

He looked into her eyes for a moment longer, then pulled away. "Sure. If that's all you want."

"If that's all I want?"

"Yeah. If you ever want a decent kiss, just let me know."

If she ever wanted—? Oh, God. She fell back into her chair and rubbed her temples, almost hoping for a headache. Headache and lust didn't go well together, and she'd prefer the headache. "You're nuts, David. Totally nuts."

He winked at her. "You like me that way, don't you?"

She shook her head, exasperated. "Sometimes I'm not sure I like you at all." Her feelings for David defied all her attempts at categorizing or cataloguing them. She was afraid to even search them too deeply. She just wanted to—

"I want to kiss you again," he said, bracing his hands on her desk and leaning toward her with that teasing twinkle in his eyes. "You know. A real kiss. One that lasts more than two microseconds."

She stared at him. Yes. He was right. It was probably the only way to get this thing between them out of the way. Really over and done with. Maybe that would be it and everything would return to normal. "I know."

"Yeah?"

"Well, you've not exactly been keeping it a secret, have you?" She felt her heart increase its pounding even before she said it. "Fine. Let's do it."

David blinked and paused, as if he wasn't sure he'd heard right. Then he straightened, and the look on his face reminded her of a confused kitten who'd just caught its tail and wasn't sure what to do with it. Not macho—but cute.

Irresistible.

Mr. Irresistible wasn't cooperating, though. He rubbed his forehead with the back of his hand and stared at her. "Excuse me?" he said at last.

Damn. He didn't get it? "You know. That kiss. Let's do it."

He just blinked again. "Huh?"

Huh?

What sort of a response was that? Had he just been toying with her? Wasn't he interested in anything but the chase? She squirmed in her chair, more uncomfortable with every second that passed. Silence bounced off the walls. David didn't step closer, didn't beckon her closer, just stood there, looking at her.

Lou crossed her arms, feeling defensive. This wasn't the romantic moment she'd been having se-cret—very, very secret—fantasies about. He wasn't even *smiling*. Just looking at her with those hot eyes, while the electricity shooting between them was prob-ably sufficient to keep her laptop running for a week.

"Well? We should just get it out of the way. I mean, it can't possibly…" She came to a screeching halt.

"Be anything like what we've been imagining for quite a while now?" he supplied, speaking at last.

She colored. Some very unrealistic visions *had* been floating around inside her head lately. "Something like that."

"Well, I suppose there's only one way to find out." He smiled suddenly, and her heart skipped a beat. "Want to come over here? Or do I make the trip?"

The distance was a whole eight feet. "I suppose we could always meet midway."

"There's that," he agreed, but he didn't move.

She stood up. Dried her damp palms on her pants and took the first step. David's eyes seemed almost silver as they fixed on her. She lowered her gaze to his chest, and saw it lift and fall with his breath.

She wanted much more than a kiss. She wanted to touch him, feel the warmth of his skin under her palms, on her lips… She wanted a whole lot more than the kiss—but at what cost?

It would be okay. She wasn't in love with him, after all. The attraction between them wasn't emotional. She *wasn't* risking her heart. And her position at Livingstone's was secure—she wasn't a greenhorn anybody could push around. A fling with a colleague shouldn't affect her standing there at all, should it? Everybody thought they were a couple anyway.

She yanked her gaze back to his face to find him smiling. Then he reached out a hand. "Come here."

The long list of risks floating around in her head melted away. There couldn't be anything wrong with the way he was holding her—making her feel safe and wanted, needed. He was warm. His chest warm against her breasts, his hands warm against her back, and he smelled so good. His lips were warm against her—

"Oh!"

"What?"

"When you said a kiss, I thought you meant—mouth to mouth."

"You've got a delectable earlobe. I couldn't resist. I've been wanting to taste it since we first woke up together."

He made it sound intimate. It *had* been intimate—in its own unique way. "Right," she quipped. "An earlobe on your pillow beats a mint anytime." She lifted a hand to his neck and traced his own ear. "Yours isn't that bad either." She pushed her hand into his hair. "Your hair is so soft. You must use conditioner. What kind?"

Conditioner? She was pathetic.

David seemed to agree. "I refuse to talk about hair products right now, Lou." He moved his head, which caused his mouth to trail from his ear to her cheek. She closed her eyes and turned her head just slightly, until she felt his lips touch hers.

"This is a kiss, isn't it?" she asked, her lips touching his with every movement.

"Not quite."

"Close enough?"

"Nowhere near."

"We're being silly, aren't we?"

"Yeah. Fun, isn't it?" His eyelashes brushed her cheek and she opened her eyes to find laughter in his. She smiled.

"Yes."

And then he took her face in his hands and kicked all traces of fun out of the room with a kiss that sizzled straight to her toes.

"Mmm," he whispered a while later, wrapping his arms around her shoulders, his lips touching her forehead. "Maybe there's something true in that old saying that everything good comes to those who wait."

She buried her face in his shoulder, leaning all her weight against him. She was dizzy—which was a good excuse—but the real reason was that she just couldn't bear to lose the wonderful feeling of his body against her.

And she wanted more. Despite the lingering fear, despite the risk of flashbacks and failure.

Why not go all the way? Give him a chance to work on her "issues," as he'd once promised? She liked David, and he knew all about her hang-ups. It was worth a try. If she didn't get back in the proverbial saddle again soon, she might as well resign herself to becoming a born-again virgin spinster.

Yes. She'd do it. Now. Before she lost her nerve—and before she did something stupid like fall in love with the damn man and get emotionally involved. *Then* she'd be in real trouble. She straightened up and grabbed his hand. "Okay. Let's do it," she said. "Right now."

David just looked confused, which was totally aggravating. "Do what?"

"You know what!"

David looked around her office, as if he'd forgotten all about the lunchtime quickies he'd once offered. "Huh?"

"Let's go to your place. It's closer. We'll take a long lunch break."

"Wait a minute. I thought you didn't like sex."

"I changed my mind. Let's go."

"I changed your mind? With one kiss? Damn, I'm good."

She punched his chest, too nervous to appreciate his joke. "Shut up, or I might change my mind again."

His sharp gaze searched her eyes, coming up with the admission she didn't want to make. "You don't want to make love, Lou," he said with dawning comprehension. "You're just pretending to. Why?"

She put her hands on her hips and glowered at him. "Cut the crap. Do you want to go to bed with me or not?"

He nodded. "I do. But not unless you want me. Not because you just want to see if you're over what happened to you once and I'm a relatively safe test subject who knows your secret already."

"Why? Aren't you sure you'll show me the error of my ways, anyway?"

"I'll certainly do my best, but not while you're thinking of yourself as a sacrifice."

She was losing her courage, and it was *his* fault. "David, it's extremely bad for my self-esteem if you turn me down."

He grinned. "I'm not turning you down. I'm just going to wait until you have the right attitude."

She sighed. "And what attitude would that be?"

"That being as close to me as humanly possible is the most important thing in the universe and you can't live another moment without tearing my clothes off."

Lou opened her mouth, closed it again, and took a deep breath. "Oh. Wow."

"Which, I might add, is pretty much how I feel about you right now."

"Double wow."

His eyes narrowed. "Are *you* making fun of *me* now?"

"No—but I'm not sure I'll ever have that attitude, David."

"Don't worry. We'll work on it."

"Oh, really? How?"

"Why are you looking at me with such distrust?"

"Because you're up to something and I don't know what it is."

"Want to come to my place tonight?"

She looked at him, feeling her eyes widen in surprise. "You just said you didn't want to spend the night with me."

"No. I said I didn't want to unless you really wanted to. We'll have to see if you really want to. I'll do my best to persuade you."

That sent a whole barrelful of shivers down her back. It also sounded somewhat surreal. "I see. A bit arrogant of you, isn't it?"

"I'm pretending to be confident. It beats nerves. I don't like losing."

"Is this a battle?"

"Yes. But we're both on the same side."

"And just how are you going to make sure I really want to?"

He winked as he opened the door. "I'll let you wonder. Seven o'clock? I'll cook."

"Okay. I'll be there."

"Cool." He started to leave, then stuck his head back in through the half-opened door. "Lou?"

"Yes?"

"If you change your mind—no problem. Okay?"

She nodded, somewhat chagrined at being given a way out. "Yes. I won't."

"Good." He sent her a scorching smile and was gone.

She was late. Not only because she had changed her mind a few dozen times, but because she couldn't figure out what to wear, what to say, what to do—none of the scripts she'd rehearsed in her head seemed to make any sense. She finally made it to David's door late—much too late for dinner. And she hadn't even called to let him know.

David looked surprised when he saw her, but smiled and pulled her inside, giving her a brief hug. "Come in. I thought you wouldn't come. I already had dinner with my cat. We had salmon. He appreciates your sacrifice."

An orange cat rubbed himself against Lou's legs and she reached down to stroke his head. "I'm sorry. I was... Well, sorry about the food."

"No problem."

Of course it was a problem. She'd been raised better than this. She didn't stand people up when they'd cooked for her. It was *rude*. "I mean it. I'm sorry. I should have called. Dammit, I should have been here."

"Hey, I understand."

"My mother would ground me for a month if she knew. You should sit me down, tie a napkin around my neck and let me eat the cold congealed salmon. The more disgusting, the better.''

"Really, Lou, don't worry about it. Plato is very grateful to you.''

Lou chuckled nervously and reached down to stroke the cat's back. "He's certainly purring loud enough.''

"Are you hungry? Do you want to order takeout?''

"No.'' She chucked her jacket on a chair and moved closer, put her arms around his neck and hugged him. His arms came immediately around her and the fear receded. She tightened her hold. "I have a few ground rules,'' she muttered into his ear. "Okay?''

"Ground rules?'' He pulled back, looking doubtful, and she buried her face in his neck again. The only way she could get through this was by being close to him but not looking at him. "Am I going to like this?''

"Probably not.''

He sighed, and his hand started rubbing up and down her spine. That's more like it. "Okay. I'm easy. List your rules.''

"Rule number one. This is not going to interfere with things at work. No matter what—we keep it separate from work.''

"Sure thing. Done.''

"Rule number two. I'm going to be on top.''

He almost jumped, and then she could feel his face light up, just by the way it felt against her cheek. "I think I'm going to like your rules,'' he said, chuckling.

"Otherwise I might get claustrophobic or something... Agreed, or not?''

"All the time?'' he asked.

"Unless we discuss otherwise. Okay?''

"Agreed." He made another attempt to disengage himself and look at her, but she wouldn't let him. She had rules to tell him, and she absolutely could not do that while looking at him. So she tightened her grasp around his neck, burying her face deeper in his neck.

"I'm serious," she insisted, turning her head a fraction so her words would be audible. "Anything else has to be discussed beforehand and I have to explicitly agree."

"Right. You on top, unless we negotiate otherwise. No problem. Next rule?"

"Rule number three. Lights stay off."

His hand stopped moving on her back, but there was laughter in his voice as he spoke. "Dammit. You just removed half the fun of rule two."

"Rule number four—"

"Wait, I'm still on rule three. What about candlelight? I mean—a guy has to see what he's doing, or he might get something wrong."

"What could you possibly get wrong?"

He shrugged. "You never know."

She paused, thinking. It really wasn't an unreasonable request. "How many candles are we talking about?"

"As many as I can get away with."

"Okay. One candle. Not for romance, mind you. Just so we can see what we're doing."

"I'm not sure one candle will provide enough light. How about five?"

"Five?"

"They'll provide even light around us. We can't mess around with one candle. It could get nasty. Imagine if we spilled hot wax on—"

She pushed away from him. "David!"

He winced. "You remind me of my mother when you say my name in that tone—and you do it a lot, you know. Almost as much as you tell me to shut up."

"You never do shut up." She crossed her arms on her chest. "I'm not bargaining with you on the candle issue."

"Okay, let's settle for three candles."

"Fine. And that reminds me. Rule number four—"

David held up a hand. "Wait a minute—just how many rules are there?"

"I don't know. I'm listing them as they come to mind. Rule number four—"

She didn't finish telling him about rule number four. He'd taken one more step toward her, and now his palms warmed her cheeks and his lips were hard and insistent and wonderful, and what they said without words was, Shut up. I want you.

She found that she was, after all, quite okay with that.

They'd never gotten to rule four.

David drew Louise closer, and she curled into him. She seemed as content as his cat after a bowl full of tuna and a half-hour tummy rub. And as sleepy.

"David?" she murmured. Not quite asleep yet, then.

"Yes?"

"You broke the rules, you know."

He smiled, his lips against her temple. He pressed a kiss there. "No, I didn't."

"Yes, you did. I'm not complaining, mind you—at

least not while you still keep to rule one. I'm just pointing it out as a fact. I distinctly remember—''

"Hey, you broke two and three yourself. Remember?" He idly stroked her shoulder and buried his hand under the hair at the nape of her neck. "Both of them. And we never got to rule four. What was it?"

"It's okay. You didn't break it," she said drowsily. "Does it matter now?"

"Yes. Better have it on hand for next time."

"Tomorrow morning?" she asked hopefully.

He chuckled. "Yes. Tomorrow morning."

"Okay. Rule number four. Don't say you love me."

His hand stilled in her hair. "What? What do you mean?"

"You know…" She could barely keep her eyes open anymore, and was too relaxed to even try. "Don't tell me the lies men tell women in bed. I don't want you to lie to me. Not you."

"I won't lie to you. Ever. Promise."

She smiled at him and cuddled closer. "Thank you. Goodnight, David."

Dammit. *Goodnight?* How was he supposed to be able to sleep now? Rules one, two and three—fine. Rule four, however… He shifted, pulling the covers over Lou's shoulders and holding her closer.

He had a feeling rule four might be a tricky one.

David was there when she opened her eyes. So was a huge orange cat—and he was glaring at her.

Her alarm clock was not there, of course. She blinked, and her usual early-morning panic engulfed her. She hated to be late. She was never late. "What time is it?"

"Good morning," David said, smiling.

She twisted to get a look at the clock and heaved a sigh of relief. "I thought I was late."

"Nah. Want to take the day off and spend it right here?"

An automatic rebuff started in her mind, but never made it to her lips. Instead she smiled and pushed her fingers into his hair. "I'd love to, but today isn't good. Another day, okay?"

David chuckled as he kissed her. "I thought you were going to say 'David!' in that outraged tone of yours."

"Yeah, so did I."

"You know, we should do this regularly," he said. "Don't you agree?"

"You mean…ah…" She tried to think of a delicate phrasing for it. "You mean we should become bedroom buddies?"

"What an excellent phrase. Yeah. How about it, Lou? Will you be my mistress?"

Somehow he managed to keep his face serious, although his eyes were sparkling with humor. She hit him with a pillow. "I don't know. Will you keep me in the manner to which I am accustomed?"

"Twelve-hour days and fast-food dinners? I suppose I could try."

She crawled on top of him and concentrated on examining his chest. "I like your muscles. They're not that apparent when you're dressed, but they sure look nice when I've got you naked. Where did you get them?"

"Why? You want them?"

"Mmm. Yes. I do." She ran her hands down his

chest to his stomach, where more muscles clenched in response to her touch. "Abdominal muscles, too. Very nice. I approve. How many sit-ups do you have to do to get those?"

His breathing was becoming labored as she explored his torso with her mouth and hands. "I like your stomach too, Lou. It makes the best pillow in the world."

"Uhm. Did you find any muscles there? Sit-ups don't seem to work for women the same way as for men. So unfair."

He tried to sit up. "Let me check... I'm sure if I look closely enough..."

"No." Gently, she pushed him back down. "Later. I haven't finished with your muscles yet. Tell me—do you go to one of those sissy gyms and lift weights while looking at yourself in a mirror?"

"Lou?" he said in a strangled voice.

"Yes?"

"You can't do that and expect me to think at the same time."

Her laugh was a vibrating purr against his skin, and as he growled and pulled her up, twisting so he could turn the tables on her, she knew with a mixture of resigned terror and pure joy that she'd somehow managed to fall in love with her new bedroom buddy.

Muscles and all.

CHAPTER EIGHT

KISSING in the elevator on their way up to the seventeenth floor was a sinful luxury Lou was getting far too accustomed to. It was one that could keep a woman happy for the rest of the day. Her face was flushed with a mixture of excitement and embarrassment when they exited the elevator. She exchanged one last smile with David before regretfully turning her back on him and heading for her own office.

Three weeks of bliss and no cloud in the sky yet. Yes, this could mean trouble. Yes, it might turn into a disaster. After all, she'd actually fallen in love with him, taking things far beyond the "bedroom buddy" stage—at least on her side. Which was another issue— she still didn't know how deep his feelings lay. But, despite all the uncertainty, her brain was somehow firmly set on "happy."

She kept humming all the way down the long corridor, almost too distracted to even notice the occasional raised eyebrow and knowing look she encountered on the way.

A bonus was that she didn't have to lie to her mother anymore. She could truthfully tell her about the things she did with David—well, *some* of the things they did together. No fictionalized plays or concerts, no lies or tricky questions to dodge. Utter freedom.

As she reached Samantha's office, and waved cheerfully to her friend, Samantha jumped to her feet and followed her. "Felix is leaving sooner than expected," she whispered as they turned into Lou's office. "Did you hear? He'll be moving up to the thirtieth floor at the end of the month!"

"Really?" It wasn't a big surprise—Felix had been expected to leave anyway at the beginning of next year. "We're going to miss him."

"Yes, yes—but you know what this means, don't you?"

Yes. Lou stopped breathing for a long minute. She should have realized as soon as Samantha told her Felix was leaving. But she'd been…distracted…lately. She breathed out. "Oh, boy."

Samantha smirked. "Yep. Either you or David will be moving into that fancy corner office." Her tone turned sympathetic. "Will this cause trouble between you?"

Lou shrugged.

"You must have thought about this—you knew it was coming. How will he feel about you maybe becoming his boss? Or how will you feel if he becomes your boss?"

"I don't know…" Her mind was racing over the implications of this. It wasn't as simple as Samantha thought. Neither option was even a possibility. The powers that be would not allow a couple to work together. This hadn't been a problem while they were just pretending—they'd assumed they'd just officially 'break up' long before the end of the year—but now…

Now they'd have to end it.

"This won't break you guys up, will it?" Samantha

said anxiously. "Please tell me it won't. I want to see him put a ring on your finger."

"Excuse me, Samantha, I'll have to go talk to David," she muttered, and pushed past her into the corridor again.

David greeted her warmly, jumped to his feet to shut the door, then trapped her against it for a long, intensive kiss. She leaned into him, returning his kisses and hugging him hard, all the more desperate now, knowing what she did—that this would have to be the last time.

"You heard about Felix?" she said, as soon as she could draw breath again. Her arms were around David's neck and she was reluctant to let go.

David nodded, and nuzzled his face into the side of her neck. "Yeah," he said, leaving her to translate the muffled words. "I should have suspected something. He's been unusually preoccupied, and Mr. Ramier is getting really anxious to get out onto the golf courses of retirement."

Lou tried to concentrate, but it was hard when he had her earlobe between his teeth. She worked her hands between them and pushed gently at his chest. David raised his head reluctantly, frowning. "What is it? Did you just decide upon rule five? We can't grope each other at work anymore?"

"That would be a smart rule," she said with a small smile, before squirming out of his arms and getting serious. She fled to the other side of the room and crossed her arms before facing him again. "You know what's going to happen now, don't you?"

"Lunchtime quickie?"

"David, be serious!"

His smile faded and she ached from the loss. "Right," he said. "Yes. I know what's going to happen now."

Lou sighed, still looking at him with hunger. She'd mussed up his hair. His shirt wasn't looking nearly as neat as it had just a few minutes earlier either, and she walked back to him to straighten his tie. "I already got an e-mail to report for an interview," David said as she reached up to smooth his hair.

"Yeah?" She glanced at his computer, excited despite herself. "Can I check my e-mail?"

"Of course."

She sat down and tapped a few keys until she could access her e-mail. "Yeah. Me too. Next Thursday at two o'clock."

David grinned at her. "I'm at one o'clock. May the best person win."

"Don't you see our problem?"

"We always knew we had this problem. The fork in the road just appeared sooner than we expected."

"That's just it! We thought we had plenty of time to 'break up' naturally, before this happened, but now…" She floundered. "After one of us is promoted, there is no way the other one will keep his or her job." She could see that he was getting her point, but pushed it home. "You know they'd never allow one of a couple to report to the other. We've seen this before. They always transfer one of the parties to a different department—or someone ends up leaving."

David was frowning. "You're right. I hadn't thought of that."

"Remember Evan and Helen? Tanya and Mick?"

He nodded. "Yes. I know. One of them was transferred, to another group. Or assigned to another boss, at the very least.''

"Exactly. And where would they transfer you—or me—to? There is no other department here for you.''

David shrugged. "I'm happy where I am.''

"Well, so am I.''

"Right.''

"So, what we need to do is break up the relationship. Immediately. They might decide to transfer one of us anyway, but if we do this quickly and quietly maybe the big bosses won't even find out we were ever involved—we might get away with it.''

"You're not serious, are you?''

"Yes!''

David was frowning. "You want to sacrifice our relationship for this promotion?''

"What relationship? We don't have a relationship!''

"What? It sure was starting to look like a relationship to *me*.''

"Of course it looks like one! We are pretending— remember?''

David's frown had become a serious scowl, and he raised his voice. "We were *pretending* for the last three weeks? We were *pretending* in bed?''

"I had some demons to slay,'' she muttered, strength draining out of her at his reminder. "You helped. That doesn't mean it's a *relationship*. It doesn't mean we should ruin each other's careers.''

"There's no need to *ruin* anything.''

"If you get that promotion I'll be transferred somewhere else. If I get it you'll be moved away. In addition, whoever is promoted will be working around the clock and won't have any time for a relationship anyway—particularly not with someone who isn't even here! Either way—it won't work. It can't work.''

David shook his head. ''Your reasoning is what doesn't work, Lou. Everybody's got time for a relationship—if they *want* it. So the only question is, do you want it?''

Oh, God. ''You're not being fair, David!''

''Fair? *I'm* not being fair? *You're* the one who wants to throw away what we have because of your *job!*''

Wasn't he listening? ''David!'' She tried a smile. ''*Our* jobs! And don't you remember rule number one? We will not let our personal relationship interfere with work. It's my golden rule, and we're in dire danger of breaking it.''

He definitely wasn't listening. His jaw was clenched and his body tense. ''Hell with your rules, Lou! Has ambition made you completely blind? Is that promotion all you care about?''

''I've been working toward this for years! Of course it's important to me!''

''More important than anything else?''

''What else is there?''

He stared at her. *''What else is there?''* he repeated, almost in a whisper, and the words sounded horrible thrown back at her. Horrible, hurtful—and terribly untrue.

There was so much else, wasn't there?

But she had her future to think about. Years of hard work and careful planning were at risk. And if they took a chance and things didn't work out—she'd be left with nothing.

Lou gritted her teeth together to keep her emotions

from bleeding through. David didn't understand how important this was—for both of them, but especially for him. There was no way of knowing which one of them would get the promotion, but she had worked more closely with Felix in the past. That gave her an edge. If she got the promotion and they were still a couple it would mean that David would be transferred, or leave for good. There was just one way to prevent that from happening.

"David, don't complicate this. Our jobs are important to us. I know you feel just as strongly about that as I do."

"Do I?"

"We shouldn't let this stand in the way of our careers. It wouldn't be fair—to either of us."

"Is that it?" he asked after a long silence, his stance somewhere between aggressive and withdrawn. She couldn't interpret the tone of his voice, but it trembled with suppressed emotion.

"Yes," she said. There was nothing else she could say. She was dying to reach out to him—but she couldn't. "You agree, don't you? When you think about it? I know how important your career is to you… You must see I'm making sense."

His gaze scorched her for a long time before he finally looked down and slammed a drawer shut. He sat down and bent over his keyboard. "Okay, Lou."

They didn't see much of each other for the rest of the week, which was probably for the best. Their interviews were still almost a week away. Everything would be clearer after that.

Or would it? Louise finished her last paperwork of

the week and glanced at her clock. Almost six. She leaned back in her chair and looked out the window, biting her lip as she wondered what David was thinking. She had no idea what he was thinking—what his final, frustrated ''Okay, Lou'' had meant.

She'd gotten what she wanted. Now neither of them would need to be transferred away. But what now? One of them would get the promotion. The other one would remain in their current position. They'd be interacting on an almost daily basis. She rubbed her face with her hands, already feeling the pain of seeing David every day—but as a stranger. As one of her staff—or as her boss.

No. She couldn't do this.

That meant there was only one option.

Her computer beeped, interrupting her concentration. It was a terse message from David, strictly business-related. It made her heart ache, especially as she thought of the fun, loving—and barely decent—messages she'd received from him throughout the day over the last couple of weeks.

No. She couldn't sacrifice the possibility of this relationship for her career. She couldn't. It might not work out—she might already have destroyed it, and even if she hadn't, it might die a natural death next week, next month. But it was still a risk worth taking.

The building was almost empty. She practically ran down the hallway toward Felix's office, only pausing to tiptoe past David's office so she wouldn't draw his attention. He was in there, bent over some files, a frown of concentration on his forehead that had her aching to go in there and kiss it away.

But she didn't have the right. Not now.

"Got a moment?" she asked Felix. He was already packing, but he seemed to be traveling light. "Only two boxes?"

"Yeah. I'm leaving all the paperwork for you to deal with," Felix said with a grin, upending a drawer into a box. A waterfall of Lego cascaded down.

"Lego?" she asked, but her heart was pounding faster. *For you to deal with.* He could mean a plural you, as in the whole department, but...

Felix inserted the drawer back in the desk. "My kids. They're three and five. They love to visit me at work occasionally. A full drawer of toys makes it a bit less likely for them to attack anything important. Not that it always works."

"Right. Your kids. I've seen them. They'll love the view from the thirtieth floor."

"Yeah." Felix gestured out the window. "How will you like this corner office view?"

Louise stopped breathing for a moment. He *was* saying what she thought he was saying. She was getting the promotion.

David would be devastated. Wouldn't he? He'd seemed to take their competition lightly, but this meant a lot for both of them, both in terms of career and salary.

But why the interviews if they'd already decided?

"Felix, are you saying I will get your job?"

He grinned. "Who else?"

"David! We both have interviews next week..."

Felix looked puzzled. "David isn't interested, so you're the only candidate."

"What?"

"He told us he had other career plans. Next thing

we knew he was talking to the guys up on the seventeenth floor. Naturally they weren't about to let go once they had him on the hook. He'll be moving there next month.''

"*What?*"

Felix shrugged. "Can't say I blame him. They have less paperwork to deal with up there, and his new position is on the same rung of the ladder career-wise as this job. It's a smart move.''

Lou left Felix with his Lego and stormed to David's office. He would not get away with this. He would absolutely *not* get away with this.

"Why didn't you tell me?" she yelled, shutting the door behind her with a louder bang than she'd intended. "What the hell do you think you're doing?"

David looked up from his file, taking a while to break his concentration. He smiled—the first smile she'd seen from him in days, and reached out for her— as if everything was back to normal. It wasn't. Her feet tried to walk toward him anyway. She ordered them to stay put and tried to focus on staying angry.

"What's the problem?" he asked.

"Felix told me I'm getting the promotion."

"Congratulations."

"Because I'm the only one left in the running."

David looked down. "You weren't supposed to find out until later. I was going to tell you this weekend. Sedate you with white wine and kisses first.''

Kisses. Too long since she'd received some of those. Lou bit her lip to remind herself of the issue at hand. "You're *quitting!*"

"No, I'm not quitting. I'm moving between departments.''

"Don't split hairs. You're quitting your job before they decide which one of us is getting the promotion. There can only be two reasons." She held up a finger. "One—you're leaving because you think I'm more likely to get the promotion and you don't want to lose to me."

David leaned back in his chair and looked at her. His expression was one of curiosity and…tenderness. "I see. And two?"

"You're leaving because you think *you* would have gotten the promotion and this is some harebrained self-sacrifice to make sure I get the promotion and not you."

"And which do you think it is?"

"I think it's the latter," she whispered.

"You think I'm leaving so you'll get the promotion?"

"Yes."

"Why would I do that?"

"Because I told you about my first job—how an office relationship ruined my chances there—and you know how determined I am never to let that happen again." She crossed her arms on her chest and took a deep breath. "David, I don't need you to protect me. You cannot interfere with my job at the expense of your own. I'm not letting you do that."

David dropped his pen to the table and stood up. "Neither of your reasons is correct, Lou. I'm not leaving because I can't stand losing the promotion to you. Nor because I want to make up for something that happened in your past."

"Then why are you doing this?"

David was staring to look exasperated, as if the answer was obvious and she should be getting it. "Why do you think?"

"I'm really not in the mood for puzzles."

"This isn't a puzzle. It's been written on the wall for a while now. You just don't want to see it."

"I don't care what the reason is. You love it here, David! You love your job and you would have loved that promotion. I'm not going to stand by and watch you sacrifice it because of some misguided—"

"This isn't such a huge sacrifice," David said, interrupting her and stepping closer. "And it's *my* choice, remember? No one's forcing me to do anything."

"It *is* a sacrifice…"

He shrugged. "That promotion was the next logical step on the ladder, but there are alternatives. I'll have to work hard for a while, but if things work out I may have opportunities at the new department that I didn't have before. The important thing is that I *want* to do this."

"Why?" she whispered.

"I don't want us to break up, Louise." He took her hands in his then, so gently, and brushed away one tear that had barely made it out of her eye yet. "Do you?"

"No…" She almost hiccupped. "Felix told me you were leaving…just as I was going to tell him I wanted *you.*"

"Yeah?" David's voice was teasing. "You were going to tell *him* that?"

Louise was amazed to find herself giggling. "I mean, I was going to tell him I wasn't interested in the promotion—talk about alternatives…a way to keep working for the firm without losing you…''

There was a light in David's eyes that told her how much this meant to him. ''You were going to do that?''

''Yes.'' She held his gaze. ''I wanted to show you that I trusted you…see if you'd give me a second chance…'' She took the last step toward him and buried her face in his shoulder. ''But now you're leaving…''

He chuckled. ''I'm moving five floors up, love. Not to another continent. We can still neck in the elevator—and we can still be together.''

''But we weren't really together before, were we? We were just pretending, and it got a bit out of hand—''

His head moved in a quick, almost violent gesture of negation, and his hand was on her neck, warm against her skin as his thumb stroked her jaw. ''Somewhere along the way we stopped pretending. Didn't we?''

''It wasn't supposed to happen,'' she whispered.

''I don't think people ever intend to fall in love,'' he said, a smile edging his voice and making her look up into his face. ''That's probably why the word is 'falling.' Love is such an accident.''

''We fell, didn't we?'' she said, her hand tightening on his. ''That's the perfect word for it. We fell. Together…''

He smiled, and she only knew it because his cheek moved against hers. She felt safe as he held her against him, safe and warm and complete—until he pulled away to look her in the face. ''You made me promise not to tell you I loved you, Louise. Would you please let me off the hook?''

Her eyes filled with tears, but she blinked them back. ''That's the last rule I have left.''

''You won't miss it,'' he assured her. ''I promise. I'll never lie to you. You trust me, don't you?''

She nodded, feeling some of the weight lift off her as she opened the invisible door, allowing him to step all the way inside. She did trust him. ''Okay. Consider rule number four invalidated.''

David's smile was sweet. ''I love you, Louise.''

''I love you too.'' Her lips were curved in a smile as they kissed, but she frowned as soon as they parted again. ''What are we going to tell our parents? This could get complicated.''

''That's the good part, Lou. We don't have to tell them anything. They were way ahead of us, you know.''

''You're right.''

''Although it would make a good story…''

She held up a finger. ''No. If my mother ever finds out she made her only daughter share a bed with a stranger…''

''She'll skin me alive?''

''No. She'll get that glow in her eyes and start sighing about fate and destiny and meant-to-be, and I *hate* it when she does that.''

''Don't worry about them. We're home free now. No telling them we've broken up. Ever. We'll always be together.''

''*Always,*'' Lou murmured. Things were working out. They really were working out, and she clung to

David, knowing with blissful satisfaction that she'd never need to let go of him again. "I like that word."

"Yep. In fact, there's just one more decision to make."

"What is it?"

He raked his hands through her hair, pushing it away from her face so he could look into her eyes without a curtain in the way. "Do you want to check out that hand-carved altar from 1815, or is it to be tandem skydiving in Central Park?"

"Hmm..." Lou mused, snuggling even closer to him, deciding she finally had the definition of perfect happiness. "Let me think about it."

Modern
romance™

...international affairs
– seduction and
passion guaranteed

Medical
romance™

...pulse-raising
romance – heart-
racing medical drama

Tender
romance™

...sparkling, emotional,
feel-good romance

Sensual
romance™

...teasing, tempting,
provocatively playful

Historical
romance™

...rich, vivid and
passionate

Blaze™

...scorching hot
sexy reads

27 new titles every month.

Live the emotion

MILLS & BOON®

FOREIGN AFFAIRS

Sultry heat, sexy men – seduction guaranteed!

Helen Bianchin
Michelle Reid
Anne Mather

MILLS & BOON

On sale 3rd September 2004

Available at most branches of WHSmith, Tesco, Martins, Borders, Eason, Sainsbury's and all good paperback bookshops.

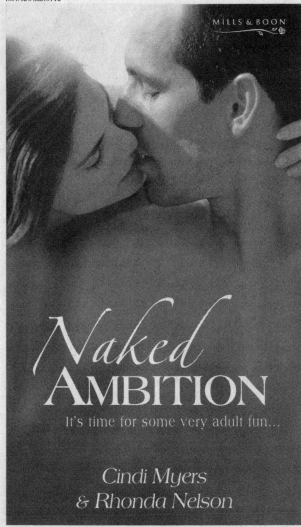

MILLS & BOON

Naked
AMBITION
It's time for some very adult fun...

Cindi Myers
& Rhonda Nelson

On sale 1st October 2004

Available at most branches of WHSmith, Tesco, Martins, Borders,
Eason, Sainsbury's and all good paperback bookshops.